Acknowledgements

Many wonderful people have helped me in the writing of this book. First I have to mention Arthur Blue for his tireless efforts to supply me with information about the Greenock area during the Second World War and also to Jenni Calder. We three went round the town together in the freezing cold imagining where everything once was. I must also thank John Burnett for his endless support in the form of helpful suggestions, accurate information and encouragement, not to mention tea. Vincent Gillen of the MacLean Museum may be entirely unaware of how our initial hurried conversation drove me on and the part the photos and subsequent information he supplied me with helped shape the narrative, but I am most grateful to him. Thanks also to Allan Barns-Graham for his time, and to him and the Wilhelmina Barns-Graham Charitable Trust for their permission to include Willie in this story. To Isa McKenzie I am indebted once again for sharing her experiences of post-Clydebank Blitz austerity, and to Clydebank Library and archives for historical information. Liz Small of Waverley has encouraged me, backed me up and been an editor with great insight and a true friend. Ron Grosset and the rest of the team at Waverley have also been outstanding. For emotional support, my daughters,

Kirsty and Jessica, have been my rock of safety in the storm of doubt and I am grateful to all my friends and family who have cheered from the sidelines. And lastly I have to thank Rando Bertoia, who sadly died in October 2013, who was the last survivor of the Arandora Star and who alerted me to the plight of Italians during the Second World War.

Rue End Street is written by Glasgow writer Sue Reid Sexton, and is the sequel to *Mavis's Shoe*, a harrowing account of what happened in Clydebank, Glasgow and the Carbeth hut community during the Clydebank Blitz and after. Sue has a background in social care and trauma counselling, and spent a decade working with the homeless. She often writes in a very small campervan in the middle of nowhere.

Rue End Street

SUE REID SEXTON

WAVERLEY
BOOKS

For everyone whose father wasn't there.

And for JXS

www.waverley-books.co.uk

info@waverley-books.co.uk

This edition published 2014 by Waverley Books, an imprint of
The Gresham Publishing Company Ltd.,
Academy Park, Building 4000, Gower Street,
Glasgow, G51 1PR, Scotland, UK

Text copyright © 2014 Sue Reid Sexton

ISBN: 978-1-84934-170-7

Also available as an eBook
ePub format ISBN: 978-1-84934-176-9
Mobi format ISBN: 978-1-84934-177-6

A catalogue record for this book is available from the British Library.

Printed and bound in Spain by Novoprint, S.A.

Before 'Rue End Street'
– by Lenny Gillespie

This story is about how my world got turned upside down for the second time. The first time was when we got bombed in March 1941. Four thousand bombs rained down on my town, Clydebank, and hundreds of people were killed. I didn't know where my mum and wee sister were or even if they were alive. While the bombs were still falling I met Mr Tait and some other people, and together we got away from the bombs as fast as we could.

That night we walked into the hills to the huts at Carbeth. This is my most favourite place in the whole world. The 'huts' there are really chalets for people to live in, and there are trees to climb, ropeswings a-go-go, and always someone to play with. It was safe. Mr Tait looked after me there until I found out about my family.

That was in March 1941. Time has passed, it's September 1943, I've grown up a lot, and disaster is about to strike again.

'Dear God,' I said, but quietly inside my head, 'please make Mr Tait not dead.' I stopped there because however upset I was I knew that was stupid. 'Dear God,' I said, 'please help.' And then I asked for the thing I had just lost. 'Please send someone to help me.' Then I waited, but nobody came.

Chapter 1

Heavy rain. Bucketing. Cats and dogs. September floods and puddles fit for ducks, the burn bursting over the path into the bushes and the air so heavy we practically had to swim home. Our new blue tammies that my mum had knitted were black and sagging down round our ears and, speaking for myself, the rain was seeping freely round my shoulders and down my spine. Mavis and Rosie and I were soaked to the bone and we still had a mile to get home.

The hedges stood in mud by the roadside, there were no trees to hide under, and the deserted cottage we could have sheltered in had a path smothered in country pancakes. There was nothing for it but to keep going or the wind would slice us in half. Mavis got the jitters first. She was only six and a half, Rosie probably a few months older, though we weren't sure, and I was nearly twice that. They had both turned a shade of grey to match the rainclouds that were pelting us.

'We'll have to run,' I said. I was worried about Mr Tait who wasn't well.

Mavis gazed up at me with her big brown eyes and trembled.

'I'm too cold to run,' she said.

'So am I,' said Rosie.

'You're too cold not to,' I said. 'But we have to dance first, like we did at school. One and two and three and turn. Remember.'

I told them a lie, that our friend Mrs Mags was coming over with the baby and some rabbit stew. That got them going, and we danced in every puddle and played chickens along the way. By the time we were in the home strait we were dog-tired and covered in mud.

Mr Tait's perfect white handkerchiefs were limp on a line inside the front window of our hut. They were fuzzy through the mist on the pane where the rough line of a funny face was left from the morning. A good head of smoke reached up from the chimney through the rain and hung there in the trees. As I started up the steps, Rosie clattered past.

'Mrs Gillespie!' she called out. (That's my mum. She's Mavis's mum too, but not Rosie's.) 'Mrs Mags!'

'Mum!' shouted Mavis.

I didn't see anyone at first.

'Mr Tait?'

The perfect white handkerchiefs were blocking all the light. The room was full of shadow. A small fire played on a pile of ashes in the little iron stove, barely more than embers. Its glow lit one of Mr Tait's boots but the room was no warmer than outside. The boot was strangely still. I had seen boots that still before when the bombing happened, but the owners of those other boots were dead. This was Mr Tait, who wasn't ever going to die, obviously, being Mr Tait.

'Lenny,' he said. His voice was even hoarser than it had been when all the houses were on fire in Clydebank when the bombing happened.

'I can't see you,' I said.

'What's wrong?' said Rosie.

'Mum?' said Mavis. 'Where's Mum? Mrs Mags?' She banged through to the bedroom to look.

'Lenny, my darling,' said Mr Tait, and then he coughed and coughed and he leant forwards and suddenly I could see him in the yellow firelight. He had one of his perfect white handkerchiefs in his hand which he coughed into, only it wasn't perfect any more and had dark splotches all over it. His face was a mass of wrinkles and I couldn't see his eyes at all because they had shrunk down into two dark hollows. He leant back again into the darkness and rattled.

'Mavis, pull the hankies down. I can't see him,' I said. 'Rosie, bring some of that wood in the box 'til we get this fire up.'

'You lied,' said Mavis, under a frown. 'Mrs Mags's baby isn't here.'

'Just do it,' I said, pulling the stove door open so a cloud of smoke puffed out. 'I didn't lie,' I lied. 'It's too wet to bring a baby out.'

Mr Tait started coughing again.

'And get a cup of water from the bucket, quick, for Mr Tait,' I said. 'Little pieces of wood, Rosie, or we'll kill the fire altogether.'

Mavis ran and brought the cup, but Mr Tait's coughs faded before he could drink it. In fact they petered out like an old car that's run out of petrol, which is what happened last year to the doctor's car, outside our school, and we all went and looked. And then Mr Tait lay there in his chair and croaked and rattled and snuffled. I offered him the water but he waved a finger at me to say no.

'Give me a peace flag,' he whispered, which is what he called his handkerchiefs. I ran to the window and undid one. It wasn't perfectly white but still had shadows of stain in one corner. But he took it anyway, put it quickly to his mouth and coughed.

'Get your wet stuff off and dry yourselves,' I said to the little ones, who were staring at Mr Tait as if he'd newly arrived from the moon, which is what he sounded like. 'Go, before you catch pneumonia.' I took the wood from Rosie. 'Here's the towel. I'll do the fire. You two go through to the room.'

Mercifully the wood had been near the stove a while and was dry. I piled it carefully into the grate and blew to make the embers flame. Soon curls of fire sneaked out.

'Lenny,' whispered Mr Tait.

'Yes, Mr Tait?'

He raised a hand from his lap to indicate I should come closer.

Ordinarily I love the batter of rain on the roof and the wind whipping round the corners of our home, because it's home and it's cosy inside and we're all in there together, but that day it was so stormy, and with the wind roaring through the trees around us, I couldn't hear a word Mr Tait was saying. His voice was always soft and gentle but somehow you could always hear it no matter what. That afternoon he was so weak I couldn't make anything out at all, so I put my finger in one ear and the other ear right up close to his mouth and waited. I felt his breath on my neck and the dryness of his lips brushed against my ear like autumn leaves. These were things I hadn't felt before because Mr Tait was never one to show affection by touching. He'd only to call me 'my dear' and then I'd know he was the best friend I could ever have.

'My dear,' he whispered, and then he coughed again and I had to get out of the way. He sounded like little farthings rattling in a collection box, and when he'd finished he was like the wheeze of the fire. He waited a moment, then gave a little nod to indicate I should put my ear back up close. I was scared, I don't mind saying so, but I always did what Mr Tait told me, usually. I heard him say 'don't touch' and 'cup' and 'keep girls away' and 'mum back' and 'Barney'. Then he sighed and I could hear his breathing like the fire again. After a minute he went on. 'Your dad,' he said, and 'not far' and 'find' and 'under bed'. This surprised me because no-one hardly ever talked about my dad. My dad was a complete no-no as far as conversation was concerned. Although we didn't know where he was and everyone thought he was 'missing presumed dead', I was absolutely certain he wasn't under the bed. Then Mr Tait stopped again and when I drew back to look at him he had sagged even further down into his chair and his eyes were closed.

'Mr Tait?' I said, and I bent down, but this time I put my mouth next to his ear. 'Mr Tait,' I whispered, 'I don't understand.' I listened for him again but he didn't speak, so I stood up and peered through the darkness at him and wondered if he was sleeping the sleep of the dead. I thought of all the people I had seen when the bombing happened and I remembered seeing an ARP man put his head on someone's chest. The ARP man had listened there for a few seconds and then given the thumbs up to another man who brought a stretcher and carried the person off. I tiptoed forwards and put my head on Mr Tait's chest. For the first time he smelled like other men, of sweat and grime, a rancid stinging smell that was not like him. He was always clean and particular, and for a brief moment I was relieved because he was as dirty as me and therefore couldn't give me a row. And then he did a little cough and whispered, 'Alive, my dear, but be brave,' and that made the tears smart in my eyes because I knew, sort of, that he must be very ill.

The fire began to crackle then so I had to check it and make sure it didn't collapse out onto the floor, and while I was down there I glanced back at Mr Tait. His face was lit up in the glow and his eyes were open and sparkling at me. He seemed to be smiling but I wasn't sure. I filled the big kettle with water from the bucket and put it to boil on the stove. Then Mavis and Rosie came through, as quiet as the grave, and went and put their dirty things into the hip bath for washing later. We should have been in trouble for being so muddy and in a way it seemed like we were. I was just wondering if God really did exist and was punishing us for getting filthy, when I heard a car outside.

Cars didn't stop outside our house. We didn't know people with cars, not even old Barney, our landlord, who always arrived on foot seeing as he only lived a few hundred yards away and didn't own a car. But this car stopped and hummed. I heard the crunch of a brake, then a shudder, then silence.

In case you don't know, you can tell my mum a mile off because she walks with a limp, and the reason she does that is she lost her foot in the bombing, a bit like Mr Tait only she wasn't a soldier and she only lost her foot, not her entire leg. Mr Tait lost almost the whole of his leg in the last war, but my mum was stuck under a house for several hours and when they brought her out her foot was mangled like jam so they took her to the hospital. The next time I saw her, the foot was gone. She had a bandage round her head too with a safety pin the size of Mrs Mags's nappy pins. Ages later they made her a new foot. It took so long because they had to fix the soldiers first and there were a good few of them needing attention.

Anyway, I heard my mum's wooden foot banging up the steps, then a man's voice, then in she came with her woolly tammy like ours all dark and heavy and wet and her brown hair like rats' tails underneath it. Her face was wet too and shone in the firelight and behind her there was a man in tweeds. He was hanging onto his hat to stop it blowing off. It was like Mr Tait's hat, a tweedy brown flat cap or 'bunnet', like lots of men wore, only without the darning at the edges, and I recognised him as the doctor whose car had stopped outside our school. He had a bag with him and a blanket. There was a lady there too in a smart coat. She had her hat tied on with a scarf that was done in a knot beneath her chin.

'Lenny, you're back,' said my mum. 'Thank goodness, and you've got the fire going. Well done. Good girl.'

This worried me all the more. I was a muddy disgrace. I deserved a row. Something important was happening.

'Wash your hands,' she went on, 'and make some tea for Miss Barns-Graham and the doctor.'

'Oh, no, no,' said the doctor in a deep voice, and he shook his head and frowned at me. 'That won't be necessary, and we don't want the infection to spread, do we?'

7

'Come in, please come in by the fire,' said my mum. 'Mr Tait, how are you? Lenny, go and get changed, sweetheart. You can take the wash-bowl with you and some water. Close the front door, Rosie, and you three go into the bedroom.'

'Actually, would you mind leaving the door open, would you, please?' said the doctor. 'The patient needs air, lots and lots of fresh air.' He smiled at the room as if smiling would make everything alright. 'There isn't enough oxygen in here.'

The draught nipped at my wet legs but I didn't want to leave Mr Tait and the doctor and Miss Barns-Graham.

'On you go, Lenny, please,' said Mum. 'The doctor's here now, for Mr Tait. There's no need to worry.'

No need to worry? She wasn't fooling me. There was plenty of need to worry. But I knew when to do as I was told.

You see, we lived in this hut in the middle of some woods in the countryside in a place called Carbeth along with lots of other huts. That's what we call it, a hut, but actually it's a proper house with rooms, only made of wood. Carbeth is the greenest place in the world in some rolling hills. Before we lived in the hut, we lived in a single-end room two floors up in a tenement on the hill in Clydebank. Tenements are tall buildings with houses piled on top of each other and a stairwell to get to the high-up ones. Our house only had one room so that there was no going next door to get changed or you'd have ended up in someone else's house, although to be fair, I'd been sent next door to the neighbour's many times if my mum and dad had visitors or important things to discuss.

But this was different. Mr Tait was not well. He was very not well and I wanted to be there. Mr Tait had stood by me many times, even when I didn't want him to, even when I thought he was just a scary old man, which is what I thought at the beginning when I first met him. But by the time he took ill he had been there beside me for two-and-a-half whole years.

In the draught of the bedroom window I threw off my dirty clothes and scrubbed my face, then got the worst of the mud off the rest of me. Mavis and Rosie huddled together on the bed and watched.

'Hey, monkey faces, cat got your tongue?' I said.

'Who are those people?' said Rosie.

'Why were you crying?' said Mavis. 'What's wrong with Mr Tait?'

Next door the grown-ups were talking quietly so we wouldn't hear.

'Ssh. They'll hear us,' I said. 'I'm not crying.' I went to the door and listened. There was silence, then they spoke again, but I still couldn't make them out. They might have said 'mop him down'.

'You were crying. I saw you,' said Rosie.

'I don't know what's wrong with Mr Tait,' I whispered. 'I've never seen him like that, but it must be serious.'

'Why?' They said this together.

'When did we last get a visit from Miss Barney?' Miss Barney, who was the landlord's daughter, was a famous artist who we'd heard was back on holiday from England.

'I didn't know it was her,' said Rosie. 'I want to see what she looks like.' She got off the bed. Mavis looked at me then at the door. There was a thud beyond it.

Rosie stopped in fright.

'She's all wet,' said Mavis. 'It can't be her.'

'Of course she's all wet,' I said. 'Just 'cause she's a lady doesn't mean she can't get wet like the rest of us. The rain it raineth on the just.'

Mavis laughed and joined in, as loud as you like. 'But also on the unjust fellow, but mainly on the just because the unjust stole the just's umbrella.' We both laughed. It was an old favourite of our dad's, though Mavis wouldn't remember that, only that we sometimes said it.

'What?' said Rosie. She hadn't heard that rhyme.

Poor Rosie. She didn't have a dad, not even one who was missing presumed dead, but the truth was we might not have had one either then, for all we knew. Rosie's, however, was completely dead in the bombing along with all the rest of her family. Poor little Rosie, and the oddest thing was that she looks so like Mavis (who looks just like me) that no-one ever asks whether we really truly are family. We even have the same hair, dark and bobbed with a fringe.

I remembered what Mr Tait had said a few minutes earlier about my dad and I thought about looking under the bed for him, but it seemed better to wait until no-one else was there in case I hadn't understood him properly.

'Lenny, are you decent?' my mum called through the door.

'Nearly,' I shouted back. I couldn't get myself dry without standing by the fire, not properly, not when it was so cold, but I pulled on my vest, pants and dress anyway even though they stuck to me.

There was another thud on the other side of the

wall and then all the adults started talking at once. I grabbed my muddy socks and shoes and ran back through.

Mr Tait was coughing again. Miss Barns-Graham had taken off her scarf and hat and coat and was holding our candle lamp over the doctor's head. My mum was kneeling on the ground with the doctor, and in between them on the floor there was a pile of blankets and shoes.

Except it wasn't a pile of blankets and shoes. It was Mr Tait.

'Hold the lamp still, Miss,' said the doctor, 'so we can secure him adequately.'

'Yes, doctor, sorry,' said Miss Barney.

'I'll take a turn,' I said, and I took the lamp before she could stop me and held it over the bundle that was Mr Tait.

His skin was like the wax candles I'd seen in chapel until we stopped going. His eyes were red-rimmed and they opened wide when he saw me.

'Lenny, my dear … ,' he said.

I took his hand. 'Mr Tait, what's happening? What are they doing?'

'Keep the light up,' said Miss Barns-Graham.

'Careful, Lenny,' said my mum, and she limped round behind me.

Mr Tait's grip on my hand wasn't strong, but I felt his fingers push mine so I squeezed back. A squall battered at the window as if it wanted to come in. Miss Barns-Graham looked up in alarm.

'If you could stand back, Miss,' said the doctor, 'I'll wrap the blanket round him and then we can go.'

Miss Barns-Graham did as she was told.

'I've been nursing him fine,' said my mum. 'I'm doing my best. He seemed to be alright. Does he really need to go?'

'I'm going to give you some aspirin, Mr Tait,' said the doctor. 'You must try to swallow it. Don't worry, it's in water. It should slip down easily enough. Mrs Gillespie, if you would, a little water in a cup, and yes, I'm afraid he really does need to go. Apart from anything else there are the little ones to consider. If it should spread … . You understand. He won't be far away.'

Mr Tait's eyes opened wider. He gazed at me long and hard and an odd sensation like an itch ran up the back of my neck.

'Where are you taking him?' I said. 'I'll look after him, won't I, Mr Tait? I'll look after you. Mum, what's happening? What's wrong with him? Why is he ill?'

'Keep the lamp still, child,' said the doctor. 'He's going to be alright, but he has something called tuberculosis and it's quite a serious condition so he needs to be in hospital. He'll come back when he's better.' Then he turned to Mr Tait again. 'Now drink this.'

Mr Tait was lying on the floor with his head on a folded blanket. The doctor reached under Mr Tait's neck and helped him up enough to sip at the cup. It was the same one I'd tried to give him before, and the doctor had to insist because Mr Tait really didn't want it and kept turning his head away until the doctor said he was being a bad example to the children, meaning us, although Mavis and Rosie were back in the other room with my mum. Obviously the doctor didn't know Mr Tait very well, because he was the best example to me ever, if only I was better at following him. But Mr Tait did as he was told. And then he stared at me again.

I knew what he was doing, too. He was trying to fill me with grit and bravery, just like he did after the bombing when I didn't know where Mavis and my mum were for days and days, and when my mum came out of hospital with only one foot and I was frightened. The problem was that this time, by trying to give me courage, he was scaring me all the more. So I turned away while the doctor fussed and asked for shoes, and Miss Barns-Graham and my mum looked about the room for Mr Tait's overcoat and his Bible, which had all his papers in it. I knew where all of those things were, and my mum probably did too, though they seemed to take forever to find them, but I couldn't help because I was blinking into the darkness to make my tears go away. I didn't feel brave, not one tiny little bit. Then I heard him again.

'Lenny,' he said. 'Lenny …' So I turned to face him and he looked smaller than he should have been and sad in a way I'd never seen before. Even after the bombing, he was only worried or disappointed when someone was unkind, for instance, but not sad. I bent down to listen to what he had to say, but instead the doctor startled me.

'No kissing!' he said. 'Good Lord, no!'

'I wasn't going to kiss him,' I said.

'Keep back please,' he said, 'and give me the lantern so I can see my way about this place. Don't you have any candles, Mrs Gillespie, or a Tilley lamp?'

Miss Barns-Graham said she would send some candles down to us. My mum said only if it wasn't any bother, which was silly because everything's a bother when there's a storm raging outside. And we still had the candle in the other room. My mum went to fetch it and lit it from the fire. There was still a wee bit of light outside anyway.

But the daylight was fading even without the row of not-so-perfect white handkerchiefs across the window. The wind blew down the chimney so that clouds of smoke puffed into the room, and when it wasn't doing that it was shoving its way in the door and making the fire seethe redder.

'Children shouldn't be in here anyway,' remarked the doctor. 'Mrs Gillespie, can you ask this child to go next door?'

'Lenny,' I said. 'My name's Lenny and I think Mr Tait wants to tell me something, don't you, Mr Tait? It's probably important. He doesn't say things that aren't important.'

'On you go now,' said the doctor. 'Mrs Gillespie? The girl.'

The doctor was ignoring me. I bit my lip and stood up to go, but when I looked back at Mr Tait his face was more than sad. His brow was pulled down over his eyes and his dry lips were squeezed together as if he was trying hard to understand something, and then I realised he was frightened. It had never occurred to me that Mr Tait might be scared of anything at all, he was always so calm. He shifted on the floor as if he wanted to get up, but then sank back onto the blanket with a sigh like a baby's rattle, so I stayed in the room but kept back in the shadow behind the stove.

Footsteps clumped up the steps to the door and someone blocked the last of the light.

'Ah, here you are at last,' said the doctor. 'Is this the lad?'

'George?' I said. 'George? What's he doing here?'

'Afternoon, Mrs Gillespie,' said George.

'Thank goodness you've come, George,' said my mum. 'I wasn't sure the message would get through. This is Miss Barns-Graham.'

'Willie,' said Miss Barns-Graham. 'Call me Willie.'

George touched his hat.

'And the doctor,' said my mum.

'What's George doing here?' I wanted to know, and why was he being introduced to everyone as if he was a proper adult when everyone knew I was much more sensible than he was. Bad George could hardly even write and didn't know any of his times tables, even before he left school and went back to Clydebank to be an apprentice in John Brown's shipyard, the biggest shipyard in the world, probably.

I looked on as he was allowed to take Mr Tait's hand and to listen to what he was whispering. I fumed by the stove while bad George went for more water for him and when he folded the blanket back round Mr Tait and made him comfortable as I had wanted to do. George, who was nasty and spiteful and did everything he could to make my life a misery, was allowed to cradle Mr Tait's shoulders while the doctor fed him the last of the aspirin, and Mr Tait seemed to forget all about me. Maybe he couldn't see into the shadows by the stove where I slid down the wall and hugged my knees, watching the pain he was in, how hard it was for him to breathe, how he leant back on George and closed his eyes and let the doctor talk as if he wasn't there, as if none of us were there except George and the doctor.

And then everything seemed to happen very fast and we all talked at once, all of us except Mr Tait. Miss Barns-Graham put her coat and hat and scarf on again and went out first, saying she'd open the car door. Then George and the doctor slid Mr Tait across the floorboards on the blanket towards the front steps. The rain came pelting down on his leg and my mum started shouting.

'He's getting soaked,' she said. 'Surely that's not good for him, doctor? Couldn't we cover him with his coat as well?'

The doctor was too busy manoeuvring Mr Tait and telling George what to do. Big bad George is what I always call him because he's bigger and badder than anyone I know. And my poor mum couldn't do anything because she had her wooden foot which she still wasn't very good with and couldn't move as fast as she would have wanted to. Mavis and Rosie were squealing behind her, especially Rosie who had lost all her family and didn't want to lose anyone else.

'Leave him alone!' she was shouting, and she pulled at her ear so hard it bled.

Mavis whimpered and bounced from foot to foot and tried to see what was going on even though everyone was in her way.

'You're going to drop him!' said my mum. 'Look out. Miss Barns-Graham, maybe you could help. They're going to drop him. Goodness, oh goodness. Oh, Mr Tait!'

'He weighs nothing,' said George, and he looked up at the doctor in surprise from the bottom step.

Once they had him down the steps I jumped down after them.

'Mr Tait!' I said, and I came along beside him.

'It's alright, young lady,' said the doctor. 'Off you go. I'm in charge of him now. There's nothing to worry about.'

'Mr Tait,' I said, not knowing what else to say.

Then they got to the car and George stuffed the bottom half of Mr Tait into the back seat then ran round to the other side and pulled the rest of him in until the last bit of Mr Tait was sticking out the side of the car and the doctor was still holding onto his shoulders.

'Bend him at the knee,' said the doctor.

So they bent Mr Tait at the knee and then George came back to the doctor and got into the back of the car along with Mr Tait and laid Mr Tait's head in his lap as the doctor told him to.

'Mr Tait,' I said.

But he didn't open his eyes and he didn't say anything. I wanted to get into the car with him too but I knew they wouldn't let me. He lay there with his head to one side like a little baby fast asleep on George's lap. Then my mum came across in the rain with Mr Tait's overcoat and went to the side George wasn't on. She opened the door and laid it across Mr Tait's bent legs, then to the passenger door at the front and handed a bundle to Miss Barns-Graham and a book that was his Bible with all his papers inside.

'Where are they going?' I said. 'I don't want him to go.'

The doctor got into the driver's seat and started up the engine. The rain grew heavier again and battered on the metal of the car

'Will you let me know how he is?' said my mum

over the noise of the engine and the rain.

'It's a little tricky, Mrs Gillespie,' said the doctor, 'because, after all, you're not family. You're not related and strictly speaking I can't give out information.'

'We're family in everything but blood, doctor. Surely you'll come back and tell me? He's like a father to these girls.'

The doctor smiled crisply. 'I'll see what I can do,' he said. 'Goodbye. Wash everything thoroughly, boil what you can and burn anything with blood.'

'Goodbye, Mrs Gillespie,' said Miss Barns-Graham. 'Don't worry, dear, he's in safe hands. And the candles, I'll send them down.'

They drove off into the rain and I followed them like an idiot, running along beside the car in my bare feet shouting 'Mr Tait!' as if that was going to stop them. They soon disappeared round the bend and we were drenched to the skin again and wretched with cold. Our Mr Tait was gone.

Chapter 2

In the following days I lost my new blue tammy, a glove and the piece and dripping I had been given for lunch. I lost the words to my favourite song, 'The Quartermaster's Stores', which I prided myself on knowing all twenty-nine verses of. I forgot six-times-nine and eight-times-seven and tripped on the skipping rope three times in one dinner time. When I tried to fix our hideout up the hill in the woods I burst my finger open with the hammer and later that day I boiled all the water out of the stovies when I was left in charge of the tea.

The doctor didn't come back with news of Mr Tait and Miss Barns-Graham forgot our candles. I guessed bad George had gone back to Clydebank and forgotten us too. My mum said no news was good news and I tried hard to believe her.

Although bad George kicked and swore around me and Mavis and Rosie, he was always super-polite in the presence of my mum, so we were extra stung that he hadn't bothered to bring her news. Mr Tait was the only person who ever got George to behave at all, and in return George worshipped the ground on which Mr Tait walked. He'd have known Mr Tait would have wanted us to know how he was getting on.

Mr Tait would probably have liked his wooden leg

too, although he said he always took it off to go to bed, which was probably where he'd been since he left us, in a bed in the hospital. He must have been sitting in his chair by the fire without it on when we came back that day, something he'd never done before and I hadn't even noticed. It was only when my mum and I went into his room later to follow doctor's orders and wash everything thoroughly that I saw it leaning on the wall. We brought it through to the front window so we could see it. It had a joint at the foot and another at the knee and it was dark brown and needed a new coat of paint, and it had leather straps for attaching it to his body. They were dark brown too and twisted with wear. My dad would have called the leg 'rudimentary' which is nothing to do with being rude.

'I've never seen it before,' I said, 'not properly.'

'Neither have I,' said my mum. 'It's pretty basic, isn't it, compared to mine, and very worn in places.'

She pulled up the leg of her dungarees so we could compare her wooden leg with his, then let it back down again. We turned Mr Tait's leg round and touched the wood with our hands. It felt wrong to do this. Mr Tait wouldn't have liked us looking. It was like we were touching him.

'How did he lose it? He never let on,' I said.

'I don't know, only that it happened in the last war. He was in France in the trenches and by the time they got him to the doctor he had gangrene and it had to be cut off.'

I imagined Mr Tait with one pink leg and one green. This was swiftly followed by a blur of horrible things I'd seen when I was running through the bombing with Rosie and Miss Weatherbeaten, things I shouldn't have seen, things no-one should ever see. This used to happen to me a lot just after the bombing, this seeing things from the past as clearly as if they were still happening, but it hadn't for donkeys. Mr Tait had taught me what to do in times like that to make the horrible thoughts go away, but I wasn't used to having to any more, wasn't expecting it, so it took my breath away. I was suddenly too cold and then too hot.

My mum turned the leg over and the foot flopped forwards. His boot was still on it, of course, and a sock. The foot smelled of leather, not cheese, not like mine when I hadn't washed for a while. I knew what that was like, but this time I had to glance round at the fire because suddenly there were other smells too, burnt rubber, singed clothes, whisky and sewers and all sorts of other things you don't want to smell all filling up my nose. But it wasn't the fire. It was all inside my head. 'Be brave, Lenny,' said Mr Tait. (He was in there too.) 'Remember it will pass.' Good Mr Tait. I stared hard at the fire and made myself remember.

We all had funny things we did after the bombing and mostly it had stopped, but my mum had been acting strangely again since Mr Tait had fallen ill a couple of weeks before. She'd been dreaming at night, and she'd talk in her sleep sometimes and wake us all up. Her dreams were mostly about the bombing and being stuck under the building and thinking she was going to die and not knowing where Mavis and I were. She'd shout for help and call our names. It was always the same and I'd have to call back. 'I'm here. It's me, Lenny, and that's Mavis beside you. We're safe in Carbeth. The other lump is Rosie.' She used to be like that all the time and then gradually it passed, just as Mr Tait always said it would. But this was different because the Germans weren't bombing us any more, even though the war was still going on, and everyone said Carbeth was the safest possible place to be.

'Lenny?' said my mum. 'Let's put this leg safely away, shall we?' she said. 'Take it back through to his room and leave it where it was.'

The leg was cold and lifeless, not so different from the logs by the fire. That's all it was, a log. I leant it in the corner by his bed.

A few days later George came back. He looked different. George was fifteen by then and he was tall and skinny (we were all skinny) with dark hair and tiny brown eyes which darted about the place like a shifty little thief. He had on the usual dark trousers and work jacket everyone wore, covered in grime from the shipyards. We were in the hideout when he came, me, Mavis and Rosie, or rather they were and I was up the tree above it testing a branch for a rope swing. The hideout was made of fallen branches stacked against the tree with a thick layer of leaves on top, all held in place by a couple of well-placed six-inch nails Mr Tait helped me with. I hooted an owl hoot through my thumbs, which was our secret signal, but they didn't pay any attention and George came striding up the hill towards us with his big long legs.

'I thought I'd find you here,' he said.

'Oh, yeah?' I said.

'Yeah,' he said. 'Everyone knows about this place.'

'Go away, George,' said Rosie, stepping out of the den. Mavis came after and narrowed her eyes.

Normally I'd have encouraged these tactics, but

George's own little eyes didn't screw up in return and he didn't call us names. And I needed to know about Mr Tait.

'I came for his leg,' said George.

'Well, it's not here,' said Rosie. 'It's in the hut, our hut, and you can't have it.'

'Cool your jets, Rosie,' I said. I heard that one in the La Scala picture house.

He gazed up at me on my branch, just as Mr Tait had done from the floor in front of our stove, and I had that same creeping itch up the back of my neck. 'Can you come down, please?' he said.

Please? Did he say 'please'? He never said please, not to me anyway. Mavis and Rosie waited for my refusal and then stared at me hard when I landed with a thud beside them on the ground. I threw the rope into the den.

'You two stay here, will you,' he said, and he started down the hill.

'George?' I called after him but he kept on going. 'George!' So I followed him. 'Stay there,' I told the little ones. 'I'll be back in a minute. George!' Behind me I could hear Rosie's feet swishing through the long grass, following.

He stopped as soon as I caught up with him. His eyes had gone small again like they always did and his mouth was tight. I thought he was going to thump me because his hands were tight fists at his side, so I kept well back. He sniffed and glanced over at me.

'He's dead,' he said. 'Mr Tait, he's …' George began to shake. His head bobbed up and down and he gulped for air. 'He's dead. He died when …'

'No, George, he can't be,' I said. 'Don't be stupid.'

'I went outside for a smoke and then … he was in the bed, by a window, it was open, lying down … .'

'Stop it, George. It's not funny.'

'It was visiting time and I went out for a minute and when I came back, the nurse, she said …'

'Don't be horrible,' I gasped. 'You shouldn't kid about things like this. I'm telling him when he comes back.'

'He gave me instructions.'

'Shut up! Shut up!'

He took me by the shoulders. 'Listen to me, Lenny, do you think I'd joke about Mr Tait? He's dead. D-E-A-D dead. He got consumption and he didn't let on until it was too late. He knew he was going. Your mum must have known. They both knew but it doesn't really matter, does it, 'cause he's gone. G-O-N gone. Doesn't make any difference now.'

His jaw jutted out and his eyebrows furrowed in the middle and I saw what I didn't want to see: that he was telling the truth, this awful truth that Mr Tait was dead. But I didn't know what he meant because of all the people in the whole wide world, Mr Tait could never die.

'The doctor said tuberculosis,' I muttered, 'not consumption.'

'It's the same thing, stupid,' he said.

I shrugged his hands off my shoulders and backed away a couple of steps and then, without meaning to, I plumped down onto the grass and stared down the hill at a man who was building an extra room onto his hut. It was Mr Duncan. He had lent us tools to build our own hut way back in the beginning. Being a quiet day with no wind, we could almost hear him scratch his lip as he stopped to consider his work. Further down I could hear Mrs Alder, one of our neighbours, whistling as she hung out her washing, something my mum thought was 'common', which it was: lots of people did it. I would have done it too if I could whistle. I pushed my lips into a pout and tried but as usual nothing came out but hot air.

'I'm sorry,' said George.

I couldn't think what he could be sorry about. He was never sorry before. I didn't expect 'sorry' from George.

I stood up again and went over to a tree and walked round it. Then I walked around it again. On my third lap I noticed George and then Rosie and then Mavis standing in a row, watching. George had his big mouth open, Rosie's hand was heading for her ear and Mavis had fixed her eyes on me over her fist. Her thumb was neatly plugged between her lips. I continued round but bumped against the tree and lost my balance so I leant against it instead. The chimney smoke from all the huts ran straight up, absolutely vertical, past the stripes of trees, those that had been left when we cleared the hill for building. Mr Duncan had stopped fixing his hut and was rubbing his head. Mrs Alder had gone inside for more washing. Two squirrels were chasing each other round a big tree further along the road, but I lost them when they went in amongst the leaves.

'What's wrong with Lenny?' Rosie's whisper sounded close to me, but when I glanced up she was still standing with the others where I'd left them. George and Mavis stared.

'I came straight to you,' he said. 'I thought you

should know first.' He waited for me to answer but a hard lump had gathered in my throat and wouldn't let anything out. My head felt strangely cold and I reached for my tammy before remembering I'd lost it.

'What's the matter, George?' whispered Rosie. 'What have you done to Lenny?'

'Nothing. I just told her … I just …'

'Don't say it!' I said, and I put my fingers in my ears and squeezed my eyes tight shut. Then, remembering this was bad George who wasn't to be trusted, I opened them again. 'Come here,' I said, and I went to Mavis and Rosie and took them by the hands and leant down so all our faces were close together. But I didn't know how to say it so I stood up again and looked back down at Mr Duncan, who was holding a log along the side of his hut to measure it. 'The thing is,' I said, bending down again. I took a big breath and tried to find some words for this terrible thing. I could hear some rooks gathering in the trees further up the hill. They seemed to be discussing the news as if it was the price of butter and not the worst possible thing that could ever have happened.

'Mr Tait's dead,' I said. The words rolled in my mouth like gobstoppers.

Mavis's eyes went all around my face. She glanced over at George and then Rosie, then back at me and for a long time we stood staring at each other, I don't know how long. She had taken out her thumb, but she put it back in again and slipped her free arm around me and held me tight. Then Rosie screamed and screamed and the noise went ripping upwards through the trees and cut through the whistling of Mrs Alder, who was out with her washing again, and the hammering of Mr Duncan at his hut. It even stopped the rooks and their chatter. Mavis and I clung to each other and I didn't know what to do or why Rosie would want to hurt us all with her noise. George put his palms over his ears at first and then we all started shouting at her to stop. But she didn't. She just shrieked, on and on. Perhaps she couldn't hear us. Then Mr Duncan shouted at us to 'turn it up', by which he meant 'turn it down', and the children from the hut next door came running to see what all the noise was about. Rosie stopped screaming and ran into the hideout when she saw them coming. She covered herself with some little pine branches we had put in there in case the Germans came, and she hugged the rope I'd thrown in like it was a teddy bear. Because the branches were over her head, all I could see of her was two eyes glinting back at me and her fingers curled round one of the sticks holding the branches in. She was only howling, not screaming any more.

'Rosie?' I said. 'Come on out.' But I didn't really mean it. I didn't want her to come out and I wanted Mavis to let go of me too. I didn't even want Mavis, my only proper and fullest and bestest sister that I had lost in the bombing and had never wanted to be parted from since I found her again.

Mr Duncan and Mrs Alder and a whole gaggle of children arrived.

'George,' said Mrs Alder, puffing. 'You again.' She was red from running up the hill. 'I might have known. What is it this time?'

I glanced at George and all the other people and Mavis, and wondered whether I should explain why George's eyes were red. Then I ran off down the hill through the trees and left them all standing there, past all the huts and all the way to the road, and then I kept on running until I came to our hut and I stopped there, panting and sweating, and tried to see in. My mum was inside. I could see her head as she jerked across the floor on her odd feet, one wooden, one real. She came to the window and started hanging Mr Tait's perfect white handkerchiefs on the string. Her head was still at last and she had a look of concentration on her face. She'd been doing this every day since he went, washing them and hanging them, and still they weren't perfect.

What had George said? 'Your mum must have known.' Her face was pale like the hankies. She glanced up and saw me but I was rooted to the spot and couldn't go in. Had she known? Why didn't she do something? I'd have to give her the news and I didn't know how to do that.

Mavis and George were calling for me. So were the others, and a little way up the hill I could see Rosie standing with a hand on her hip and a fist in the air. So, instead of going in to my mum, I ran further along the road and around the bend so they couldn't see me any more. Then I went over a dry stone wall and into the field by the loch and across the field to the farm on the side of the hill. The field was wet from all the rain we'd had and difficult to run in because of all the hummocks the cows had made. By the time I'd got to the farm my legs felt like ton weights because of the mud caked round my shoes. I leant on the back wall of the barn for a second to catch my breath.

'Lenny!' Their voices rang out to me across the distance. I could hear the farmer with his herd on the other side of the yard. They were coming closer, probably heading for the field, so I jouked into the hay barn and climbed up into the loft. No-one saw me. I hurried to the very back of it and huddled under the straw.

In those days, when Mavis got scared she sometimes called me Linny instead of Lenny. It was a leftover from when she was wee and it got worse after the bombing. I think for a while she decided she didn't want to grow up after all and tried to be a baby again. It used to annoy the life out of me, but at least I always knew when she was scared. That day I heard her underneath me tiptoeing into the barn.

'Lenny?' she said, and 'Linny?' and gave a big sniff.

That peculiar lump happened in my throat again. But I couldn't come out of hiding, not even for her.

'Lenny, come on out,' said George. He was there too. 'Don't be so stupid. What about the others? What about your mum? She'll be wondering what's going on. Lenny? Are you there? Look, Mavis and Rosie are upset.'

I could hear Rosie crying, loud but not screaming. 'She must be in here somewhere,' she said between sobs. 'This is like my uncle's barn. He had cows too and they had a field with lots of mud too and … ,' Rosie went on and on and on, as she always did.

I thought about coming out. I was worried about her and Mavis being on their own with bad George, but I couldn't. I had to hold my breath until my whole body hurt, so that they wouldn't hear me, and I had to let the snotters run onto my lip and the tears down my dress without doing anything about it so that they wouldn't find me.

'Linny?'

'Lenny?'

'Lenny, come out now or I'll come in and get you,' said George.

They all stood and listened for me. And I stayed where I was and listened for them and then the farmer came and shouted: 'What are you doing in my barn? Get away out of there!' And away out they went and just as I had breathed out at last, I heard Mavis again.

'Linny, I'm scared. Come out. Please.' We both waited for ages and ages.

But I couldn't, not even for her, and then the rustle of the hay told me she'd gone and I heard bad George on the other side of the wall outside with the farmer, but I couldn't make out what they said.

And then I thought I'd die from holding my breath. It was as if my breath had decided to hold itself and there was nothing I could do. And when I did start breathing again it was like being sick but worse, as if someone had a hold of me and was shaking me all about, like George did once when I told Mr Tait he'd stolen someone's overcoat and got on the bus with the money in the pocket for the fare and I'd seen him do it. Only this was even scarier because there was no Mr Tait to tell me what to do or make it alright afterwards.

And my brain started going in loops. 'I'll go and ask Mr Tait what it means that he's dead,' I thought. 'Mr Tait will sort George out.' It's not like I don't know what being dead means. I saw lots of dead people during the bombing and I know that being dead means not coming back. It worried me all the more that I was being so daft. Then I heard Mr Tait talking to the farmer, I was sure it was him, and the dry shoosh of his feet in the hay down below in that uneven rhythm of his from having a wooden leg. I heard the tap of his boots on the stepladder. Then George said, 'I don't see her up here,' and I realised it was George I'd heard and not Mr Tait after all. I felt silly for thinking it was him but glad George hadn't seen me. George's feet went back down the ladder and then the cows started making a hullabaloo out in the yard, so I let my sobs out because I knew no-one would hear me and because I couldn't stop myself anyway.

And then the hullabaloo rolled off into the field with the farmer, and George and Mavis and Rosie must have gone home, and because there was no wind at all to whistle through the eaves of the hay barn I heard nothing at all, only the most enormous silence. After a bit my heart stopped beating like the thresher at harvest time that we saw last year and I listened to my crazy upside-down thoughts and wondered.

What did it mean that Mr Tait was dead? What did it mean he was never coming back? These thoughts tumbled about like the autumn leaves that were starting to fall. Mr Tait always came back. He was my Mr Tait.

Chapter 3

One of the things I wondered about was what Mr Tait would tell me to do right then at that precise moment. This was just the kind of situation I would have asked him about. If he'd been there he'd have comforted me with his soft voice and probably said a prayer before we did anything else, and then he'd have gone back and told my mum that he was dead. Then I realised this was one of those circular thoughts that were making me so dizzy.

But he would have prayed, that much was certain, and even though my mum didn't really do that I knew she didn't mind if Mr Tait did, or if I did too. They'd sort of agreed about that, in the end.

'Dear God,' I said, but quietly inside my head, 'please make Mr Tait not dead.' I stopped there because however upset I was I knew that was stupid. 'Dear God,' I said, 'please help.' And then I asked for the thing I had just lost. 'Please send someone to help me.' Then I waited, but nobody came.

I waited a long time in the loft of the hay barn, enough for the mud around my feet to start to dry. This wasn't as long as you might think because the mud was encrusted with straw too and it was warm up there, so with the help of a loose nail from the roof over my head I scraped most of it off. Fighting with my feet also helped me calm down and I could think more clearly.

I sat there a while longer and cried again. It was fierce and sore and made my stomach ache and it went on so long I thought I'd never stop. It made everything hurt and curled me up in a ball so tight I thought I'd be stuck like that forever. A heavy rain started, so heavy it was like bricks falling on the roof and it scared me because it was like the bombing, and I thought my head would explode with the noise and with my sobbing. But after a bit I could breathe almost properly again and my arms and legs and body stopped being so tight and sore, and I felt heavy and tired instead, as if I'd walked all the way home from school into a strong wind like the day they took Mr Tait away, only all by myself.

But then I remembered Mavis and Rosie were alone with bad George and I thought I'd better get out of there fast. Coming down the ladder I could hear voices in the yard outside, and when I got round the corner I saw it was the farmer and a delivery man with a lorry chatting as they unloaded sacks of grain into another barn.

'Afternoon,' I said as I raced past them, and they shouted something back I didn't catch.

I calculated the farm track would be easier than crossing the muddy field again. A row of little heads popped up over the garden wall of the farmhouse.

'Hi, Lenny,' called one of the heads, Laura, from my school, a nosy girl my age who'd been pals with George at the outdoor swimming tournament in the summer. (Mr Tait said we all deserved medals just for going in, which was all George did.) I didn't want her, of all people, to see me. Being red-eyed was not something I did. I was usually brave and sensible. Mr Tait said so. And anyway, I was too old for crying.

At the bend in the road the huts appeared, lined up along the side of it beneath the trees as it swooped off down the hill towards the main road and the Halfway House pub and Clydebank and Glasgow. Down at the bottom near the next bend I saw George carrying a log. Mrs Alder's children were with him and so were Mr Duncan's girls. They were leaping up trying to catch the log, and that's when I realised it was no ordinary log but Mr Tait's leg, held aloft with the foot waggling about at one end. I stopped and held onto my tummy to keep its contents from emptying onto the road. I should have gone down there and sorted him out. I should have made him bring it back, but I was too busy gawking and trying to keep breathing. Then suddenly they drew back from George and I saw him shake the leg at them so they all screamed and ran back up the road shouting 'Lenny!' I stood with prickles up my spine and a chill gripping my stomach. I wanted to hide and have Mr Tait deal with it. But he wasn't there.

I raced to our house before they got to me and banged the door shut. Rosie was chattering by the window. I wanted her to be quiet, or not be there at all, which was terrible. After she lost all her family in the bombing, she used to chatter away as if they'd just popped out to the shops, not understanding that they were all dead and gone. I wanted so badly to tell her so she'd know the truth, which seemed more important than anything else, and every so often I'd try and she'd look up at me as if I was speaking double Dutch. Then time passed and she stopped asking for them, but she never stopped talking. And here she was again: blah, blah, blah.

'Lenny's back!' she announced, as if I'd arrived for a party. Mavis and my mum turned from the fire where they were warming themselves.

'Lenny,' said my mum.

Her face was blotchy and her eyes were red from crying. She had a pair of scissors in one hand and Mavis's head in the other. She'd been trimming Mavis's hair, but the fringe was all up and down, much worse than it had been before. I took the scissors and held my mum tight. I wasn't much smaller than her any more. She had her old dress on from before the bombing, all stitched up under the arm where the seams had burst because of the crutches she used to have, and big woolly socks to cover her wooden foot. She heaved a sob and then so did I, and Mavis hugged us too and then Rosie on the other side, and we all heaved and sniffed and wailed. Then Rosie started howling again, like the packs of dogs I'd seen running about Clydebank lost with no owners, hungry and wild.

'Rosie, stop it!' said my mum, drawing back. She was shaking the way she does when her legs get tired and she needs to sit down, so I had to get a chair. She was closest to Mr Tait's chair so that's what I got. Mavis slid up against her with her thumb in her mouth and fat tears running down her cheeks.

'Rosie, stop howling,' I said, shoving the tears off my own face with my fingers. 'You have to stop doing that. Rosie? You're big now. You know what this means.' Her noise filled the room so I had to shout to make her hear me. 'But we're still here. We're not going to die, not for years and years. You're staying with us. Mr Tait would want that, wouldn't he, for us all to stay together? Wouldn't he, Mum? Mavis? Wouldn't he?'

'Of course he would, Rosie,' said my mum. 'Please stop screaming, Rosie. I can't bear it.'

I went right up close to Rosie's ear, like I did with Mr Tait when he was on the floor ill and I took both her hands, one of which was pulling on her earlobe like there was no tomorrow.

'Rosie,' I said, taking hold of her face. 'Look at me,' I said. She was trembling from head to foot. Her face was hot and sticky and her hands twitched beside mine as if they didn't know what to do with themselves, but she stopped howling and looked up at me with her face all twisted up as if she expected me to hit her. But just like before about her own family, I couldn't find the words and instead just stood there like an idiot saying her name and crying too. Then she put her arms around me and we hugged each other. When we were calmer and our breathing was even, she reached out to touch my face where the tears were.

'Your face is covered in mud,' she said, and did a little laugh like the air coming out of a kettle. 'There's straw in your hair.' And she laughed again.

Mavis came and looked. 'You were in the barn,' she said in a sad little voice. 'Why didn't you come out?'

'I'm sorry, Mavis,' I said. 'I couldn't, I just couldn't.'

'Why?' said Mavis.

'I don't know.'

'Why?' she said, not understanding that I didn't know everything, not even about myself.

'I'm sorry.' I picked up the scissors where they'd

fallen on the floor. 'Come on,' I said. 'We need to straighten your hair.' But she batted my hand away and hid behind my mum.

'Leave her just now,' said my mum. 'You should have come out. In fact you shouldn't have left them in the first place.'

I slumped down on the bench Mr Tait had made from five little birch trees. 'Sorry. I couldn't.' This was no lie. 'They were only up the hill. They're not babies any more. I just didn't think. It's Mr Tait. I mean, it's our Mr Tait. My Mr Tait.' I shook my head and felt my mouth go to jelly again. 'What did George say? What happened?' I said, gathering myself. I wanted to ask *Why did Mr Tait die?* But I couldn't, not out loud.

'George said ...' Mum stopped as soon as she started. I waited as she stilled her voice. Rosie took my hand and squeezed hard. Mavis furrowed her brow and we all gazed at our mum. 'He said Mr Tait had TB, that's tuberculosis, and pneumonia, which are chest things that make it hard to breathe properly.' She was so short of breath I was suddenly scared she might have it too. 'He said Mr Tait had gone to sleep in the hospital in his bed when it was visiting time. He said hardly anyone visits and that he, George that is, had gone outside to smoke a cigarette and when he came back the nurse told him.' She stopped and took a gulp of air.

'Told him what?' said Rosie.

Mum's voice was all broken and shaky and it took her forever to get going again. 'That Mr Tait wasn't going to wake up.' I thought how Mr Tait must have been the best friend she'd ever had too. 'He wouldn't have been in any pain, I don't think. He just drifted off.

George said it was like Mr Tait was there when he left him and gone when he came back.'

'I know what death is,' I said, eyeing the little ones. I always hoped they'd forget what they saw during the bombing. 'You can tell me later.'

'But that's what happened, Lenny, honestly. There's nothing more to tell. He died in his sleep. He fell asleep and just never woke up again.'

So he was sleeping the sleep of the dead, and this time it was real.

'Stop pulling that ear, Rosie darling,' she said.

Rosie allowed her hand to be removed yet again and leant in to my mum on the other side from Mavis. Her little chest was rising and heaving like she was getting ready to scream again and her mouth was upside down like a cartoon from the *Sunday Post*.

When I thought about it, it seemed right that Mr Tait should die in his sleep, so peacefully, and in a proper bed in a hospital instead of the pallet he slept on in our hut. It must have been a quiet way to die, like he was always calm, except for that last day when the doctor came for him.

Mum limped over, sat on the bench beside me, put her arm around my shoulders and drew me close.

'I'm scared,' I said, as I shook and let her steady me. 'Mr Tait was filling me up with grit and I didn't let him. I looked away because I didn't want to be brave. I didn't want him to be ill and lying there on the floor. And now he's gone and it's too late and I'm scared. I shouldn't have looked away. Poor Mr Tait. I couldn't even be brave when he needed me. And George is away with his leg. Where is he taking it? Why did you give him it? He was shaking it at the Duncan girls.'

'Lenny, Lenny,' she said, sniffing. 'Mr Tait knew you'd be upset. He didn't want you to see him in that state, but the doctor took much longer to arrive than we thought. I had to sit in the hall in the big house for ages before the doctor came. You must have run all the way back from school that day.'

'I was worried. I knew something was up.' I pushed my tears away. 'I just knew it.'

She pulled me in close and ran her fingers through my hair.

'The funeral director needed the leg,' she said. 'George took his Sunday suit as well.'

I knew what that meant. It meant he wasn't being laid out in our house. He was somewhere else. He was not with us. I had seen people laid out before and I knew what happened. It didn't happen after the Blitz because people had no homes to lay their dead people out in, and they often had no dead people to lay out because the whole of Clydebank, or a lot of it anyway, was burnt to the ground. But we did have a home. Mr Tait had a home, our home there in Carbeth, even though it was only a hut. It was a big hut and Mr Tait had his own room that he could have been laid out in. He had built it himself with help from me and George and some of the neighbours. I changed my mind about his dying in a comfy bed in a hospital. He should have been with us on the pallet in his room.

'Why?' I said, feeling wee. 'Aren't we going to lay him out like Grandad?'

'George says the funeral is on Monday,' she said, so we all started crying again.

We went to church the next day, which was something we didn't do as often as Mr Tait would have liked, but there were people from the huts who went every week and some of them helped me push my mum's wheelchair that Mr Tait had made for her from an old wooden chair and the wheels of a pram. My mum still liked to go in the wheelchair sometimes when she was very tired. The church wasn't actually a church. It was a barn at Home Farm near the main house. The minister walked from Blanefield, which was a good distance and all uphill and is probably why his face was so red. Mrs Alder led the singing because there was no organ. Old Barney was in the front row on a chair and the rest of us sat on hay bales which made us itch.

'And our thoughts are with Mrs Gillespie and her family at this time of sadness at the departing of their good friend Mr Tait,' said the minister. His eyes were red too. Perhaps Mr Tait had been his good friend as well. Everyone turned and stared at us. I heard Rosie take a big breath.

'Thank you,' muttered my mum and wiped her nose with one of Mr Tait's big white hankies.

Rosie started howling again and Mavis joined in this time, so I had to take them outside in case they drowned out 'Abide with me', which Mr Tait hadn't, even though I felt like howling too. The rain had stopped but the ground was wet and squishy. We leant against the outside wall and I felt as small as the little mouse that ran past our feet.

Chapter 4

The funeral was on Monday, as George said, but the day began as if Mr Tait had never been. We got up, I made the fire, my mum drew her chair over so she could make the porridge while Mavis and Rosie and I got washed and dressed. We were quiet, even Rosie. There was nothing to say and I for one was concentrating very hard on not thinking about Mr Tait, which meant I thought about nothing else. I tried drawing another face on the window but the mouth bled at the edges so I scrubbed it off.

Then my mum put on her best dress and her coat and a nice grey hat she had borrowed from next door, and Mavis and I stuck some little feathers we'd found into the rim of it. We closed up the fire and bumped the wheelchair down the steps onto the road and set off for the bus stop near the Halfway House pub. We left the wheelchair behind a hedge for later because my mum couldn't take it with her. As a treat, I suppose, we got to go on the rumbly old bus, but of course Mavis and Rosie and I had to get off at the school. The journey passed in silence, Rosie still mercifully quiet. No-one on the bus spoke either, even the people we didn't know and who had probably never even heard of Mr Tait and his dying.

When we were nearly at the school we passed a

funny-looking man in a brown suit. He was tall and his jacket stuck out at the shoulders and flopped down his arms, and a flash of white leg showed where his trousers were too short. The bus crunched to a halt just as Miss Read rang the school bell (that was honestly her name). I said goodbye to my mum and we all hugged her and waved goodbye from the side of the road. She was going all the way into Glasgow and getting the tram all the way back out to Clydebank. Luckily there were other people going to Mr Tait's funeral too who would help her.

The man in the odd suit turned out to be George. Rosie and Mavis crossed the road and had already found their pals. My pal Senga, whose name was back to front, was wandering along from the village. She was always late. I stopped by the roadside and watched George in his borrowed suit hurrying along, then without so much as glancing at me he started up the little path along the burn beside the school which I knew went all the way up and over the hill, past Cochno, past Hardgate and down to Clydebank, where we all used to live. It was the path I came over with Mr Tait and Rosie and Miss Weatherbeaten when the bombs were falling on Clydebank.

George was going to Mr Tait's funeral. It wasn't fair. There was no question of me going. Girls of twelve didn't go to funerals. I had been told in no uncertain terms that I would not be going, no matter what. So I was going to school instead. But George was on the path on his way to Mr Tait's funeral and he wasn't a grown-up either. He was only fifteen, which wasn't much older than me, and the fact that he was working made no difference, or that he'd built his hut mostly

42

by himself. In my opinion he had no more right to go to Mr Tait's funeral than I had.

I ran across the road and followed him up the path when I was sure no-one but Senga was looking.

'Lenny!' she shouted and started to run, but not fast. She lived on a farm so they were never short of food.

'George!' I said when I got close enough.

I startled him. Maybe he was lost in thought, but he seemed surprised to see me. I clambered over the stile, ripping the hem of my dress (again), and ran after him.

'Stop. Where are you going?'

'Where do you think I'm going?'

'I know where you're going.'

He came to a halt. 'So why did you ask?'

I stopped too and stared back down at the school. I could see Mavis at the side of the playground with her thumb in her mouth gazing up at us. Miss Read's bell rang out and they formed the line.

'I'm going to the funeral,' he said at last.

'I know that.'

'Stupid question then,' he said in a tired voice, and he stayed there on the hillside looking down at me.

'Leave me alone,' I said. 'I'm tired. Why do you always have to be like that?'

I was tired because of waking up all through the night. It had been a still night, deathly still, except for my mum dreaming out loud and Mavis whimpering, and then Rosie had sat bolt upright and screamed blue murder until we talked her into lying down again.

'We're all tired,' said George.

I looked away. As well as everything else, I'd dreamt

that Mr Tait was snoring in the next room, and then I'd had to realise all over again that he wasn't there and it was only a bush outside rubbing in the wind.

George looked like he hadn't slept either. He was an odd grey, a bit like his brown-grey cap.

'Mr Tait said … ,' he said. He started, then stopped himself. 'Nothing.' He pulled his bunnet off his head, Mr Tait's cap that is, and scratched his crown the way Mr Tait used to when he was thinking. He was only fifteen but he thought he was a proper man.

'Mr Tait said what?'

'Well,' he said. 'He … um … he …'

'What?'

'Never mind.'

'What did Mr Tait say?'

Bad George looked down at his fingers. He shifted his lunch parcel so far under his arm that it must have been squashed.

'He said I was to look after you.'

'Look after … ?' I stood up very straight. 'That's ridiculous. Mr Tait would never say that. I can look after myself.'

'He didn't mean just you. He meant Mavis and Rosie and your mum too, all of you. How are you going to live now he's not there to provide for you?'

George put a lot of emphasis on the word 'provide' which I thought was unfair. You see a long time ago, after the bombing, Mr Tait promised to provide for me, but I was only nine and didn't know what he meant by 'provide'. So I kept telling everyone, hoping someone would explain. On this occasion George was taking the micky.

'We'll manage,' I said. I looked off up the hill so

that he wouldn't see that this was something else I'd been trying not to think about and therefore thinking about all the time. 'I'll get a job. I'll get a Saturday job or a paper round. We'll manage. We'll find Miss Weatherbeaten.'

It was his turn to laugh. Miss Weatherbeaten, whose real name was Miss Wetherspoon, had wanted to adopt Rosie who had no-one at all after the bombing except me and Mr Tait. That was before we found Mavis and my mum. Miss Weatherbeaten was from my school in Clydebank and she had no-one after the bombing either because her very close friend who was nearly family had been killed. But adopting Rosie hadn't worked out because Miss Weatherbeaten got her old job back in a school in a different building from the school she had been in before and went to stay with a friend from the town hall. Rosie was left with us, and Mr Tait and my mum had sort of adopted her instead. Rosie never liked Miss Weatherbeaten anyway because she was strict, so Rosie kept making trouble for her without really meaning to and after a while Miss Weatherbeaten stopped coming back at the weekends.

'I've got to go,' said George.

'No, wait,' I said. 'I'm coming with you.'

'You can't,' he said. 'Children aren't allowed. Your mum'll be there. She'll know you didn't go to school.'

'I don't care. I'm coming.'

'No you're not. Piss off.'

I gasped. 'I'm telling … ,' I said. But I couldn't tell Mr Tait.

'Suit yourself,' he said, 'your funeral.' And then all the colour drained from his face. He turned and started off up the hill in great lollops and I had to run after him.

'That's horrible!' I shouted. 'You have to wait for me.'

'No, I don't,' he said without even looking back.

There were trees beside the path and they roared in the wind as I passed. It was the biggest hill I'd ever climbed. I glanced back down from the brow and saw Mavis and Rosie at the end of the line as they went in the school door backwards, staring up at me. I had to stop and lean against a big old beech tree for a second to catch my breath.

'Wait!' I shouted.

But bad George kept going, shifting the parcel under his arm every so often, and as he went into the distance I realised his suit was Mr Tait's. I didn't know what to do then, but I was so out of breath and incapable anyway, I sat down and watched him skirt along the side of a field where the cows watched. As soon as I could breathe again I ran after him.

'George!' I shouted. 'That's Mr Tait's suit! You've no right. Stop!' But of course he didn't stop, not until he got to the flat rock, which was miles from where we'd started. But you couldn't walk that path and not stop at the flat rock because you could see right over Clydebank and Govan and Glasgow. You could see all the churches and their spires and the smoke from the tenements and factories and shipyards, and the light bouncing off the very Clyde itself like a ribbon of pure silver. You could even see the White Cart River where it joined the Clyde on the opposite bank. A few houses nestled beneath the hillside on the way down and over to one side, beyond fields and walls and cows and clumps of trees and the crater where a bomb landed and threw mud and stones all over the place, you could just make out the farm where Mavis ended up during the bombing.

George stood facing me with his back to all of this and his little eyes all screwed up into his face. Perhaps it was the fact that the sun had suddenly come out and was glaring at us from every leaf and muddy puddle that made him squint. He threw his hand out at me with the fingers all splayed like a fat star.

'You are the most annoying person I've ever met in my whole life!' he yelled. 'Leave me alone. You know you can't come. You're too young and too stupid.'

'I'm not too young. Mr Tait wouldn't have said that.'

'And you're a girl and he wouldn't have let you come. Of course he wouldn't have. Anyway, it doesn't make any difference now because HE'S NOT HERE!'

He stared at me with eyes like burning embers inside his head, as if Mr Tait dying was all my fault. Then he turned away and a terrible noise burst out of him. It was like Rosie's wail only worse because it was George, and sore as if it was splitting him open, and it came scraping out of him like something breaking. He swung round and lurched towards me and stood over me with his fist in the air ready to punch my lights out. His eyes bulged wide. His fist shot towards me. I ducked and covered my head and I heard him breathe like an angry bull, felt his heat close to me. Then his boots swished off through the long winter grass and I knew he was gone.

My heart thumped in my chest. I stayed where I was until I was sure he wasn't coming back then picked myself up. I don't know how I ended up on the ground. My face was wet too, as his had been, and I was trembling and hot. I thought about all the angry things I could shout after him, that I'd tell my mum on him, how he looked ridiculous in Mr Tait's suit, how stupid and despicable he was and all Mr Tait's work on him had been wasted. And that I was upset too, and it wasn't just him. But I was too scared.

For the tiniest of moments I worried that Mr Tait would give me a row when I got home for sneaking off from school, and that made me plonk back down on the rock and cry that he was gone. There was no-one to tell about George except my mum and she didn't believe me about George because he was always very extra nice with bells on for her.

Mr Tait had taught George and me lots of sensible things, useful stuff like building huts and how to behave in certain circumstances. But Mr Tait was gone and couldn't teach either of us anything any more. We had to work it out by ourselves and I didn't know how to do that.

I hurried down the hill after George. By then he was a brown speck in the distance, dotting in and out of the trees, but he knew I was following him. I knew he knew I was there because he kept glancing over his shoulder, but I was too clever for him and kept my eyes fixed on the back of his big hateful head ready to duck out of sight behind a bush. I knew where he was going, too, so I didn't care if I couldn't keep up, which I couldn't.

There was no hurry. Everyone else had to come from Carbeth and it was a long way if you got the bus into Glasgow and out to Clydebank again and didn't walk directly over the hill. I came down Kilbowie

Road which runs over the hump of the hill and on towards the river, stretching down in front of me to John Brown's shipyard at the bottom with its cranes reaching upwards like arms silhouetted against the green fields on the bank opposite. Closer by, the big white La Scala picture house stood surrounded by rubble where the buildings used to be and then the chimneys and clock tower of Singer's further on. A coalman's cart was struggling up the hill, the driver's eyes white in his black face. Two motor cars were stuck behind it. The coalman grinned white teeth at me and passed by. Then a tram came sneaking up behind me. 'Ding' it went as it passed, and the conductress laughed when I jumped. I straightened out my dress as if I'd meant to jump and ignored her.

There was a long pile of rubble down one side of the road where the tenements used to be and a neat row of red sandstone houses on the other. You had a bit of money if you lived in them.

Halfway down the hill was the church. I saw George go in, but he'd only been in there a couple of minutes when he came dashing out again and ran off down the road towards John Brown's. He was in such a hurry he even took his bunnet off. I decided to wait in the rubble and perched myself on a black chunk of tenement. There was no place to hide properly. A couple of old neighbours passed by and said hello and asked why I wasn't in school, so I said I was waiting for my mum, which wasn't entirely untrue.

After the bombing happened, my mum said we didn't need to go to church again. She said, 'How could there be a God if He let that happen to us?' When my dad was still there we used to go to chapel sometimes on a Sunday. They talked in a language I didn't understand and neither did my mum. Maybe my dad did. The chapel had hard seats and a little bench to kneel on and none of my friends went there. Then, when my dad left to fight in the war, we used to go to this church instead, the one on the hill where Mr Tait's funeral was going to be. My mum said it was like going home. I liked the singing. We all liked the singing. But then the bombing happened and we didn't go to church anymore. Sometimes we went to the makeshift one in the barn but not often. Mr Tait would say prayers sometimes, especially at dinnertime, but my mum never joined in. She said it felt like lying and only went to the barn to please him.

While I was perched there, a tram stopped a little way down the hill. Three women got out and one of them was my mum. I stood up, then sat down, then stood up again. I should have been helping her, but I shouldn't have been there too and I'd be for it if she saw me, so finally I crouched down and kept still. They stepped back from the road and waited for the tramcar to continue on its way, then crossed over. A few minutes later, when I was getting tired of crouching and keeping still, I saw a horse and cart with two men on it and lots of people walking behind and I knew it was Mr Tait and all the neighbours and friends going to the funeral.

As it drew close I saw the big wooden box on top of the cart and some flowers lying beside it all jiggling about. The box was brown, like Mr Tait's suit that bad George was wearing, and it was flat on top. There were rope handles on either side. The horse was straining up the hill with the weight of Mr Tait and the box to pull and I worried that Mr Tait was going to fall off. It was a very steep hill and the horse made the cart shake and shudder and the flowers twitter and twitch until a sprig of yellow broom landed on the road. No-one seemed to notice. I nearly went and told them that Mr Tait would fall too if they weren't careful, but I knew that would upset my mum who already looked upset and that she'd send me straight home. So I held still and didn't breathe. All the people in the street had stopped. The men had taken off their hats and the ladies bowed their heads to show they knew what was happening.

The cart turned into the side street and stopped by the church steps and the men on the cart jumped down. They were completely dressed in black apart from their starched white shirts and looked sombre and serious. One of them went to the horses and held onto the bridles and the other went round the back and spoke to some of the men. George was there with Mr Tait's trousers that were too short and the bit of leg showing. Another was Mr Duncan from Carbeth, but I'd never seen any of the other men. They slid Mr Tait in his coffin off the back of the cart and put him on their shoulders then started up the steps of the church. I thought he was bound to fall this time because the two men at the front were so much higher than the others and because Mr Tait's head was down the hill. I leapt up, my tummy fluttering like a butterfly, and thought how uncomfortable that must be for him, and I remembered standing on my head for too long at the back of our hut once and having a sore head for the rest of the day. George was in the middle, at Mr Tait's waist, and when they stopped at the top of the steps to the church door, he turned and looked straight at me with his tight little eyes and his face all red with the weight of the coffin. Then they all went inside. When I looked for my mum she was standing near the cart with her hands clasped together, almost as if she had been praying, as Mr Tait would surely have been if he hadn't been inside the coffin. Maybe she was praying he was alright in there and not all scrunched up on his head and that they wouldn't drop him all over the road and the steps. Then she followed him in along with the others, and everyone who wasn't with them put their hats back on their heads and carried on about their business as if nothing had happened and Mr Tait wasn't dead.

I suddenly thought I could smell Mr Tait, his whiff of toast and poached egg in the morning, or carbolic soap.

'Go on then,' he said. 'You know what to do.'

I looked behind me. There was no-one there. There was no-one anywhere in the rubble except me so I guessed I must have heard his voice in my head, but it was so real I had to listen again. Nothing came, only the echo of what I'd already heard: 'Go on then. You know what to do.' He had said this to me often, but only when he was still alive.

'Mr Tait?' I whispered. 'I don't think I do.'

But I knew what I wanted to do, go into the church and say goodbye to Mr Tait, because, after all, that's what funerals are for. So I crossed the road and went up the steps. The minister was in his pulpit at the front and everyone was listening. He wasn't talking about hell-fire and sinners like I'd heard him before. He was talking about 'our brother' and 'God is welcoming his son' and things like that. And because you wouldn't dare not listen to him, no-one paid any attention to me sneaking in the back. I picked up a blue hymn book and sat in the back row beside the door and opened the hymn book in front of my face.

We sang and then we prayed and then we listened to the minister again, or tried to, and for once I heard most of what he said because he was talking about Mr Tait going home and I remembered what my mum had said about going home to church, but I was wishing I was going home to Carbeth with Mr Tait. Then we prayed again and sang again, except I couldn't because I had a big gloop in my throat and my voice kept going all wavery. Then the minister did more talking and I couldn't listen to any of it and suddenly everybody stood up to leave so I had to get out of there as fast as my legs would carry me before I was seen.

This time I went down the hill, which was silly because there was nowhere to hide down there and still be able to see what was going on, but when they carried Mr Tait back out of the church George was on the other side of him so he couldn't glare at me. Once he'd put Mr Tait back on the cart, he turned and looked for me on the other side of the road and then whispered something to my mum. She looked over there but of course I was gone, then she put her arm round George and gave him a squeeze. I'd never seen anything like it. Then she handed him one of Mr Tait's big white handkerchiefs and he started away from the crowd and down towards me. I didn't know what to do so I didn't do anything at all. I just stood there gawping as if I was meeting the queen, frozen to the spot with my teary face cold in the wind. He put his hand against a wall for a minute and I thought he was going to be sick. He was swallowing hard and kept standing up extra straight then flopping down again. I heard that strange noise from him that I'd heard on the hill. His hands were shaking. I felt the blood drain from my face and the cold wind blew up my dress. George rubbed his cheeks and then pressed his hand against his mouth, I suppose to stop the noise getting out.

While he was standing there I saw the cart starting to move off with all the people following it. I wanted to say, 'Hurry up or you'll be left behind.' He was scaring me. It made my eyes burn to watch him and I began to swallow too. But I didn't want him to know I'd seen him that way and I looked about for somewhere to hide. Then he stood up straight and tugged Mr Tait's jacket down so it was neat, which made the bottom of his trousers flap, and he turned back up the hill and hurried round the corner after the others. I don't think he saw me even though I was right in front of him. I hurried to follow.

There were lots of places to hide in the graveyard but funnily enough lots of other people seemed to want to hide too or at least not get close to the grave. They hung back as if they were just waiting for a bus in the sunshine, and I'm pleased to say it was sunny, but windy too. So I had to wait by the gate, which meant I couldn't hear what they said about Mr Tait and putting him in the ground. I had to wait until everyone had gone back out before I could go and say goodbye to him myself. I hid behind the gatepost while George and my mum went past holding each

other by the arm. I don't know who was keeping the
other one up.

Chapter 5

The other gravestones all had humps of earth in front of them or plain old grass. Some had jam jars with flowers and one was planted with little white star-like blossoms like I'd seen in the woods at Carbeth. I decided to plant those on Mr Tait's grave too. I was sure he'd have liked that.

But when I got to the grave there was no grass or mound of earth, just the biggest hole you ever saw with straight sides making a huge rectangle of darkness and lots of mud around it and footprints going in all directions. A mound of earth was on the grave next door. Huge it was and high as if a fat person was buried underneath. The gravestone at the back of Mr Tait's had the name 'JOHN TAIT' in squinty letters and a date from long ago and I wondered if they'd got the date wrong. John was Mr Tait's Christian name but only certain adults were allowed to use it, mostly men. Perhaps it was his dad's name too. There were other names on the gravestone, two Elizabeths and a James, and a milk bottle with some flowers sat beside it.

When I got close I gazed into the hole and deep down inside was Mr Tait's coffin with a piece of paper stuck to the top that said 'John Tait', a number and a date. Splatters of mud were all over the length of it.

I wondered why they would leave Mr Tait in such a mess and thought how clean he always was and how upset he'd be at that important moment to have mud all over the place.

It was a long way down. If I'd stood up straight in it my head might have reached the rim. I crouched at the edge and thought about how cold it must be and dark in that box with a lid shut tight. Once, at my old school, some bigger girls locked me in a coal bunker and I thought I'd be there all day and all night and no-one would ever hear me shout, and someone would find a skeleton in a hundred years' time and wonder why I was there. This actually happened to someone in a big old house in the middle of Glasgow, but the teacher let me out at the end of lunch when she heard them laughing about it.

A bit of muck peeled off and landed on the coffin with a whisper. Then a great splop of rain hit the paper with Mr Tait's name on it and the ink ran away everywhere. I went to lean on the stone for safety and watched as more rain fell and the blue ink brightened and spread until you wouldn't have known who was in there at all and the paper was like clouds of cigarette smoke.

'Mr Tait,' I whispered into the downpour. Although I tried, I couldn't quite say goodbye. I felt like he was standing there beside me, which is how I often felt when he was alive, as if he was with me even when he wasn't. So instead I said, 'I wish you hadn't gone,' and I stayed there trying to think what else to say until the shower stopped and I was wet right through to my bones and my teeth were clacking against each other.

'Bloody Eyeties,' said a voice.

I ducked behind the gravestone.

'What's that?' said another.

'The Italians,' said the first. 'All very well changing now.'

'Most of them won't have wanted to join Hitler,' said the second. He was about my dad's age and had a shovel and a rake on his shoulder.

The first one was as old as Mr Tait, and lurched down the path using his shovel like a walking stick. 'Cowards every one, you mark my words,' he said. 'No backbone, the lot.'

'Och, away you go,' said the other. 'There're elements in this country would've joined the Nazis as quick as Bob's your uncle. You know that. It could have been us. We shouldn't be too quick to throw stones.'

'No. Never. Not us. The Scotsman is a socialist through and through. Wouldn't happen here.'

'Not if we had our own government, no, but we don't, and the ones we've got ...' He broke off. 'Oh, would you look at that.'

The gravediggers stopped and stared at me so I came out of hiding.

'Soaking wet,' said the younger, and he swung his spade and rake to the ground and leant on them the same as his friend. 'You're like a drowned rat.'

'You'll catch your death, young lady,' said the older. His spade sang on the cobbles.

'Hey, watch what you're saying!' He elbowed his friend. 'You alright there?' he said to me. I nodded. 'We should take her in, let her dry off at the fire,' he went on.

'No, send her home,' said the old man. 'She

shouldn't be in here anyway. You don't want to encourage them.'

'This your dad, then?' said the younger, nodding at the grave.

I shook my head. Raindrops flew off my hair.

'Grandad?'

I shook again and something slithered down my back.

'I see,' he said, though he couldn't have done. 'On you go then. Get yourself home. Do you live close?'

Suddenly I felt like Mavis who stops talking when there's trouble. I tried to say 'no' but my throat had gone dry and nothing came out. I wanted to say, 'This is my special friend who was like a grandad and provided for me and my family when we had nothing,' but my voice seemed to have disappeared altogether. I tried a smile instead.

'It's not a playground, young lady,' said the old one.

I backed behind the gravestone, though my legs had turned to jelly.

'Don't run,' said the younger. 'Come back! You frightened her, you eejit.'

I kept going until I couldn't see them any more and then stopped against a wall. When it seemed safe I sneaked a little way back and watched them. They shovelled the mud pile into the hole on top of Mr Tait. It sounded like potatoes in a barrel at first and then a shoosh as if Mr Tait was about to speak and they didn't want him to. I could have said, 'Goodbye!' or 'Stop! I'm not ready,' but instead I just watched as they trod the earth down over him as if they were planting bushes in a garden.

'Luigi was a laugh,' said the younger man, who was doing most of the work.

'Right enough, his chips were good,' said the other.

'I heard they sent him to Australia. The Australian sun'd suit him. He was always complaining about the weather. It was always better in Italy.'

'Should have gone back then, shouldn't he? Anyway, I heard it was Canada. That'd freeze the bollocks off him.'

'There's a crowd of them out at Helensburgh at the forestry, and Dunoon. Always fancied that myself. There are worse places to be right now than up a mountain cutting trees. Better than shovelling wet earth over dead people in the rain.'

'Damn the rain. Makes the work that much harder.'

I wished they'd hurry up and go away and I could be with Mr Tait. I willed the rain to start again so they'd have to go. At last they did, and I went back to find the earth piled up and the flowers knocked over.

I set the milk bottle right, crouched against the stone and whispered to Mr Tait again. 'I don't know what to do,' I told him, 'or what to say. I wish you were here to tell me.' I wiped my eyes on my sleeves and dried my hands on my dress, stood up to go and waited for a little robin to finish his song on the next door grave.

'Goodbye,' I whispered. I let the tears run freely and turned towards the gate and home.

Leaning against the gatepost was my mum still wearing her borrowed hat and feathers.

'Lenny,' she said. 'There you are. Thank goodness. George said you might be here.' I ran and fell into her arms and sobbed and sobbed and we stood there for ages, even though her legs must have been hurting terribly, and then we went and got on the tram and then another tram and then the bus and she kept her arms around me all the way, right in close, until we got home.

Chapter 6

Auntie May once called my mum headstrong and reckless. Gran said she agreed wholeheartedly. Because I was only wee at the time I didn't understand 'reckless'. I thought of ships that sank without trace. When our house was bombed, I thought it meant not even having a wreck, in other words homeless, which is what we were. Gran and Auntie May never came to visit us in Carbeth. They said my mum was being reckless again. They wrote to tell her so. I saw the letter. Mum was so furious about it we all read the letter, even Mavis who was just learning.

'There ... will ... be ... talk,' read Mavis, only she said 'talc'.

'Tongues ... will ... wag,' read Rosie, only she said 'tong-goos'. So we all laughed and waved the fire tongs at each other. All except Mr Tait. Mum put the letter in the fire.

It was because of Mr Tait. They were confused about him, same as I had been. They thought he was a bad man who wanted to take advantage of my mum when in fact he wanted to look after us. He knew we wouldn't make a good job of it ourselves and would probably have ended up in the poor house or at least on the parish. Mr Tait rescued us from all that.

Auntie May said my mum had nearly ruined her

life by marrying my dad, because he went to chapel and we went to church, and she said that now my mum wanted to complete her downfall by 'living in sin' with Mr Tait, made even worse by the fact that she was already married. They didn't say that in their letter. That's what my mum told me on the way home from the funeral when I asked her if we'd have to go and stay with Gran. She was upset at the very idea.

'Mr Tait knows all about sins,' I said as quietly as I could. 'He was very careful to avoid them. I think the sins in our house are all by me, Mavis and Rosie.'

The bus stopped to pick up a boy from my school and his mum.

'Hello, Mrs Gillespie,' said the lady, and she patted my mum on the shoulder and left her hand there. 'So sorry to hear about your Mr Tait. You will be staying in Carbeth won't you?'

'Thank you,' said my mum. 'Yes, for a bit, I suppose.' She turned her face away to blow her nose and they passed on to the back of the bus and I heard that song in my head, the one about the back of the bus they canny sing.

'He wanted to marry me,' she said. 'We have to keep an eye out for the girls, by the way, so we can stop the bus for them.'

'Marry you? But what about Dad?'

'Shh!' She glanced at the other passengers. There were plenty of them but they were mostly quiet, staring at the heads in front of them. 'Gran and Auntie May thought I was …' Her head fell forwards, then back up. 'Living in sin is when … . Maybe we better talk about this at home.'

'No, tell me now. What does it mean?'

She thought for a moment and then leant into my ear and whispered. 'They thought Mr Tait and I were living as if we were married.' She looked into my face to make sure I'd understood and I stared back and tried.

'Well, you were though, weren't you?' I said. 'He went out to work at Singer's and you sewed at home on your machine for people in town and looked after the house and us.'

'Yes, but …'

'Isn't that being married?'

'Yes,' she said, 'that's part of it, I suppose, but it's not what they meant. Let's talk about it at home.'

I had to think hard about this. They didn't sleep in the same bed, if that's what she meant, like Senga's mum and dad and like when my dad was still at home. We'd all slept in the same bed in the alcove, but that wouldn't have been right with Mr Tait. And we all slept with my mum anyway, Mavis and Rosie and me, and the bed was only pallets, like his, so there wouldn't have been any room. And he was a man.

'I couldn't anyway because of your dad.'

'Because of Dad, no. But surely if he's …' I was going to say the 'D' word, D-E-A-D dead, but she was peering out the window, wiping the mist off it so she could see.

'Stop, driver, please!' she called out. 'There are the girls, Lenny. Go and tell the driver to stop.'

So I just had to figure it out by myself.

Mum cooked up square sausage for tea that night with Mrs Mags's onions and Mr Duncan's tatties. The butcher had been generous because of Mr Tait so we ate our fill and Mavis burped and we all laughed, which Mr Tait would never have allowed.

'That's rude,' I pointed out. 'Mr Tait would send you to bed.'

'Good,' said Rosie. 'I want to go to bed.'

'We had physical education today,' said Mavis grandly. 'Miss Read called you wilful.'

'Really?' I said, not surprised. 'What did you do then, for PE?'

So we tried their physical jerks, stretching and lunging while my mum arranged the accumulators for the radio close to the fire to charge them for the news later. When I glanced at her she was staring at something on the wall as if the radio was already on. She didn't tell us off for making noise or knocking her chair. I packed Mavis and Rosie off to bed and told them a story about three little pigs in a house made of wood, but without the big bad wolf. When I'd finished and Rosie was snoring and Mavis was still as still, I went back through. My mum had moved into Mr Tait's chair and was staring at another spot on the wall.

'Mum,' I said, ready with a battalion of questions.

'I miss our old house,' she said. 'I miss Clydebank.'

'Do you?'

'Yes, I do, and I miss going out to work, which is just as well because I'm going to have to get used to it all over again.'

'Won't you get more sewing work?'

'There isn't any. They only gave me it because of my leg and most of it came from people Mr Tait knew round Clydebank. Bearsden and places like that. No, I need something better, more secure and I won't get that here, not with only one foot.'

'I could get a job,' I said. 'I could ask Barmy if they need a maid. I could be a maid in the house. They'd probably feed me too.'

'Barney, darling. Don't call him Barmy. You have to go to school.'

'Everyone always thinks I'm older. And I know everything there is to learn at school now. We keep repeating everything for the wee ones. It's a complete waste of time. Apart from geography of course. That's always good.'

I had a plan. While trying not to cause myself maximum panic by thinking about it, I had in fact thought a lot about money and living and getting by with no proper wage-earner in the family. It stopped me thinking about Mr Tait being D-E-A-D for a start, and how much I missed him. My mum was doing a fine job with the dressmaking, but since the latest austerity measures came in last year there was no fabric to buy and everyone was skint anyway. There'd been less and less work for her and more and more walking for me delivering her work further and further away. This could continue if someone lent me a bike. I could also speak to Jimmy Robertson, my friend who ran a shop from his bus at the side of the road where, by the way, he slept too, although obviously I'd never seen him do it. He would help. I didn't look twelve. Maybe it was the bombing that made me grow up, though it didn't work for George, but I could pass for fourteen which meant I could get an office job. There was bound to be an office in the village somewhere.

'I've got a plan,' said my mum, and she shifted back in her chair.

Her plan was different from my plan. This is often

the case, I've noticed, with adults. The things they think are important make my head spin. Mr Tait, on the other hand, said we should stay in Carbeth at least until the war was over, in other words forever. This was my view too.

'Mr Tait hadn't planned on ... leaving us,' she said. 'Things are different now. I'll have to go back to Singer's.'

'They probably don't take children in the worker hostels,' I pointed out. 'In fact I bet they don't take ladies either. We'll have nowhere to stay and you'll have to spend all your money and time getting back here.'

'I've made some enquiries about rooms,' she said. 'There's an old friend of mine down near Beardmore's, and Miss Weatherbeaten owes me a few favours.'

'Miss Weatherbeaten?'

Oh dear.

'You could go back to your old school,' she went on. She smiled as if this was a good thing. She had no idea. I hadn't liked to bother her about the coal-shed caper when it happened because I had put up a good fight, and because she was worried about my dad not coming back. I was going to have to tell her, perhaps add a few embellishments.

'I don't think that's a good idea,' I said as sensibly as I could, keeping the dread out of my voice.

'You'd be with your old pals. You keep saying there's nothing left to learn in Craigton except geography. I bet at your old school they're doing history and art and cookery. You like cookery.'

I didn't want to do history or art and I was sick to death with cookery because I did so much of it at home, thank you very much. 'I don't want to do history. Who cares what happened hundreds of years ago? And I can do art already.'

'Maybe your friend in the bought houses could put us up for a bit. What was her name?'

I told her I couldn't remember and that she'd been evacuated and I was tired and needed to go to bed.

'Lenny. Lenny? Lenny!'

'What?' I said from the bedroom door.

'Nothing,' she said. 'Sorry, darling, you must be exhausted. Go to bed and I'll be through in a minute.'

She wasn't through in a minute. I heard the radio come on and the murmur of news and I lay listening to Mavis snuffling and Rosie snoring and cried. It was like I'd been bombed out again, my whole world blown apart. But then I heard Mr Tait: 'Save your tears for later and be brave.' And I remembered Mr Tulloch, a farmer near us who'd told me to always eat a good breakfast and make a plan and that planning was very important. So I went back to my plan and put some flesh on the bones and that made me feel better. At last I began to drift off.

Not long afterwards I heard Mr Tait in his room. He was tossing and turning, which he did a lot when he was ill. His elbows kept banging against the wall and then I thought he must have got up because I heard a scraping sound on the floor.

I shuddered awake to silence. Mavis dug her fingers in my side and Rosie kicked.

'Ssh!' I said, although neither of them was awake. The room was hazy with no curtains, and a hint of candlelight marked the shape of the door. Our hut was scarily quiet without his snores and not even any wind in the trees. But then the rain started again, whispers at first and then it battered on the roof as if fairies were up there dancing in hobnail boots. I unwrapped myself from Mavis and Rosie and went to find my mum.

She was on Mr Tait's bed with her coat pulled over. We'd burnt Mr Tait's blankets after he went to hospital, just like the doctor said. She was on the bare mattress we'd made out of old sheets and straw from the farm. We should probably have burnt that too. I crawled in beside her. She put her arms round me and I listened to her breathing and waited for her to go to sleep so that I could too.

'Lenny?' she whispered.

'What?'

'Mr Tait wanted to marry me so that I could have his pension if … if anything happened to him,' she said. 'I wish I had now. He must have known how ill he was. I just couldn't face the truth.'

'But you're already married.'

'Yes, exactly, so it was impossible anyway.'

'But he's probably dead.'

'Don't say that, darling.'

'Sorry.'

The rain had died back. She stroked my hair a moment then stopped. Then a deep silence.

'He's not dead, you know,' she said in a dreamy slurry voice.

I opened my eyes and saw a slither of moon like a cut in the wall.

'Mr Tait?' I whispered. 'Mr Tait's dead. I saw his coffin. I saw the earth go in. I saw his name on the bit of paper and his dad's name on the gravestone.'

'What?' She was awake now.

'Mr Tait. He's dead. You said he wasn't dead.'

'Oh dear, what did I say? I said he's not dead, did I?'

'Yes, you did, but he is.'

'Well, of course he is, of course Mr Tait is …'

'Don't say it!'

We listened to the silence now the rain had stopped. A streak of moonlight made a line across the coat. She blinked and blinked again.

'Who, Mum? Who did you mean?'

'I didn't mean Mr Tait, oh dear, Lenny, no. Of course he's …' She didn't finish. I waited. This waiting was a technique I'd had to develop with Mr Tait himself. He was always slow to speak when there was something important to be said. 'I meant your dad, darling,' she said. 'Your dad is alive. I didn't mean to tell you but I suppose you're old enough now. How stupid of me talking in my sleep.'

Nerves stabbed at my fingers. I sat up. The coat fell off me. A taste of cold touched my lips.

'Dad? What do you mean? Where is he? Mum?' I gave her a little shake. 'Mum, please. Tell me. How do you know he's alive?' The cold wrapped itself round my shoulders and a million thoughts crowded my head. I suddenly remembered Mr Tait's saying something about my dad being under the bed. I'd thought he was jibbering and hadn't even looked.

She shook her head. Her eyes were closed.

'Mum, please, I want to know.'

She rolled over and tried to pull me back down. 'Oh dear.'

'Why didn't you tell me?' I said. 'Please, Mum, it's important.'

I waited while she got back up on one elbow and pulled the coat over our legs. I leant back against the rough wall beneath the window. She was frowning but awake, biting her lip. Finally she propped herself against the wall. There was just enough light to see each other. She cleared her throat and breathed a long sigh out and a quick one in.

'Right, now listen to me, Lenny, and listen carefully because I don't want you talking to anyone about this at all, not even Mavis and certainly not Rosie and her big mouth. This is very serious. Perhaps you are old enough now to be trusted not to tell anyone, but this is the biggest secret you'll ever have to keep, alright?'

I thought about all the other secrets I'd ever had to keep, like when I stole the best biscuits from my gran, or when Mavis lost her ugly new hat from Auntie May accidentally on purpose, or when Miss Weatherbeaten told me not to tell Rosie all her family were dead. That was probably the biggest so far, about Rosie's family. I'd had a lot of trouble keeping that one.

'Okay,' I said, cautiously. 'Where is he?'

'I don't know. I only know he didn't die when they said he did and that he's not coming back. The government thought he was dangerous so they locked him up.'

'Why would he be dangerous?' I pictured him sitting on a riverbank singing lullabies to Mavis when she was a baby and how he used to run his big rough finger down her perfect cheek to get her to close her eyes. And then I remembered the furious arguments he and my mum had the last time he was home, but not what was said.

'Is he a spy?'

'No, he's not a spy. He's an idiot.'

I closed my eyes. He was my dad. She shouldn't call him names. Suddenly I wished Mr Tait was there. She wouldn't have said that if Mr Tait was there.

'Sorry,' she said. 'No, he's not a spy. You'll only worry if I tell you the whole thing. I had news today that might change things, that's all. That's why it's on my mind.'

'News? Did you get a letter then? Did he say where he is?'

'No, Lenny, just news on the radio. Listen, forget it. It doesn't matter right now. When the war is over maybe we can see what's what, but just now you don't need to know any more. In fact it might even put you in danger. And he's not coming back. He's made his choices. I'm sorry. I know this is hard but you're going to have to trust me on this. Now let's go back through to the girls and get into bed properly. I don't know what I was thinking coming in here. We should burn this mattress as well. I'll do it tomorrow. Or maybe the next day. I have to go back to Clydebank tomorrow and meet someone in Singer's.'

She wouldn't tell me any more, and once we were back next door in our own bed I had to be quiet and not wake Mavis and Rosie. It felt like I was full of bombs again just waiting to go off, which is how I'd felt after the Germans flattened Clydebank. I had to lie very still in case I set them off, so I lay all night long and hardly slept a wink.

Chapter 7

Rub-a-dub-dub, three girls in a tub. Not at the same time of course. It wasn't big enough for that. We went in strictly in order of age, youngest first. And always on a Tuesday.

Mum was late back from Clydebank, but that didn't stop us. Neither did the fact that I was dog-tired because I'd hardly slept for trying not to think about my dad. Or about Mr Tait and that ache I felt of missing him, an ache that threatened to engulf me at any moment. Instead I'd been wondering how to keep us in Carbeth. Planning.

First, I needed a job.

The butcher, the baker, the candlestick maker, which was it to be? When we did the tinker, tailor, soldier, sailor game at school the week before, I got beggar man and thief and I didn't want to be either of those. And anyway, what about welder, checker, rigger, riveter and draughtsman, or for that matter teacher, nurse, dairymaid, secretary and shop assistant?

Miss Read, the teacher, had given Mavis a letter for my mum about my sneaking off the day of Mr Tait's funeral. I hadn't gone the next day either. Rosie told Miss Read I had flu but Mavis just said I'd 'gone off'. Thanks, Mavis. After our bath we put the letter in the fire and watched it burn, finishing with the signature.

Mavis was right. I walked halfway to school and then doubled back across the hill past lots of other huts including Mrs Mags's and the big rope swing tree at the top of the hill and the Connors' hut. They were bad George's parents and only came at weekends. I went through the pine trees behind them and on down the other side of the hill, through more huts, across the field, past the loch and the hay barn where I'd hidden when I found out about Mr Tait, then back up onto the road. This meant that I cut out the bit where our hut was.

A lorry roared up beside me and the driver offered me a lift into the village so I said thank you very much and climbed in thinking what a good start this was.

The cabin smelled of engines. The man at the wheel was round in every way, round face, round belly and peculiarly round fingers. I asked him if he had any work he could give me.

'What, a scrawny little thing like you?' he said, making his eyes round too.

I stuck my nose in the air and tried to look composed. That's what you look like when you haven't got bombs going off inside.

'Can you lift a sack of coal?'

'Of course I can,' I said, but he didn't have a black face like a coalman and his sacks were clean.

We were almost at the bottom of the hill. He pulled his lorry in beside a long low farm building of pale brown stone and turned off the engine. The whole thing shook so much it made all my bones bang together.

'Alright,' he said. 'Can you lift a sack of grain?'

'If you can lift a sack of coal,' I said with false

heartiness, 'you can lift a sack of grain.'

'You think so?' he said.

I nodded.

'You're on,' he said, and he opened his door and jumped down. 'Out you get!'

I pulled the handle and the door swung out and nearly hit the barn. Then I turned myself round and felt with my feet for the steps. It was a high door and a long way down and my foot slipped on some mud I must have put there on the way in, so I landed in a heap on the ground. He laughed and closed the door.

'Beveridge' was written big red letters across it. By the time I'd got myself up, Mr Beveridge was standing at the back waiting for me.

'I'll give you a chance,' he said. 'I'll lift it off the lorry and load it onto you. Turn round. Bend a little. Hands at your shoulders.'

'I know how to carry coal,' I reminded him.

'Oh. Sorry. Forgot I was dealing with an expert.'

I should have looked at the sacks before agreeing. It was a hard lesson to learn. I heard the sack sliding along the tailgate. I heard him gasp as he lifted the sack, then felt it land on me and half a second later I was flat out on the ground underneath it. I heard him laugh as if he'd burst, which I wished he would. 'Hahaha!' he shrieked, as if he was at the circus. I thought I might die. Maybe he was sitting on top of me. I thought of my mum underneath the building.

And then suddenly the laughter stopped and there was an explosion of shouting and someone shoved the grain sack off me. They helped me up but I could hardly breathe or stand straight and plonked straight back down on the ground. Then Mr Beveridge and his lorry took off down the road and left me wailing on the ground with the farmer who I didn't even know. I wanted to shout and scream after Mr Beveridge.

'There there,' said the farmer, as if I was a lion needing tamed. 'Better get up, then.' He patted my head while I swayed and spat mud and grit out of my mouth. Then his wife came out.

'What in the name of God?' she exclaimed. 'Is she hurt? Did Beveridge hit her? Help her up, for goodness sake, and don't stand there staring.'

'Are you okay? Maybe we shouldn't move her,' he said. 'Maybe she's got something broken.'

'I don't know,' I managed. Everything hurt. The farmer's wife helped me up. 'My knees!' I said. I could see red blood pushing its way through the gravel and muck that were stuck to them.

'What were you doing with Mr Beveridge?' he said. 'Is he a relation?'

'I was looking for a job,' I sobbed, picking a pebble out of my knee.

'With Mr Beveridge?' he said. His wife burst out laughing.

'Yes,' I sniffed, 'with Mr Beveridge. He gave me a lift so I asked him for a job, on the off chance.'

'A very bad choice, if you don't mind my saying so,' said the wife. 'You any good at picking peas?'

'Peas?' I said, wiping the back of my hand across my nose.

'Yes, peas. Little round things. Green. About that big.'

She took me inside to a white enamel sink in a clean and orderly kitchen and washed the cuts on my knees with a spotless rag and warm water. Then she sent me into a bathroom with a bowl of water and a pair of overalls (which Mr Tait would never have let me wear), a towel, and a jumper that was too small and had been shrunk in the wash. While I was in there I counted the bruises. It didn't give me the same kind of pleasure as usual. When I was clean and dressed she gave me a basket and a pair of scissors and sent me into a field to pick peas. It wasn't difficult, picking peas, and soon I felt better. I had a black-and-white farm dog for company who kept interrupting me to be stroked, and a large extended family of rooks in the sycamores nearby. As I picked I thought about the things we could do with the money I was going to make harvesting everything on all the farms and how pleased my mum would be when I gave her it.

'Fourteen you say?' said Mrs MacLeod. That was her name, and although she lived on a farm she was small and thin and tired-looking as if she'd been working hard through the night in Singer's.

'Uh-huh,' I said, not looking at her.

I'd finished the picking already and we were shelling the peas and putting them in a bag made of tight netting. My dress was drying on a string over the kitchen range and my coat had been scraped of mud and hung on a chair beside it. She rested her hands on the table a moment and looked directly at me.

'You sure? You don't look it. What school did you go to?'

'Craigton,' I said.

'Craigton,' she said. 'Miss Read.'

'Yes,' I said.

'George Connor,' she said. (That's 'bad George' to you and me.) 'He pulled the swedes for me last year.'

'Hmm,' I said. 'I've got two wee sisters and my mum and Mr Tait. He's … not with us any more and my dad's … gone.'

'Why don't you get a proper job then?' she said. 'Go into Glasgow or something. You'll have to sign up for war work, you know, and they'll send you where you're needed.'

'I don't want to go into Glasgow,' I said, trying not to sound sulky. 'I want to stay here. Carbeth is my home now. We came from Clydebank.'

'You'll only get farm work here,' she said. 'D'you want farm work?'

'Yes, I do, definitely,' I said. 'Do you have more peas to pick?'

'No, but I've got some carrots. You can help me with them if you've any strength left.'

She gave me a bowl of purple beetroot soup and a thick chunk of bread and we hung the peas from a hook in the ceiling to dry. Then she gave me another sack and took me on a cart to a field. She told me to pick carrots, put them in the sack, then carry them back and empty them into the cart. She left me there saying she had cows to milk. I thought my back would break completely in two. I was sticky all over with sweat. And then at three o'clock when she came out with a drink of milk for me I said I had to go home and see to my wee sisters, which wasn't true. But she didn't seem to mind and gave me back my clothes. She handed me a bag of peas and carrots too but no money. I wished I'd told her before I started I wanted money for my work but didn't know how to say so.

'Come back any time,' she said.

Well, she would say that, wouldn't she? I work hard.

So that's what I'd been up to and why we had to burn the letter from Miss Read, because I didn't want my mum to know anything until I had a proper job with money to keep us there.

Mavis and Rosie and I ate the carrots and peas as soon as I got home, those I hadn't already eaten. They were sweet and crisp, the veg that is, not Mavis and Rosie. Mavis and Rosie were stupid and annoying. They also asked lots of questions about where our mum was and why, so I had to tell them some of those white lies my mum always talked about, only I was beginning to wonder about white lies and whether they were as alright as she said.

All lies are about keeping secrets and I had started to care less and less what colour they were as long as they were keeping me from the truth. And on top of that I didn't want to lie to Mavis but I had to find a way of keeping us there, and I had to find the truth about our dad, and I had to do all of this without worrying Mavis's worried little head any more than it was already worried.

So I sent them both up to the hideout as soon as they'd finished their carrots and put the kettle on for that bath. Then I took a candle and peered underneath our bed for my dad, keeping my ears open in case they suddenly came back. Obviously he wasn't there. There was only a handkerchief under the pallet, all stiff and dusty, and some mouse droppings, but old ones so nothing to worry about. I tried the radio for news too, but the accumulators were dead.

Later, after the bath, when my mum came in she thought we were sickening for something because we were so full of peas and carrots and didn't want any dinner. Being covered in bruises was quite normal for me so I didn't have to tell her about Mr Beveridge.

She made herself a cup of hot sweet tea with the remains of our ration and said she'd been to see Miss Weatherbeaten, and that Miss Weatherbeaten was in a sad and sorry state.

'What does that mean?' I said, not really fussed about Miss Weatherbeaten's well-being. No-one ever called her by her real name, except Mr Tait. She escaped from Clydebank with Mr Tait, Rosie and me when the bombs were falling and the town was on fire.

Rosie was all ears and not mouthing off the way she does twenty-five hours a day. She stood right up close beside me so I had to move and nearly burnt my hand on the fire.

'I went to ask her why she hadn't been sending me my money,' said my mum, 'and what she thought I was going to feed Rosie on if she didn't keep her end of the bargain.' She took a large gulp of tea and slouched into the back of Mr Tait's chair with a sigh. We waited. I opened my mouth. Rosie spoke.

'Well? What did she say?' Rosie tugged at her ear.

'Come here, Rosie,' said my mum, and she took Rosie up onto her knee even though she was far too big for it. 'You belong with us now.'

'I know that,' said Rosie. 'I never liked Miss Weatherbee.' This is what Rosie called her two and a half years ago when she was only four. 'I don't want to be adopted by her anyway. I like Mr Tait. And you. She wasn't nice to me and Lenny and she shouted and …' and Rosie began to relate all the terrible things Miss Weatherbeaten had ever done to us, some of which I didn't quite remember, and we couldn't get her to shut up again no matter how hard we tried.

Finally Mavis shuffled past with her rag doll and unplugged her thumb long enough to say, 'You talk too much,' before continuing to the window seat, for which Mum and I were grateful because Rosie stopped and glared at her long enough for us to speak.

'So what did Miss Weatherbeaten say?' I asked again.

'Do you remember the little girl Mavis used to play with down our street?'

'Doris? Dora? Dorothy? Yes.'

'Miss Weatherbeaten broke her arm.'

Mavis came running. Rosie nearly fell on the floor. That 'rrright good seeing to' that we all used to talk about and Miss Weatherbeaten used to threaten everyone with: she had finally done it.

'She did it!' I said. 'The cow! What happened?'

'Lenny!' said my mum. 'There's no need for that.'

'Yes, there is,' said Mavis. 'Poor Dora. A broken arm? What happened? Is she going to be alright?'

'Dora is fine,' said my mum. 'She's got a sling and a plaster, apparently, but she'll mend.' She gazed into the fire and shifted in Mr Tait's chair. 'Miss Weatherbeaten is a poor misguided … . She's selfish. And twisted. That's all. We don't need to have anything more to do with her.'

'I don't like her,' said Rosie. 'She's nasty.'

'And dangerous,' said Mavis. 'I hate her.'

'I hate her too. She's … she's violent,' said Rosie with a great shake of her fist. Then she stopped and looked round at us expectantly and we all stared.

Then my mum snorted a laugh. 'Girls!' she said.

But Rosie and I copied Mavis: 'She's violent!'

'Poor wee Dora,' I said, once we'd had enough of that.

'Miss Weatherbeaten lost her job at the school,' said my mum. 'They sent her home without pay until they can find her another job somewhere else.'

'Somewhere else?' I said. 'They can't let her teach somewhere else, not after that.'

'What about Dora?' said Mavis.

'I didn't see Dora, but I heard she's back at school already.'

We all thought about Dora who had fabulous ringlets and was almost as cute as Mavis when she was four.

'Miss Weatherbeaten's stuck in her digs now,' my mum went on. 'She has to wait until they find her something. No-one's speaking to her.'

'No wonder,' I said.

'That's why she wasn't at the funeral, because she was hiding, even though it was Mr Tait and he's been so good to her in the past. But anyway the whole upshot is she says she can't afford to pay me so I told her I can't afford to pay for Rosie either and what are we supposed to do? She adopted Rosie in everything but the law so she has a responsibility. But she said she couldn't possibly afford to give me anything on no wages at all and hardly any savings so I told her I had no wages at all too and absolutely no savings and three other mouths to feed on only what I can scrape together with the sewing.' She came to a halt and flopped back on the chair again as if she was completely exhausted with the telling.

'And?' I said. 'What did she say to that?'

'She said you can't get blood from a stone.'

'And?'

'Miss Weatherbampot,' said my mum, sitting up straight again and tugging on the straps of her dungarees, 'is not used to living on nothing like the rest of us. She's giving everything she has for her lodgings. She's right. You can't get blood from a stone and Miss Weatherbee is as cold and hard a stone as you'll ever come up against.'

'And?' I said.

'Now, don't be upset,' she said, seeing my consternation. This is another of my dad's words and it has a lot to do with being stern. I waited for her to go on. 'We'll have to go back to Clydebank.'

'No!' This was Mavis, surprising us all. 'No, no, no!' she said, and she flung her rag doll into the corner, then ran a circle round the room.

'I'm going to see the council man tomorrow about somewhere to live ...'

'I'm not going!' said Mavis.

'I'm not going either,' said Rosie. 'There's nowhere to live and ...' and Rosie was off on one.

'Quiet, Rosie!' said my mum, but it made no difference. Rosie went on and on and on and she stumbled round the room bumping into Mavis who was still in her circle. 'We'll have to give this place up too,' she went on, as if getting every possible piece of bad news out at once made it easier. 'We can't afford two rents.'

Everyone started talking at once, but the only person making any sense was me. I told my mum about the peas and carrots and the farm but I don't think she heard me. I told her I was going to find a job and that my job would keep us there, along with her sewing, and I'd try everywhere the next day for more work. I told her about my plan, but suddenly we were all shouting at each other and I had to run away into Mr Tait's room and hide behind the door until they'd all stopped. It was like Miss Weatherbeaten all over again, shouting and making noise and everyone being unkind, as if her violence had infected us all just by the mention of her. Then suddenly our last candle died and Mavis and Rosie were sent next door to ask Mr Duncan for one of his while my mum banged about at the fire muttering to herself, heating more water to add to the bath that was still sitting there cold and waiting for her. They didn't want to go for the candle. I could hear them arguing. As they left I heard my mum shouting to all of us.

'I'm doing my very best for us!' she yelled. 'I don't want to go any more than you do!'

But I didn't believe her because if she really wanted to stay she'd have listened to my plan and tried to keep us there. I knew I'd have to do it all myself and maybe that way I could convince her we didn't need to go.

The girls came back with the candle, Rosie still talking fifteen to the dozen and Mavis as silent as the grave, and were sent straight off to bed. I stayed behind Mr Tait's door and listened and tried not to fall asleep and, to stay awake, I checked under Mr Tait's bed again with my hand. I pulled the pallet away from the wall too, as carefully as I could so no-one would hear me, but there was nothing there either. I lay down on the floor in the gap I'd made and listened to the wind and watched the dark shapes of the trees merge with the night.

Beautiful Carbeth, my beautiful Carbeth. I couldn't

bear it, the very thought of leaving. There had to be something more I could do, more than earning peas and carrots. And then I had one of those crazy thoughts: if only my dad had really been under Mr Tait's bed then he could have come out and looked after us and we'd all be together again. He'd make sure we stayed in Carbeth, I was sure of it, if only he'd known how desperate we were and how beautiful Carbeth was. I'd just have to find him. Then everything would be alright.

Chapter 8

The next day we ate breakfast in silence. Then, without even pretending to go to school, I said goodbye to Mavis and Rosie a little way down the road and turned in at the long sweeping path between the trees to the big house. Thick and tumbling bushes deadened all sound except the little birds hiding amongst them. The front of the big house seemed to be at the back and when I arrived there I climbed the steps to the front door with its fancy pillars on either side and knocked. A tall man with a thick moustache opened it. He had a tweed suit on like Mr Tait's and the mouth beneath the moustache was wide, made wider by a smile.

'What sort of services?' he said.

'Anything,' I said. 'I'll do anything. We need money.'

He eyed me sideways. 'Shouldn't you be at school, young lady?' he said.

I squinted back up at him. 'I'm too old for school,' I said.

'Really?' he said, and he twisted his mouth and the moustache to one side. 'We'll put you in the kitchen then. We have guests for lunch and Willie needs help. We don't have a cook.'

Willie was not a man. Willie was Miss Barns-Graham, the same Miss Barney who'd been there when Mr Tait was taken away. She recognised me instantly.

'Hello, young lady, remember me? Sorry, awfully sorry to hear about your dad. You must be frightfully upset.' Without waiting for a reply she set me at a large wooden table, scrubbed pale with use, and handed me a knife and some potatoes. 'Peal 'em and cut 'em up good and small. I can't seem to get this stove going well enough today so it'll have to be small and mashed.'

I did as I was told.

'We're having pheasant. I found this one on the road two weeks ago. Must have been hit by a car but it seems alright. What do you think? Look, isn't it beautiful, bronze and sleek.' She pronounced 'sleek' with a special flourish like a big tick and grinned at me. I smiled back. 'There are six of us for lunch so we need six big carrots from the garden and a bit of spinach too. I like a bit of spinach.' Then she dived out the door and came back a few minutes later with the veg wrapped in newspaper. 'Voila!' she said and grinned at me again. 'The apples are a bit sharp but they'll just have to do. Stewing'll help. Now, where was I? The pheasant. Do you think you could pluck it?'

I gulped. We had done this before, or rather, my mum had done this before and I'd helped. Mr Tulloch gave us a hen once that had been caught by a fox. The fox got every single one of the hens and left them lying dead or nearly dead. It was a terrible waste. I don't understand why foxes are so wasteful. Why not just kill one and come back the next day when you're hungry again?

'Fill the sink with hot water from the kettle then put in the pheasant. It opens the follicles so the feathers come out more easily.' She pointed at the kettle and the sink as if I didn't know what they were.

I did as I was told. It was a thoroughly horrible thing to do. The feathers stuck to my fingers and got up my nose. It wasn't just the feathers that were colourful either. Slimy bits of orange, purple and green pheasant skin came off in my hand and when I'd finished there were blotches and holes all over it. It also stank to high heaven and made me hold my breath. It was almost impossible not to think about people who'd been stuck dead under the rubble in Clydebank and the awful cloying smell there had been when I went back there two weeks later to try and find Mavis.

I'd been in Willie's big kitchen an hour before I realised I hadn't said a word since, 'I'm too old' on the doorstep. 'Finished!' I said as soon as I was, glad to hear the sound of my own voice again, glad to unsticky my fingers under the tap.

'Smashing!' she said. 'What next?' She looked about the room, tapping one finger on her lip.

'Um, excuse me,' I said.

'Yes?' Her gaze fell on me.

'I'm looking for a job.'

'A job?'

'Yes, I need to earn a living for me and my sisters and my mum, so we can stay in Carbeth.' I didn't tell her Rosie wasn't really my sister because she was as good as, and either way I had to find money for her too.

'Well, good for you!' she said. 'What kind of job?

'Um, this kind,' I said. 'Anything really. I just want, um, to be paid, you know?'

'Paid?' she said. 'Shall I ask our guests if they know of any jobs? How old did you say you were? Paid?' She tapped her finger on her lip again.

'Fourteen.'

'What's your name?'

'Lenny. Lenny Gillespie.'

'Well, Lenny Gillespie, I don't believe you really are fourteen but well done for trying. We can't pay you, I'm afraid, because we don't have any money either, but I can give you some of our veg, if that would help. You live in that hut, don't you? And you were bombed out.' I could see her thinking it all over.

She promised me a big sack of stuff from her garden if I'd help her peel the apples. So I did. I rescued the spinach that was boiling dry, and I got the stove going properly too. She was trying to save wood for some reason even though we were surrounded by trees. She was very kind but not good at staying on the job in hand, like me when I'm at school, I suppose.

I was scrunching up the newspaper so that I could tease the fire back to life and get the pheasant to cook when I noticed a headline.

TIGER IN EXEMPTION APPEAL

I had to look. Fenella the tiger was a circus tiger with a Miss Overend for a trainer. Miss Overend must surely have been a trapeze artist when not taming tigers. Miss Overend had been called up for war work. I wondered if I could have her old job.

Then Willie came back and gave me my pay: eight large potatoes, four huge carrots and a cabbage. I noticed little smears of paint on her apron and suddenly remembered she was A FAMOUS ARTIST.

'Thank you, miss,' I whispered.

'I'll come and get you if I need help again, if I may. Look what you've done with my fire!' She clasped her hands under her chin and beamed at me. 'How wonderful you are!'

As I wandered back along the sweeping driveway picking the mud off one of the carrots so I could eat it, I reflected on my uselessness as a woman of business and determined to do better next time. Nice to be called wonderful though.

My next stop was Jimmy Robertson in his shop-come-bus-come-bedroom. I stood on the bottom step and smelled old milk and biscuits and offered my services. He said he had no need of help. He was fine thank you very much.

'What about the papers?' I said. 'I could deliver papers.'

'Hmm,' he said. 'I hadn't thought of that. Maybe. Maybe not.'

I waited. He sat back in his driver's seat and smiled at me. I could do it. I knew I could. He didn't know how much I needed to.

'No,' he said and scratched his beard. 'Wouldn't work. How would you get them up the hill? Good luck though! I'm sure you'll find something.'

Disappointed, I hoped he was right.

Then I tried the tearoom next to the Halfway House pub. But it was empty except for a lady waiting for customers to arrive.

'How old are you?' she said.

'Fourteen.'

'Come back on Saturday,' she said, looking over my head.

'Alright,' I said.

'We're busy then. You can work in the kitchen.'

But I knew I had to get something before then.

So I went to Mr Tulloch's farm. Mr Tulloch was a bit on the round side, like horrible Mr Beveridge only nice. His head was like a ball and his unshaven face was matched by the stubble across his head and down his neck. Very useful, he said, for keeping your hat on.

'Come back at four,' he said.

'In the morning?' I said aghast, another of my dad's funny words, for when things are really horrible.

'No, no, you daftie,' he said. 'This afternoon. You can help with the milking. You ever milked a cow?'

'No,' I said, 'but I can learn. How much will you pay me?' I said. It seemed so cheeky to ask, especially when Mr Tulloch had always been very kind to us and it was thanks to him and his brother that we got Mavis back. 'Halfway to Helensburgh,' he said she was, then he had to explain that Helensburgh was miles away along the Clyde River, and he promised us we'd only really been a short distance apart.

He burst out laughing at my request for a wage. 'Well,' he said. 'How much would you like me to pay you?'

I looked at the sky. I closed my eyes and scratched my head. I kicked my toes one into the other and pulled my lip. 'Um,' I said.

'Um. That's no use. I can't pay you in "ums". Come back at four and if you're any good I'll give you a penny.'

'Thank you!' I said.

'You can do the cleaning up and if you manage alright I'll show you how to milk.'

'Thank you!' I felt dizzy with excitement and nearly

fell over a mounting block on my way out of his yard.

'Watch where you're going!' he called after me. 'Slow down and keep your wits about you! You can learn some common sense too.'

For good measure I stopped at the Halfway House pub where a huge fire roared in a wide grate, a lady stood behind a bar and three men leant on it chatting.

'I'm fourteen,' I said to the lady. 'I need a job. I can cook and clean.'

They all fell about laughing and I stumbled out the door, the excitement of going to Mr Tulloch's farm all gone up in smoke.

Chapter 9

'Sometimes good things come out of bad, my dear, don't you think?' said Mr Tait. 'Even the bombing. If the German's hadn't bombed us we wouldn't be here together under this tree eating your mum's best dumplings and watching George mess up the roof of his hut because he won't ask for help.'

George had no idea we were watching. There was a sudden yowl then a thud as he threw down his hammer. And I had no real idea what Mr Tait was on about. The bombing was straightforwardly bad. How could it be anything else?

'Oh dear,' said Mr Tait. 'That looked like a thumb this time.' He leant forward the better to see and reached for his stick. George disappeared behind a tree. His hut was a skeleton made with bits of old wood he'd carried over from Clydebank, piece by piece, from places that had been bombed. There were three green strips along one side that looked like they'd once been a park bench. The whole thing was not much bigger than two single-end alcoves stuck together. George was only thirteen at that time but determined not to live with his parents Mr and Mrs Connor or Mrs Mags his aunt, which is why Mr Tait kept an eye on him instead.

We finished our dumplings, me and Mr Tait, just as

George lifted his hammer again.

'That'll never do,' said Mr Tait. 'If he puts that there it'll be in the way of the door.' Mr Tait went on in this way, but I didn't catch most of it because it was mainly too technical for me and the dumplings were making me drowsy. Mr Tait went down and helped George while I lay back and snoozed in the grass.

But George's hut was long finished, Mr Tait was gone and I sat under the same tree all by myself and waited for four o'clock to come. When I thought it must be time I made my way down through the trees and across the fields to Mr Tulloch's farm.

Mr Tulloch's whistle, which normally rang out wherever he went, was almost impossible to hear above the rising wind as it hurtled through the trees around the farm buildings. But add to that the happy mooing of his cows as they were herded into the old byre and he was easy to find.

'Ah,' he said, standing by the gate to the back field with a stick in his hand and Molly the collie dog at his feet. 'My new milkmaid.'

'Hello, Mr Tulloch!'

'Hmmm,' he said, looking me over. 'Skinny little thing, aren't you? We'll need to put some muscle on you if you're going to be any use with cows.' His eyes fell on my legs with all the bruises from Mr Beveridge's little joke.

'I'm tougher than I look,' I told him and smiled. It was a fake smile. I was overcome with nerves. And then I was overcome with nerves because of being overcome with nerves, which I wasn't used to being. Normally I'm first in the queue for anything new, and this should have been the best thing in the world since I rode Senga's dad's Clydesdale home from the field last year.

Mr Tulloch pulled the gate shut behind the last of the herd and shifted his cap so far back on his head it should have fallen off but for the stubble.

'The first thing you have to do is wash those hands,' he said. I followed him past the herd to the front of the queue. The cows were at a standstill at the byre door, which he now opened. 'There's a tap over there,' he said, pointing along the wall. 'Keep out the way of this lot or you'll get trampled. They're a placid bunch really but heavy and stupid and they'll put a foot right through you without actually meaning any harm.' He dived inside.

I pressed myself against the stone of the byre while the cows sauntered in, each one swaying to a halt to look me up and down before deciding I was nothing of interest and moving on past. They had big square noses, round dark eyes that seemed to be all pupil and tufts of curly hair between two horns and two ears. Their hips were triangular with the skin pulled tight over them and underneath hung huge wobbly udders heavy and straining with milk. They had impossibly skinny legs and no feet.

There was a clank of metal inside the barn and they all stopped. The middle ones bumped into the ones at the front and two at the back started mooing, as if they were arguing over an important family matter.

There was a rustling of light chains. Mr Tulloch whistled away, stopping every so often to mutter a few words to the cows. I rushed to wash my hands at the standpipe then squeezed past the largest brown cow and followed him in.

'Now, no sudden noise,' he said. 'If you upset one of them you upset them all and that makes 'em dangerous. They're not bad, just clumsy, so talk softly and don't shout over to me. They'll get used to the sound of your voice.'

I nodded.

'Got that?'

I nodded again.

'Well?'

'Yes, Mr Tulloch.'

He looked at me and frowned.

'Another thing. Don't come at them from behind. They don't like it. They don't know what's going on back there. The best thing to do is just keep talking all the time so they know what you're up to.' He eyed me and frowned again. 'If you don't know what to say you can sing. How's that? That okay?'

I nodded.

'Right,' he said.

Ordinarily I would have been wildly excited to be in Mr Tulloch's byre learning about milking, but it was like all the happiness had been sifted out of me and all I could do was nod miserably. I was tired too. The thought of singing with Mr Tulloch did not cheer me up either.

'Tough losing Mr Tait, was it?' he said, gazing down at me.

I looked at him.

'He was a good man, he was,' said Mr Tulloch. 'Very solid, if you know what I mean, very kind.'

I felt my lip tremble so I nodded extra low.

'Right then, no crying in here. You don't want Tulip over there getting upset.' Tulip twisted round to look at us with her big soft brown eyes.

I wiped my nose with my sleeve. He patted me on the shoulder.

'You want to be careful of these things too,' he said quietly, tapping Tulip's horns. 'Lethal.' He pursed his lips. 'Keep your eyes on 'em.'

The barn was warm from the cows and dark and smelly, and the cows were lined up in their stalls waiting patiently for us to begin, three on each side with chains hung loosely round their necks and attached to the wall. Suddenly there was the sound of running water, only it wasn't running water. It was the making of a country pancake right there on the stone floor at my feet, on my feet actually, to be more exact.

'Oh,' I cried out.

'Shoosh now,' he said. 'What did I tell you about noise? Now, that's the other reason for not standing behind them. You never know when that's going to happen. Back out to the tap and wash it off your feet. My apologies, young lady. I should have given you some gumboots. You go now to the house and ask my wife why she's not down here yet and if she has any spare gumboots, which she does. Off you go now.'

So off I went. Mr Tulloch and I had songs we liked to sing. I'd had lifts on his milk cart loads of times. The very first time we had sung songs and chatted and he'd given me some very good advice about finding my mum and Mavis who were both still lost at that time. Then afterwards he had gone round all the other farms where other people from Clydebank were staying after the bombing and asked if they had anyone called Mavis aged four, and it was his brother who said yes. That's how I found Mavis in the end. So

Mr Tulloch was kind and a good friend. But for some reason the idea of singing filled me with dread that day and brought me out in a sweat. I had no idea why.

As I crossed the yard I squinted between the buildings, trying to catch a view of the huts on the hill opposite, but the farm was in a dip in the valley and hemmed in by giant sycamores turning for autumn and I couldn't see beyond them.

When I reached the farmhouse door I considered forgetting the whole thing, accepting my fate and returning to Clydebank to my old school with its bullies, to the rubble and the stink left behind by the bombing, to living in someone else's house and not having the woods to run about in and the rope swing on the big beech tree at the top of the field. Perched on the doorstep I imagined giving up any idea of staying in Carbeth and wondered whether my mum's plan wasn't the best after all. But I wasn't there long before a stout lady in a pinafore and pink slippers opened the door.

'Hello,' she said. 'What can I do for you?'

'I'm … I'm … I … I …'

'You must be the girl with the sister,' she said. 'Come on then. We're late enough already. Look at the state of you. Here, put a pair of these on.' She shoved me towards a line of gumboots of all shapes and sizes. 'Woops! Not much of you is there, hen?' she said as I clattered against the wall.

'Sorry,' I said to the wall and grabbed a pair of boots that looked my size.

Mrs Tulloch lifted a pair of boots too. Hers were shiny with fresh mud and she kicked her pink slippers off into the space they left, slipping first one chubby stockinged foot into a boot and then the other.

Plumping down onto the step I pulled at my shoe buckles, yanked off my shoes, straightened my socks, which were wet and brown, and shoved my feet into the boots. They were far too big, but there wasn't time to choose another pair. Mrs Tulloch was already haring across the yard faster than you'd imagine someone that size could.

'Right, at last,' said Mr Tulloch. 'Take this bucket into the store on the other side of the yard where there's a big sack of grain. Fill it, bring it back and put a little feed in each of these mangers so they've got something interesting to do while we sneak back and get their milk. On you go.'

Mrs Tulloch took a little three-legged stool from a shelf and got down beside one of the cows. 'Come on, young Dahlia,' she said in a singsong voice. 'Give us your milk, then. Go on, for the sake of the children and good strong bones.'

I took Mr Tulloch's bucket and went for the grain. A flock of little starlings followed me across the yard. The bucket rattled in my hand and the door squeaked open. I filled the bucket from a sack marked 'Beveridge', which made me shiver, and staggered back to the byre with the starlings all chit-chattering around me. Mr and Mrs Tulloch were both milking and the milk skooshed into their buckets rapidly and rhythmically as if they were racing against time, or at least against each other. Neither of them spoke so I did as I'd been told and filled the first manger with grain using a scoop that was hanging on a peg.

'Talk to 'em, Lenny,' said Mr Tulloch in a quiet voice, 'so they know you're there. Tell them what you did at school yesterday, anything.' There was a low moo.

'Oi, Tulip, mind your p's and q's. Ladies present.'

I didn't know what to say. I'd been picking peas the day before instead of doing my twelve times table. There was nothing to tell. A heavy silence followed.

Mr Tulloch started to whistle. Mrs Tulloch sang along. I resigned myself to not speaking and to being in trouble for not doing as I was told. I could be silent. There was nothing wrong with silence. Why talk if you have nothing to say? I knew the song they were singing. It was 'Ye Banks and Braes'. I even knew some of the words, but I couldn't sing. Absolutely not. There would be no singing from me.

'Come on, Lenny,' said Mr Tulloch, and he sang; 'Ye banks and braes o' bonnie Doon, how can ye bloom sae fresh and fair?'

'Maybe she doesn't know the words,' said Mrs Tulloch. 'Maybe she's shy. Are you shy, girl-with-a-sister?' I didn't answer. 'There you go, she's shy. What did I tell you?'

'Lenny's not shy, are you, Lenny?' said Mr Tulloch. 'Lenny? And we've sung that song before.'

Another silence.

'Maybe she's shy today,' Mr Tulloch went on. 'She's not usually shy, are you Lenny? Lenny?'

'N ... n ... no,' I said with great difficulty. Somehow the words just wouldn't come out.

'See? Told you.'

I kept still, my hand and the scoop poised over a manger, and wondered what was happening to me. My mouth had become thick and spongy, like when George knocked me flat against a tree stump last year when I stole his last sandwich for Mavis. (It was the same day he and Laura from the other farm had been carrying on down at the pool. It was his own fault really and Mavis was starving from swimming anyway.)

'You alright, love?' said Mrs Tulloch. There was a pause in the skoosh-skoosh in her bucket.

'Mmm,' I said.

It was like there was no breath left in me. My body was heaving, trying to do its work, but my mouth had clamped itself shut and wouldn't open. There was a loud long moo from one of the cows waiting outside as if to say, 'Get a move on and never mind her.' It made me jump.

Mrs Tulloch responded by skoosh-skooshing into her bucket with even greater speed.

'Sss … ,' I began. I wanted to say sorry for not speaking, for not singing, for not being able to breathe. For not being the normal cheery person I usually was having fun learning how to milk cows, which was something I'd wanted to do for ages, ever since I'd visited Mr Tulloch one time not long after we arrived in Carbeth. It was after he brought Mavis back. Mr Tait and I went to take him a present of some oranges to thank him.

Neither Mr Tulloch nor his wife spoke. I edged back round the cow whose manger I had just filled until I was in the middle of the byre near the country pancake with lots of cows' behinds facing my way. I didn't know where to put myself and I couldn't see either Mr or Mrs Tulloch because they were both bending down to their cows, so I tiptoed back towards the door and leant against the cold stone wall and trembled.

'Sss … ,' I said, but I don't think they heard me. 'Sorry!'

'Lenny, where have you got to with that feed?' said Mr Tulloch. 'The cows need their grub just like you do.'

'C … c … coming!' I said.

But the nearest cow was not standing straight in its stall. It had its head against one wooden partition and its back-side against the other. Danger at both ends.

I began to hum. I hummed 'Row row row your boat' which was one of my favourites. It should have been sung noisily and sometimes we did it on the floor at school rowing a pretend boat, but that day I just hummed it and probably no-one caught anything, not even the cow, who stayed exactly where she was. She turned towards me and fixed her big brown eyes on me as if she was daring me to move her.

'Sc … sc … scuse me,' I said.

'That's Nasturtium you've got there,' said Mr Tulloch. 'We call her Nasty for short because she's always difficult. I'll do her.' He put down his own bucket, which was full of creamy milk, then took the feed bucket and scoop from me. Then he shoved Nasturtium out of the way so he could fill her manger.

'There you go.' He gave me back the bucket. 'Try Poppy over there. Go on. She won't bite. She's a darling.'

There was a clear space past Poppy so I filled hers no problem. Mr Tulloch went back to milking, whistling. Poppy turned her big head to look at me and I saw she only had one horn. The other had broken off right at the root so there was a dip in her head. The skin was brown and scabby round about. It was like things I saw in the bombing and afterwards when people arrived in Carbeth and stayed in our hut, the one we borrowed when we first came. Poppy's wound was dark and grimy, like the wounds on someone's leg, and I thought I could smell that burny smell like meat you've forgotten on a stove, which is daft because I couldn't have smelled things like that because I was in a byre. It gave me such a fright I dropped the bucket. Poppy lurched away and swung her head round to me so her nose bumped me hard in the tummy. Then Nasturtium started mooing, as if she was saying 'leave Poppy alone', then Tulip, and they all started up and Mrs Tulloch cried out and stood up and raced back to the middle of the byre with the milk slopping out of her bucket.

'What in God's name happened there?' she said above the din of mooing and rattling chains. 'Lenny, get out of there,' she shouted. 'Davie? You out?'

I came out of the stall and ran to the back wall. Mr Tulloch, whose name was Davie, stood in the middle leaning against a divide.

'I'm alright. I'm with Tulip,' he said, 'dozy as a dormouse.'

The mooing spread to the herd outside like a chorus in a round. Then Mr Tulloch began to sing too, in a quiet voice, not low, not a bass like my dad used to sing, and not soft and gentle like Mr Tait either, but somewhere in between, slow and sweet, so that to begin with I thought he'd gone loopy or was crying. It made the hair prickle on my neck but the cows began to calm down.

'The Lord's my shepherd,' he sang, 'I'll not want. He makes me down to lie.'

Then Mrs Tulloch joined in. 'In pastures green, He leadeth me.'

And I sang too, but in a teeny tiny whisper. 'The quiet waters by.'

Mrs Tulloch picked up my bucket and quickly filled the remaining mangers, and between the singing and the grub, a miraculous amazing thing happened: with a tinkle of their chains the cows swung quietly back to their mangers, even Nasturtium, and were soon crunching happily on their feed, as if the commotion had never happened.

Mr and Mrs Tulloch continued singing. They knew all the words whereas I, in my panic, had forgotten most of them and could only hum. Mrs Tulloch pointed at a brush that was leaning in a corner along with a shovel and gave me a little push in that direction so I did as I was told and set about brushing up the feed that had fallen all over the floor. But what they probably didn't know was that I had sung that hymn not long before at Mr Tait's funeral, which made it difficult to sing again, impossible actually, if you want to know the truth. And what's more I wanted to be as far away from Poppy and her wounded head as I could possibly be, and it took all my strength to stay cleaning up the mess and not run out of there as quickly as quick. To make matters worse, the tears started falling down my cheeks while I was down there sweeping so I couldn't see the grain or the floor or anything else for that matter. Mrs Tulloch came and took the bucket from me and then the brush and shovel which was full of grain and straw and was shoogling about in my hand ready to empty itself back on the floor.

Mrs Tulloch gave me a little squeeze and, still singing, lead me out of the byre and back to the house. Molly the collie dog followed us, leaping and barking as if the most exciting thing in the world had just happened.

'You get your shoes back on and I'll be back to you in a jiffy once we've got these cows milked. We're late already and they get sore and impatient if they're left too long. Big deep breath, okay? No more tears?'

I nodded and sat on a little stool that was in the porch and started to push the first boot off with my toes.

'That's a good girl. Then we can have a nice cup of tea and you can tell me what's wrong.' She patted my head. Then she patted Molly's head too and Molly looked up first at her and then at me and pushed her wet nose under my hand, licked the snotters off my face then bounced after Mrs Tulloch's retreating back.

As I watched them go I thought about how stupid I was, how alone, the indignity of it all and how cold it was without Mr Tait to go home to. I sat there on the doorstep for a few minutes and cried and wished there was a big hole that would open up that I could fall into and go to sleep forever.

What was wrong with me? Why didn't I just sing along and fill the feeders?

Chapter 10

I didn't wait for Mrs Tulloch to come back that day and I didn't go back the next day at milking time either. I didn't go to the Halfway House tea room at the weekend like the lady had said or to any of the other farms as I'd planned, not even Mrs MacLeod with her carrots. In fact I completely stopped thinking about finding work, went to school as normal and accepted my fate.

But strange and horrible things kept happening to me, especially at school.

Miss Read asked me to take a message to the bleach works over the road. Apparently we were clean out of matches. So off I went.

'Mm … mmm … Miss Read,' I said. 'Sent me for mm … mm … mmmatches.' I clamped a hand over my mouth.

In her pure white pinny, her white headscarf, her white hair and her very pale face, the lady at the bleach-works looked like she'd been bleached herself. She looked at me in surprise. Her pale thin eyebrows shot up her forehead and she laughed.

'Michty me!' she said. 'That didn't want to come out.'

My face burned. I tried a smile. She went inside to fetch the matches and I turned my hot face to the wind.

'Thanks,' I mumbled when she came back, and scurried off.

That afternoon I was asked to read the register. This was a treat awarded to the best behaved person in the class. I had never done it before, but that day I hadn't wandered off when I was sent for the matches or stayed too long at the bleach-works or bothered people for apples. (The people next door had a tasty apple tree completely covered in fruit.) I hadn't talked in class either because I hadn't talked at all because I was scared to try in case this strange horrible thing happened to my mouth again and it went to jelly.

I stood up and went to the front of the class. The blood seemed to drain from my head down to my feet and then quickly back up again. Senga, my back-to-front friend from the farm, gave me a big thumbs up. For the second time that day my face was scorched and my throat tightened like the day Senga decided strangling me with my scarf was funny.

'Anne Sc … Scott,' I said.

'Here!'

'Mm … mm … May Goodson,' I said.

'Yup!'

'Here will do nicely,' said Miss Read.

'Here!'

'Enough!'

'Jjj … jjj … John Harris,' I said.

'Hh … hh … here!'

Sniggers rippled round the room. My throat ached. I paused. Tears were forming, hot in my hot face.

'Sss … sss … sss …'

'Stop being silly, Lenny,' said Miss Read.

'Sss …' I took a deep breath. 'Senga!' I had to shout

this to make sure it got out.

'Right, Catherine,' said Miss Read. 'You can take over. Lenny, go, you, and sit down immediately.'

'Sss … sss… sssorry.'

They all fell about laughing and I stumbled back to my seat and hid my face in my hands.

At the end of the day I tried hard to sneak off but Dougie, bad George's wee brother, came and stood in my way.

'L … L … L … look at L … L … lippy L … L … Lenny,' he said.

'That was so funny,' said Senga, pushing him out the way and dragging me by the collar. 'Where d'you get that idea? Miss Read was furious. My uncle does that all the time. Nobody talks to him any more. He's a complete freak.'

'Thanks, Senga,' I said without difficulty. 'I wasn't joking. I don't know what happened.'

'D'you wanna go to the ruined cottage today? John Harris stole his dad's cigarettes.'

'Cigarettes?'

'Shh. Miss Read's only through that door.'

I stared at her miserably.

'Suit yourself,' she said. 'You've been a dumbo recently anyway.'

She flounced out through the door.

'Lenny?' It was Miss Read. 'Can you come and help me put the slates back in the cupboard please?'

I knew what that meant. It meant a big bad row.

But I was wrong.

'Now, Lenny, what happened in there?'

'N … nothing.'

'You're not pretending, are you? Or are you?'

'N ... no, Miss Read, honest I'm not.' Speaking very fast I got to the end of my sentence.

'Careful with those slates. We have too many broken already.'

They were heavy because I was trying to carry as many as possible so I could get away.

'Why weren't you here those couple of days last week?' she said.

'Mmmy mmmum was sick,' I said.

'I was worried. Rosie said it was you who was sick and Mavis said you were trying to find a job. What really happened?'

'N ... nothing,' I said. 'Honest.'

'You can't afford to miss school. You miss most of what's said to you when you're here.'

'No, I don't,' I said, miffed, suddenly finding my voice.

'Yes, you do,' she replied sternly.

I put the last of the slates in the cupboard. 'C ... can I go now?' I said.

But she made me set the fire for the morning first. I brought in the wood from the outhouse and twisted the newspaper into balls and sticks for kindling, hurrying to get away.

'I have to catch up with Mavis and Rosie,' I said. But they were waiting for me in the shelter in the playground playing chuckies. And then the rain came on.

There was a picture in one of the newspapers that I didn't recognise. I sat down and crossed my legs for a better look. It seemed at first like lots of dark squiggles with arrows pointing upwards. I couldn't make sense of it at all. Then I realised it was a map of Britain but on its side and the arrows pointing up-the-ways were actually pointing from east to west, from places on the coast of Europe to places on the coast of Britain. It was how the Germans might go about invading us. **SOMETHING BIG IS BREWING** it said. My stomach leapt. I held my breath and checked the date, but phew! It was January 1942, more than a year and a half earlier, and I sagged in relief and remembered the darkness of two winters before, our first in Carbeth, and how we had worried. When the bombs came down, some people thought there were German's under the parachutes and not just huge fifteen-foot parachute bombs that blew apart the whole street.

Last summer in those brief moments when George wasn't building his hut or making my life a misery, he used to practise bayonet charges with the other boys. One of them had a newspaper cutting called **COMMANDO TRICKS YOU OUGHT TO KNOW** with little drawings about how to tackle a Nazi, in case we met one unexpectedly, because even last summer we still thought we might be invaded and find real live Germans wandering about the countryside, scaring people from behind bushes. I'd tried some of these tricks on Rosie and Mavis. We even made these exercises into a new form of gymnastics, lunge and thrust, until one of the girls next door got hurt and I wound up with the blame as usual. They seemed like handy tricks to know when George was around.

But the same day we had our swimming tournament this summer and Mr Tait told me we all deserved a medal for going into the pool at all, he also told me we weren't going to be invaded by the Germans and that Britain was winning the war and that God was on our side. I don't know about God but Mr Tait was definitely on my side and he was right about most things, so I stopped worrying about Germans in the bushes.

When I'd finished laying the fire, Mavis and Rosie had given up and started for home. But they were so slow I caught up with them well before we got there.

The house was empty, my mum still making plans in Clydebank. I gave them both a piece and jam, sent them off next door to play with the Duncans and sat on the little birch bench and thought about what Mr Tait had said about my dad. I looked under the beds, then searched everywhere else. I didn't know what I was looking for and the only thing I could find, and this under the springs under the cushion on Mr Tait's chair, was my mum's old blue leather handbag that she'd been clutching the night she was under the building. She had it when they took her to hospital and all our money and papers had been inside it. A square had since been cut out of the leather on both sides and attached to the elbows of Mr Tait's blue work overalls. Several long strips had been cut out and attached to the wrists to stop them fraying. All the papers were gone.

I turned what was left of it upside down and shook it, thinking all the time how silly it was to keep this old wreck of a thing with not much leather left to use. The tattered lining flopped forwards, like my gran's petticoat that had seen better days, and hung limp and grey, little fronds of thread sucking back and forth as I leant forward and peered. I gave it one last shoogle for luck, ready to shove it back where I'd found it, when something landed in the sack the lining had made. I went to the light at the window, set the bag on my knee and pulled out an old brown envelope so withered round the edges its contents emptied themselves into my lap before I could stop them.

And there staring up at me was my dad.

My heart thumped up into my throat. My dad! What was he doing there? I never knew there was a photo of him. Oh, Mr Tait, thank you!

He looked almost as young as George and he beamed with bright twinkly eyes that seemed to stare right into me and laugh. I found myself jumping off the seat and laughing back. He had lots of thick dark hair, some of which was falling forwards over his face in a great loop.

'Dad,' I said, blinking back a tear and realising one of my hands was flat across my head and I had no idea how it had got there.

The photo was fixed onto a piece of card with four big staples. They were old and rust had seeped out of them across his chest and on either side of his head. Above him it said 'NAME *(Surname first in Roman Capitals)*'. This was odd because we'd been learning about the Romans at school so I knew they were long gone.

Underneath this, on a dotted line, someone had written 'GALLUZZO, Leonardo' in bright blue ink. But my dad's name was Leonard Gillespie. Everybody knew that. Leonard not Leonardo, Lenny for short, Big Lenny to save confusion if we were both there at once. And our surname was Gillespie, not Galluzzo.

'Galluzzo,' I said, 'Galluzzo,' and I turned it over in my mouth, saying it as many ways as I could. 'Leonardo Galluzzo. Lenny Galluzzo. Gal Us Oh.'

My dad was gallus alright. That's not one of his words, by the way, but everyone in Clydebank says it. It means cocky, which fitted my dad well. He was always pushing his luck, especially with my mum.

The name Galluzzo wasn't a bad name, but it wasn't ours, even if it did have a certain glamour with two double letters and not just one as in Gillespie. But the fact was it was the wrong name.

Some other bits of paper had fallen with the photo and when I put them together they made a notebook. But maybe they didn't all belong together because on one of the bits of paper it said '*Nationality:*' and someone had written 'Italian' next to it, and there he was in his army uniform, the British Army. So 'Italian' was wrong too, and it said he was a welder when in real life he was a rigger. But his birthday was right, and there was our old address in Clydebank, the house that was blown to kingdom come along with everything we owned. I flipped over the photo page and on the back, which seemed to be the front of the little book, were the words 'CERTIFICATE OF REGISTRATION' and 'Aliens Order, 1920' and a list of occasions when the book had to be 'produced' for the police. All of this was strange and difficult to understand and probably about someone else. I couldn't tell, the problem being what was my dad's photo doing in there along with his date of birth and our address? Who was he pretending to be? I opened it again and gazed at his cheery face inside, glowing with fun and mischief, and wondered, uneasily, if maybe, perhaps, he was a spy.

'Oh, Lenny,' I heard my mum say. She had a different way of saying it when she said it to him, like she was laughing and telling him off at the same time.

'Dad,' I whispered, and remembered how it felt when he was there, as if everything was in the right place.

I set the little notebook on the bench beside me. It was soft, almost fluffy, round the edges and tiny fragments of the card had flaked off onto my cardigan. The envelope was worse. I had another poke around in the bag and found one more thing, a picture postcard with a message scribbled on the back. I couldn't make out the date but the picture was pretty, a seaside town with a hill behind it, and the message read:

DeareSt Peggy,
So Sad not to See your Sweet Self but hope you, Lenny and MaviS are all Safe and Sound. I will alwayS be cloSe and waiting.
Love, aS alwayS, Uncle RoSS.

This was pretty strange too. I don't have an Uncle Ross, or none that I know of and I always made it my business to know all my aunties and uncles. They were generally good with sweeties or even the occasional penny, at least before the war, apart from my Auntie May who was what you might call 'nippy' not to mention mean. But there had never been any mention of an Uncle Ross. And whoever Uncle Ross was he had the peculiar habit of writing the letter 'S' extra big when it should have been small.

I read it through again and examined the picture on the front. Maybe I'd recognise it. But the rain began battering on the roof and drummed all sense out of me.

I read the message one more time, slowly, with my dad's picture beside it, and suddenly I knew why Uncle Ross had such silly S's. Uncle Ross wrote his silly S's the same way my dad wrote silly S's, with little flicky bits at either end. I had forgotten this but actually I used to do it too when I wanted to be fancy. At first I thought Uncle Ross must be a long lost brother of my dad's, but then I saw the truth.

Uncle RoSS *was* my dad. It was a Secret meSSage to my mum. He was letting her know he was still alive and maybe where he was, if she knew the place, which I didn't.

If Uncle Ross was my dad that meant my dad wasn't missing presumed dead. He was alive, just like my mum said. Or did it? I squinted at the date on the post-stamp, but couldn't make it out even though I held it up to the window and opened my eyes so wide they hurt.

The rain made such a racket I didn't hear Mavis and Rosie until there was no time to hide what I'd found.

'What's that?' said nosy Rosie.

'Who's that?' said Mavis, peering over. Mavis didn't know her own dad, but then she was only three the last time she saw him. I was nine which is old enough to remember, plus we used to have special days out, me and him, when we'd go walking in the Kilpatrick Hills.

'Nothing,' I said. 'Nobody.' I shoved it all quickly together and hid it under my arm. The bag was behind me on the birch bench. Mavis poked my arm with a damp finger and eyed me suspiciously.

'Are there any more carrots?' she said.

'My grandad's friend had a little book like that,' said

Rosie cheerfully. 'He got taken away by the police and no-one ever saw him again.'

'Oh,' I said, wondering how to get the envelope back to its hidey place. Rosie was four when she last saw her whole family. She wasn't a dependable source of information, and Mavis was best kept in the dark until I knew more.

'Yes, Mavis, there are more carrots but get your wet clothes off first and hang them by the fire,' I said, which gave me time to get the book and the photo and everything all back into the bag and under the cushions on Mr Tait's chair.

I redd up the fire and got the tatties boiling. Once we'd eaten we did some of those Commando exercises from the papers but not for long because I was so tired, and then I thought the time of the last bus must have passed because the light was going. I wondered what could have happened to my mum who should have been on it. She had a job in Singer's again, but nowhere to stay so she had been coming back in the evenings and leaving early in the morning. She was so tired she'd fallen asleep on the bus the day before and no-one noticed her slumped sideways on the back seat until they were all the way to the terminus at Drymen, a few miles down the road. A Glasgow man dropped her off on his way to town, which took forever, of course, because of the blackout.

We watched the wind blow black leaves across the sky and listened as it roared through the branches over our heads, and to the tick of the clock over the fireplace until it said eight o'clock, which was well past our bedtime.

So we washed our faces in the bowl just as if my

mum had been there and went and crept into bed and cooried into each other. We were quiet, even Rosie, all wondering why she wasn't home, hoping she'd just fallen asleep again, but I knew it wasn't true.

'Maybe she's gone to the pictures,' said Mavis. That's where she was the night of the bombing. Mavis stuck her thumb in and gazed at me over her fist.

'No, she's found someone to stay with and been too tired to come home,' I said.

'Maybe she's doing night-shift. My mum did night-shift,' said Rosie, panic making her talk. 'And they have to work extra just now because of the war and making guns instead of sewing machines.'

'Yes, Rosie, I suppose,' I said with a yawn.

'See,' she rattled on, 'we don't need sewing machines as much as guns just now because people can't make clothes because of the rationing.' This is what Mr Tait had told us.

'Quiet, Rosie, I'm sure there's nothing to worry about.'

Oddly, she was quiet and lay rubbing her ear between her fingers.

So on top of wondering where my dad was and whether he was alive or dead, now I had to worry about my mum too. I wanted to take his picture back out and stare at it for ages and remember him, and look at the strange things written in the little book and at the picture postcard to see if I could squeeze a memory out of my head, but I couldn't because of the little ones. So I lay between them and waited until Rosie got to wheezing and Mavis started snoring, but then I was stuck tight between them and they'd have woken if I'd budged an inch.

A great hole appeared in the darkness and into it drifted the picture of my dad, as clear as day. I stared at the ceiling and remembered teaching him clapping songs I'd learnt at school and picnicking in the hills before the bombing. But that was before he wasn't coming back, before the war had even started.

A wave of fury washed over me for my mum who wasn't coming home, even though something awful might have happened. I realised with a start that I'd known when Mr Tait died that she would go eventually and leave me in charge. She always used to leave me. She did it the night of the Blitz. I was usually good at looking after the wee ones and she knew she could depend on me. It was true she hadn't gone anywhere since we'd lived with Mr Tait but that was because she had him for company. Now she only had me and Mavis and Rosie and that wasn't enough.

And as for Mr Tait, well, I was, of course grateful that he told me, sort of, that there was something to know about my dad. But. Hmm. This is hard for me to admit but I was angry with him too. This was something new, being angry. I'd been annoyed before if he was telling me off when I didn't deserve it. But he was always right, usually, in the end. Not this time. He knew things about my dad and he went and D-I-E-D died before he told me the truth. Until then Mr Tait had always told me the truth.

Chapter 11

The next morning, Mavis and Rosie were up before me and the wooden spoon was tapping hard against the pot. I staggered blearily through to see what they were up to.

There was enough food, for the time being anyway. We had a big flour tin full of oats for porridge and another one full of flour, two-thirds of a sack of potatoes and half a caddy of tea. I had already estimated this would keep us going for about a month, apart from the tea. That would last maybe three days. Unfortunately we had forgotten to soak the oats overnight so Mavis was standing over a pot stirring frantically, then beating the sides as if this would make it cook faster. Rosie was on Mr Tait's chair pouring the last of the tea into the pot. I grabbed both from her.

'Hey, I'm doing that!' she said. 'That's my job.'

'You don't need all that tea, stupid,' I said. 'There'll be nothing left at that rate.'

I peered in at the porridge. Half-crushed grains scooted to the surface then sank back to the bottom. The stove was almost cold. I checked inside where a pile of blackened kindling sat on a scrunch of brown newspaper. Mavis poured another jar of water into the pot.

'Oh no,' I said.

'What?' she said.

'Nothing,' I said. The clock ticked. 'Great idea. Porridge for dinner. That's about when this'll be ready. We'll have it then. Good forward thinking. We need more like you on the team. You, Private Rosie. No tea for you this morning. No time. All into battledress quick as how's-your-father and we'll have turnips behind the ruined cottage. Come on, there's no time to hang about. Private Mavis, down tools and follow me. Attennnnnnnntion!' Mavis set the water jar on the stove and stood to attention as stiff as a post. Rosie, who had a hairbrush stuck in her hair, froze too. 'Private Rosie!' I shouted. 'At the double!' Rosie let the brush hang and stood with Mavis. 'Excellent, chaps!' I said. 'Now walk this way.' I waddled and kicked my feet up behind me and they did the same and we giggled our way into the bedroom to get dressed.

'Don't forget your cardies,' I said. 'We're into autumn now.'

We lifted our coats and scarves from the pegs by the front door and I looked with longing at their blue tammies which, unlike me, they had not lost.

On the way to school we stopped at the ruined cottage and sneaked round the back where a field of fresh turnips was waiting to be harvested. I'd brought a knife with me and picked and chopped the nearest one and we sat against the cottage to eat, Mavis perched on the window ledge. A giant raincloud hovered over some trees at the other side of the turnip field.

'Mind and chew it fifty-nine times,' I said, passing strips to them. 'Or you'll get bellyache. I won't have shirkers on my watch. No, siree. And no telling,' I said, biting on a fresh strip, 'anyone,' I chewed, 'about

Mum not coming,' munch munch, 'back.'

'Why not?' said Rosie.

'Never mind why not, Private Rosie,' I said. 'It's an order.'

'Orders is orders,' said Mavis, which we'd heard in a film once. We hadn't actually been to many films since the bombing because there was no picture house in Carbeth so we had to go all the way into town. The last time was around my birthday in April when we had a trip to Glasgow to see *Casablanca*. So romantic, so sad, and Mum cried.

At school they had started without us. Miss Read wheeched her specs off to give us a stern look before flinging them back and going on with the lesson.

Of course I had no plan for lunch so we had to beg and borrow and bargain with Senga who always had loads.

Two more days passed in this way. Mavis and Rosie seemed to like being Privates and we defended our hut with our commando lunges if anyone came calling.

Mr Duncan next door came to ask for our mum. I told him she was sick and couldn't go out and it was catching so he couldn't come in either. He shouted good health to her through the window. We always checked the windows before we went out and shouted 'Bye, Mum!' so the neighbours wouldn't ask difficult questions.

'Sssh,' I said. 'She's asleep. I'll pass the message on. Th … thanks.'

On the Friday afternoon, battle squad Gallus, as I had by then named us, were passing the Halfway House tearoom on our way home when the thin lady who worked there appeared from nowhere.

'I thought you wanted a job,' she said without saying hello first.

'Hello,' I said and waited for her to do the same.

'Well? Do you?' She looked over my shoulder as if there was someone there.

'Y ... yes,' I said, glancing at the empty road behind me.

'Eight a.m. tomorrow then,' she said. 'Don't be late.' She turned to go.

We all laughed. 'Don't be late!' we mimicked under our breath.

'Be clean!' she said in a sharp voice. 'Eight.'

We kept walking 'til we were out of earshot before shouting 'Be clean!' and 'Eight!'

There was a rap on Jimmy Robertson's window as we passed.

'Halt!' I shouted.

'Nine!' said Private Mavis.

'Thirteen!' said Private Rosie, and they erupted into giggles again.

Jimmy Robertson came panting down the steps of his bus-come-shop. 'Lenny,' he said. 'Did you find anything yet?'

'No,' I said.

'Ah, well, then,' he said, in a resigned tone. 'All the best!' And he went back inside.

We carried on in silence until Mavis said, 'Ah well then,' which for some reason was unbelievably funny.

And then, when we were nearly at the Cuilt Brae where our hut was, we heard hooves clip-clopping on the road behind us and Mr Tulloch came flying round the bend on his cart.

'Whoa, whoa, there, whoa!' he said, pulling back

on the reins. The horse snorted and shook her head in annoyance at the interruption. 'There you are, young Lenny,' he said once they'd stopped. 'Mavis, Rosie. I thought maybe you'd disappeared back to Clydebank.'

'Hello, Mr T … Tulloch,' I said. 'Say hello then, you two.'

'Hello, Mr Tulloch,' they chorused.

'Fancy another shot at the milking? My wife's not up to it and won't be with, you know, with …' He tapped his foot on the front of the cart and then cleared his throat. 'With the baby almost come,' he said at last. 'I need to train you up.'

Ah. I see. I knew what that meant. It meant she was having a baby. And soon. I had thought she was just fat.

'Um … ,' I said.

'We'll have no more of your ums young lady either,' he said with a smile. 'She forgot all her songs,' he told the squad. 'What do you think of that? Forgetting her songs!' He stood there and shook his head and whistled the tune to 'Scatterbrain', which was a favourite of ours, finishing with 'Isn't it a pity that you're such a scatterbrain?' and laughed.

I wanted to forget my last milking experience. My face was hot just thinking about it.

He reached over behind him and pulled out a metal cup. 'You can have some of this as a down payment,' he said and he lifted the top off a churn, scooped out some milk and handed it to me. 'You can bring the cup with you, clean of course, when you come tomorrow, okay?'

I nodded.

'You got an alarm clock in your house?' he said.

'Yes, we've got Mr Tait's,' said Rosie.

'Alright, six tomorrow morning. That do you?' he said.

'Six?' we all three said together.

'Yeah,' he said. 'It comes just before seven. Almost light. You'll love it. See you then.'

The horse was already straining forward, tugging on the reins, and needed no encouragement to turn and speed back down the road, leaving us standing there with our mouths open.

We closed them and went home. Rosie washed some tatties and Mavis brought more wood in, while I lit a fire the way it's meant to be done. One of the newspapers I scrunched into a ball said **WITHOUT LEGS MAN CAN STILL FLY**. The man in the picture had no legs but no wings either although it said he was getting them later in the week. I kept that sheet aside so I could figure it out later.

We boiled Rosie's tatties, rolled them in oats and roasted them in a pan. Very delicious I can promise you. We were settling back, at ease, on the birch bench by the window when Willie, Miss Barns-Graham, arrived at the door panting and wheezing like nobody's business. She came inside and coughed.

'Hello there? Anyone at home? Still no candles?'

My heart leapt into my mouth. The last time Miss Barns-Graham was in our house was when she brought the doctor for Mr Tait. Maybe she had bad news now about my mum.

'Wh … why?' I began.

'Hello, young lady, how are you today? I brought you two,' she said in a loud smiley voice and handed me two candles from her pocket. 'Y'aright? S'only me.

No need to look so alarmed. Is your mum in? Mrs Gillespie? You there?'

'She's ... she's sick,' I said with an awful feeling that this had all happened before.

'Oh dear,' she whispered, a hand over her mouth. 'Sorry for making so much noise then. Not seriously sick, I hope?'

'It's alright,' said Rosie, not whispering at all. 'She won't mind. She's very kind.'

'I'm sure she is,' said Willie.

'She adopted me,' said Rosie

'Really?' said Willie, bending down for a closer look at Rosie.

I thought this was big of Rosie, given my mum was the latest grown-up to vanish out of her life.

'And did she adopt you two as well?' said Willie.

I was just about to say that actually it was me who had done all the adopting round here, and that even though I was only twelve going on fourteen, actually I might as well be thirty-two and a half, which was my mum's age at the time. But my mouth went to jelly.

'Oh no,' Mavis piped up, whipping the thumb out of her mouth. 'She's our real mum, hers and mine.' The soggy thumb flashed between us. 'Rosie didn't used to be our sister but she is now.'

'I see,' said Willie. 'She's very like you. No-one would ever guess.' She looked round at us all. 'My goodness,' she went on. 'And now you've lost your dad, you poor things.'

'No, we haven't,' said Mavis. 'Mr Tait wasn't our dad. He was our friend. Our dad's gone camping.'

'Home on leave then, is he? What is he, a soldier?'

Mavis stopped and glanced over at me for help but

I was too busy wondering what she was on about.

'No,' said Mavis, 'I don't think so. Well, he was a soldier for a bit.'

'He was definitely a soldier,' I put in.

'But now he's gone camping,' said Mavis.

'Really?' said Willie.

I made a face at Mavis to stop. Rosie was tugging at her ear and looked like she was about to go off on one, so I cut in:

'C … can I give my mum a message when she wakes up?'

'I wanted to ask if it was okay for you to come and help me again tomorrow night in the kitchen. We've got guests, important ones. D'you think she'd mind? I'd give you a bit of money and you can have dinner too. Chicken this time. One of the dogs got out and went on the rampage at Home Farm.'

'She wouldn't mind at all,' I said, too stunned to have a jelly mouth.

'Super! Let's say five o'clock. Alright?'

'Oh,' I said. 'I may have to go m … milking at four.'

'Milking too? What an enterprising young woman you are. Just get along as soon as you can then.'

By the time she left it was almost dark and the rain had started again, but she didn't seem in the least bit bothered and waved a cheery goodbye, pulling her hat around her ears against the wind.

'Well, well, well,' I said, running through all my new jobs. 'We're going to be as rich as kings, you wait and see, and there'll be no more talk of leaving Carbeth. Tomorrow's Saturday so you two have to stay here and don't wander. Just say Mum's ill and accept all offers of food. Got it?'

They glanced first at each other and then at me.

'Look, you know where I'm going to be and you know I'm not making it up, don't you? I never go anywhere and I always come back.'

Rosie's hand was back at her ear and Mavis glowered at me from behind her fist then went to the window and stared out into the dark.

'I bet Mum comes back tomorrow afternoon anyway,' I said. 'You'll see. She won't just go off and leave us.'

But I was scared too. I wanted her to come home. I wanted to know she was okay.

'What do you mean Dad's camping?' I said, swinging on Mavis.

'I don't know,' she said and backed into the corner.

'Yes, you do. You must have meant something. What do you know?'

'Nothing. Leave me alone.'

'What? What is it?'

She stuck that stupid thumb of hers firmly in her mouth and wouldn't budge. And then, completely from nowhere, I had a sudden need to thump her across the head. I'm not proud of this but suddenly she was just about as annoying as any one single person could be, apart from maybe George. I'd already had enough of being in charge.

'She's just making up stories,' said Rosie. 'She didn't mean anything really. Your dad's dead, same as mine, everybody knows that.' And on she went.

'Shut up Rosie,' I said. My fingers twitched to thump her too now. 'It's none of your business. He's not your dad.'

'Yes, he is,' she said. 'If your mum's adopted me

then your dad must be my dad too.'

I hadn't considered this possibility before. It made me feel slightly sick and dizzy. I sat down in Mr Tait's chair and put my fingers in my ears so that I could think this crazy idea through. It turned out even Mavis knew stuff about our dad that I didn't know, and now I had to share him with Rosie too and we didn't even know whether he was alive or dead. I'd been there a few minutes listening to my heartbeat thundering in my ears when I felt a damp hand round my wrist.

'Lenny,' said Mavis, as she pulled my hand away from my ear and blinked up at me. 'Linny ...' Two tear lines ran down her cheeks. 'Lenny, Daddy's gone camping. George told me. And then he told me not to tell you. I'll be in trouble now.' She chewed her lip.

'George? What do you mean George told you?'

'Don't be angry,' she said.

'I'm not angry,' I said, and I wasn't, not any more, just confused and frustrated. 'I'm sorry, it's just a bit strange, that's all, and I don't understand. I don't seem to know anything about my own dad.'

I got her up on my knee on Mr Tait's chair and we stared at the fire in the grate. Rosie stayed on the bench by the window pulling at her ear and rocking back and forwards. Every so often she'd mutter something. 'He's going to be my dad too,' she said. 'Everything will be alright. Lenny will look after me.' I don't think she meant Big Lenny.

'Mavis,' I whispered. 'What did George say to you? Tell me exactly what he said, word for word.'

She thought for a long minute. 'He said, Your dad's in a camp, and he said, He won't come back and he might die there.' She pulled at her lip. 'But I thought he was already dead.'

'A camp? What else?'

'He might even be dead already,' she said. 'That's what George said. That's all. And he said if I told you he'd tell everyone Mum had gone to Clydebank and we'd be sent to the poor house or Miss Weatherbeaten.'

'When did you see him?'

'Day before yesterday. He came past the school.'

'You should have told me, Mavis.'

Chapter 12

I fell into a deep, deep sleep that night, roasted between Mavis and Rosie and lulled by the hum of the wind. Mr Tait's alarm went off at five thirty. I'd left it by the stove so that I'd have to get out of bed to put it off. It had two little bells on top and a hammer that banged so hard back and forth between them that the whole thing jumped off the shelf and onto the floor, narrowly missing the water bucket.

'Turn it off!' shouted Mavis before I could find the knob in the dark.

I put on the spare dress my friend Mrs Mags had given me a few weeks earlier that had belonged to her sister's sister-in-law's stepdaughter, or something like that. It was pale green with little yellow flowers all over it and I liked it a lot. It matched my dark green cardigan, made me look at least fourteen and was clean into the bargain, and I reckoned if I kept my coat on at the Tullochs' farm I should still be able to arrive at the tearoom in a clean enough state for work. If I was really careful I might even get to the big house in it. I kissed them goodbye and left them sleeping, grabbed my coat and scarf and set off in the moonlight for the Tulloch's farm.

In the porch of the farmhouse I rubbed my arms against the cold and pulled on a pair of wellies.

Mr Tulloch was whistling beyond the front door and nearly fell over me in the dark when he came out.

'Whoops!' he said. 'There you are! Good morning to you!'

Molly the collie gave a single bark and a nip at my elbow.

'M ... morning.'

'But those'll never do,' he said bending to peer at my boots.

'N ... no?'

'Not unless you have two left feet.'

I examined them in the light from the door and saw that he was right enough.

'Okay then,' he said, once I'd found a proper pair. 'Go into the barn and fetch the bucket and fill it like you did the last time in the grain store and do the mangers. If you do it quick you'll be done before I bring the cows in. Go on now.'

I took a huge lungful of air so I could speak properly. 'Yes, Mr Tulloch,' I said in a loud firm voice.

'That's the way!' he said, and he disappeared into the darkness towards the fields with Molly sleek beside him.

Feeling slightly more in command of my voice I sang a marching song on the way to the barn. Quietly. 'I had a good job and I left and it jolly well served me right ... right ... right.' And then on the way back I went: 'It jolly well served me right 'cause I had a good job and I left ... left ... left.' But slower, because the bucket was heavy. I decided to keep singing no matter what. It was 'Away in a Manger' next while I filled the mangers but I stopped when Mr Tulloch came back because it wasn't Christmas.

'Mrs Tulloch is trying to get up, but just in case she doesn't make it, I'm going to show you what to do right now. You ready?'

Deep breath. 'Yes, Mr Tulloch.'

'You're very polite this morning,' he said.

'Yes, Mr Tulloch,' I said.

'Good. Keep talking. What did you have for breakfast?'

This was a tricky one. I hadn't had any breakfast. I paused just long enough for him to realise.

'I've told you about this before, haven't I?' he said, but not angry. 'A good breakfast is very important. What was your mum thinking letting you out with nothing in your stomach?'

'I … I don't know.'

'Right, we'll get you some milk in a minute, but we have to get it first.'

Oh dear. I knew what was coming. Warm milk, straight from the cow. Yuck. And I'd forgotten to bring the cup he'd given us.

'This is Forsythia,' he said. He slapped Forsythia across the bottom. 'Move over. Forsythia. Forsythia, this is Lenny.'

Deep breath. 'Hello, Forsythia!' I said. Forsythia took her head out of her feed, paused, then stuck it back in again.

'Not so loud, Lenny, in case you scare them.'

Mr Tulloch put a three-legged stool on the ground beside Forsythia and sat down on it himself. He put a bucket underneath her and made me crouch down beside him so I could see what he was doing. This is what I saw:

Forsythia's udder was huge and pink and hard, fit

to burst, and it was muddy as if she'd sat down in the soggiest part of the field. Mr Tulloch's bucket was full of soapy water and a cloth.

'See all this muck?' he said. 'You got to make sure none of it goes in the milk. So it has to be clean, alright? Like this.' And he showed me. Forsythia carried on munching as if there wasn't someone fiddling about with her udder. 'No standing behind her, remember. Always from the side. You can go round the other side if you need to. On you go now. Your turn.'

I got down on the floor and washed the teats. They were hard but soft too, like my gumboots. And they were rough like Mr Tait's hands. I sloshed the soapy water up over the dirt. It was mostly country pancake, if you want the truth, but I washed her anyway. Mr Tulloch didn't say a word but watched me all the time.

'Perfect,' he said when I'd finished. 'You're a natural. Now carry on round and do the others and I'll follow you with the luggie.'

'The luggie?' I said.

'The milk pail,' he said. 'What a townie!'

So I washed the other cows' udders, and I can tell you I earned my penny that day and washed my hands very well afterwards. When I'd emptied the soapy water, he told me to come over and he'd show me something.

'This is how you do it,' he said. There were two cows left. We got down beside one of them, who was called Forget-me, Mr Tulloch on his little stool and me crouched beside him.

He spread his fingers wide and gripped the top of one of the teats between his thumb and the knuckle of his hand then pulled the other fingers in below, one after the other. A squirt of milk hit the side of the bucket and stopped as soon as his little finger joined the others in what looked like a fist.

'Pull and squeeze. Come on Forget-me,' he said. 'That's short for Forget-me-not.' He showed me again: 'Pull, squeeze, then release it, pull, squeeze, release, so the milk comes down.' Then he did the same with his other hand with another teat. 'Grip it tight at the top so it can't escape back up,' this he did, 'and again,' squirt went the milk, 'then the other one again,' squirt, 'and this one, and so on. You try it.'

I sat on the little stool. Mr Tulloch leant over me to watch. I could smell his sweat and his tobacco smoke even over the smell of Forget-me-not. My hands looked puny beside her great swollen udder. She chomped on, still ignoring us.

'Lean your head into her. Go on then,' said Mr Tulloch. 'Grip her hard. She's expecting it. You won't be surprising her.'

I leant my head against her side and felt her warmth, then took another deep breath and gripped the teat in one hand. I fanned my fingers down in the way Mr Tulloch had shown me, one after the other. It was squishy and bendy and nothing came out. I was scared I'd hurt her and she'd kick in pain. Mr Tulloch made me try again.

'Harder. Pull. Bring the milk down. Each squeeze of a finger pushes it further. You'll get it. Tight at the top and push it down. That's the way.'

'Oh!'

Forget-me stopped munching for a second as if she was surprised too.

'That's it,' he said.

'It's working!' I couldn't believe it!

'And again. Don't stop.'

'Look!'

'Keep going. Get into a rhythm.'

'Oh!'

'That's my girl. Well done. I knew you'd do it. Don't stop.'

'Skoosh!' I said.

'Make sure it all lands in the luggie. Look after the drops and the gallons look after themselves.'

'Oops! Sorry.'

'I need to deal with Nasturtium over there. She's getting tetchy. Doesn't like being last. You just keep going. I'll be listening.'

So I kept going with a slow but sure skoosh-skoosh into my luggie and soon there was a respectable amount of milk in it and Forget-me-not's udder had shrunk up-the-ways to almost nothing. As the flow of milk grew less and less, the ache in my arms got worse. Mr Tulloch sang 'Ye Banks and Braes' and then something about blue skies over Dover, which made me think of one of my favourite counting-in rhymes. So I summoned all my courage and waited for him to stop.

'Eenty-teenty, heathery-beathery, bamfaleery, over Dover, ram Tam, toosh Jock, you are it!'

Mr Tulloch laughed his head off and said I'd have to teach him that one. By then he'd finished milking Nasturtium and went to empty his luggie into the big vat next door in the dairy. I looked in mine and gave Forget-me-not one last squeeze.

Finally there was nothing coming out.

'Great, young lady. I'll just finish her off,' he said.

He sat on the stool and went skoosh-skoosh-skoosh from Forget-me-not into my luggie and stood up and beamed at me. 'Look at all that yummy creamy milk. You did that. Come back at four and we'll see what else you can do.'

Deep breath. 'Yes, Mr Tulloch.'

I came reeling out into the sunshine. Mr Tulloch could probably in fact have milked twenty cows in the time I took to do my one, but I had MILKED A COW and not only that: I had MADE SOME MONEY. Plus the sun was out and I had more work to go to.

I had walked almost the whole half-mile to the main road before I realised I was still wearing their gumboots and had to turn back. Mrs Tulloch was in the dairy by this time, talking loudly across the yard to the grain store where I could see Mr Tulloch's back. I changed back into my shoes without being seen.

'We should get some Italians,' she said. 'Or Germans. They're probably glad to be prisoners of war and out of the worst of it. I've heard they're just ordinary lads like ours. They can't all be lazy. What do they want with the war? And they've nothing to do in the camps and probably glad to get out. I'll be back on my feet soon enough, but if it's not costing much I can't see why you have any objections. Stop whistling and listen to me!'

Italians, Italians! Why was everyone talking about the Italians?

I ran back down the road and up to the Halfway House tearoom.

'At last,' said the thin lady, and she glanced down the road and pointed a sharp finger at a clock above a counter. I was five minutes late. 'Let me see you.' I opened my coat. 'Nice dress. Turn round. Ach. You have mud, or something, all up and down the back of your legs. The bottom of your dress is mucky. Go and wash. Hands.' I showed her my hands. 'Oh my good God! Through there at once.'

She was beginning to sound like Miss Weatherbeaten. Therefore I obeyed without question, scrubbing my legs, hands and dress as hard as I could at the cold tap, even though my hands were already spotless.

'Turn round,' she said, when I came out of the bathroom. 'Hands up!'

I checked over my shoulder in case she had a gun, Commando lunges at the ready, but she had what looked like a small tablecloth which she wrapped round my middle and tied tight at the back.

'There. Perfect,' she said. 'Off you go into the kitchen then and you can get started.'

I looked round for a door and there one was. It had a round glass panel in the middle of it which was completely steamed up. Pushing my way through I found no-one on the other side, just a huge pot of boiling water on a big stove and a large window which was also steamed over. Three loaves of bread sat neatly side by side on a table with the biggest slab of lard you ever saw. Presently she followed me in.

'I'll slice, you butter, thin mind, every second piece.' We worked in silence, which suited me. Not only was my mouth in a state of jellified terror but the rest of me seemed to be frozen rigid too so that I kept dropping the knife or putting the bread together all wrong. And every time I did, she hit my fingers with the back of her knife. Then when the bread was done she gave me a basket of potatoes and told me to wash them under the tap at the back door with a little scrubbing brush. Very soon my fingers were blue with cold and red with grazes where I missed the tatties and got my fingers instead. When I'd finished those there was another basket of carrots and two huge fresh turnips. Next was chopping. The turnips were as crisp and hard as you like and, because Mr Tulloch had forgotten to give me any milk, I still hadn't eaten and couldn't help eyeing up the little chunks I was cutting for soup, especially the carrots. I had just thrown two squares of it in my mouth when she came back through from the tearoom.

'What's your name?' she said.

She was smiling, and seemed to have thought better of being such a cow, although I realise now what an insult to cows that was, having just learnt they were perfectly friendly and placid. I shoved the lumps of carrot on top of my tongue so I could speak. 'L … Lenny,' I said.

'Well, Penny, go out the back and clean out the WCs. There are two. Ladies and Gents. They must be spotless. I want to see my face in them.'

I'd like to see your face in them too, I thought.

'Cleaning equipment under the sink, except for the mop which is by the door. Off you go now. No. Wait. Come here. Turn round.' She undid the tablecloth from round my middle and hung it over a chair by the wall. 'Put this back on when you're finished. I don't want it ruined in there. Go.'

I don't think those cludgies had been cleaned in a month. Ours at the hut was never like that and we didn't even have water. It was worse than our communal one on the stair in Clydebank that we shared with the rest of the close before it was bombed to bits. I will not describe her cludgies to you. That's how bad it was. To make matters worse I could hear Mavis and Rosie playing amongst the trees behind the building. I had told them to stay at home, but there was nothing I could do. And then, by the time I finished that revolting job, the front of my beautiful dress was as dirty as the back.

A bowl of soup was sitting on the table when I came back in. I was starving, absolutely, and cold, and generally miserable and cross. I was particularly miserable and cross with myself because I hadn't even told her I needed paid for my work. The soup was developing a skin. I hoped it had been left for me. I went to the little round window and peered out. To my great surprise, all six tables were full of people. The thin lady was smiling at everyone as if she was goodness itself. I ran back to the table and started shovelling the soup into my mouth as quickly as I could. It was watery and needed salt, but when you're starving, all food is fantastic. Then I quickly washed the bowl and spoon and put them in a cupboard.

She came back, the smile wiped clean off her face.

'Where's my soup?' she said.

I was ready for this. 'I put it back in the pot, Mrs ... ,' I said. How annoying not to have her name.

'No you didn't,' she said, 'You ate it. Liar.'

I was also ready for this. 'That's not fair. I don't lie,' I lied. 'I was taught not to. I did put it back in the pot. It had a skin, and I washed the plate and put it away.'

She paused for the briefest of seconds. 'Nonsense,' she said. 'You have some on your dress.'

I looked down and saw that this was true. This too I was ready for. 'It must have splashed going back in,' I said.

She began to laugh. 'Onto your chin?'

This would have been the moment to falter but I had already decided that enough was enough when she kept hitting me with her knife earlier on. I decided to change the subject.

'How much are you paying me for doing this?' I said.

'Pay? How much?' She seemed to be thinking. 'Tuppence,' she said. 'You're not worth tuppence, but there it is.'

'A penny will do. I've done everything I'm doing.' I held out my hand.

She laughed again. 'Your working day has hardly begun,' she said, and she made a strange noise with her nose. 'Fill the sink and put the cloth back round you, then go and clear the tables.'

'It's nearly two o'clock,' I said. 'I'm hungry and tired and you're rude.' I hadn't meant to say this last bit. It just slipped out, and once it was out I tried hard not to look sorry for saying it, even though I was. I almost wished my mouth would turn to jelly again and shut me up.

'And you're a liar. Get to work.'

'My penny please,' I said, going to the corner and taking my coat from the rack.

'Get back to work.' She turned and left through the round windowed door. Now I was furious.

I followed her through and in front of all those people I said, not loudly, 'I'm going home now and I want my pay.' I held out my hand, which to my great annoyance was shaking. The customers looked up, every one of them.

'Be quiet, girl, and get back in the kitchen,' she said under her breath.

'No,' I said.

'I'm docking your wages for leaving early,' she said.

'Hello, Lenny, what are you doing here?' I looked up to see my friend Mrs Mags who was bad George's auntie. She had her baby with her and a lady in a hat.

'Hello, Mrs Mags,' I said. 'I'm working. I just started but this lady isn't very nice so I've decided to stop again.'

'You need to finish your shift, Lenny,' said Mrs Mags kindly. 'You can't run out in the middle of a shift and leave her in the lurch.'

'Yes, I can,' I said. 'She keeps hitting me with her knife.'

'That's terrible,' said an elderly man at the next table. 'What a thing to do to a young girl. Look at her hands.' I held up my hands for everyone to see.

'Poor wee lassie,' said the man's wife. 'That's a sin. I've some ointment in my bag that would help that.'

'Thank you, that's very kind,' I said.

'I thought you said you were leaving,' said the thin woman.

'I just want my penny. It's not much for six hours of work, is it?'

'Shocking,' said someone behind me.

'I'm not paying someone who runs out in the middle of a shift,' she said. 'Absolutely not.' She turned and went back into the kitchen.

The room fell silent. The lady put her ointment on the table.

'Give me your hands, dear,' she said, reaching out.

I felt my lip go. It trembled and froze. I felt stupid. I was trying hard to go on being grown-up and brave when Mrs Mags's baby suddenly yelled and made everyone jump and stare and forget about me. I put my coat on as quickly as I could and made for the door, gulping in my pride.

'S ... sorry,' I said, to the ointment lady as I fled. 'S ... sorry.'

George was in my way, the final straw. I pushed past him and clumped down the steps to the road and then turned back up the hill between the pub and the tearoom and went in search of Mavis and Rosie.

'Mavis!' I shouted. 'Rosie!' Tears of rage flowed down my cheeks and then Dougie, bad George's little brother, appeared on the path in front of me.

'They went home ages ago,' he said. 'What happened? What's wrong?'

'Nothing,' I said. 'Nothing at all.'

Chapter 13

This is what happened next. Dougie told me afterwards. He went to join George and Mrs Mags and the baby in the tearoom. Mrs Mags was trying to calm the baby down but little Calum, who was already two and a half and so not really a baby any more, had bellyache, probably because of the thin lady's bad cooking. He didn't want to be quiet. After a bit the thin lady came out and asked Mrs Mags to keep her children in order. By this time George had been given the run-down on the old bat and her not paying me, so he followed her into the kitchen and gave her a piece of his mind. George's mind is pretty mean even on a good day so I'm glad it wasn't me he was giving his mind to, which it usually is. Anyway, he said quietly to her that he was going to start shouting too, along with his little cousin Calum, who is normally cute as a button, I promise you, if she didn't give him, George, my penny IMMEDIATELY. He probably got that from Miss Weatherbeaten because that was her favourite way of getting you to do stuff, by shouting IMMEDIATELY and making you jump out of your skin.

So George got my penny. When Dougie told me this I was furious at first, not expecting ever to see the penny. And then Dougie pulled out of his pocket a warm shiny slightly sticky penny with King George the Sixth on one side, and the lady with the fork on the other.

But I'm away ahead of myself because this didn't happen until well into the next day.

After I left the tearoom and went in search of Mavis and Rosie, I didn't find either of them at the rope swing or any of the huts as I thought I would, and then I thought I'd run out of time and had to get back to Mr Tulloch's farm. In fact I was early and had to hang about in the porch, waiting.

By then I was a lot dirtier than I'd meant to be, apart from my hands which had been scrubbed and rubbed and whacked and so on for several hours. I thought that was probably enough to make me clean enough to milk cows for the whole of the next week but Mr Tulloch thought otherwise and sent me straight to the tap.

I washed all twenty cows and milked Forget-me-not again until Mr Tulloch finished her off, or 'stripped' her as he called it, which sounds sore but he says isn't.

While we were milking he was very quiet, just humming 'Ye Banks and Braes' over and over, so I hummed along too and when he fell silent I sang the words, those I could remember, more to keep myself awake than anything else. The warmth of the barn made me sleepy and I was glad to be able to sit on a stool and lean my head against Forget-me-not's side. Mr Tulloch seemed sleepy too.

He gave me a penny and a cup of milk and made me drink it there and then seeing as I hadn't brought him back his cup from the day before. He told me to come back in the morning and bring the cup with me and he'd show me how to do the milk dishes.

'Yes, Mr Tulloch,' I shouted, though I couldn't remember seeing any dishes and I went back down the lane. As soon as I hit the road I pulled out my penny and rubbed it between my fingers. Nineteen twenty-five, it said, with another King George on it, this one with a fancy moustache. I kissed it, put it in my pocket and held it tight all the way home shouting 'Mavis!' and 'Rosie!'

As our hut appeared through the trees I saw smoke billowing out of the chimney like it does when it's newly lit, or like when George set his on fire and he ran out screaming and Mrs Alder had to run in with a bucket and throw water on the fire before it burnt the whole hut down.

Just then one of Mr Duncan's girls came bouncing down the hill and onto the road in front of me.

'They're in the hideout,' he said. 'Your mum's been shouting on them for ages.'

'My mum?' I said. 'Oh, yeah, of course. Good. Thanks for telling me.'

But Willie was waiting. I decided Mavis and Rosie were alright if my mum was there. So I took the shortcut to the big house and went in by a back door straight into the kitchen.

'Ah, there you are,' said Willie. 'Great, and what a pretty frock. Stick your coat over there and give your hands a scrub in the sink. Look lively.' She beamed at me and wiped a few stray locks from her forehead with a floury hand, leaving a streak of white. The kitchen had three huge windows, each one probably higher than the other, and the biggest stove I've ever seen. I knew all this already, but what I noticed this time was how much smaller it seemed with the mess she had made in it. There were three recipe books lying just visible on the vast table, but they were half-buried in newspapers and cabbage leaves. The sink was full of gritty pink water and chicken feathers that I also noticed in several corners of the room. They were under the huge kitchen Aga, at the windows even, and in little flurries under the chairs. In fact I kept finding little feathers for the rest of the evening no matter how meticulously I picked them up when I saw them.

On a pale oakwood Welsh dresser stood two roasting tins. Willie lifted their lids to show me what was inside and for a second I thought she was going to bang them together like a pair of cymbals. Luckily I was wrong.

'Look!' she said proudly. 'Not bad eh?'

There was a plump chicken in each one, with most of their feathers removed.

'W … well …'

'I plucked them myself.'

This didn't surprise me.

'F … f …' This was ridiculous. Willie was the least scary posh person I'd ever met. I took a deep breath so I could join in with her fun. 'Fantastic!' I said, louder than seemed polite.

'I'm tremendously pleased with myself,' she said.

'Look,' I said, still too loud. 'That one still has feathers.'

Her smile fell.

'It's okay,' I said. 'I'll do it.' I was being far too loud but it was the only way I could get any words out.

'Oh dear, is it very bad?' she said.

'It's very good!' I shouted.

Then she banged the tin lids together after all, making my head buzz painfully.

'Sorry,' she said, seeing my alarm.

I decided being quiet might be the better option.

While I sorted out the chickens, she left the room saying she had an idea. When she came back I was chasing a feather that had floated upwards on the heat from the stove as I was throwing in a handful to burn.

'Oh, how lovely. What a game!' she said, and together we chased after it until she, being the taller, captured it and dropped it into the fire. 'What on earth happened to your hands?' she said, turning them over in her own.

'I've been working very hard all day,' I said. I didn't want to tell her about the café or the toilets. She might have made me clean hers.

'Very admirable,' she said. 'I thought so. Why don't you get that paper over there and put all the feathers into it. The place is a pigsty ... . And I'll finish the pudding. Apple crumble. Yumble! You hungry?'

I nodded enthusiastically. She brought me a cup of tea and a piece toasted on the range and made me sit for five minutes before doing anything else. While I was eating I noticed the front page of one of the papers: **POULTICE ITALY'S TOE**. I knew a bit about poultices, having taken a few knocks in my time, but also because of my mum's leg which often gets sore and swollen and needs one. But the paper's story was boring stuff about invasions and things, so I had a look inside. I had just found the Wee Macs, my favourite cartoon, when Willie came back. She gave me a broom and got me to sweep up the feathers.

This was not easy and they seemed to spread

themselves out all the more. Some made their way down the corridor, even as far as the hall, as if they were trying to escape. While I was there I heard men's voices and a layer of cigar smoke slithered through a half-open door, following the feathers on their way to the front door.

'Pst, Lenny,' said Willie from the kitchen. 'Come back here. Look what I've got for you.'

I took my fistful of feathers back to her. She held up a dress for me to see. It was very sombre, dark grey, in a beautiful fine material with a fancy lace collar.

'I know it's a bit dull,' she said. 'Your frock is so much prettier but it's not ... it's not very ...'

'It's f ... filthy,' I said, which made her laugh.

'Yes, it is rather. This is an old one of mine. I never liked it much. Much too serious, don't you think? But, you can't help in the dining room in that thing, lovely though it is. And we could keep this here for you and it would always be clean when you needed it.'

'Um ... alright.' I said. 'Thank you.'

There were six people for dinner including Willie. One of the others was Barmy Barney, who was her dad. There was a man in little short trousers called plus fours that only went below his knee. He had thick green socks and a checked shirt that didn't match and hardly any hair. His face was red and he laughed all evening when he wasn't talking. The other man hardly said a word, in fact I can't even remember what he looked like, and then there was a young couple who didn't say much either and squeezed hands under the table. I saw them do it. He was in a uniform, RAF I think, and she was so pretty with red lipstick and high heels with sequins on the toes and beautiful sweet perfume that filled the whole room, that I thought I'd faint just being close to her. The perfume wasn't Willie, definitely not. Willie smelled of turpentine and cooking.

There was a feather in the pretty girl's crumble which I didn't notice until I'd put it down in front of her. Willie noticed it at exactly the same moment and made a squinting face at me then opened her eyes wide. We both glanced round at the other puddings and I saw another feather in the plus-four man's cream. Luckily everyone else was talking too much to notice.

'What's that noise?' said Willie, interrupting them.

'What noise?' they said.

'There,' she said. 'There it is again. It's coming from up there.' She pointed at a corner of the ceiling.

'I can't hear anything,' they said.

'There ... and again,' she said. 'Surely you can hear that. You must all be stone deaf.' She stood up and put her head to one side and started towards the door as if she was in a trance. The rest of them were so daft they all got up and followed her.

'It's coming from upstairs, I think,' she said.

'But what's it like? What are we listening for?'

'It's there, listen ... no, it's gone again. It's like a hoot, or a whistle.'

'Well, which is it? A hoot or a whistle? It can't be both.'

'It's a kind of whistling hoot. Can't you hear it?'

'Oh yes,' said short-trousered man. 'I think I can. There. You see?'

It's amazing how stupid people can be.

As soon as the last person was through the door I whisked the feathers from their plates and checked all the others. Only Willie's was feather-free. Then I went into the hall where they were all standing with their heads cocked to one side listening up the stairs and took a deep breath.

'Excuse me,' I said. 'Your c ... crumble will be going c ... cold.' But if they heard me, which I doubt, they ignored me, as was only right. It was none of my business. There was a tiny vase on a shelf in the corridor back to the kitchen, so I put the feathers in that, as if it was a bunch of tiny violets, for Willie to find later and laugh at.

'Do you know I think we've scared it off, whatever it was,' I heard her say. 'I can't hear it any more. Let's go back in and get our crumble.'

They stood a little longer in silence listening for an indescribable sound that wasn't there and I tiptoed back to start the washing up. Then Willie came through and told me that there was a plate of dinner in the oven for me. And what a plate! Chicken and gravy and carrots and cabbage and, best of all, roast potatoes. I tried hard to go slow but there was no way. The plate was empty in five minutes flat. Then I started cleaning up the mess we had made trying to do the crumble.

I had so much fun that night I completely forgot about the tearoom lady or going back to Clydebank or my mum or George or even my sore hands, even though I was fetching and carrying all night long. I forgot I had to get up early and go back to Mr Tulloch's farm and do the milking. I even forgot about Mr Tait, and when I suddenly remembered him on my way home I felt a pang of guilt that stopped me in my tracks. But then I realised he'd have been happy for me to be with nice people and having fun and he'd have been proud of me for making it all happen.

What a long day it had been. I rubbed Mr Tulloch's penny in my pocket and the thruppence Willie had given me, turning them over and over, and listened to the little 'tink' noise they made when they fell against each other.

But I hadn't forgotten my dad because everything seemed to be about Italy. While I was serving steaming hot dinners on fancy plates with blue Chinese houses and birds on them, the dinner guests had been talking about Italians and camps and the difference between Italians who were prisoners-of-war and other ones who were internees and had been arrested and whether they were all fascists or not. Prisoners of war were soldiers and pilots, like the man in the uniform, only he wasn't Italian, and internees were Italians who were living in Britain. They were all in camps. There was some confusion about these camps and where they were and what should be done now about Italy. Now was different. And then I heard the news my mum must have heard but wouldn't tell me. Italy had stopped being Germany's friend and had decided to be our friend instead. This was how Willie explained it to me when I asked her, casually, when we were serving up the crumble. This was probably why I wasn't paying proper attention and all those feathers got into everyone's dinner.

I asked her why Italians who lived here would be in camps and she said they might be secret friends of Hitler's so, just in case, they had all been put in camps.

'In tents?' I asked.

'I don't know,' she said. 'Maybe. I don't think so.

It just means lots of people together, but don't worry, they can't get out. They put barbed wire fences round them. Most of them were sent to Canada anyway. You don't need to worry about them.'

I had this dizzy feeling of everything fitting into place, like finding all the lost pieces of a jigsaw. Things suddenly made sense, but I hoped my dad hadn't gone to Canada. That would be too terrible.

When I went to clear the pudding bowls away, they were still talking about the Italians.

'Do you think the internees will be brought back?' said the pilot.

'I doubt it. Not yet,' said the plus-fours man. 'They might release some of the ones in camps here, those they're sure aren't Nazi sympathisers. Some of them are contributing enormously to the war effort in forestry and farming and suchlike. They're a valuable asset when all's said and done and we need all hands on deck.'

'I agree,' said the thin man. 'It's time they came back and made us some of that delicious ice cream of theirs to go with this fabulous crumble.'

I decided it was time to pay George a visit.

Chapter 14

Everyone was asleep by the time I'd found my way back home. I wound up Mr Tait's clock, turned on the alarm and crept with enormous gratitude into bed alongside my warm little family.

My mum, exhausted from working all week, only grunted when I came in. Then suddenly she woke up. 'Lenny?' she said. 'Oh, thank goodness. I was worried.' She gave me the biggest hug.

I was just about to say 'You were worried?' in a sarcastic voice, when I realised I wasn't worried any more, only tired. Then we both fell sleep as easily as falling off a log.

It seemed like only five minutes before the alarm shrilled through the wall again and I had to haul myself out of bed and leave those three warm bodies behind.

I stumbled back down the road in the same green dress with the yellow flowers; there wasn't time or light to find my everyday one. At the Tulloch's door I pulled on a pair of boots, filled the grain bucket and did the mangers. Then I filled another bucket with soapy water and waited in the dark for Mr and Mrs Tulloch to appear. Mrs Tulloch wasn't there long and said she was just too tired and went back to bed.

Again I managed Forget-me-not, again Mr Tulloch

had to strip her for me, but I managed Tulip too, by which time he was through in the dairy whistling and cleaning up. Again he said, 'Come back at four,' but remembered this time to give me a warm cup of milk, just delivered, to be drunk there and then, and another telling off for not eating breakfast. I promised to bring his other cup back to him later on and wandered sleepily back down the lane to the main road and past Jimmy Robertson's bus.

Jimmy Robertson was standing at the window. He looked surprised to see me and had sticky-up hair. He cocked his head by way of a question, so I gave him a grin and two thumbs-ups, but he waved for me to come in. A terrible stink hung in the air, old cabbages, I reckoned, or he'd spilt a pint of milk and hadn't cleaned it up. I stopped on the bottom step.

'Now,' he said. 'There's an old man up your way who needs his paper. Can you take it?'

'Just the one?' I said.

'The others'll come down for theirs,' he said, 'and they'll buy their bread when they're here.' He handed me a fresh crispy roll. 'Tulloch says you don't eat.'

'Thank you,' I said, and I was so hungry I forgot all my manners and sunk my teeth into it straight away.

Jimmy Robertson laughed. 'Did you find a job yet?'

I nodded as I munched.

'Knew you would,' he said. 'Here.' He rolled a paper, tucked it under my arm for me and gave me directions to the old man's hut. 'Tell him he can pay me later. On you go.'

'Thank you,' I said again, and hopped back down from the smelly bus.

The roll was gone in a flash. Warmth spread from

my tummy outwards and I began to dawdle. It wasn't as cold as usual and the trees were pretty, just taking on their autumn colours. I took out the paper and unrolled it to look at the front page.

I couldn't believe my eyes.

This is what it said: **ALLIED TROOPS PUSH NORTH FROM SOLERNO TO CUT OFF LEG**.

Cut off leg? My heart pumped hard in my chest and an old familiar sick feeling gripped my stomach.

You see, I never saw my mum's foot after it had been smashed under a building. I only saw the leg after they'd, you know, taken off the foot. In fact by that time it had mostly healed and didn't even need gentian violet any more. It was round and smooth, apart from a giant scar, as you'd expect. I think I would probably have fainted completely on the spot if I'd had to look, although the nurse who came to clean it and do the bandages did try to make me. I had various methods for avoiding thinking too hard about how the foot came off and tried one there on the hillside. It was simple: I put my fingers in my ears, closed my eyes and kept very still. It didn't work, of course, it had never worked, and I was too old by then to believe it ever would.

So I leant against a fencepost and started reading.

The news was good. It was not about an actual real live human leg being cut off and even the leg in question was, strictly speaking, so far only a foot. It was the foot at the bottom of Italy, and by pushing north the Allied Troops were hoping for a more serious amputation. I'd never heard of Solerno but there it was on the map next to Rome. This is what the story was really about: our troops were pushing north through Italy. Our troops were chasing Hitler away back north out of Italy and back to Germany where he belonged. Because Italy was our friend again. And my dad was an Italian. So if my dad was an Italian, why was he fighting in the British Army? I can assure you he was because I saw him in his uniform when he came home on leave. (This always struck me as odd, that 'leave' meant coming back home instead of leaving.)

'What have you got there then?' It was Dougie, bad George's wee brother, a nosey wee parker if ever there was one.

'Papers,' I said, folding it back under my arm. 'Where's George?' I always liked to know where George was so I could be somewhere else.

That's when he told me about George and my penny. I put it in my pocket with the others and they tinkled together like a man's pocket.

Mavis and Rosie were further up the hill shouting 'Be clean!' and 'Eight!' and other numbers and daft things and then they started up a tree clinging on like two little monkeys.

'Are you going back to Clydebank then?' said Dougie. 'To live, I mean. I knew you would. I said so to George.'

'Mind your own business,' I said, hurrying away from him.

'So you are!'

'Mind your own business. No, we're not.'

'George says you are.'

'Get lost!' I said.

'Suit yourself.'

And he went.

Back at the hut I decided I had to ask my mum some of the questions that were buzzing round my head like a cloud of bees. She had washed our clothes and hung them across the veranda outside the window.

'Mum?'

There was no answer.

The fire was going but the windows were open.

'Mum?'

Something bumped in the bedroom.

'Why are you in bed?' I said.

'What?'

She rolled over and gazed at me as if I was a picture on the wall.

'Are you not well?' I said, feeling a twist in my stomach. 'Shall I go and get the doctor? I've got fivepence to pay him.'

'Not well?' she said. 'No, I did the washing. I just meant to lie down for a couple of minutes.'

I knelt on the floor beside her.

'Okay,' I said. I waited a minute, trying to figure out what to say. 'Mum ... I just wanted to ask you something.'

'Come and have a cuddle,' she said, as if I was four.

So, even though I was twelve, I got onto the bed beside her and cuddled in.

'Mum?' I whispered, knowing she was already fast asleep again. 'I've got so much to tell you, and to ask.'

I waited for the first snore and decided I could probably ask her later, even though it was warm and snug in there and sleep seemed like a very good thing. But I was supposed to be delivering a newspaper, so I sat up and slid as carefully as I could off the bed.

The rain had started again. I put the newspaper

inside my coat and went in search of the old man. It seemed the old man was hiding, but after several tries I finally found him in a hut just above George's.

George was down below by the road with an axe above his head that went 'thwock!' as it landed on a stump of wood. It scared me so much I changed my mind about asking him questions about my dad.

I chapped on the old man's door. The sun was back out so I couldn't see into the dark inside. The old man peered out at me, hanging onto the door jamb. His mouth spread into a grin and I saw he had no teeth, not a single one.

'Thank you so very much,' he said slowly, seeing the paper. 'I know you. You're Lenny. Mr Tait's girl. He was a lucky man indeed to have you, a lovely girl, so kind, so kind. Thank you!'

'Th … thank you, sir,' I said, and wondered why I addressed him as 'sir'. A lump pushed into my throat.

'You're very, very welcome,' he said. 'And tell that Jimmy Robertson to get himself a proper shop. Or a proper hut. One or the other. Sleeping with the groceries. Tut.'

'Yes, sir, I will do,' I said. 'I'll do that.' Although I'd no intentions.

'And tell George he should have listened to Mr Tait more. He needs to put his back into it if he's going to do anything but hit the wood. He needs to slice it, you see, slice down hard with the axe. And he needs to swing it sideways, round and back over his head so there's momentum, and then down.' He stepped out of the doorway and demonstrated how. 'He needs to use the momentum of the axe's weight.' He made a chopping movement with his right hand against his left. 'Chop chop! You tell him. Go on then, you tell him, chop chop.' He laughed at his own joke and turned to go back inside. 'Thank you,' he said and closed the door.

Then I went down to George, swallowing back the lump in my throat, and sat down on a tree root a little way off. It was never a good idea to get too close to George.

Thwack! went the axe.

I had three reasons for coming to see George. 'Thanks for getting me my penny,' I said. That was the first one.

Thwack! went the hammer. I watched him doing his chopping all wrong.

'The man up the hill gave me a message for you,' I said, wishing he hadn't, and wishing I hadn't mentioned it. It wasn't one of the three important things and it seemed like the wrong moment to deliver it.

Thwack! He winced as the axe bounced off the log. One of his beady little eyes turned on me. I made sure not to laugh.

'Well?' he said, leaning on the axe.

'He said you have to swing the axe round sideways,' I mimed how, 'round and back and ...'

'I know how to chop wood, thank you very much. I don't need you to tell me.' He picked up the axe again.

Thwack!

I resisted the temptation to point out how obviously he didn't know how to chop wood because I needed him to talk.

He took one last swipe at the log, but the axe bounced off it and shuddered right out of his hands. I saw the shock travel up his arms and his face twist with the pain. He turned away and straightened so I wouldn't see. I'd seen him do this before, this turning away. It meant he was going to be extra-super-mean when he faced me again, like he was putting on his meanest face specially for me. But this time I was wrong.

'What do you want?' he said, with a sigh as if he was only tired. 'You're putting me off.'

'Sorry,' I said. 'I was just wondering what you knew.' I stopped here. It seemed such a strange thing to say, 'about my dad'. I realised I had never talked about him to anyone, not even Mavis really. It was like he was completely taboo, as if to say the words 'my dad' was against the law.

'About what?' said George.

He was the last person I wanted to say this to, but I had to if he was the only person alive who knew, but just at that moment my mouth suddenly went to mush again and I couldn't get the words out.

'M ... m ... my ...'

'What?'

I took a big deep breath. 'My dad,' I shouted. 'What do you think? My dad, of course.'

'No need to shout,' he said quietly. 'I can hear you. So the little piglet squealed, did she?'

'She's not a piglet.'

'She is in my book,' he said. I suppose he hadn't forgotten how she threw grit in his eyes when he was picking on her down at the canal in Clydebank. It was the night of the Blitz, just before the bombing started, and he'd lost his balance and fallen in.

'She's too wee to keep secrets,' I said. 'Look, keys, George, keys. Can't we have a truce for a minute? Just for once?' I crossed the first two fingers on each hand. I had stiff fingers and they were sore with all the work, so crossing them was difficult. As soon as they were crossed I held up both hands up for him to see. 'Keys,' I said again.

He looked at me for a minute and burst out laughing. Then he went and picked up the axe where it had fallen and swung it up onto his shoulder. 'I haven't got time for this,' he said. 'I've got firewood to chop and I'm lining my hut. Some of us have to work for a living and only have a Sunday to do everything else. I don't have time for keys.' He laughed again and I tried hard not to spit out everything I'd been up to for the past two days.

'I've been working too,' I said, as casually as I could. 'You know I have.'

But he laughed again and started towards his hut. So I followed him all the way inside.

George's hut was very like ours with a brick fireplace at one end, but it was much, much smaller with only a bench to sit on and to sleep. There were thick wooden supports for the walls on which he had attached various boards and planks for the outside layer. Part of the inner wall had been put in place too. This was what he must have meant by 'lining his hut'. There was a gap of two inches between the two layers.

The third thing I wanted to ask George about was his newspapers. I knew he read them because Jimmy Robertson once told me he gave George his old ones. There they were, a stack of papers, and the top one was today's with the *Cut Off Leg* headline.

'I'll trade you,' he said. 'Scrunch up those papers, except today's, and stuff them down inside here.'

He showed me the space between the inner and outer walls. 'Like this,' and he tossed the top paper to one side and showed me how to take a sheet of newspaper from the pile and turn it into a ball, as if I was a very stupid three-year-old.

'Okay,' I said, biting my tongue. 'So, my dad?'

He stuffed the rolled-up paper down into the space in the wall.

This is what he told me while we filled his wall:

One day when Mavis and Rosie and I were all at school and my mum was over at Mrs Mags's, and George had thought Mr Tait was up at the big house visiting old Barney, George took himself up to our hut and went inside.

'I was just being nosy,' he said, as if that made it alright, 'but I found this old bag with strips cut out of it and inside there was ...'

'Yes, I know all that,' I said. 'You shouldn't have been nosing about.'

He glowered at me a moment. 'What did Mr Tait tell you?'

'To look under the bed, only that's not where it was.'

'That all?' he said.

I nodded.

'He told me not to tell you,' he said.

'He changed his mind,' I said. 'The day they took him away. When he was on the floor by our fire sweating and coughing and ill. You remember. It was before you came in that he told me. Before my mum came back with Willie and the doctor.' Suddenly I felt very hot.

George sighed. 'You're not doing the papers.'

'I will, I will,' I said, and I did.

'Your dad is an Eye-tie,' he said. 'Push them down harder. Like this. His real name is Leonardo Galluzzo and he's from Cantabria, which is somewhere in Italy.'

'No, he isn't. He was born in Hull, in England,' I said. 'We went there.'

'Well, his dad must have been Italian then. I don't know. I'm just telling you what Mr Tait said.'

I stared at him a long time and tried to keep breathing and not fall off the bench. Why had Mr Tait told George all this and not me? But that would have to wait.

Here's the gist of what George knew:

When the war broke out my dad had joined the army and gone to fight the Germans. I knew that.

My dad had come home on leave three days before Italy joined up with Germany.

Some family (Gran and Auntie May and the baby) had arrived the same day, just before Italy signed up with the Germans, and there had been an almighty row. I remember this row but I was at school when it happened. There was another when I came home. We went to Rothesay the next day, me, Mavis, Mum, Gran, Auntie May and the baby. We left my dad behind. When we came back three days later, he was gone. George said my mum had never forgiven herself for leaving him. He said my dad had been arrested.

'What on earth for?' I said. 'Why would anyone arrest my dad? He's not a criminal. He's very law-abiding. He joined the army. He's funny and kind. Everyone loved him. Loves him. He's still alive.'

'You're not filling the walls,' said George. 'I'll have to stop telling you if you don't stuff paper in the walls. They arrested him for being Italian.'

'Which he isn't, but even if he was, being Italian isn't a crime.'

'It is if we're at war with Italy.'

'I suppose so.' I thought for a minute. 'But we're not at war with Italy now.'

What had Willie's plus-fours man said? Something about forestry and farming and he'd wondered whether they'd be released.

'That's probably why Mr Tait thought it was okay for you to know. Stuff the walls, or get out.'

'So, how come you told Mavis he'd gone camping? That wasn't very nice, telling her something that's not even true.'

Very annoyingly, George laughed.

I threw a ball of paper at him.

'He's in a camp, stupid, a work-camp, a prison camp for prisoners of war,' he said. This was what Willie had told me about. I didn't want it to be true. I pictured barbed wire and mouldy bread and cold and no shoes. George picked up a piece of wood and positioned it between two of the supports at the bottom of the opposite wall. 'They get better food in there than we do,' he said. 'Same rations as men serving in the army.' He pulled a nail out of his back pocket and positioned it at one end of the plank.

'But he wrote to my mum,' I said. 'They don't allow that in prison do they? Do they allow letters? Or cards?' I was thinking about the picture postcard.

'Did he? You sure?' He banged the nail in with three little taps then three huge thumps.

'So where is this camp?' I said once I'd recovered from the noise.

But George had no idea. All he knew was my dad

had been arrested along with lots of other so-called Italians, even though he was a soldier for Britain, and they'd all been taken into Glasgow. I told him my dad said he'd be court-martialled for desertion if he didn't go back to the army when his leave was over, but George reckoned that was nothing compared to the trouble he'd be in now. He said he'd heard the Italians were put on a train for Liverpool. This was terrible news because Liverpool was bombed just like Clydebank and lots of people died there too. But George said they were all put on ships and sent to Canada and Australia, and would probably never come back. He said one of the ships had been sunk by the Germans.

'How do you know all this?' I said, barely able to breathe.

'Richie told me,' he said and he stuffed a ball of paper far down into the wall.

'Who's Richie?'

'He does the river patrol, the bit between Greenock and Cardross. I do Clydebank to Cardross and sometimes we have to pass on information.' As he said 'information' he rolled his shoulders as if they were heavy from carrying so much information, and thwacked the next newspaper into his hand three times.

I watched and waited for him to go on.

'He's an apprentice, same as me, but in Greenock. That's further down the river. It's where the troopships come in.' He thumped his paper two more times, sniffed and went back to stuffing the wall. 'He says it's where all the survivors are brought into as well, from sinkings and wrecks, like the one that went down with the Italians.' He paused and watched my face, which I kept very still. 'I'm not really supposed to tell you any of this, in case you're a spy.'

'Don't be stupid. I'm only interested in my dad,' I said, keeping the tremble out of my voice. 'Go on.'

'It went down off Ireland. Richie said there were only a handful of survivors. Before the war it was a big fancy liner for rich folk and it had the best name, the *Arandora Star*. Anyone who survived was brought back to Greenock.'

'What happened to them after that?' I said.

'Dunno,' he said.

'Can you find out?'

He shrugged and banged another nail into the other end of his plank.

'Someone must know,' I said.

'It was ages ago. No-one cares. They're our enemies, don't forget.'

'But they'll have records, won't they?' I said. 'They'll know if he survived, or at least if he was on it, won't they? Like the town hall in Clydebank after the bombing. He's a swimmer anyway. He taught me. He can do fifty lengths just like that. He'd have swum to the shore and hidden.'

'Why don't you ask your mum?'

'She says he's not coming back.'

'But not why.'

I pushed a ball of paper down into the wall.

'Maybe it's because of your Uncle Ross in Helensburgh,' he said with a smirk. 'I always said your mum was a tart.'

I was old enough to know what that meant and also that it wasn't true, so it gave me great pleasure not to rise to the occasion but smile sweetly instead. You see, not only did I know something that he didn't know, that Uncle Ross was my dad, but he'd also told me where the postcard came from too. Helensburgh. My dad was in Helensburgh, or had been.

George gave me a cold potato he didn't want, because I was hungry, and he let me tell him what the old man up the hill had said about the axe. But all the time he stared at me with his little black eyes narrowed. So I asked him if I could go out and try it myself, just to see if I'd heard the old man right.

The axe was the heaviest thing in the world, apart from the *Queen Mary* liner.

'He said it's all in the momentum,' I said.

I swung the axe out sideways and hit myself on the head with the handle. The whole thing dropped over my shoulder with a clunk and scudded against the back of my legs. This made George laugh his stupid head off, so I rubbed where it hurt and stared at him long and hard, just like he'd done to me. I glanced up the hill in case the old man was watching which luckily he wasn't, only a few crows who seemed more interested in each other.

'I'd like to read today's front page,' I said, giving myself a shake. 'It might tell me about my dad. He's a hero, you know, and very, very funny. I don't believe he'd dead. Not for a second.'

So I left George with his axe and went back into his hut and read the front page, and then I read the other pages and then it occurred to me that some of the old newspapers we'd just stuffed in the walls might have stories about Italians and could even tell me where the camps were, because George said there were lots of camps but no-one was supposed to know. But someone must have known because someone had to be guarding them, and that person had to be married to someone or have children and those children might want to know where their dad went to work every day and that dad might have said, 'Oh it's in such and such, or somewhere-or-other.' And maybe even the people in the newspapers might make mistakes sometimes, and forget what they're not supposed to write in their papers, which is what happened when they printed the number of people who died after Clydebank was bombed.

We had stuffed all the other papers inside the wall so, carefully, I tugged a few sheets back out and scanned them for 'Italians' and 'Italy' and '*Arandora Star*' and things like that but hardly found anything at all, only a map of Italy, but without Cantabria on it, and stuff about Italian rail strikes and another map of how much of Germany we could bomb from Italy and an ad for special tablets that I thought might help my mum with her nerves. I folded the map and put it in my pocket. Then I heard George coming back and couldn't get all the papers stuffed back in again before the door opened.

'What are you doing?' he yelled. 'Look at the mess you've made!'

If he'd been anybody else I'd have said sorry, but this was bad George. 'What mess?' I said, pretending innocence. 'I stuffed 'em in, I can take 'em back out too.' I ducked from his blow and squeezed past him and out the door.

He went on shouting like that as I ran off down the road. It was time for Mr Tulloch's milking anyway and I wanted to better my cow score.

'Bye, George,' I shouted from a safe distance and blew him a kiss.

Chapter 15

That afternoon I milked three whole cows, well, Mr Tulloch had to strip them all for me. They were, in no particular order, Forget-me-not, Tulip and Asparagus (Mr Tulloch wasn't sure how an asparagus flower looked, but he liked the name). I was so pleased with myself I finally found my tongue and started talking nonsense to the cows. Here are some of the daft things I said:

'This afternoon we stuffed George's walls with newspaper and then I pulled some of them out again. The news is very interesting don't you agree, Asparagus dearest?'

'The animals went in two by two, do you? Moo moo?' which I sang.

'This is the story of Jack who sold his cow for five measly beans. Now don't be alarmed because we're not selling you, are we Mr Tulloch?'

('No, not Tulip. She gives the most milk.')

I described, in detail, my search for the old man. That story nearly sent us all to sleep.

Then we went into the dairy and did the milk dishes. This is not dishes as you might know them. Oh no. This is everything to do with milking, big and small, and involves lots of cold water and blue hands, but no actual dishes, just tubes and buckets and things.

Mr Tulloch gave me another penny to add to my collection and said that starting the next day he'd give me a ha'penny for every cow I milked. I went skipping up the road to tell Mavis and Rosie about Forget-me-not and Asparagus and Tulip, and everyone, especially my mum, about all the work I'd done and how we could stay in Carbeth forever after all.

But there was no smoke above our chimney and the washing had been taken off the line. I speeded past George's hut and up along the road to home with a million possible explanations flashing through my head.

No-one was there. Mr Tait's chair had been pushed back against the wall. The water bucket and bowl were empty, the floor swept and all our crockery, such as it was, gone, even the sewing machine. Only Mr Tulloch's cup sat alone on the shelf. A huge bundle wrapped in a blanket stood on the bench by the window as if looking out. My footsteps echoed around the walls and the thin autumn sunshine strained through the glass.

'Mum?' I said, quietly, to no-one. 'Mavis? Rosie?'

Mr Tait's room was empty apart from the pallet. I noticed the remains of a bonfire outside where my mum must have burnt his mattress. There was still a bed in our room, the pallet and mattress, but no bedding and no clothes piled in the boxes in the corner.

Mr Duncan's geese squawked outside the window. There was a knock at the door.

'Mr Duncan,' I said. Mr Duncan hardly ever came to visit us. He was very thin, which was why he wasn't allowed in the army.

'Lenny, hello,' he said, and he touched his cap, probably because of Mr Tait. He hadn't been in our hut, which was really Mr Tait's, since Mr Tait had died. 'I've got a message for you from your mum. She couldn't wait until you got back.'

I knew what the message was before he said it. It was the message I had been dreading all this time. I was to put the bundle on my back and go down and get on the bus to Clydebank. Mr Duncan had a tiny piece of paper for me and on it was written the address I had to go to. I glanced at it and stuck it in my pocket beside the money. Mr Duncan thought he was telling me good news. He had no idea that I was all broken up inside, that I had finally lost absolutely everything, all in a little split second, and my life would never be the same again.

'You'll be back at the weekends no doubt,' he said with a smile. 'I hope so. You'll be missed. Oh and she left this for you, for your fare.' He handed me a silver sixpence, which was more than enough to get me to Clydebank.

'Thank you,' I said. 'When's the last bus?'

He told me and said I should hurry because it wouldn't be long. Without thinking, I looked for Mr Tait's alarm clock on the shelf but all that was left was a box of matches.

'You want a hand down there with that bundle?' he said.

'No thank you,' I said. 'I can manage.'

He left me there and I sat on the bench made of little birch trunks and leant on the bundle and stared hard and long down the road and through the trees that were turning for autumn and off to the Campsie Fells where Senga and I had gone tramping one day over the summer. My mind wandered through our adventures on that trip and the swimming tournament, and all the other days when I did all those other things that had seemed so wonderful or terrible or ordinary since I'd lived in Carbeth. If I'd ever written a diary, this would have been like reading it. We had been there a whole two and a half years, so it took me some time to revisit all those days. But when I'd finished, I realised I had a plan and I hadn't even been trying. If only I could have told him about it, Mr Tulloch would have been extremely impressed.

Obviously I didn't get on the bus. Instead, I unwrapped the bundle and put the blanket back on the bed, climbed in and went to sleep. There was nothing else I could do because I had stared at the hill until all the daylight was gone, and I had no food, no candle and no-one to talk to who wouldn't have given me away. Fortunately I was so completely exhausted I fell asleep in no time and because I'd gone to sleep so early I also woke the next day with the birds, even before Mr Duncan's geese were up, which meant I could go down the road in time to milk the cows with Mr Tulloch.

I managed the same three cows I had milked the previous afternoon. Mr Tulloch had no idea what was going on. A penny ha'penny he'd give me, and another penny ha'penny or even tuppence I'd make later in the afternoon if I kept it up.

After I did that morning's shift I went down to Mrs MacLeod's farm on the other side of the hill and offered my services there. There were still some tatties to be brought in and put in cloches, so I spent three days doing that. She gave me thruppence that day for the pleasure and a huge plate of soup at lunch-time with meat in it, rabbit I think, thick broth with some of those peas I'd picked and chunky brown bread. It was hard going back to work afterwards.

For five days, Monday to Friday, I milked the cows twice a day, increasing the number milked to four by the Friday. Amazing! Each day when I'd finished I washed all the equipment, the churns and buckets and so on, and on the last two days I mucked out the byre too and Mr Tulloch made my money up to half a crown for the week. I gazed at this shiny silver thing in amazement that it was mine and that I had worked for it, before stuffing it in my pocket along with the other coins.

Bad George had gone back to Clydebank, probably on the very bus I should have been on, and I knew he would be gone all week, otherwise he'd have lost his job. So one evening, after the afternoon milking, I went into his hut and pulled the newspapers back out of his walls again and looked for clues about my dad. I kept the pile of scrunched-up papers in a corner ready to be put back in.

The awful truth is I found almost nothing I hadn't already found out, but what I did find scared me. Here's the worst of it: the day Italy decided to join Hitler, people in Britain had gone to all the Italian cafés and chippies and ice cream parlours and they'd smashed them to pieces, everything, not a thing left unbroken, and stolen all their ice cream. There was even a picture of a café in Edinburgh with the window all over the pavement. People had stolen what was inside too and the police had been called to stop the riots. Perhaps those Italians really were friends of the Nazis, I had no idea, but I knew my dad wasn't a Nazi because he'd gone off to fight them as soon as he was able. It didn't make sense. But if he really was Italian, which he wasn't, I began to see why my mum would not want me to know. I wasn't famous for keeping my mouth shut and they might have arrested her too for marrying him, or me and Mavis for being his children, because if he was Italian, didn't that make us Italian too?

And all the time I missed Mavis and Rosie terribly and worried about them and wondered what they were doing. I kept thinking how annoying they were but also how much they'd be missing me as well. We were all missing Mr Tait so much already that it seemed mightily unfair to lose Carbeth and each other too. Plus there was a good chance I'd lose the note with the address and never be able to find them again. My mum's head must have been mince if she thought going back to Clydebank was a good idea. Maybe she was missing Mr Tait so much she wasn't thinking straight. I was missing everyone so much I couldn't think straight myself.

George had no curtains so Mr Duncan must have seen me in his hut.

'What are you doing here?' he said.

'Mrs Mags gave me a message that I should just come to Clydebank when I was ready. From my mum. And I'm not ready.' This was as close to the truth as I could get.

'I'd sort of worked that out,' he said. 'But what are you doing in George's hut?'

'I'm stuffing his walls,' I said. He eyed the pile

of scrunched and unscrunched papers. 'I'm very interested in the news.' I picked up a page with another map of Italy I'd found. Above it were the words **65,000 BRITISH PRISONERS**. 'My dad's a soldier,' I said.

He looked surprised.

'These are great,' I said, spreading a Broons cartoon over the map. 'Much better than the Wee Macs.'

'Och, yes,' he said. 'But Oor Wullie's the best!' And he squatted down beside me to read.

Mrs Mags came over to our hut at teatime the next day with little Calum. Teatime didn't really exist because I had no tea, only a jar of porridge left by my mum, and no pots to cook it in.

'Well, young lady,' said Mrs Mags. 'What's going on here then?'

'Nothing,' I said. 'I don't want to go to Clydebank.'

'I can see that. I meant, don't put words in my mouth.'

'Sorry, Mrs Mags,' I said, cursing Mr Duncan for his tale-telling. But I was sorry. Mrs Mags was one of my favourite people in all the world. 'I'll go over this weekend, I promise.' I meant it too.

'Your mum'll be working seven days a week, you know,' she said. 'She needs you for the girls. What would Mr Tait say?'

'Sorry, Mrs Mags,' I said.

'Oh, stop being so sorry all the time. I know exactly what Mr Tait would have said. He'd have said, "Stay in Carbeth, Peggy, where it's safe," wouldn't he? Of course he would, but Mr Tait's gone now and you have to do what your mum says, especially her with her leg. He'd have said that too.'

'I know,' I said. I did know. I just couldn't go.

'Someone's been into George's hut and trashed it too,' she said.

Little Calum looked up at me and beamed and offered me a corner of his soggy blanket.

'I'll put them all back,' I said. And I did plan to.

But on the Friday night I was still frantically searching the papers for news, trying not to get stuck on Oor Wullie, The Broons and Thae Twa (which means Those Two) when the old man from up the hill arrived and then Mrs Alder's children arrived, and then Mr Duncan again and they all wanted to know what I was doing there, and Mrs Alder brought me some Moulton pie for my dinner and sat until I'd had every last mouthful of it, which didn't take long, so she could have the plate back. I managed not to let any of them into George's hut because I had a pile of important stories which they might have seen. But then darkness fell and there was no moon and I had to get back to my hut for some sleep before milking in the morning which wasn't easy.

And I forgot, sort-of, to re-stuff the walls, and the next morning I was bundling up my belongings in the blanket and setting off, and to be fair I was only half awake.

That morning my mouth turned to jelly again and it wasn't just the cold.

I only milked two of Mr Tulloch's cows even though I tried hard. But my mind was full of the day ahead so I couldn't think of any daft nonsense to say to them. Mr Tulloch sang 'Ye Banks and Braes' for them but I forgot all the words and had to hum instead. Mrs Tulloch was there too and she sang 'Good Kind Wenceslas' but with silly words because it wasn't Christmas.

'Got to do something to get the little 'un going,' she said. 'You look a bit peaky. You alright?'

I shrugged as if to say, 'you know how it is', the way I'd seen grown-ups do, and hoped her baby didn't come that day.

At the end of milking she went back indoors and I went to the dairy for the milk dishes. Mr Tulloch followed me in.

'Mr T ... Tulloch?' I said.

'Yes, Lenny,' he said. 'What's wrong with you today? Only two? Miss Tulip was sorry not to have your company. I was going to give you ten shillings for the week, but I may have to think again.' Unfortunately he was only joking.

'Mr T ... Tulloch,' I said. And I sighed for all the effort just to speak. 'Mr Tulloch, c ... can you k ... keep a secret?'

'Y ... yes,' he said.

Was he taking the micky? No, he looked too surprised for that.

'Go on,' he said.

I took a deep breath. 'I can't do the milking any more because I have to find my dad,' I said.

'I didn't know you'd lost him,' he said, sitting down on an old wooden chair against the dairy wall. He took his cap off and wiped his brow with his hand, then put the cap on the back of his head like I'd seen him do so many times before.

'I don't know where he is,' I said, 'and I thought he was d ... dead, but it turns out he's not, or probably not, and I'd like to know.'

'I see,' he said. 'Where did you last see him?'

'In Clydebank about three years ago,' I said. 'I can't tell you any more because you might not like me if I did.' But he said he liked me just fine and that he always had and that nothing I could tell him about my dad would make him like me less because it was me he liked and not my dad, who he didn't know.

'Really?' I said.

'Yes, really. I've never met him.'

'No, I mean …' Then I saw he was making fun and we laughed at each other. 'I think he might be in a camp for people who live in Scotland but whose parents came from somewhere else.' I was hoping this was clear enough for him to understand but vague enough for him to not get the Italian part.

'Well that's clear as mud!' he said with a laugh. 'But I think I can help.'

I hoped so too. He had, after all, found Mavis after the bombing and he probably knew lots of farmers. Maybe he had more brothers too.

So while I finished the milk dishes, Mr Tulloch went back into his house for a minute and came back with a book in his hand that turned out to be a map the size of a window once he unfolded it. He sat on his chair against the wall and we looked at it together in the sunshine. It had place names and brown mountains and blue for the sea and patches of green trees, and Carbeth was on it and Carbeth Loch and he had put a little cross where our hut was, mine and Mr Tait's that we had built and lived in for two and a half years. The pub was there, tiny and close to Mr Tulloch's farm. Clydebank was by the river and there was Greenock and Helensburgh and Dunoon and lots of other places I had heard of but never been to, and

Rothesay where we'd gone with Auntie May and Gran. I noticed the route from Clydebank to Helensburgh had a black train line.

'Thank you, Mr Tulloch,' I said. How kind he was.

'But he could also be on the Isle of Man,' he said. 'Some of them were taken there, in which case you need to talk to someone official.' I bit my lip. 'Italy isn't at war with us anymore. They're with us now. You won't be arrested.'

But I had already decided to take no chances. After all, Italy might change its mind again. 'You won't tell anyone, will you?' I said.

'No, but what I'm going to do for a milkmaid I don't know,' he said. 'I'm going to give you a florin for luck because you've worked hard this week and I know you'll come back. Bring the map when you do.'

'Oh, thank you!'

'Good luck!'

I added the florin to my pocket and did some mental arithmetic, five shillings and sixpence. I could last for ages on that! I hadn't spent a thing all week.

'Thank you! Bye!'

Molly the collie followed me across the farmyard. I was nearly gone when Mr Tulloch called me back.

'I wish you wouldn't go,' he said. He seemed to be thinking very hard.

'Why don't you ask my friend Dougie to help with the milking?' I said, and I told him which hut Dougie was in.

'No, no,' he said. 'It's not that. I'm worried about you. Young girls shouldn't be wandering about on their own, especially not now with a war on. What does your mum think of all this?'

'I'll be alright,' I said as cheerfully as I didn't feel. 'She'll be ...' What? Furious? Delighted? Not even notice I've gone?

So he made me promise to tell her where I was going. 'Where are you going anyway?'

'I don't know. I know he was in Helensburgh,' I said.

'Very nice. Very pretty. Just don't you be going there by yourself.' He paused a minute, and we watched while Mrs Tulloch waddled out of the house with a bucket of scraps for the chickens then went back in again. 'You've been very lucky coming to Carbeth. I hope you know that.' Molly stuck her nose in his hand and he patted her and pulled her ears.

I nodded that I'd understood. I told him that was precisely why I had to find my dad, so we could stay in Carbeth, and I listed all the things I loved about being there, the friends I had, the safety from bombs, all the places there were to explore, the ropeswing on the big beech tree at the top of the hill, and the fresh clean air with no factory smells. I knew how lucky I was.

'Yes,' he said quietly, 'it is all that. But it's not like that everywhere else. There are lots of bad people about, bad men in particular. The troops, you know? Especially in Greenock. They get a bit wild when they're off duty. You're not used to dealing with things like that.'

He took his bunnet off, shook his head, scratched the stubble at the back of it and put his bunnet back on. He said even Helensburgh was busy and there were prisoner of war camps up the glens and all sorts of people wandering about that nobody knew. He said a friend of his had counted all the ships on the Clyde one time and there were more than three hundred, which made me think Mr Tulloch's friend must have been telling porky pies, but he said no. There were a lot of very important things going on and it wasn't safe for me to go there.

'Why can't you wait, or get your mum to come with you? Or hang on 'til the war's over and I'm sure he'll come home.'

I didn't know what to say. I needed my dad now, not in a few years.

'But if you have to go just be careful,' he went on, seeing I wasn't going to change my mind. 'No talking to strange men and keep well away from Greenock and servicemen off duty.'

I chewed my lip again and nibbled on my thumbnail.

'Ach, what am I saying?' he said. He stood up and ruffled my hair. 'They'd never let you travel without a pass anyway. Just keep yourself to yourself and don't go on your own. Always make sure you can get home.'

I gulped and nodded, but somehow couldn't find any words.

'You can stay here, you know,' he said. 'We've got the baby coming but there's room. You could help with it when it comes.'

'Thank you, Mr Tulloch, that's very kind but I do need to go. Don't worry. I'll make sure I don't get into any trouble.'

Famous last words.

Chapter 16

Being a Saturday, no-one was at school. The road and the woods round our hut were teeming with everyone I'd known for the last two and a half years, but no-one bothered me as I made my way home to pack up the bundle and leave. I'll be back, I kept telling myself. This is just for a while. There are things that need done.

I headed back down the long sweeping road, waving goodbye to anyone who noticed, and onto the main road towards Glasgow. Jimmy Robertson gave me the thumbs up, I ignored the café and at Mr Tulloch's road-end I paused and gazed down the track, but saw no-one, not even the cows, who must have been in a back field. At the turn in the road I looked back one last time at all the huts dotted about the hillside in the gentle sunshine and listened to my friends playing, their voices carried easily on the still air, and I wished I could wind back the clock. For a second I thought of staying, but that wouldn't work either, so with heavy steps and a heart full of dread I turned towards Clydebank.

Miss Read was in her garden beside the school, clipping away at a bush with a pair of something snippy when I sneaked along the path that goes up and over the hill. She was singing 'Mairzy Dotes' under her breath and I thought she hadn't seen me.

'Leonora,' she called, which is my Sunday name, after my dad, Leonard.

It was rude of me but I kept going because I didn't want to explain what I was doing and why I hadn't been at school. When I arrived panting at the big beech tree at the top of the hill I swung the bundle onto a dry patch of ground underneath it, sat down and scanned the horizon. Two women came up the hill behind me. Neither of them was Miss Read, so I pretended there was something interesting happening in the other direction.

'Morning,' said a voice I didn't recognise.

'Good morning,' I said, and they passed on by.

There was no-one else on the path so I spread Mr Tulloch's map over the bundle and had a look, tracing Carbeth to Clydebank with my finger then Helensburgh, Greenock over the water, Port Glasgow, Paisley and Govan on the other side, and then Glasgow where the riverbanks met. Then someone popped over the hill from Clydebank so I folded it quick and hid it in the bundle. Maps were strictly not allowed in case they fell into enemy hands.

Once I'd recovered from the struggle up the hill I set off along the path again, stopping every so often to shift the bundle from one shoulder to the other.

I was coming through a little thicket of trees, thinking that the weather would be turning wintry soon and the leaves would be gone and perhaps this wasn't the best time to be setting off on a great journey, when I saw two small people wandering along arm in arm discussing something with great seriousness. One had blue eyes and the other brown and they both had the same dark bobbed haircut that I had. I dropped the bundle and waited for them to see me. Mavis was the first to look up, Rosie being too busy enjoying the sound of her own voice.

Mavis's little face cracked into a smile and she let go of Rosie and ran to me but in the short distance between us her smile faltered and fell and finally crumpled into a silent wail, then she slammed against me, hugged me hard, held on and howled.

'Lenny!' said Rosie, ignoring Mavis's cry. 'We were coming to get you. Your mum's having kittens because there's no-one to look after us, so we said we'd stay in the house ourselves all day today and never go out so that we could come back over to Carbeth without her knowing and stay with you.'

'What?' I said. 'You should do what she tells you.' This was a tiny bit pots and kettles.

'You wouldn't believe the boys in our school, by the way,' she went on, 'and guess who's the head teacher?'

'Miss Weatherbeaten!' wailed Mavis.

'Miss Weatherbeaten?' I said. 'That's terrible. They can't let her teach. She's a …' I didn't know what she was. 'She's a lunatic,' I said at last.

They both stared up at me, maybe imagining what Miss Weatherbeaten might look like now her madness was full-blown and obvious.

'But we're not going back to Carbeth just yet,' I said. 'And you two have to stay with Mum for a few days while … while I sort something out.'

'Sort what out?' said Rosie.

'You're going to find Dad, aren't you?' said Mavis.

'Well, yes,' I said. 'How did you know?'

But Mavis only gazed up at me in that way only she knows how and slowly the thumb went back in.

'Was that who the photo was?' said Rosie. 'I knew it. I said so to Mavis. I said, Mavis that's your dad. Don't you remember your dad? And then I thought, I don't remember my dad either.' She looked away over at the hill I had just come down and pulled at her ear, with her eyebrows all squeezed up in the middle.

'I'd forgotten my dad's face too,' I said. 'And you were only wee when he …'

'I wasn't that wee,' Rosie interrupted, and off she went about how big she was at the time of the bombing and how she'd found her own way back from Clydebank to the flat rock where Mr Tulloch's brother found her. Rosie was like a homing pigeon, with me being home.

'Right, Squadron,' I said. 'About turn. We're not going to Carbeth today. We have an important mission elsewhere. *I* have an important mission and I need absolute obedience in the ranks.'

Rosie shut up for a minute and eyed me in a way similar to George. Mavis swatted the tears from her eyes and listened.

'I'm in charge of this battalion,' I said, 'and foot soldiers must do as they're told otherwise the enemy will take over.'

'The Germans?' said Mavis in a shaky voice.

'No, silly,' I said, seeing her fear. 'The Germans aren't coming any more. Mr Tait said so.'

'Mr Tait's dead,' she said.

'I know,' I said, feeling less and less like the sergeant major who must be obeyed. 'He told me at the swimming pool in the summer.' They glanced at each other. 'It's all over the papers,' I said. 'Haven't you heard? But the thing is, I have to find Dad, so you have to stay with Mum and do what she says.'

'I thought your dad was dead,' said Rosie.

And Mavis and I both said: 'So did I.'

'I knew he wasn't dead really,' I went on. This wasn't entirely true. 'Well, he might be, but I'm going to find out.'

Mavis, whose thumb had fallen out of her gaping mouth, frowned and squeezed her mouth shut and put her damp hand in mine.

'Mine is,' said Rosie, as if this was something to be proud of. 'Mr Tait said so, but I don't want to go to Clydebank and that school and your mum is …' She broke off.

'What?' I said.

'She's cross all the time and goes out,' said Mavis.

'She's working,' I said. 'She's tired. She has her leg.'

'Sometimes she goes out with lipstick on,' said Rosie.

Mr Tait would not have approved. I knew more about what this meant than I used to. It meant she didn't believe my dad was coming back. It probably meant she still wanted to go to America, which is what she used to want. It meant dancing, maybe with a man who wasn't my dad, though she wasn't that good with only one foot. Whatever it meant, it certainly wasn't good.

I needed to get the squadron moving again but Mavis had stuck her thumb back in and Rosie said she wasn't going anywhere if it wasn't Carbeth, and she thrust her chin forwards which she only did when she really meant business.

'We're not going back to Miss Weatherbeaten!' she shouted.

'You're going to have to for a few days,' I said. 'There's nothing else for it. You can manage a couple of days.'

'No!' she said. 'It's alright for you. You're not going to be there.'

'You have to go back to Mum,' I said. 'I'm only twelve.'

'I don't want to! I don't have to!' shouted Rosie.

'Yes you do!' I shouted back.

Mavis took her thumb out every so often to say, 'Stop it, stop shouting.'

But Rosie was off and loud, pausing only briefly for air and to tweak at her ear.

'Attennnnshun!' I said.

But she kept on.

'I'm not going back to Carbeth!' I shouted over the top of her. 'And you'll get court-martialled if you're not careful!' I picked up the bundle and swung it onto my back. 'Get in line. We're going to Clydebank. One two one two. Except you, Private Tomlin,' I said, changing my mind. Tomlin is Rosie's surname. 'You have to stay here.' This was a trick.

Mavis came trotting after me, the long grass whispering round our legs. We trudged on in silence with the birds rushing between the little birch trees and me with my breathing heavy under the bundle.

'I'm not coming!' Rosie shouted. 'You can't make me!' Her voice became small amongst the trees until she stopped.

'I don't want Rosie to be court-martialled,' said Mavis.

'Shoosh, Private Gillespie,' I said.

After a few minutes we slowed down.

'I don't want to leave her,' said Mavis, still worried. 'What if a bad man comes?'

'We're not leaving her,' I said, and sure enough soon we heard twigs crackling underfoot behind us. 'Don't turn round,' I whispered. The footsteps grew closer. I couldn't go fast with the bundle anyway. 'The animals went in two by two, hurrah, hurrah,' I sang but not loud, having hardly any breath. Mavis joined in and then Rosie did too when we got to the animals going in three by three, the wasp, the ant and the bumble bee, and we all pretended nothing had happened, for to get back to Clydebank.

The trick was if you told Rosie to stay where she was, she always followed you. It worked every time.

Soon we were at the top of Kilbowie Road which would lead us all the way into Clydebank. From there we could see the mess where our house used to be and when we got over the brow of the hill we saw Singer's and John Brown's with their towers and scaffolding sticking up through their own smoke. But I knew that if our house had still been there, from our window on the second floor we'd have seen all the way down the river where it opens into the sea, maybe all the way to Helensburgh.

Somewhere distant there was the rumble of something mighty being moved. A motor car puttered up the hill towards us then turned off, and a rag and bone man came by on a cart with his old horse's hooves loud on the road. For a second I considered tossing my bundle on the back but thought better of it. I'd need it later. We continued over the hump of the hill. I didn't like coming to Clydebank and seeing the rubble still there from the bombing and the hole in the field where a bomb missed the buildings, and it was so much smokier and darker than Carbeth which was full of brown leaves and green grass. We passed Mr Tait's old street and I remembered how much nicer Mr Tait was once I got to know him from what I thought when we first met.

Another motor car came roaring past us giving us such a fright I dropped my bundle and we all landed in a heap on top of it. I remembered what Mr Tait had said about getting frights, that you just had to wait and the fright would pass and your heart would stop beating the way it did and everything would be alright. But before I'd had a chance to make myself wait and be calm and not panic, Rosie had burst into hoots of laughter and was rolling joyfully on the ground on the other side of the bundle with Mavis spread across her, also giggling, neither of them the worse for wear. So I had to join in.

'Little Miss Puddle, all in a muddle,' I began. And then another car went past and a lorry and we all screamed with stupid laughter again.

Until suddenly I felt idiotic for behaving like that with Mr Tait dead and my dad missing and my mum with only one leg and not being able to live in Carbeth any more, and I was twelve after all, nearly thirteen, and too old for such silliness.

'Squad!' I said as I bounced to my feet. 'This is indecorious!' This was something Mr Duncan said once and has something to do being daft. 'Last one up's a turnip lantern!' I said.

'What's a turnip lantern?' they said together and went into further fits. There had been no turnip lanterns since the war began.

'I'll tell you when this war's over,' I said, feeling vastly superior in my knowledge of the war's progress now that I had read lots of papers, although mostly only headlines.

But because there was still so much rubble along the roadsides, the sight of which filled me with horrible memories, I was glad Mavis and Rosie were with me and silly. We made our way down Kilbowie Hill but didn't turn along Second Avenue towards our old house. But we did pass the beautiful La Scala picture house standing by itself amongst the wreckage made by the bombs. Memories flooded back. I sheltered there in the bombing, and looked for Mavis and my mum in the foyer which was dark because the lights went. There were so many people, living and dead, and for a second all this came rushing through my mind. I took Rosie's hand thinking she might need comfort because she had been there too.

'I spy with my little eye,' she said, 'something beginning with … G.'

'Grunter,' shrieked Mavis. 'Ground. God.'

The pair of them fell about laughing again.

I put my bundle down on a block of sandstone and tried to catch my breath. That old familiar sick feeling came back and I paused a moment with Mavis now tugging on my sleeve and thought I smelled all those stinks the bombs made, the singeing, cloying stench that stuck to everything.

'Giant,' said Mavis, hanging on my arm. 'Good.' Then after a moment's thought she added at the top of her voice and with no warning at all 'Glory Glory hallelujah!' and it made me jump all over again.

'Stop it!' I shouted. 'Shut up!'

The laughter stopped.

'You always make so much noise,' I growled. 'I can't think properly with you screaming.'

After a moment Rosie did a little dance around me: 'Lenny's in a ragie, put her in a cagie.'

Mavis let go of my arm and stood rigid beside me, but Rosie went on.

'Silence in the gallery, silence in the street! The biggest monkey in the house is just about to speak.'

'Quiet or I'll make you quiet!' I shouted.

Finally she was.

'That's a terrible way to behave,' said a lady passing. 'What a noise to make. I don't think your mother'll be happy when I tell her.'

I put my head down and shook with fury. None of us spoke until we heard the lady's feet retreating.

'Who was that old nosey parker?' I said.

'I heard that, young lady,' said the nosey parker.

We all looked at the ground again and waited. I thought I'd burst waiting but finally she was gone and we all breathed raspberries.

'Right, let's go,' I said sternly.

'George,' said Mavis.

'Yup. Your turn,' said Rosie.

'George? What are you doing here?' I said.

'Go jump in the canal,' said George. 'What d'you think I'm doing here?' He had a pile of newspapers tied up with string that he dropped beside my bundle with a thud. I shoved my fingers under the knot at the top of my bundle where I'd tied the corners and swung it on my back.

'Come on, you two. We don't have to bother with this dunce.' I might have been nicer to George because of the mess I'd left in his hut, but I could still smell the bombs even though they weren't there. I really, really wanted to get away.

'Hi, Lenny!' It was a girl from my old school. She had fat pigtails that didn't sit right and a fat nose and fat red lips. She hadn't changed a bit. 'Fancy seeing you here. Wanna come down the canal later?' We used to chuck stones in together to see who could make the biggest plop. Really, Kilbowie Road was like Sauchiehall Street on a Saturday, which is THE big shopping street in Glasgow.

I glanced at George. He had a hand on his hip and his cap in the other while he scratched his head.

'Yes ... no ... maybe,' I said.

She laughed. 'Which is it? Yes, no or maybe?'

'Dunno,' I said. 'No. I've got to go somewhere.'

'Where? Can I come?'

'No, it's secret. Top secret.'

'She's going to look for our dad,' said Rosie.

'Rosie! Shoosh!' I said. 'No, I'm not.

'I thought your dad was dead,' said the girl.

'So did we,' said Rosie and Mavis.

'She your cousin then?' said the girl.

'No,' I said, 'and I'm not going to look for my dad. Don't you lot ever listen?' I glared at Rosie. I could see George sniggering out the corner of my eye.

'Suit yourself,' said the girl. 'We're staying with my granny in Old Kilpatrick now. What school you going to?'

'Dunno,' I said.

'Don't know much, do you?'

Why didn't she just go away? Why didn't she take George with her? Why didn't Mavis and Rosie do as they were told?

Mavis was dancing on and off the kerb, whispering something under her breath and not paying attention when a car went past and beeped its horn at her. She jumped and grabbed me. The car slowed, stopped, waited a second and went on again.

'Whoopsadaisy!' said the girl. 'Better keep an eye on that little one. What's her name again?'

'Mavis. Which way were you going?' I said, holding Mavis tighter than I needed to.

'Suit yourself,' she said. 'See you later.' Off she went.

'Not if I see you first,' I muttered.

I was shaking now from head to toe. 'What are you grinning at?' I said to George. 'Come ON, Mavis, Rosie. We need to get home.'

George pulled a cigarette out of his top pocket and straightened it before sticking it in his mean little mouth.

'Want one?' he said.

I said nothing.

'Please yourself,' he said and laughed like he was Mavis's age. 'Off to Carbeth, of course. Can't wait. Just the business after a long week's graft.'

I was about to lose my dignity and call him for everything when I remembered the mess I'd left in his hut. 'Well, I'm sure your hut'll be warm after us stuffing the walls and all,' I said, and grinned as wide a smile as I could manage.

His own smile flickered and faded.

'See ya!' I said.

'See ya, bad George,' said Rosie.

'See ya, Rotten Rosie,' he replied, and then he and Rosie did something strange. They slapped their right hands together, then their left hands and then turned a circle and slapped both their own hands with each other, finishing with a thumbs up and a shake of the head.

Mavis snorted but I could see she thought it was funny.

I picked up my bundle and turned down the road in disgust, not caring if they followed.

At last they came, grumbling and complaining but dancing to their own reels all the way to the bottom of Kilbowie Hill. I, for one, kept schtum. I had nothing whatsoever to say. Except of course I had lost the piece of paper with the address and needed them to take me there.

Chapter 17

Having nothing to carry they were soon well ahead of me and I had trouble keeping up. We turned along Dumbarton Road then past the town hall, Hall Street baths and the Library going west. I knew it was west because my dad used to always say he was going west when we came out of the baths then stagger about as if he was dying. Then we'd go under the underpass under the canal and back home to our old house for soup or sausages. But this time we passed by the underpass and kept going quite a way before turning right and left and right again.

The street was full of children and smelled of onions cooking, sausages and soup all mixed up with coal fires. A girl was beating a rug against a wall making the dust fly and I recognised a boy from our old street and a girl from school. They circled round and stared.

'Who's that then?' said one.

Mavis clung to me. I hung onto my bundle and we edged along the street. A breeze lifted our hair and smelled of cludgies.

'This is Lenny Gillespie,' Rosie announced. 'She's our big sister. I told you I had a big sister, didn't I? She knows all twenty-nine verses of 'The Quarter Master's Store'.' This started an argument about how many verses there were in 'The Quarter Master's Store' but I couldn't join in because my mouth turned to jelly again.

We turned in at number forty-three. We were on the ground floor, the best place to be when the bombs dropped, although it didn't make any difference in our old close which was burnt out from top to bottom. Instead of breenging in like it was our own house, Mavis stood and knocked and when there was no reply, knocked again. With a glance at me she opened the door.

The hallway was completely dark but she pushed open another door and a blaze of sunshine burst through.

'This is our room,' she said.

It wasn't a big room, our room. There was a high bed in one corner with our blanket over it, and only one chair, my mum's wheelchair. No coal scuttle was by the fire, only a box that said 'Brasso' on it with some bits of wood, some old papers, a few chunks of coal and a little shovel. The big tall window stretched almost to the ceiling. In one corner there was a small pile of clothes, our clothes, neatly folded and stacked. I dropped my bundle on the floor beside it.

It was a lovely room, not Carbeth, but bright and friendly all the same.

'Mrs MacIntosh lives in the kitchen,' said Mavis. 'She has that all to herself and we only get in there in the morning and at night to make dinner.'

'Is she nice?'

'Yeah. So are the Weavers.'

'Who are the Weavers?'

'They live here too in the other room,' she said. 'Where's Dad? Why didn't you tell me that was him in the photo?'

I undid the knot on the bundle and everything flopped down. A quick glance round the room and I didn't see the blue leather bag. I got up on the bed, dangled my legs off it and slumped down like a sack of potatoes. It had been a long walk. The room smelled of old onions cooked the day before. Up on the mantelpiece I noticed a book, Mr Tait's Bible, and caught my breath.

'Quick, Lenny,' said Mavis, 'tell me before Rosie comes in. Where's Dad?'

She stood facing me, legs apart, and leant on my knees. I ran my fingers through her hair and told her about the postcard, not a lot.

'Don't talk to anyone about this,' I said. 'Not even Rosie and her big mouth.'

'I want to come too,' she said.

'You can't, Mavis. I don't know where I'm going. I need to speak to Mum first. This place is alright. You'll be safe here.'

But she leant her head forward into my lap and began to cry. 'Please,' she said.

'I'll be back, I promise,' I whispered and I pulled her up onto the bed beside me and we lay down and cried together.

'I miss Mr Tait,' I whispered, glancing at the mantelpiece.

'Me too,' she said. 'But I miss you most.'

And then, not surprisingly after walking so far and all that carrying, we fell asleep.

But not long after that there was a loud knock at the front door and Rosie came barging in with a crowd of other people. They stood round the bed and sang:

'It's raining, it's pouring, the old man is snoring. He

bumped his head on the back of the bed and couldn't get up in the morning!'

'Get out!' I screamed at the top of my lungs. 'Get out or I'll knock you all flat!'

There was a tiny silence then they laughed and a girl with a dark fringe like mine stepped forward.

'Who are you then?' she said. 'The Queen of Sheba?' Everyone laughed again as if no-one had ever said anything so funny. She did a little jump, waving her dark red polka-dotty skirt about as she did, then they all stared at me.

'This is our room,' I said, getting up on my haunches. 'Get out before I make you.'

Light flashed in her eyes. Perhaps it was only the sun through the window, which seemed especially brilliant, but I thought I saw red in them.

'This is my gran's house,' she said. 'I'll do what I like.' She moved away from the rest and did a quick highland fling, whistling as she whirled on the hearthrug.

'This is my mum's room,' I said, standing upright on the bed.

'Lenny … ,' said Mavis.

'Lenny, don't,' said Rosie, who had pushed to the front.

'Don't?' I said. 'I'll don't you! I'll don't you all! Get out now! Get out, the whole lot of you! Scumbags!'

Three little boys scuttled off, but not the girl doing the jig: she froze, one arm over her head and the other curved under like a monkey. I thought of that stupid teapot song. 'I'm a little teapot, short and stout.'

'Make me, then,' she said, and grinned.

Two girls hurried out of the room. As I sailed

through the air towards her I heard 'FIGHT!' yelled out the front close and when I landed we fell together onto my bundle. She banged her head on the hearth stone and her face contorted like a witch's and came swiftly towards me. Her forehead landed hard on the bridge of my nose. A pain shot across my face. I'd never been in a proper fight before, not since I was wee in Clydebank. I didn't know what to do. But pain made me move. We flung fists and slaps and feet and knees, pulled hair and scratched, and soon we rolled onto other people's feet and they squealed and scrambled back.

'Fight!' they shouted. 'Go, Ella!'

It was to the death, like we were drowning, and the blows rained down in torrents, first me on her and then her on me. She had me pinned, sitting across my chest as if I was Senga's dad's horse, but I thudded my knee in her back sharp and she fell whumph across my chest, so I grabbed her hair and pulled till my hands were full of rats tails.

Everyone shouted. 'Get her Ella! Give her back!'

Mavis screamed, 'Lenny! Lenny! Lenny!' and bounced on the bed.

And Rosie shouted, 'Go on Lenny!'

Halfway to standing, the girl grabbed my dress, the pale green one with the yellow flowers, and it ripped at the hem so that I stopped long enough to see what she had done and open my mouth to shout but she slapped me hard across the cheek. Someone cheered so they all cheered and she slapped me again. Coming to, I thwacked the third slap out of the way and followed it with a few slaps of my own. Blood trickled down her forehead from a gash. I wiped the blood from my own nose with the back of my hand and reached back to swing at her the way I'd learnt from my 'Commando Tricks for Nazis'. She reached back too. In the pause before we let fly she cracked a smile, her eyes gleaming at me, and dropped her fist.

'Shake,' she said, holding out her hand.

I screwed up my eyes and peered at her. Was she having a laugh?

'Go on then, slow-coach, I haven't got all day,' she said.

I dropped my punch and gave her my hand and she shook it, then yanked it towards her pulling me off kilter. I flew past her onto the floor, my hands skiting across the rough wooden boards, and I landed with my bloodied nose on a white bed-sheet in my mum's neat and clean pile.

A cheer went up, then a shriek from Mavis, then the countdown: 'Ten, nine, eight …'

I rolled over and brushed off the blood running down my lip and stood to face her. Again she smiled and held out her hand. I glared at it and slapped it away so hard mine stung like a wasp.

But then I saw the little coal shovel soar over Ella's head and draw back above Mavis who was standing behind her taking aim to land the thing as hard as she could on Ella's crown. Much as I hated this Ella, I didn't want her actually killed. Quick as a flash I shoved her over and caught the shovel on my own temple instead.

Suddenly everyone withdrew as if the air had been sucked out of the room, and when Ella and I staggered to our feet we found a large Mrs MacIntosh livid in the doorway behind us.

'Look what she did to me, Gran,' wailed Ella,

pointing at her head, her face a mask of misery, streaked with red.

'Oh my good God, look at the blood!' breathed Mrs MacIntosh, her eyes large and glaring at me. Then she swung on Ella. 'You! What on earth have you been up to? Look at the state of this girl. What'll your mother say?' She poked a finger three times into Ella's chest while Ella backed off into the corner. 'You and your old tricks! I thought you'd learnt. You're old enough. It's about time you grew up and stopped causing all this grief.' She turned back to me, large and heavy. 'And who are you anyway?'

Her breath was warm and damp on my face and tasted of rotten potatoes.

'L … Lenny,' I said.

'Lenny, is it? I've heard about you.'

Mrs MacIntosh was as wrinkly as an old prune but she took us into her kitchen and sat us on her smelly brown box bed, one at each end. She gave us a cloth each to dab at our wounds then made us take turns at the sink to wash them properly ourselves. It was clear she had no sympathy for either of us. She leant on the draining board, towering colossal over us, and directed proceedings as I washed first and then Ella.

'You're a disgrace to humanity,' said Mrs MacIntosh.

She put gentian violet on us that made us look as idiotic as we were and stung like billy-o. There would be no hiding it from my mum or anybody else. My nose had swollen up and gone a funny orange colour and an inch-long gash pulsed just above my left eye. Plus various bruises appeared the length of me over the rest of the day, not to mention a couple of giant splinters in my right hand from the floorboards.

Rosie had gone straight back outside with the others but Mavis clung guiltily to my side with her thumb in her mouth.

'What happened, Mavis?' said Mrs MacIntosh, dabbing my cheek with purple. 'Did you see? Who started it?'

But Mavis was too scared to say anything and hung about like one of those hovering bees you only get in the countryside.

'I don't know what you thought you were doing,' Mrs MacIntosh went on. 'You with your mother all on her own trying to make a living. She needs you to be grown up and help. You're old enough! How old are you?'

Luckily she didn't wait for an answer because that jelly freeze thing was happening again. 'And you, young Ella, you're definitely old enough. It's high time your dad came home and gave you a proper leathering. That'd sort you out.' She carried on like this as she worked, and once she'd finished she gave us all a cup of water and a quarter of bread with dripping. But she never asked Ella or me what had happened, not in the way you have to answer. I mean, it wasn't me. I'd have told her that if she'd asked me directly. But neither of us dared say a word.

'Ella, get home to your mother and help her with the tea.'

Ella put her cup on the sink and went to leave. Mrs MacIntosh was busy kennelling the fire so as she passed us Ella slapped me and Mavis on the head before darting out the door. I had more sense than to react.

'How old did you say you were?' said Mrs MacIntosh.

'T ... twelve,' I said.

Mrs MacIntosh stood up straight and looked me in the face.

'T … t … twelve,' I said.

She had watery grey eyes the same colour as her hair which was mostly stuffed in a hair net.

'Well, you'd better go and sort the mess you made in the room before your mum gets here.'

The beautiful room was transformed. There were spots of blood on the hearth and our belongings were thrown all over the floor and the bed. Even the papers for the fire were disturbed. **THE LEG THAT WOULDN'T HEAL IS WELL AGAIN!** declared one sheet, not Italy this time but an ad for ointment. I scrumpled it up and put it in the grate. The neat clothes pile in the corner had been knocked over so I tidied it and added another pile beside it of my own. Mavis tried to help.

'Leave it,' I snapped. 'I'll do it. You're making it worse.' I took my workaday dress from her and folded it properly, trembling, and put it in the pile. She backed against the wall.

Outside, distant in the street, I could hear 'Charlie Chaplin went to France to teach the ladies how to dance'. I was sore all over and I was fizzing, fuming, furious and ashamed, and scared of what my mum might say or do. But I was more scared of myself, and the possibility of exploding like that again, all those bombs going off inside me, and of the fact that Ella would make sure it happened again and I'd be helpless in the face of her and her army.

Mavis slipped from the room as if I wouldn't notice. A triangle of broken mirror sat on the mantelpiece beside Mr Tait's Bible, the only things undisturbed by the fight. I laid my hand on the Bible and felt my shame all over again, then took the mirror down. I was a strange combination of glowing apple-red cheeks and blue shadows beneath my eyes, red wounds still spilling and bright gentian violet. How could I look for my dad with a face like that? I went to the window to shake my head at myself.

Mavis was crouched alone in the back court poking at a puddle with a stick. The skirt of her dress dragged in the dirt and she leant her elbow on her knee. My Mavis. There were other people out there, ignoring her at the puddle, and every so often she wiped the bottom of her nose with her hand. Little Mavis. Then she put her thumbs in her ears and her fingers over her head and rocked herself back and forwards. I held my breath, fuming and scared, scared of what my mum would say and scared of Mavis being so miserable, scared of what I'd done.

None of this would have happened if Mr Tait just hadn't gone and died like that. I kicked the panelling beneath the window so my foot hurt. How could he? And he must have known. Why didn't he warn me? Why didn't he tell me what to do? Why didn't he tell me about my dad? Somehow, the more I thought about Mr Tait the clearer it became that it was me who started the fight, and I knew that because every time I glanced at Mr Tait's Bible I was ashamed.

I gathered up the bloodied clothes and went through to Mrs MacIntosh. Mrs MacIntosh was not slow when she saw an able body.

'There's a wash-house out the back,' she said. 'You'll need some elbow-grease for that lot.' She gave me a scrubbing brush and some salt and a tiny piece of soap. 'Don't waste it! And seeing as you're here, Lenny, you can see to the supper. Your time is between five and six this week and it's nearly that time now. After that you need to skidaddle for the next hour while the Weavers make theirs. Cooking, eating and washing up, all done by six. Got it?'

I nodded. 'Wh ... when is my mum coming back?'

'Well now, she's working until five, so she'll miss part of her dinner hour here. You'd better get started I suppose. Then she's joining me at the choral at seven. I suppose she'll be back in between times. If not I'll see her there. So you better get on with it.'

Right. I got that. Get on with it. Thanks.

'There's a box under your bed.'

What did she mean? I ran back through, excited at what I might find, but the box had a handful of tatties and not much else, no secret letters or photos. I took the tatties to the sink and scrubbed them and put them in a pot. Then I went out the back and found Mavis and even though I was tired and had to make our dinner I took her through a little hole I found in the back wall and into a lane and we sat there for ages, just the two of us, not even Rosie, and I told her all the stories I could remember about our dad, especially the one about going up in the Kilpatrick Hills behind Clydebank with him for picnics, just him and me. I told her everything I knew all over again about where he might be and I told her about the milking and the café lady and George getting my penny for me and the newspapers in his hut. I made her laugh over Willie pretending about the noises upstairs and the chicken feathers that went everywhere.

'Lenny's hennys,' she said.

'Mavis's schmavises,' I said, which is what my dad

used to say, but she didn't remember. She really didn't know much about anything.

Chapter 18

I was thoroughly ashamed of myself. I had to make amends. Not to Ella, obviously, but to someone. Mavis, maybe, for scaring her and being a bad example, to my mum for not being there when I was needed, to Mr Tait for letting him down in so many ways I couldn't bear to think of them, and for being annoyed with him. I didn't want to be annoyed with Mr Tait. It just kept happening. But as he himself pointed out, sometimes it's hard to know the difference between good and bad. I was certainly having trouble with knowing right from wrong.

I brought Mavis in so we could rescue the tatties but Mrs MacIntosh had already saved them. We had made a pact not to talk about our dad to anyone else, not even Rosie, and I knew she would stick to it.

But I still had to find him because first of all he was our dad, and because secondly some people didn't have a dad any more and other people had never had one to start off with, like Betty, a girl in my class at Craigton. Then there are people who didn't want the dad they'd got, like Senga my back-to-front friend whose dad was angry all the time and hit her even when she hadn't done anything wrong. Lots of dads were being killed in the war too. I knew plenty of people like that and some of them made do with someone else for a dad, like us with Mr Tait. Lots of the dads were away for one reason or another and the ones who were there worked seven days a week so they might as well have been in Timbuktu for all the difference it made. Some people didn't miss their dad's, but I missed mine. Or I used to when he first went. I missed him loads then. Then I had Mr Tait instead and it wasn't as bad, but then he died and I was left with an ache I couldn't even describe.

I had this idea that if I could just find my dad then everything would be alright. He'd know what to do. In this topsy-turvy world of mine where very little made sense, that seemed important. At least if we were all together my mum wouldn't have to work these long hours herself. We'd all have him there with us, if I could find him. We'd all be together.

I decided to talk to my mum that evening but she didn't come back at dinnertime and I fell asleep before she came in later. In the morning she was up early again for work.

'Lenny,' she whispered. 'You awake? Wake up.'

'Mum!'

'Ssh.'

'Where are you going?'

'Early shift. So glad you're here. Look after the girls, won't you?'

'Where's Dad?'

'Oh Lenny, don't keep asking about your dad.'

'I have to. He's my dad. Is he in Helensburgh?'

'I've no idea.'

'But really?'

'He was. He may still be but he's probably been caught by now.'

'But you don't know?'

'Well … no.'

'Why not?'

'It's just … you see …'

'He's my dad.'

'I know that. I'm doing my best, darling. Look, I've got to go or I'll be late and they dock your wages if you're even five minutes. See you tonight, after five.'

'Mum!'

'Ssh. I heard about the fight. My goodness look at your face. What happened? Mrs MacIntosh said you went for Ella.'

'It was nothing,' I said. 'Just a carry on.' Sometimes lies are alright, she taught me that.

'Be more careful next time.'

She kissed me and was gone.

Right, I thought. That's it. I'm off. Helensburgh here I come. How could I not? Or could I? I lay between Mavis and Rosie and bit off the end of both thumbnails and quickly followed a crack in the ceiling from one side and back again. Could I do this? On my own?

Mavis rolled over towards me.

Yes, I could. I had to. I sent a quick apology in my head to Mr Tulloch, glanced at Mr Tait's Bible and slipped out of bed.

I put on my green and yellow dress, all washed the day before, even though it had a rip in the hem, and my dark green cardie, coat and scarf and I pinched Rosie's hat because I needed it more than her that day. My coat pocket jingled with the money so I wrapped my hand around it. The other pocket bulged with Mr Tulloch's map. From the doorway I blew kisses to Mavis and Rosie and ran my eyes round the dark room. Those papers had to be somewhere but there was no cupboard or drawer for them to hide in and the wheelchair had no cushions. There were only the two piles of clothes, mine and theirs.

I went back and slid a jumper off their pile then lifted the rest and felt underneath. Nothing. I undid every bit and felt through them all until at last, in the pocket of my mum's Sunday dress, I found them, the postcard and the little book with the photo. There was no bag. I took the map out of my own pocket and slipped the postcard and the book with the photo into its place, then opened the map as quietly as I was able and had one last look. I tried hard to memorise all the place names, Helensburgh, Greenock, Port Glasgow, Paisley, and when I thought I had them all in my mind, I stuck the map under Mr Tait's Bible for safekeeping.

'Thank you, Mr Tait. Thank you, Mr Tulloch,' I whispered.

I tiptoed back to Mavis. It broke my heart to leave her. She stared up at me from the bolster so still I was scared she was dead, so I bent down and put my head next to hers.

'Don't cry, Mavis,' I said. 'I'm coming back. Stick with Rosie and Mrs MacIntosh. I'll be back before you know it.' But we both shed a tear and I hugged her again, and left with my mouth in a different state of jelly.

Mrs MacIntosh was asleep in the kitchen so I couldn't wash, so I ran out to the wash house and put my back to the wall and cried until the salt ran into my cuts. When I was done I washed my face as carefully as I could under the tap and took a long drink. Then I stood up straight in the twilight to watch the stars fade as the sun rose and to gather up all my strength. It was time to go.

I went down to Dumbarton Road, a big wide road that runs all the way from Glasgow through Clydebank and on to Dumbarton. I wondered what to do. There were trams and buses going in both directions and crowds of men going into Beardmore's yards, like John Brown's, and the noise of the riveters at work already, hammers on metal. I started walking because the noise was battering off the tenements and making my head hurt. But by the time I got to Dalmuir station I realised I had no time to waste and decided to spend some money on a train.

'H … Helensburgh, please,' I said.

'Upper or Central?' said the man in the railway hat.

'Um.'

'What street are you going to? Have you got an address?'

I tried hard to say 'Central' because the centre seemed like a good place to start, but all that came out was a slithery snake sound. Fortunately a gang of soldiers had just arrived behind me and were all talking at once.

The railway man glanced over my shoulder at them.

'Makes no odds anyway,' he said. 'It's the same price, but you need the next train for Craigendoran for the ferry or Central, or change at Dumbarton Central if you want Upper.'

'R … right,' I said. 'Th … thank you!' Then I shouted: 'But I'm going to Helensburgh.'

'No need to shout,' he said. 'I just thought you

might want the ferry terminal for the boat to Greenock or somewhere, though you'll need a pass.'

'No, thanks. Helensburgh, please.'

I could see he was surprised at my shouting. 'You'll need to ask someone on the train where to get off,' he said in a quiet voice as if he was telling me a secret. 'There are no signs on the platforms, don't forget.' This was to try and fox the Germans, but it meant people kept getting off at the wrong place.

He told me where to go for the train so I went and stood on a platform and hoped it was the right one. The gang of soldiers followed me and stood against a pillar smoking. They were quiet now, glancing up and down the tracks, serious and thoughtful. At last, in a blizzard of steam and noise, the train arrived, chuntering like a factory, then wheezing like an old man. The soldiers shouted above it, their voices mixing with the black smoke that pushed against the station roof.

I chose a different compartment with some ladies in it and sat by the window. One of the ladies had a cat in a wicker basket with mesh tied over the top so he could see out. But I had too much to worry about right then to think about cats. With a scream of the whistle we were off.

'You going somewhere nice?' said the lady in the seat opposite.

I took a big breath. 'Hhhelensburgh,' I said and pulled my tammy over my ears.

'You got family there?' She had big lips and curly hair that bounced.

'My dad,' I said.

She didn't seem to be listening. 'Change at

Dumbarton for Helensburgh Upper. I'll keep you right.' She nodded at my cuts. 'What happened to you?'

'F … fell.' I wiped the steam from the window.

'Aye, right!' she said. 'I've heard that one before.' She and the other lady laughed. 'Who won?'

'I don't know,' I said.

'Not the other guy, but?'

I couldn't help grinning, even though it made the cuts hurt, even though I wasn't proud of what I'd done.

'I'm going to see my boys at their gran's,' she said and she smiled and looked out the window. 'Where did you say you were going?'

'Hhhelensburgh,' I said all over again. 'I'm going to see my dad.'

'It'll be good when this is over,' she said. 'Won't be long now, they say. Then we can all get back to normal.'

Normal. What would that look like?

'Where's your dad stay?' she went on. 'Is he working out this way? More often it's the other way round, isn't it, people heading into Dumbarton or Clydebank.'

'Y … yes. He always does things b … back to front.'

'He's a man, isn't he?' laughed the cat lady.

'Is he billeted out there?' said the lady with the curls, but serious, not laughing, taking me seriously. 'There's no model, but there is a big house they requisitioned.'

She meant the model lodging house for workers. I hadn't thought of that. We had them in Clydebank. I glanced out the window at all the ships passing each other on the river. They were mostly grey against the green bank on the other side.

'I can tell you where it is,' she went on, taking my silence for a yes.

'That's up by the monument, isn't it?' remarked the other lady. The cat in the basket was hers. He hadn't moved the whole time. Perhaps he was dead.

'That cat alright?' said the lady with the curls.

'I poured some whisky down his throat for the journey,' said the other lady, who had light ginger hair the same colour as her cat.

'You never did!'

'Works a treat.'

'That'll be some head he'll have on him when he wakes up.' They laughed and talked about their men, which was a relief because I didn't want any more nosy questions.

But then I realised I had lots of questions myself and the only way to find my dad was to ask as many people as possible, which is how I found Mavis. Even if half of me was Italian I'd just have to risk it. I listened to them until we were past Dumbarton and their chat lulled, by which time I'd convinced myself this was the right thing to do.

'Excuse me,' I said, too loud.

'Yes?' said the lady with the curls. They both turned to face me. Just then the train pulled into a station and the door suddenly opened, two men peered in, then closed it again just as rapidly without anyone getting in.

'Not good enough for them,' remarked the cat lady.

'Ach, we don't want any men in here anyway,' said the other. 'So, young lady, you were saying?'

Their two faces were pointed at me.

'I … I … ,' I said. 'I'm looking for my dad. I don't know where he is. He might be in Helensburgh.'

'Might be?' said the curly lady. 'I see.'

'Yes. We had a postcard and someone told me it was Helensburgh.'

'Doesn't your mum know?' said the cat lady.

I shook my head.

'She working?'

I nodded, not sure what that had to do with it. Everyone was working.

'So what did the postcard say?' said the curly one.

'Nothing really.' I dug it out and showed it to them.

'This is from your Uncle Ross, not your dad,' said the cat lady.

'It's Helensburgh alright,' said the other. 'Look, there's the pier and there's Dino's on the front. Just think, when all this is over we can have his chips again. His were the best. Shame for them, what happened.'

'No, it's not. They were all Nazis, the Eyeties, along with the Germans.'

I had the little book with the photo in my hand ready to show them but quietly stuffed it back in my pocket. They argued for a minute about the price of fish while I tried to pick the photo off the card inside my pocket without them seeing.

The river widened and I could see a town on the other side. Something in my pocket tore so I took my hand out not to make it worse.

'Where's that?' I said, pointing over the river.

'Port Glasgow, and that's Greenock further on,' said the cat lady. 'It's crazy down there,' she said to the other lady. 'Our Davie went over there to work and never came home.'

Mr Tulloch's map appeared in my mind.

'What, you mean he …?' said the other.

'No, it was work. There's loads of work in Greenock

and hunnerds of folk coming and going.'

'Ah,' said the curly haired woman. Then she looked at me. I turned back out the window where fence posts flicked past in a sea of greenery. 'So how're you going to find him, love?'

'Dunno,' I said, and suddenly wondered when the return train to Clydebank might be and whether I shouldn't just get on it.

The train stopped again.

'That's me then,' said the cat lady. 'Nice to meet you. I hope you find him.'

The ginger cat opened one eye as he passed me. The lady threw the carriage door open and left. No-one took her place.

I decided to risk it and pulled out the alien book, quickly tore the photo from the card and showed it to the curly lady. She didn't seem to notice the book but took the photo between finger and thumb and brought it close to her face then out at arm's length. I stuffed the book in my pocket. The train set off again, tick-tick, tick-tick, then ticketty boom and on we went across open fields.

'I know that face,' she said.

My heart beat like the train.

'I think so, but I can't be sure. There was a man up on my uncle's farm ...' She smiled, mirroring his smile. 'He's a cheery one, isn't he? Good-looking too.'

'On a farm?' I said. 'Y ... you saw him on a farm?' Ticketty boom, the world went by in a blur, everything fuzzy except her face. She stared back at my dad and didn't say another word. I held my breath.

She handed me the photo and wished me luck.

'But you said ... about your uncle's farm.'

'Och, there was a man on the farm who looked a bit like that, but there are all kinds of men all over the place. Americans, Italians, Canadians, you name it, they've been down this river. He could be anywhere. Try the police. They'll know.'

'But which farm?' I said.

'Oh, it's not him, love. Sorry. There are so many men!'

As if to emphasise the point we pulled into a station that was full to the brim with servicemen in all sorts of uniforms. A gang of soldiers went past the window, none of them laughing like the other lot had.

'And you know … ,' she said with a glance round the empty compartment, '… we shouldn't really be talking.'

'He's funny,' I said. 'Was this man funny? He's always making people laugh. Everybody loves him. You'd remember if you'd met him, honest.'

'But I don't, darling, I don't. I wish I did. Sorry.'

I bit my lip and stared out the window where a mist was settling over the water, the towns on the other side fading into it.

'He sounds English, bit like this, northern,' I said, in my dad's northern English accent.

'There, that's us at Central,' she said. 'Ask the police. It's round to the right outside the station.'

'Thank you,' I whispered.

The train wheezed and grumbled to a stop and we got off. As soon as she landed on the platform her boys came shrieking towards her. I stepped quietly to the side and went out onto the road. I don't think she had any idea who my dad was at all.

There was no police station that I could see so I

stared down the other direction, squinting through the people who swarmed past me. I tried to summon the courage to go and look for it, but couldn't. The street was much narrower than Dumbarton Road and the pavement narrower still. Instead I stared at the pub over the road until I thought I'd go cross-eyed trying to decide what to do.

Chapter 19

A man came out of the pub and stared right back at me so I hurried off in the other direction and quickly found myself at a crossroads. This meant I'd made the decision, without even meaning to, not to go to the police until I'd tried everything else. The problem was I had no idea what everything else might be.

Helensburgh was completely different from Clydebank. There were no high tenements or factories that I could see, only shops and low buildings and a dark grey sky hanging over them. A storm was brewing, or at least heavy rain, and people were holding their hats against the wind. I drew in my coat. A busy road lined with shops lead up the hill, reminding me of how Kilbowie Road used to be. The crossroads was blocked with traffic. A man on a cart shouted for everyone to get a move on. In the other direction, at the bottom of the hill, the sea shone silver, a little slice between the buildings, and on it there were ships the same colour but darker.

Not knowing what else to do I began looking at all the faces because, you never know, maybe my dad would just happen to be there, running an errand for his boss or delivering something to a shop, and there we'd be, face to face, surprise! Anything was possible. I took the photo out to remind myself then stuffed it back in again.

The building behind me was the town hall. It had pretty turrets and stonework over the doors, important-looking but nowhere near as big as Clydebank town hall. I thought about going in but then saw a sign with POLICE on it which stopped me in my tracks. Heart thumping, I hurried away, down towards the sea, crossed a street, passed some shops, and jouked in amongst some ladies with prams. Then I crossed another road and all the time kept my head down because it was buzzing like a beehive and I was scared. At last I smacked against the seafront wall, buried my face in my hands and wondered what on earth I was doing there.

When I looked up I was amazed to see hundreds of ships spread out across the sea, all shapes and sizes, and a long pier with a couple of small fishing boats alongside. It was just as Mr Tulloch's friend had said. The town on the other side was completely obscured by mist, but I knew it was there because of Mr Tulloch's map.

Of course, after a short time I remembered exactly what I was doing and realised I had to find some courage and grit if I was going to get anywhere at all, and the quicker the better. Maybe Mr Tulloch was right and I shouldn't have come alone. But there I was anyway, and being a scaredy wasn't going to find my dad. I swivelled round and looked back up the street so I could prepare myself for bravery.

There was a row of shops going off to the left, facing the sea and beyond some grass, but there was probably nothing in them, being the war. In the other direction, on a corner, just beyond a church was ITAL in big bold letters on a corner above a shop window. The full word was ITALIAN, of course, and peering inside I saw tables, but not set for dinner. Instead, queues of people were on one side and ladies in uniforms on the other. The room was full of smoke and there were no chips or ice cream to be seen anywhere. I positioned myself so I could see some faces, but my dad wasn't amongst them. Then I noticed a small hand-written sign which said 'LABOUR EXCHANGE'. It seemed a horrible place with walls of bare bricks.

Not knowing what else to do I started along the row of shops I'd seen on the waterfront. The rain was gathering and I was getting cold, so I decided to walk quickly about town and look at everyone I met. As I sped along I must have seen a hundred faces coming towards me before the shops ran out, and on the way back I crossed the grass to the walkway by the shore and stared in panic out to sea instead and wished I was in Carbeth. If it hadn't been for a motor car honking its horn, which naturally I had to investigate, I'd have missed Dino's café altogether. I quickly took the postcard from my pocket and compared it to the real thing. Dino's. I went back across the grass and went in.

'Can I help you?' said a lady behind the counter.

I could smell the chocolate, but there was almost none on display. She didn't sound Italian at all, but then neither did my dad. I showed her the photo.

'He looks like a cheery chappie,' she said.

'Oh he is,' I assured her. 'But I don't know where he is. He's I … he's Italian. He's my dad.'

Her eyes went large and round. She put my dad face down on the glass counter, sniffed and looked over my head. I glanced round at the other customers. An old man caught my eye and turned away. I took my photo quickly and put it back in my pocket.

'Filthy scum,' I heard the lady mutter as I walked away. 'Coming in here …'

I ran out and stood shaking on the pavement and felt my eyes burn. It was definitely time to go home. As soon as I could get my legs to work I would head for the station.

'Excuse me,' called a voice behind me. 'Excuse me. Young lady? You with the gentian on your face.'

It was the old man in the café who'd turned away. My shoulders shot up around my ears.

'What?' I said, and I looked at him with eyes like bad George's, small and tight.

'Don't mind her,' he said. 'She's embarrassed because she got Dino's café to run. Everybody loved Dino, really, you see. Let's see your photo. Maybe I'll know him. Who is it you're looking for? Go on then, I don't bite. I don't even have any teeth.' He grinned broadly at me and I saw that this was true, so I gave him the photo.

'Nope. Never seen him in my life. Sorry.' He seemed pretty sure. 'There are a few Italians at Blairvadach, though it's mostly Germans.'

'Germans?' I said.

'In a camp,' he said. 'Prisoners of war.'

An old lady came and stood near us. She seemed to be listening in. We shouldn't have been talking about this kind of thing, I knew that, but I thought she might be his wife and anyway I had to break the rules if I was going to find my dad.

'Gracie, mind your own business,' he said. 'Away

223

home to that man of yours and his gout.'

Not his wife then, just a busybody.

'I'm just doing my job,' she said. 'You watch what you tell her, Archie, and don't be an old fool.'

'Ach, away you go!' he said. 'She's only young. Who's she going to tell?' The old lady moved a little way off and stood in a doorway. A horse and cart went past with a car stuck behind them. 'Now, where was I? Oh yes. Germans, prisoners of war. That's them on the cart now, see over there. You don't usually see them this time of day. They come down the loch in the morning, hundreds of them, no exaggeration, and off through town to the farms and so on. Usually on foot. Those men must be sick to be on the cart.' He scratched his chin. 'You don't sound Italian.'

'I'm not,' I said. 'Which way do they go?' I stared after the cart. Real live Germans.

'Oh, anywhere at all,' he said. 'Wherever there are farms. That lot are going up the hill.'

The cart lingered on the corner, then turned up the hill and vanished from sight.

'What's your name?' he said. 'What's your dad's name?'

'Lenny,' I said. 'We're both Lenny.'

'Both of you?'

'I'm Leonora and he's Leonard or … Leonardo.'

'As in Da Vinci?'

'Pardon? No, as in Galluzzo. Is there another Leonardo?'

'There are probably a few, but I'll look out for Leonardo Galluzzo.'

'Tell him to come home,' I said, which made a lump appear in my throat. A drop of rain hit my face.

'Alright, Leonora. Be careful. Bye!'

I left him and ran after the cart. It wasn't moving fast so I caught up easily but hung back, scared to get close. Eight or so men huddled together on the back, one with a patch over his eye. They were young, not much older than George. None of them spoke and nobody paid them any attention. Maybe they didn't realise there were Germans in their town.

The rain pelted down so I stood in a doorway which smelled of pee and waited for it to pass, which it soon did. What was I doing following Germans anyway? One of them pointed at me and they all began to wave. I fell back against the door again and yanked my hat over my eyes. What if someone saw and thought I was a spy?

But I needed these Germans to help me find the Italians so I ignored Mr Tulloch's good sense and chose Mr Tait's instead, in other words I drew up all my bravery from my boots and followed the cart up the hill, even though it had already disappeared round a corner.

The road wound on another half-mile past cows in one field and a bull in another until I came round a bend where the country pancakes lay thick and plentiful. I was surrounded by brown newly ploughed fields and others full of workers picking tatties in one and peas in another. A track lead off to the right so, avoiding the cow pies and with no other plan, I wandered along between thick green hedges until I came to a farm. There in the yard was the cart with the Germans. I turned and ran back the way I had come, tiptoeing furiously over the pancake pies.

'What are you doing here?' someone shouted. It

was a man's voice, slow, deep and broad. I looked round for someone built to match but instead saw an ordinary little man in farm clothes, dark trousers and jacket, with mud up to his knees leading the world's biggest horse. It was bigger even than back-to-front Senga's dad's horse. The ground was awash with 'pie' so the whole place stank to high heaven. Mr Tulloch's hardly ever smelled like that.

'I'm looking for my dad,' I said.

'I beg your pardon?' he shouted. Carefully, I went closer.

'I said I'm looking for my dad. He sounds English but he's Italian and he's on a camp and I don't know where he is.'

'I'm sorry, I'm awful hard of hearing,' he said. I was practically in front of him. He must have been stone deaf.

'Are there any Italians working here?' I shouted. 'Italians?' The horse didn't even flinch.

'Italians? They were late today but they're in the top field.'

It seemed easier to shrug my shoulders and show him my palms than to actually say 'and where would that be?' especially since my heart was in my throat again. He followed suit and directed me with his free hand without saying another word.

The Italians were dotted about a big field, mostly bent double picking carrots. The field swooped off in all directions with a perfect hedge running over the brow of a hill. I felt oddly close to the sky especially as I could see another shower on its way. None of the Italians noticed me. I tried to see if any of them was my dad but they were all too far away. A horse stood by the gate with a cart full of carrots. I waited there and gazed out over the field to the river below and all the big ships spread across it and over on the other side the green hills above Greenock.

There were no soldiers guarding the Italians so I knew if anything happened I was on my own. At last one of them stood up and swung his sack onto his back and started in my direction. I got behind the cart just in case. Closer he came until he banged into the cart and shifted the sack off his shoulders onto the orange pile of carrots, making them drum against the sides of the cart. He pulled himself straight with some effort and looked over at me.

'Hello, love, have you come to give us a hand?' he said in perfect English, in a perfect English accent.

'I'm looking for the Italians,' I said, confused.

'This is Scotland,' he said. 'You're in the wrong country. Best go back the way you came.' He leant over to one side to stretch his back and then the other.

'Oh,' I said. 'Isn't this the top field?'

'Who told you about the top field?' he said. 'The top field's top secret, you know. You don't want to go blabbing about the top field.'

'Sorry,' I said. 'It's just I'm looking for someone. He doesn't seem to be here. The man at the farm said to go to the top field.'

'Sh!' he said, leaning on the rim of the cart. 'There you go on about the top field again. These fields have ears, you know, especially that one.' He nodded to the cornfield next door which was full of stubble. 'Used to have ears anyway. Used to. Who are you looking for?'

'The Italians,' I said.

'What, all of them? There's a few million, you know. You might want to choose one.'

I laughed.

He took his hat off, shook the rain off it and stuck it back on again. 'What about Rocco?' He tapped his chest with both hands. 'Won't I do?'

'You're not Italian,' I said.

'Yes, I am,' said Rocco.

'No, you're not.'

'I am, actually, and I should know, shouldn't I, seeing as I am me and therefore something of an expert.'

A shiver came over me and I straightened and looked across the field at the other men. Two more were making their way towards us. I was warm from climbing to the field but the wind was already racing through my coat.

'Don't bite your lip,' he said. 'Have a carrot instead. Much better for you.' He offered me one across the cart but I was too busy trying to see if any of the others was my dad. Rocco sighed and tossed the carrot back on the cart. The other two dumped their carrots in the cart then stretched. 'Who are you looking for?' said Rocco.

'My dad,' I said. 'He's Italian. He has an English accent but it's not like yours. It's northern.'

'Well, that makes you Italian too. Fantastico! Fortunati voi!' Suddenly he sounded like a proper Italian.

'Nae luck!' said one of the others. They threw their sacks onto the cart then leant backwards to stretch. 'What's the story?' he said, pure Glasgow.

'Che cosa sta succedendo?' said the third.

'Ha perso il suo papà,' said Rocco.

The other two took off their hats, crossed themselves and stared at the ground.

'No, no! Non è morto! No, no. Perso! Lost.'

They all laughed, and the two newcomers wiped the sweat off their brows and put their hats back on and leant on the cart with Rocco. Suddenly they were all proper Italians, talking Italian and fast, so I couldn't understand a word.

'They say none of us are old enough to have a grownup daughter like you,' said Rocco straightening. 'And we're all too ugly anyway.'

'Except maybe Gio who started young,' said the Glasgow one and got thumped for his trouble.

So I told them my story, that we were from Clydebank, that my dad had joined the army but then he'd been arrested when he was home on leave, that I thought he was somewhere around Helensburgh because of the postcard and I hadn't known he was Italian.

'Wha ha detto?' said one, which was followed by a storm of Italian. I waited 'til they'd finished then brought out the photo. My hand was trembling. What if they grabbed it off me and wouldn't give it back? What if they grabbed me?

'What's that you've got there?' said Rocco. I passed it to him over the carrots. 'Ah, Leonardo,' he said.

'Oh,' said the others and they all three stared at me, serious at last.

Chapter 20

Rocco and his friends argued in Italian again, then gave me directions to another farm not far away. They said my dad had been staying there but wasn't any more and someone on the farm would know where he'd gone, probably. Then they argued again.

'Ask for Jean,' said Rocco. He'd stopped smiling and carrying on. 'I should come with you.'

'Aren't you a prisoner?' I said, my heart thumping in my chest. It somehow seemed rude to point this out. 'Don't you have to stay and work?'

'Yeah, but he might let me go, under the circumstances, special dispensation by his majesty Mr Gregory.'

So Rocco came back to the farmyard with me and it turned out they all lived in a little bothy at the end of a barn and not in a camp after all. There was a guard called 'Bud' who visited once a week but otherwise they could move about the farm freely, but couldn't leave it, even to go to the other farms.

'Bud wouldn't allow it!' shouted Mr Gregory. 'The authorities will send you back to the camp if I do that.'

'She's a child. Don't you think I should go? She's too young to go on her own.'

'What?' said Mr Gregory.

'She's too young,' shouted Rocco.

'What?' said Mr Gregory. 'No, no, no.' He wandered into a byre and was greeted with a moo.

Rocco shook his head and produced carrots from his various pockets and stuffed them into my own. 'Say ciao to your papa for me,' he said. 'I'm sorry I can't come with you.' He watched me go. 'You be careful now and come back and tell me how you get on.'

I washed a carrot in a ditch and hurried along the lane, crunching on it. I wished I'd listened to Mr Tulloch and not gone alone. But maybe I was actually going to find my dad after all which was just the most exciting thing in the world ever.

'A row of trees full of rooks,' Rocco had said, 'the only trees on that side of the road. The last cottage after the farm.'

I saw it in the distance, higgledy-piggledy against the side of the hill, a farm, the trees and a row of cottages. The family of rooks above the trees seemed to call me to join them. So this was it.

The track from the road was sludgey and there was a stink like Mr Gregory's farm. I kept to the roadside even though my socks were soon wet from the long grass. Five hens came out to greet me. One even pecked my toes, but I didn't care. There were hens at Carbeth. Then a cat came slithering round the gable end and after that a black-and-white sheepdog who barked and ran in circles. I wasn't scared of dogs either, not this one anyway because once it had finished running round me it ran round itself and chased its own tail.

Beyond the farmhouse there was the row of stone

cottages, as Rocco had said. I passed by them until I came to the last which was a little up a hill and had tatties growing in the garden and straggles of nasturtiums by the path. The dog followed as I passed through a gate in the hedge. A toddler in muddy dungarees came round the corner of the house with a slice of apple in his hand. He was a little tiddly thing all wobbly on his legs and very serious with lots of pale curls and two fat sunburnt cheeks. He stopped by the vegetable patch when he saw me. The dog ran up and licked his cheeks and the toddler looked at the dog and laughed. The sun had come out and the wind shook great drops of rain at us from the chestnuts nearby.

'Hello,' I said to this little ragamuffin. The dog seemed keen to lick my face too so I stepped out of his way. Then a lady came out and stopped still with her mouth open.

'Can I help you?' she said.

Here goes, I thought. Deep breath. I did consider pretending my dad was someone else, like my friend's dad instead of my own, but it might have got me into even more trouble. 'I'm looking for my d ... dad,' I said. I had my fingers crossed behind my back.

The lady wore grey dungarees like my mum's and had a basket on her hip and inside it I could see potatoes. She was turning one over in her hand and for a second I thought she was going to throw it at me. Instead she stared with these big brown eyes she had. They seemed to get bigger and browner the longer we stood there and I felt prickles up my back until my face burned. Then an old man with a garden fork came up behind her. He stopped and leant the handle of his fork against his stomach so he could roll up his sleeves and stare at me.

'Who's this then?' he said, wiping his hands on his apron.

'What's your name?' she said. Her eyes were fixed on mine. The little boy tottered forward with his wiggly nappy-bottom and offered me a bite of his apple.

'Lenny,' I said.

The lady seemed to stop breathing. Her mouth clamped shut.

'L … Lenny Gillespie,' I said. 'It's my dad's name too. I'm looking for my dad.'

I went into my pocket for the photograph. The toddler dropped his bit of apple and bent to pick it up. His little hands had trouble with it being slippery so in the end I had to crouch down and get it for him. In return he gave me the biggest beamer ever and reminded me of Mavis when she was wee.

But then a big strong arm came swooping round his middle and whisked him off the ground and away from me. The bit of apple flew through the air and bounced off my hair and onto my shoe. And while I was gazing at my toe where it landed I heard a great man's hawk, like my dad when he'd been smoking, and a big glob of spit landed beside my shoe.

'Filthy scum,' he growled. 'We've had enough of you Italians round here.' He turned to the lady. 'Get the wean into the house, Jeannie. I'm not having any of this.'

Jeannie stood staring at me, the basket on her hip, but her hand had stopped still inside it. I got ready to duck but I was shaking from my head to my toes and back again.

'She's looking for her dad, you know? There's nothing wrong with that,' she said at last. 'I'd do the same if you went missing.'

'She doesn't have a proper dad to find, and they're all the same, you know. It's in the blood,' he said. 'And look at the state of her. She's got scars the length of her face.'

I'd forgotten about my cuts, and this was an exaggeration, but either way I just stared at this horrible man who had spat at me. I couldn't move.

'It's not in the blood. What about the wean? He's a good boy. Look at him. You can't say the wean's bad. This wee lassie's Lenny's girl. You can't blame her wanting to find her father.'

'Be quiet and get him in the house.'

But she wouldn't and instead they argued about my dad and whose fault it all was and the little boy cried as if he was joining in, until suddenly the lady put down her basket of tatties and took the boy from him. She bounced him on her hip and held him tight, but still he cried. I was rooted to the spot like the gate post.

'It's your own damn fault not seeing the type of man he was,' said the father.

'You were happy enough to share a glass of his beer and have him working for you for nothing,' she replied.

'He was a foreigner. What did you expect? I thought you'd more sense.'

'Foreign as far as England.'

She turned her back on him and ignored him telling her not to. I pulled my hat down over my ears and held on.

'Your dad was arrested,' she said to me. 'We called him Gallus Galluzzo because he was always so cocky. We just never realised how cocky he really was.' She laughed at this and shook her head but I think she was angry. I couldn't tell.

'Aye, cocky's about right,' said the dad.

'I was left with this,' she said, and she nodded at the wee boy who was winding up to another scream.

'No,' I breathed.

'There's probably a whole lot more where that came from too,' said the man.

'No, there aren't. I'd have been told,' she roared at him. 'He'd have stayed if it wasn't for you listening to gossip.' Then back to me. 'This is your brother,' she said to me, 'your half-brother. His name's Robert. Wee Bobby. My wee Bobby.' She chucked him under the chin even though he was bawling and arching his back. 'If you find your dad tell him not to come back if he wants to live but give him my love and I'll be ready when he's able and the war's over.'

'Give him your love? Are you thick in the head? This lassie's the proof of the gossip, you stupid eejit.' Then he turned and started towards me and I bounced off the ground and staggered away from him, backwards and all over the place. 'Tell your dad to come back for the hiding he deserves, if he's man enough,' said the old man. He was big and I could smell him where I stood already. I'd backed off so far I was jammed into a hedge.

'Get away!' I shouted. 'Leave me alone!' My tummy churned and I screamed as loud as I could. 'It's not true! That about my dad! You're lying!'

But he'd gone back and was shouting at her again.

She seemed not scared at all and was arguing back, just as loudly. I pulled myself out of the hedge and stumbled backwards out of the path and watched them in amazement. Calling each other names, yelling and not listening. Until finally they were quiet, glaring at each other while the wee boy howled.

Then she rocked little Bobby again and sang, 'hush little baby, don't you cry', but not in that nice way my mum used to do.

'Where will he be?' I shouted once I had some breath, though it was more of a squawk. 'Where will I find him?' I blinked back my tears and wiped the snotters away with my sleeve. 'Please? Where is he? I need to …'

She was swinging wee Bobby round and back on her hip as if she wanted to shake the air out of him altogether and singing and all the time he wailed and wriggled.

So I shouted again. 'Where did he go? Please, just tell me and I'll go away. Where did they take him?' Until finally the man picked up his fork and the basket of tatties and went back round the side of the house with the dog.

'Bloody fools!' he roared as he went. 'How would I know where he is?'

She waited until he'd gone.

'Get on with your work!' he shouted from out of sight.

She waited a minute more, then came through the tattie patch to the gate and gestured for me to come back.

'Sorry about my dad,' she said, with a glance over her shoulder. 'But listen and I'll tell you. They took

Lenny to the police station in King Street. They say he played cards all night and won all their money and then lost it back to them again before the morning.' This made her laugh for some reason. 'Then they put him on a boat to Greenock. I've never heard from him since. He knows where I am and I'll wait. I know he'll come back to me. You know where I am now too, and now you've met your wee brother.'

I didn't know what to say and anyway I couldn't take my eyes off little Bobby, the new wee brother I didn't even know I had. So like Mavis.

'He can't be … ,' I started, but all the breath seemed to have gone out of me, so I just shook my head. What did she mean, little brother? That was stupid.

'We thought your mum was dead until my dad met some man in the pub,' she said. 'We thought she'd died in the raid.'

'My mum's not dead,' I said, suddenly alert. 'Mavis isn't dead either. Neither am I.'

'I can see that,' she laughed.

'He's my dad,' I said. 'I just want to know where he is. We thought he was dead. Dead presumed missing, I mean missing presumed dead. I heard the old lady say it.' Words were just coming out without my meaning them to. I gulped them back in. No-one ever told me why my dad wasn't coming back but I overheard 'missing presumed dead' and always thought it was that. 'He's funny and kind and good and …'

'I know. Isn't he great?' she said, interrupting. 'Everyone loved him. He worked really hard here and kept everyone cheerful. I miss him so much!' She gave wee Bobby a jiggle. Bobby was quiet now, sniffing and playing in her hair.

'I miss him too,' I said, but it didn't feel right, telling her that. I think she meant something different from the way I missed him. And anyway he was mine to miss and not hers. 'He's my dad,' I said, 'not yours, or his.' I nodded at the baby.

She ignored this and started telling me how they had worked together and a load of other stuff but I didn't hear much of it. I just looked at her with her little boy who was like Mavis and I thought of my poor mum who looked older than her and who couldn't have stood there swinging a toddler round when she only had one leg. A knot twisted up my stomach when I thought of my mum. I didn't understand. This was all wrong. Jeannie must be lying or thinking of someone else, not my dad. It couldn't be true.

'Jeannie!' shouted Jeannie's dad. He wasn't nice like my dad, but then maybe mine wasn't nice either. I didn't know. Maybe I hadn't understood anything at all. Maybe the world was upside down and inside out again, like when the bombing happened. A great gust blew through the trees and pulled my coat across my legs and then almost immediately the rain arrived. Jeannie glanced over her shoulder.

'Good luck!' she said to me. 'I hope you find him. You look so like him. Those eyes. So sweet.' She hung on the corner of the house a moment beneath the eaves, holding her little one close. Bobby, quiet at last, watched me with his eyes like Mavis's. Then they both disappeared round the corner and left me standing there in the muddy lane with torrents coming down round my shoulders.

'Jeannie!' called the old man. 'Get that wean indoors!'

'Alright, I'm coming!' I heard her yell.

I stood a moment longer and stared at the corner of the building wondering if I'd imagined it all. Then I turned and gazed out through the rain over the tattie fields where people were running to the trees for shelter and I pictured him there lifting tatties or maybe bringing the cows in to milk. It didn't make sense. The idea of him being there at all, with this Jeannie, with a baby. It was all nonsense. It had to be.

And why wouldn't he have sent for us? Of course he would have. Why didn't we live in one of those houses in a neat little row with tatties growing in the garden?

The rain thundered through the trees and even though I was already completely drenched I went down the road with my legs stiff like logs to the nearest chestnut for what little shelter it offered and wondered what had just happened and whether I wasn't going completely mad myself to have dreamt up such a terrible thing. He was so like Mavis, cute and yummy like Mavis was, the same eyes. How could that be? I sank onto the chestnut roots and held my head in my hands and put my thumbs in my ears to cut out all the horrible thoughts. But it didn't work. It had never worked, and I was left with a million stupid explanations without proper questions, and absolutely no answers.

Chapter 21

A bomb had gone off in my life and no-one had sounded the sirens. Everything was blown to pieces and all those pieces flung to the many winds, far beyond anything I could understand.

I squeezed my eyes and thought about my mum, but all I could see was little Bobby and his apple, Jeannie in the garden and her dad's spittle landing by my foot. They seemed to be a bubble inside my head, completely separate from anything else, and I wondered whether it had really happened. Perhaps I had imagined it, a dream, the whole thing. But there was Rocco and his friends. They must have known. That's why Rocco wanted to come with me.

I wished I hadn't come. I wished I was home with Mavis, Rosie and my mum, wherever home was. I wouldn't care as long as I was with them. My dad didn't matter. I didn't want my dad now. I wanted him to go away and never have existed at all. I wanted Mr Tait never to have made me look for him. I wanted Mr Tait.

A gust shook the chestnut and a flurry of leaves flew off towards the town and did cartwheels along the road. Three rooks swooped down and bounced back towards me. One came close and put his head on one side, the way dogs do, as if to say, 'What is that sitting there? I don't understand.'

'You and me both,' I thought. 'This doesn't make sense.'

It couldn't be true. I mean, why would he go and have another wife when he had my mum at home waiting? Why would he make another baby with someone else? I'd have been over the moon with a new little brother, but this made my heart hurt trying to understand. Bobby was so like Mavis it was easy to love him, but he wasn't mine to love, same as my dad wasn't Jeannie's to miss.

You see, I knew then, roughly, about that unmentionable thing that made babies happen and I knew that men seemed to like it a lot and obviously that my dad was a man. I stared at his photo. He seemed so certain and dependable and fun. I wished it wasn't true. But that was silly thinking. That was like wishing Mr Tait wasn't D-E-A-D dead, which made me close my eyes and wish it all over again. I'd rather have wished my dad was dead, which made more sense. I threw a stick at the rooks and they squawked and flew away.

'Bastard!' I heard bad George say in my head, which is something he often said.

'Bastard!' I said out loud, but it felt silly, saying bad words with no-one listening, so I put the photo away, pulled my collar up, wrapped my arms around my knees and sobbed and rocked.

After a bit the rain stopped and I ran out of tears. The rooks were back. They had brought several of their pals and were digging about in the mud or swirling above me in the tree. They seemed to be laughing, but there was nothing funny about this.

I squeezed the photo in my fist and wanted to tear it up, but knew I had to bring it safely back to my mum. Then I remembered she knew he was alive. Maybe she even knew about Bobby. Why hadn't she just told me? I tried to remember things she'd said. Maybe there were clues. But I couldn't think of anything except little Bobby and his eyes like Mavis's.

It was time to get back to Clydebank.

I wobbled to my feet, squeezed out my hat and set off quickly in the hopes of warming up or at least drying out. Luckily it was all downhill.

'I had a good job and I left … left … left,' I sang under my breath to drown out other thoughts as I marched along, though I kept muddling the words.

Back in Helensburgh I went straight past the police station and the town hall and into the railway station. There was a queue at the ticket desk, two sailors, an old lady and a dog, and they all seemed to have trouble buying their tickets. Suddenly it was my turn.

'Yes,' said the ticket lady at her little window.

I opened my mouth to speak but nothing came out. 'Well?' she said.

I bit my lip and shook my head. 'Sorry,' I said. 'Just a minute.' I ran away from the desk and threw myself against a wall outside.

I still wanted to find him. He was my dad, for goodness' sake. Of course I wanted to find him, if only to tell him how furious I was and ask him for the truth. Maybe Jeannie was lying. Maybe she meant a different Lenny from my dad. Maybe my dad didn't know about the bombing and my mum's leg and losing Mavis, or he couldn't find us because we went to Carbeth. I thought of Jeannie standing there with her baby and I stared at the rainwater rushing down the gutter, the way it bounced off a stone that was lying there and ran on round it and the stone didn't move. It didn't make sense. Maybe my dad could explain.

But I had to find my dad. Even Mr Tait wanted me to find him, didn't he? I mean, why else would Mr Tait tell me to look under the bed? My dad was my dad. I had a right. He wasn't going to hide from me. I was going to find him if it was the last thing I'd do. And he'd better be ready. Maybe he'd even come home with me.

I went to the police station. The doors were dark wood with brasses on them so shiny I could see my face. I took a deep breath and went in. A huge tall policeman was standing behind the counter holding a piece of paper as far away from his eyes as he could manage, which was quite far because his arms were so long and his head pulled back on his neck. Only his eyes were moving, side to side, across the paper.

I stood so long I thought I might burst. And while I stood, he read. And then he turned to a set of drawers and started rummaging. When he found what he was looking for he looked at the paper again, clutching it as before at the end of his arm. I looked at the poster beside him: 'Deserve victory!' it said, with a picture of Winston Churchill, the prime minister. Okay, I thought, I'm trying, really I am. At last he noticed me.

'Hello,' he said. 'What can I do for you, young lady?' His quiet voice seemed to fill the room. He leant on the counter and gazed across at me.

'Hello,' I said. 'I'm looking for my dad.'

'Your dad?' he said.

'Yes,' I said. 'He was here. In Helensburgh I mean,

not in the police station. Maybe he came here too, I don't know.'

'What's his name?'

'Gillespie,' I said. 'Lenny Gillespie. Same as me only he's Leonard and I'm Leonora. He's my dad.' My mouth seemed to be working but wasn't attached to my brain.

'Why do you think he came here?' he said softly, and he smiled.

So I explained about the postcard and I said he'd been on a farm, or maybe a farm camp. It seemed safer to be vague. I didn't show him the photo or tell him about being Italian because I suddenly ran out of courage.

He stood up so straight I thought he'd go right through the ceiling. 'I don't know anyone by that name,' he said, at last.

Relief was what I felt, perhaps only because I was breathing again. I was just about to say goodbye and thank you very much when he leant forward once more.

'But we'll just check the register, shall we? Lenny. Something familiar about that. Not so common a name, is it? When would he have been here?'

'I don't know. There's no postcard on the mark, I mean, no mark on the card.'

So he said he'd do some checking and I should come back later in the day. Then he smiled again and I knew it was time to go.

'Lenny,' he muttered. I turned back. But it was himself he was talking to, not me. 'Lenny Gillespie.'

I came out feeling sleepy and confused. Perhaps I should go back and show him the photo. Scared and unsure, I bumbled along the street until I was back down at the sea wall staring dumbly across the water at all the boats lingering there at anchor. The long pier ran out towards them and a single boat lay at the end of it. I guessed it was early afternoon. I ought to have gone home. I was still only half dry and the wind was racing through me. I'd catch cold. Another giant rain cloud was hovering, even though the sun was suddenly out.

A man was leaning on the wall close by.

'Excuse me,' I said. 'Is that boat going to Greenock?'

'No,' he said, 'and I can't tell you where it is going either. That would be against the law.'

'Of course not, sorry,' I said.

He took out a pipe, poked his finger into it then lit it with a match, his hand drawn carefully against the wind. 'But it's not going to Greenock,' he said. 'I doubt you'll get across there today.' He nodded out over the water. 'Mind you, you could practically walk over, there are so many boats. ' He poked the air with his pipe. 'It's Craigendoran you want, the beautiful *Lucy Ashton*, but she's not going to Greenock either.' He winked and one side of his face squidged up like a prune. 'You'll need a pass, of course. Leaves in thirty minutes.'

'Thank you!' I said and started to run. Greenock. That was it. She said he'd been sent to Greenock. I wasn't ready to give up. I screeched to a halt. Mr Tulloch said not to go there. Then I sped on again. What else could I do?

The sun had vanished in a wash of white cloud. The beach was stony and half-covered with seaweed so I slithered over towards the water's edge and hurried along the shingle, dodging waves as I went. A train whistled behind the houses. Another far bigger pier was visible some way along and a khaki-coloured crowd was gathering there. As I neared, I picked my way up the beach to the ferry office. The rain arrived suddenly and sang on its roof so I had no alternative but to shout.

'Return?' said the man. He was old and had a cigarette hanging from the corner of his mouth. He looked like Clark Gable.

'No, thank you,' I said. 'One way.' (One way? I thought. What if I never came back?)

'Pass?' he said.

'P … pardon?'

'Louder, dear. I can't hear you. It's raining, in case you hadn't noticed.' He pointed at the roof. 'You need a pass, otherwise you can't go. This is a special. You could be an enemy alien.'

I slumped against the counter.

'I don't have one,' I said.

'Pardon?' he said.

'I said I don't have one,' I said. 'But I'm not an enemy. I'm only twelve.'

'You look fourteen at least to me. Anyway, you might be acting on orders.'

'Please? I'm looking for my dad. I think he's in Greenock.'

'You look like trouble. Where d'you get all those cuts?'

I sighed and walked away.

By then the rain was vertical, making it suddenly dark, and I couldn't hear the sea any more.

This was stupid, what I was doing. I'd no idea how

I'd get home even if I did get on the boat, or where I'd go in Greenock. But somehow I didn't care. I just couldn't give up. I stood in the doorway while the rain battered on the roof and watched the soldiers shuffling across the pier, men like my dad, dressed as my dad had been last time I saw him, and made a silent apology to Mr Tulloch.

There were several boats at the pier but I guessed the biggest one was the *Lucy Ashton*, for Greenock. So many people swarming about and everyone shouting over the rain, it was hard to see anything at all.

'Hurry up at the front,' they yelled.

'Move along. Keep it coming!' bawled a sou'westered ferryman.

Greenock had vanished completely in the rain, and as I gazed back along the shore Helensburgh was fading fast. A motor car came round the side of the ticket office, jet black like the rooks, and the soldiers got out of the way. Without meaning to, I left the doorway and followed it. Meaning to even less, I joined the cavalcade of one, and shadowed the ferryman, holding my head high and trying to look like I was meant to be there.

'Make way! Watch your back there!' said the ferryman.

The crowd parted enough for the car to get through. I smiled graciously at anyone whose eye I caught, as if the car was mine, and followed it as it murmured over the rain-soaked pier. My world was so inside out it might as well have been mine.

We reached the gangplank, and the car stopped. I wasn't sure what to do. A man in a fancy cap got out of the driver's seat. Ignoring his look of surprise, I beat him to the door handle at the back and before I knew it, I'd opened it and stood back smiling at the passenger inside.

'Who are you?' growled the driver in my ear. He was old and smelled of putty.

'New cadet,' I smiled back. 'Special.'

A man in uniform got out of the car. I saluted with my left hand and took the smile off my face. The man looked at me with some surprise.

'Good afternoon,' he said.

I was about to say hello when the driver poked me in the ribs and a voice from the gangplank called over my head.

'Welcome, sir. I'm Captain Carter, sir. This way if you don't mind.' He had a plummy voice like the doctors in the hospital when I went to find my mum after the Blitz.

'Of course, Captain, lead on!' said the important man, and he turned to me. 'My suitcase, young lady, in the boot. And remember, always salute with your right hand. Never the left.'

'Yes, sir, of course, sir, right, sir, will do,' I said.

The driver glared at me then went swiftly round the back and opened a door there. I followed him. Luckily it was a small suitcase, but heavy. I lifted it out with two hands and waddled towards the gangplank. Behind me the back door banged shut, then the side, then the driver's. I turned to see the car back through the crowd then turn and leave the pier.

'Excuse me!' I said as loudly as I could, and wobbled my way up the rutted gangplank and onto the deck. The ship's funnel gave two loud blasts and the crowd folded round the gangplank. It was all I could do not to duck with every sudden noise.

'That way, love,' said a sailor in a duffel coat on the ship's deck. The captain and the important man had disappeared. I followed where the sailor had pointed and knocked on a door. The important man and Captain Carter were talking and ignored me as I hovered, until the captain nodded at a corner by porthole so I put the case there. That done, he glanced over the important man's shoulder and indicated the door with his eyes.

Back on deck I felt the ship's engines rumble into life and everything underneath me shook, like when the bombs fell. I gripped the handrail and scuttled behind a lifeboat to hide. Freshly blackened boots shuffled past beyond the curve of the lifeboat. I thought hard about Mr Tait and not being scared and how everything always passes, no matter how bad. But this was idiotic.

'Full up inside!' called a voice. 'Use the upper deck! No complaining please, it's a short crossing.'

The rain battered on the lifeboat's tarpaulin and slid in globes off the side. There was just enough space for me to squeeze underneath. 'Yet another fine mess,' I thought, my sudden courage all evaporated like steam from a kettle. This was stupid, illegal and dangerous. I had to get off. I'd just have to brave it, get my head up and go. I gulped some air and stood up.

'You'll have to wait for the next one, mate,' said the ferryman to some soldiers. 'There's no room even up on top. Go back to the terminus and wait. There's no way I'm risking the safety of these men by overloading.'

The four men argued with him but he blocked their way on the gangplank. I thought about sneaking round him, and off the boat, maybe no-one would notice, but he was too big, so instead I ducked back under the lifeboat and shivered. Then a scraping noise and a 'thunk' told me the gangplank had been pulled back onto the pier.

'Oh no!' I whispered.

'Cast off aft!' I heard.

'Aft cast off!'

The engines roared louder and the boat shook off the pier side. The hiss and gurgle of water churning removed all possibility of shore. I was going wherever that ship was taking me and I had to hope it was Greenock. There was no going back. But the other side of the water and all the boats in between had disappeared into the rain. How were we to avoid ramming all those other ships? We were sailing blindly into a white blanket of rain as if we were going off to heaven. I thought briefly of throwing myself overboard and swimming back to the ferry terminal to save my life. Seagulls turned around the boat, girning and chasing each other like children in a game. Then the ferryboat blasted its foghorn as if it was yelling 'Stop raining!' at the top of its voice. Another boat hooted back out of the mist and a couple more from goodness knows where. The boat began to shoosh through the water and I looked over the side at the spray building up beneath me. Suddenly we lurched to one side and then the other and I knew we were out in the open sea. I was glad to be close to the lifeboat in case I needed it.

Ships loomed out of the mist. Some of them were small but others were huge and rose above us, grand and unmovable, solid cliffs of smooth grey metal with giant chains straining into the water. Some were top-heavy like castles, piled high with lookout stations and guns and turrets, making the men on them seem like tiny little ants. The ships hummed as we went past, or clanged with metal like a blacksmith's, and one played a series of bells like in church. A small boat slowed down as it passed and the people on board waved. I didn't mean to wave back. I did it without thinking, just being polite, but of course they weren't waving at me. They were waving at the people on the upper deck and I had given myself away.

A lady was driving the little boat. 'You've got a stowaway!' she shouted to the people above me and pointed.

'Is she good-looking?' someone shouted back, and people laughed, then the little boat zoomed away towards Helensburgh.

We were in the middle of the sea and both Greenock and Helensburgh were lost in the mist. I hugged myself tight and shivered against the wind, hiding my head in my knees, all my gallusness gone. My next problem was how I was ever going to get off without being arrested and sent to a camp forever.

But suddenly the rain stopped and the clouds lifted like the curtain at the La Scala and the sun beamed through and I saw hundreds of ships spread out in front of me like silvery trinkets set on the pewter sea. Greenock town was behind them with cranes and chimneys and factory buildings and smoke and noise exactly like we had in Clydebank, and the green hills rose steeply above, dotted brown with autumn and lined with houses.

The ferryboat stopped rocking and the closer we got to the shore the slower we went, passing between two towering warships and lots of little puffers whose chimneys bulged with black smoke like a train. When I looked back for Helensburgh it was gone, wrapped in the blanket of mist we had just left.

They cut the engines and we drifted to a standstill against the side with a thud that nearly shook me overboard. Men were shouting fore and aft. Smoke from the funnel swooped down around my head, hung a second then flew off into the breeze. I waited for someone to either arrest me or cheer that we had arrived safely, but no-one seemed bothered. Having considered handing myself in, I decided instead to try the head-up thing again and walk casually off the boat.

But three soldiers had other plans.

'Hello, sweetheart, did you have a nice trip?' said one.

'How much d'you think we'd get for this one then?' said another, looking me up and down.

'Got anything interesting under that coat of yours?' laughed another.

'Aw, don't make a face like that,' said the first. 'We're only having a laugh.'

'Throw her in irons! She can walk the plank!'

They laughed and so loudly it was like a clap of thunder. I waited until they'd finished and then, trembling inside, said as sternly as I could, 'I'm looking for my dad,' as if it was them who had stolen him.

'Yeah, but the captain's looking for you,' said one. He grabbed my arm and set off towards the captain's cabin, dragging me along beside him.

'Let go,' I yelled. Ella flashed into my mind and I kicked and twisted, which made them laugh all the more.

'I found the stowaway, sir,' he said, at the cabin door.

'Not now,' said Captain Carter and he glanced at the important man, then back at me. 'Good God, what have you done to her?'

'Nothing, sir, she was like that when we found her.'

The important man turned to face me and took the pipe from his mouth.

'Ah, the new recruit,' he said, without getting up. 'Did you have a pleasant trip?'

No-one else spoke. Captain Carter pointed at the door and the soldiers let go of me and left.

'Yes, sir,' I said.

'Come here child,' said the important man. 'Let me look at you.'

He stared at me for ages as if each streak of purple was extremely important. I reached up and flattened my hair and straightened my coat. He was smart in his important uniform with gold edging, but he had smudges of pipe ash down the front and one yellow finger which he poked into his pipe for a second before reaching into his pocket for a box of matches.

'If you want to go impersonating people you have to study your subject first,' he said. 'The first lesson for any new recruit is how to salute an officer. You got that wrong. I must applaud your bravery, however.' He paused a moment and I had to force back the smile that was trying to spread across my face out of pure nerves. 'But this is a very serious breach of security at a time when we need absolute dedication from all our citizens and especially our armed forces who must be allowed to operate without distraction, not to mention time-wasting.' He sat back in his chair and lit his pipe. 'What are you doing here anyway?'

'I'm looking for my d ... dad,' I said.

'On this ship?' he said.

'No,' I said. I glanced at the captain who nodded. 'No, sir,' I went on. 'They sent him to Greenock.'

'They?' A layer of pipe smoke oozed across the room at me. It was sweet, like my gran's toffee.

'The p ... police,' I said, and gulped.

'The police? That's interesting.'

A pause passed.

'I hope you find him,' he said.

'Thank you, sir,' I said. 'S ... so do I.'

'I'll have her taken back, sir,' said Captain Carter. 'We can keep her in one of the engine room lockers on the journey.'

The air fell out of me. In a locker?

'There's no need for that,' said the important man, getting to his feet. 'Surely you can phone Helensburgh Constabulary from here? Or hand her over to Greenock.'

'There's the refuelling to see to, sir. We're due at four.'

'You see the important time you're wasting, young lady?' said the important man.

They went on discussing what was to be done with me as if I wasn't there. Outside the porthole I could see the gangplank, empty, and beyond that a huge building, the ferry terminal perhaps or a station entrance.

'Let me see the log,' said the important man and they started peering over something on a table, not a log as far as I could see, and discussing whatever was important about this, that and the next thing. I stepped slowly backwards until I was at the door, then in one careful move I was out, along the deck, around the back of the cabin and down the gangplank.

'Hey, you!' came a voice. 'Stop her!'

I had walked briskly all the way, as if I was meant to be there. I slowed then and straightened my back as if this was the kind of thing I did every other day, leaving ships with important errands to do. I turned and waved to the man who'd shouted from the upper deck and gave him the thumbs up.

'Won't be long,' I called, like a big fat liar, then I nipped behind a crowd of soldiers there so I couldn't be seen.

'Stop that girl!' he called.

Chapter 22

Men in uniforms I didn't recognise were waiting there in rows, slouched on bundles or hunched on the ground. They were a bedraggled lot and gazed up at me through drops of rain that fell from their hats. The sailor's voice was soon lost in the din and no-one else seemed to notice me. Soldiers stood over the unhappy men. One of them said something to me I didn't understand and I realised they were Germans! More Germans! I stared at them and one of them smiled. It made the hair creep on my neck and I backed off down the pier not sure what to do. Then I saw the sailor on the ferry coming down the gangplank so I hurried away. I wanted to run but couldn't risk drawing attention.

A little further on, a gangplank rose to another ferry and down it came men who looked like someone had thrown black paint all over them. But in amongst the black there was red too, and grey bandages, and the whites of their eyes staring out. They helped one another down, limping and hanging on to each other. No-one was smiling. One of them came down on a stretcher and I thought of Mr Tait on the steps at his own funeral. But I didn't want to get caught, so I followed where they went and kept low amongst the crowd. The biggest ships were out at anchor but the quayside was lined with all sorts of other boats.

A fancy building with balconies and pillars stood further along the dock. It looked fit to burst. Men were queuing to go in at one door and still more came out at another. It had to be the ferry terminal but it was also the station, and when I sneaked in it was the giantest, noisiest, dirtiest, busiest railway station I have ever been in. I guessed it would make the perfect place to hide.

But I was wrong. Apart from some WVS ladies at the entrance serving tea, a couple of ladies at the ticket office and two more with buckets near the toilets, it was all men. I stuck out like a sore thumb but didn't realise until I saw two policemen watching me. They started towards me. A train roared its engine and a huge cloud of smoke shot up to the roof. I glanced about for which way to escape.

'This is no place for youngsters!' said one of the policemen. 'What do you think you're doing here?'

'I came on a boat,' I said. It was too late to run. 'Where's the way out?'

'No you didn't,' he said. 'How did you really get here?'

I didn't wait to answer, but darted round the soldiers and out a side door.

'Hey!' shouted the policeman.

Not looking where I was going I ran straight into a sailor, smack against his chest so that I burst my lip and it started to bleed and swell. I wiped it with my hand. The sailor wore a dark jumper that rolled at the neck and a dirty white cap.

'Oh my word, I've caught a little sprat,' he said, blocking my way. 'What are you doing here?' He only had one proper eye. The other one didn't open at all, like an everlasting wink. 'Are you running a message?' he said, pinning his one eye on me.

'Yes, sir,' I said, so he laughed at me saying 'sir'.

'Well, no wonder you've got so many cuts. Look where you're going.'

'Yes, sir.'

He laughed again. 'Are you a spy?'

I nearly said, 'Yes, sir,' and, 'What do you think, sir? Of course I'm not a spy, sir,' but thought better of it. I was in enough trouble.

'You'll be taken for a spy. Go on. I'm watching you. Off you go. Quick before they catch you.'

'I'm not old enough to be a spy,' I said. I put my hand in my pocket and squeezed my dad's photo.

'If you're not old enough to be a spy, you're not old enough to be hanging about here. You should be in the kindergarten with all the other babies.'

'I'm not a baby. I'm looking for my dad,' I said.

'Well, there's plenty to choose from here,' he said, nodding at a row of soldiers who were lined up against a wall.

'I don't think my dad's one of those,' I said.

'Why not? Is he a conchie, then?'

'No,' I said. 'He's … he's a … he's an …'

'Well? What is he? Tinker, tailor, soldier sailor?'

'Um …'

'Rich man?'

He picked up a steaming hot cup of tea from a window ledge and took a slurp. There was a chunk of bread in his other hand. I wished the tea and bread were mine. He took a bite and talked as he chewed.

'Not a rich man then?'

I shook my head.

'Probably not a thief then either.'

I shook my head again.

'Where have you come from?'

Unfortunately my mouth had gone to jelly again and no matter what I did, no matter how big a breath I took I couldn't get any words out.

'C … ,' I went. 'C …' A rush of heat filled my head and I thought I'd faint right over and fall on the ground. 'C … C …'

'Kilcreggan?' he said.

'C …'

'Cardross? Kilpatrick? Cartsdyke? Crinan? Campbeltown?' He went on and on and named all the places he could think of that began with C and I stared at him with my mouth open not even trying. And with every name he laughed all the more until he got to Clincarthill and the tears were rolling down his cheeks. He was laughing so much he had to put his tea back down on the windowsill because it was spilling over.

'Canada,' he laughed. 'Canberra. Kansas!'

I was just about to scream CLYDEBANK and CARBETH at the top of my voice when another man appeared between us and pinned the sailor to a wall by his neck.

'She's a wee lassie!' growled the man. 'Leave her alone!'

I waited a moment and held my breath and saw the ferryboat leaving behind them.

'I was only having a bit of fun,' the sailor man protested. 'No need for that!'

I wished I'd stayed on the boat. Too late! Instead

I ran away from them along the pier not caring who noticed me, past piles of boxes, barrels so big you could drown in them, ropes, bollards and hundreds of men in strange uniforms standing in rows. Then I reached the end of the dock and had to turn up towards the road. There was a close doorway so I threw myself into it and blammed against the wall. I shook and raged and wiped the blood from my lip until half my hand was red and I sobbed until I thought I'd choke.

Oh Mr Tait! I thought. *What have I done? Mum, I'm so sorry. What was I thinking? Mr Tulloch, why didn't I listen? Mavis, Rosie, I'm so sorry. I hope you're alright. What am I going to do?*

A motor car went past with its horn blaring. Then the rain started pelting down and some soldiers clattered by all talking at once, their boots echoing round the close. I edged back to the doorway and washed my hands in the rain. No-one paid me the slightest attention.

I needed to get home, but I was too scared to go back into that station. I was too scared to go to the police for help either. It was even worse than before, the daughter of an Italian stowing away in a ship. I decided the town hall might be best, if I could find it, if the rain would only stop.

Eventually, of course, it did, and by that time I'd managed to stop crying and found some of my courage, enough to tidy myself and start up the street.

At the end of it, the biggest tower you ever saw stuck right up into the sky, and I thought it might have the town hall underneath it, but the bombers had done their work in Greenock too and the streets between the waterfront and the town hall had buildings with walls missing and no roof. Wallpaper and fireplaces were uncovered for everyone to see and there were piles of rubble and mess still there beside the roads, same as Clydebank. And as if that wasn't bad enough, the town hall had been bombed too and a whole row of buildings beyond it. I stood in front of the town hall trying not to smell all the things I'd smelled in Clydebank or see things hiding in the strange shapes of the debris, the arms and legs and heads, but that's another story. I was trying so hard not to see it that I forgot I could just run right out of there.

Then an old woman came along. She had a stick to hold her up and a bright woollen scarf tied tight around her head to keep her hair down in the wind, out of which her face bulged.

'If you're looking for the town hall,' she said, 'they're in a special office down there past the police station.' She pointed with her stick. 'There's a notice on the police door telling you where.'

'Thank you,' I said, and down a little street saw a sign with POLICE on it and a huddle of policemen in dark uniforms beneath.

'What's the matter? You look all undone,' she said.

'Um,' I said.

'You looking for someone?'

I nodded.

'Go and ask the police, then. They're only down there.'

I shivered and looked at the ground.

'Why not? Are you in trouble?'

I thought about this. 'Yes, I suppose. I don't know.'

'For brawling?'

'No,' I said, putting my hand to my face.

'That looks sore. Ooo, your lip's still bleeding. Don't you have a hanky? What happened?'

Where could I start?

'Come on, love. Cat got your tongue? Who is it you're looking for? Come on, you can tell me. I'm just an old woman in the street trying to get up the hill and home.'

I had to wonder if she was a spy. She didn't look like one.

'I shouldn't have come here on my own but I need to find my dad,' I said.

'Ah, I see. Is he in the services? He'll be down at the docks or maybe up there at the barracks. Depends what kind of service man he is. They don't stay long. They go off in trains every day, all nationalities, talking every language and most of them don't understand a word I say, even the Brits.' She chuckled to herself. 'There's all sorts based here. From all over the world, Americans, Canadians, Norwegians, French. You name it. I don't understand half of what they say either.'

'He's Scottish,' I said. 'No, British, English, I think, sort of, not quite.' I shook my head to get my thoughts in the right order.

'Hmm. Impressive. A citizen of the world,' she said, 'just like the rest of us.'

'He was in the army, the British Army. He was, but I don't think he's in it now.'

'That way,' she said, and poked her stick back towards the docks. 'Down there for the town hall offices. Good luck! And you watch yourself, specially down at that Rue End. There are too many men in this town.'

'I will, thank you,' I said. 'What's the Rue End?'

'It's where all the trouble starts,' she said, 'pubs and ... och, just don't you go there. Go along that way instead.'

I sooked up the blood I could feel oozing on my lip and followed the line of her walking stick.

'Where's your mum?' she said when I didn't move.

'She's at Singer's, in Clydebank,' I said.

'Singer's? You've come all the way from Clydebank? Well, you're some lassie. I worked in Singer's myself a long time ago. Married a man from Clydebank, but he's long dead. Died in the last war.'

I dabbed at my lip with my sleeve.

'Tsk, don't do that, love, you'll get it all over your clothes and it'll never come off!' She took a hanky out of her pocket and patted the blood away. It wasn't a perfect white one like Mr Tait's and smelled distinctly not nice. 'I'm up there,' she said and pointed up the hill. 'Near the top on the right, number twenty-two, top floor, if you need any help. Mrs Strachan. Don't be slow in calling.'

'Thank you, Mrs Strachan. Twenty-two. I'm Lenny,' I said.

'Lenny? That's unusual for a girl. Are you a Roman Catholic then?'

'I don't think so.'

She laughed. 'You don't know. That's nice.'

Then she turned and started up a steep steep hill at a slow pace and I wondered if she'd ever make it.

But time was hurrying along, so I had to hurry too. I started down the road then stopped. Mrs Strachan had taken two steps to my twenty and put her bags down. Her cheek bulged out of her scarf. She coughed and her cheek wobbled. She wiped her nose with the same hanky and bent, slowly, to pick up her bags again. I went back.

'Mrs Strachan?' I said.

She put down her bags and straightened to look at me.

'Can I help?' I said. I glanced up the hill and felt Mr Tait smile at my good deed. Then I heard a train chunter by and saw thick black smoke above the hill, reminding me I should go home.

Mrs Strachan laughed so her cheeks both wobbled like bags of water and she wiped a drip off her old nose with a pointy finger. 'No, no,' she said. 'You're in a hurry. Lenny wasn't it?'

'It's no bother,' I lied.

'Yes, it is,' she said.

'No … ,' I said.

She smiled again. 'It is, though, isn't it?'

I wanted to say, *Do you want my help or not?* but in my head I saw Mr Tait's face wrinkle with disappointment. I lifted the bags and smiled back. 'It's fine,' I said. 'My dad's been a long time lost!'

'All the more reason you should hurry,' she said, and we set off together.

The bags were both string bags with lots of old newspaper holding everything inside. There were probably ten tons of tatties in there and another ten of turnips. We took a couple of steps together then she told me to go on ahead and leave the bags outside her door.

So I did. The hill was as long and steep as the hill at Carbeth and the door to number twenty-two had a slanty step. I went in and up the stairs until I found a door with Strachan written on it. I leant my head against the door until I caught my breath then dropped the bags and leant against the wall for my heart beat to slow. It was dark and damp in there with no stair-lights and I didn't like it one bit, so as soon as I could, I set off back down the stairs.

Mrs Strachan was still near the bottom of the hill but from outside her close I could see the river and the bank on the other side, maybe Helensburgh, faintly through the mist. This was a relief. I had almost believed it had been taken away and that there was no way back. The clouds had lifted a little and across the water I saw boats and ferries and battleships, small in the distance or giant up close. Then, as I watched, the cloud slipped over again.

I ran back down the hill.

'Thank you, Lenny,' said Mrs Strachan. 'What a kindness!'

'You're welcome,' I said.

'Now you know where I am if you need me,' she said.

Chapter 23

The rain clouds seemed to sit over Greenock and the water like a thick grey blanket stealing all the light. The four big policemen were still outside the police station as if they had no thieves to chase. I slowed down and walked past them with my face pointed at something interesting on the other side of the road so they wouldn't see me, then ran round a corner to another door with a handwritten sign on the outside. 'Town Hall Tempry Office' it said in letters that seemed about to fall forward on their faces. I leant my head to read the list of opening times below. It shut at five. I peered through the window and saw a clock which said ten past five. The door rattled in my hand.

I stared at the notice for some time, willing it to change, then stared at the clock. How ill thought-out the whole thing was. A shudder of fright ran through me and left an ache that wouldn't go away. Then a deep rumble from some huge machinery at the docks made the ground shake under my feet. Another train whistled by up on the hill, racing along with its smoke lying along its back, then vanished behind the buildings. Soon there would be no more trains for the day and I would be stuck there overnight.

There was a sign for a railway station further down the road on the opposite side. I'd go straight there and get on the next train home.

As I went down the street, one car honked and another one rattled. A man bumped my shoulder and two ladies tutted. Another man with rubber legs (drunk) swayed round me and almost into the road so another car hooted like a foghorn. A huge tall man in overalls grabbed the rubber drunk by his shirt front and swung him back onto the pavement and against the building.

'Stay off the sauce, eejit!' he said.

'No harm, pal,' slurred the rubber man, patting the big man's chest. 'Just trying to get home.' He started singing, his hand by his mouth as if he was pulling the sound out with his fingers.

The big man let go of him and walked away.

My eyes were so busy following this bulk of a man that I didn't realise my feet were following him too. He was crossing the street towards the station, where I was going. Unfortunately trams, unlike cars, don't make any noise except their bell and I didn't hear any bell until it was far too late and a tram had come right up behind me. The big man turned and swept me out of its path as the bell rattled by my ear and its wind tried to suck me along with it. I was hot then cold then hot again. He set me straight while I took in what had happened.

'Watch where you're going!' he said in a friendly voice. Some other people stopped to stare.

'Is she alright?' said another man.

'She got a fright,' said the man, 'but it missed her.

I blinked and stared at them.

'Give her a minute,' he said.

'Oh dear, what happened to you?' said a lady in

lipstick who seemed too close.

'Nearly run herself over,' said the man.

'Aw, wee chook,' said the lady, and she touched my chin with two dirty fingers.

I stepped back from them, looked at my feet and wondered whether anyone's heart had ever broken their ribcage.

'She'll be alright,' said the man. 'You won't do that twice, will you?'

'You okay? I don't think she's okay,' said the lady and she peered in at me and smelled funny. Whisky like my dad, that was it.

'I'm fine,' I said, only my voice seemed to have finally disappeared. 'Thank you.'

'What?' she said.

'Leave her be,' said the man.

'And since when is it your business?' said the lady, her voice rising.

'It's not your business anyway,' said the man.

'And who's business is it to decide whether it's my business or not?' said the lady. She was sharp and slurry at the same time. I ducked into a doorway as the argument heated up then slid along the wall and off down the road.

I hadn't gone far before a boy ran out of a side lane and then another boy, both grinning from ear to ear, and rushed past me so close that I dropped my photo which I'd just taken out of my pocket. Then a third boy came flying out after them and didn't see me bending to pick up the photo. Luckily I already had it before he fell right over the top of me.

'Out of the … !' he said as he went down with a thud. A bread roll bounced away from him along the pavement. He picked himself up as quickly as he could, grabbed the roll and his cap, which had tumbled after it, and peered down at me. 'Sorry. You okay?'

'Stop! Thief!' shouted a man in a white apron. He didn't see us down there but then suddenly he did. 'Ah-ha,' he said. 'So there are four of you.' He yanked us to our feet by our collars, his fingers tangling in my hair. So I screamed. I didn't scream a little scream. I screamed a big one and I didn't even plan it. It was like Ella all over again. My brain switched off and I fought for my life, kicking and punching and howling like a dog. I bit the man's hand, which was floury because he was a baker. I'm not proud of this but at least he let go of me and I took off down the road. The boy came running down the street after me shouting to anyone who was interested 'I've never seen her before in my life, honest!' and laughing like a hyena, which is a special kind of extra cheerful dog that you only get in Africa, according to Miss Read. I ran across the road to get away from him and nearly got hit by another tram, then scuttled down a side street before either of them could come after me.

There I stopped on a corner to get my breath. Greenock seemed to be every bit as dangerous as Mr Tulloch had said, if only I'd listened. Another train went by on the hill, but then a man passed me who looked exactly like my dad. I only saw him from behind but he had the same dark hair and stood very upright and walked with a lilt as if one leg was longer than the other, which my dad's wasn't, but that's the way he walked. I followed him because I wasn't sure. It seemed too unlikely, too easy, too good to be true, to just bump into him in the street. He went the way I had just come and was moving fast, so I had to hurry to keep up.

Back on the main road there was no sign of the baker or the boys, and it was so busy I nearly lost the man who looked like my dad and even had his quickness.

Then I saw a sign that said 'Rue End Street' and had to stop and think what Mrs Strachan had said: Don't go there. That's where all the trouble starts. But I had to keep following too, in case it was my dad, even though he'd never have gone to a place with trouble.

There was a pub on the corner and another pub on the next corner too, but there were churches in between, so maybe it was alright. Maybe I could go to the church if there was trouble. The man seemed to be on urgent business and then, without warning, he crossed the road and turned into one of the pubs. Then, almost as quickly, he came back out, backwards. There was a shout, then another man staggered out past him and landed against a lamppost near the door. The man who might have been my dad didn't even look but carried on straight back into the pub and I stopped where I was to watch. The other man hugged the lamppost but then straightened himself and rubbed his forehead where he had banged it. He was unsteady on his feet, lurching to one side like the rubber man I saw earlier. He looked about, as if he was lost, so I smiled when he looked my way in case he needed help. Then he crossed the road and staggered towards me.

'My God,' he said. 'You girls just get younger and younger.'

This was clearly not possible but he lurched past me

before I could say so.

Another tram came past with its bell tinkling and two soldiers hanging off the back. 'There's one!' they shouted as they went past waving. This time I managed not to wave back but leant against a wall and concentrated on watching the pub door in case the man who might be my dad came back out.

It was so noisy there. Three horses and carts clattered past carrying the biggest barrels you ever saw just as something huge in the shipyards made the ground shake like an earthquake. Two men were shouting to each other from one end of the street to the other and most people were in uniforms. There were dockers too in ordinary bunnets and overalls like Mr Tait's. Every so often the roar of some giant engine would sound from the docks or the howl of a foghorn or the clang of metal. Smoke from the houses and yards hung in the mist and pulled at my throat.

The man did not reappear.

Two girls about sixteen came up to the door. They had flowery overalls sticking out under their coats and a pencil line up the back of their legs which wasn't quite straight. They stood outside whispering to each other and fiddling with their hair for a moment, then joined hands and went together into the pub. Into the pub! Maybe Mrs Strachan was wrong. Maybe it was alright to go in. Maybe I could too? There was a hurry, after all. I had to get the last train and it was already nearly dark.

I pulled my fingers through my hair, straightened my hat and rubbed the mud from my shins.

'Don't even think about it.' It was a lady in a coat that was too small for her. It was open at the front and her blouse wasn't buttoned properly. 'How old are you?' she said, and she blew smoke through fat red lips so that we were both suddenly in a cloud.

I put my hand to my nose. She was close enough for me to see little lines of red escaping up the creases round her mouth, even through the smoke.

'Go home,' she said, while I watched her lips. 'This is no place for nice girls.'

'I'm looking for my d ... dad,' I said.

'That's what they all say,' she said.

'No, really,' I said.

'They say that too,' she said.

'Why?' I said. 'Why would they say that if it's not true?'

Her brow crinkled beneath a crimson scarf. She pursed her painted lips. Then she leant in even closer so I could smell her heavy perfume.

'My God, you look like you've been through it,' she said.

I waited while she examined me. 'I really am looking for my dad,' I said. 'I think he went in there.' I pointed at the pub, noticing its name for the first time, The Lomond Bar.

She stood up tall and from the side of her mouth took another draw from her cigarette, gazing at me over her hand. 'What's he look like?' she said.

I showed her the photograph.

'He's a nice looking fellah,' she said, and she blew more smoke around me. 'Sorry, she said, batting it away, 'never seen him. I'll go and ask for you, if you want. Give us that.' She swiped the photo from my hand. 'You wait here.' Squeezing her cigarette out between her finger and thumb, she put the rest in her pocket and crossed the road.

'Thank you!' I said.

'What's his name?' she called back.

'Lenny Gillespie,' I said. ' Or …'

'What?'

'Nothing. That's my name too.'

While I waited, the two girls came out with a couple of soldiers in uniforms I didn't recognise. They seemed to know each other well. They laughed and chatted and walked along the street arm in arm. Arm in arm. With two soldiers. Even though they were too young to be in a pub in the first place. Mr Tait would have had something to say about that.

As if to emphasise the point there was a crash of glass shattering and raised voices further along the street. I couldn't see what had happened and pushed back against the wall as a man with a wheelbarrow full of giant bolts rolled past, then it was quiet again.

Ten minutes later the lady in the crimson scarf hadn't come back. Because of this terrible fact, an ache crept up the back of my neck and I felt sick. I was freezing cold too, still damp and starving. I felt like a ton weight but also slightly dizzy. A picture of my mum, Mavis and Rosie tucked up in bed at Carbeth came to me. It was almost blackout. Soon there would be no more trains.

So I crossed the road and went up the steps to the pub. A great stink came towards me of dirty men of all kinds, like my dad asleep at the fire after the pub, damp and smoky and sharp and sick-making like old cheese. The roar of them all talking at once made me want to stick my fingers in my ears.

I couldn't see the lady anywhere.

'Where's Rita?' someone shouted.

'Don't ask!' came a reply, and everyone laughed, though I couldn't see anything funny.

'You know this boy in the photo?' said the man nearest the door. He wasn't talking to me but the old man beside him. They were grimy and their elbows were worn through and needed mending. My mum could have helped, and made some money too.

'No,' said the old man. 'What photo is that?' He tipped the contents of his glass down his throat.

They all had their hats on, even though they were indoors. None of them looked even slightly like my dad.

'Rita had it. This one,' said the first man, searching along the bar. 'It's gone. She must have taken it with her. Some wee girl lost her dad. Not the first. Rita found her outside.'

They didn't notice me. I knew where the photo had gone. It was on the floor amongst the fag ends and dirt, leaning against the bottom of the bar. The old man's filthy black boot was right up beside it, the heel hovering inches from his face, ready to slam down on top of him the next time he cleared his throat.

I started forwards to get it, not caring who saw me.

But suddenly I was grabbed by the scruff of the neck and swung off balance so that I fell backwards and thudded into a man.

'Oh no you don't,' he said. 'Not in there you don't.

My coat cut sharp into my throat. He clutched the back of it and tugged.

'Good God, look at the size of you!' he said. 'You're barely out of nappies! May the good Lord have mercy on us all.'

I tried to scream but my throat was blocked. The men at the bar glanced over as if they saw this every day and turned back to their pints. And as I fell back down the steps, still in this man's grip, I saw the old drinker's boot shift round, turning its owner towards the bar for another glass.

'My, but you have the devil himself inside you,' said the voice behind me. 'May the Lord bless you and forgive you your sins.'

I was hauled backwards along the pavement with my arms like windmills and my feet half dragged and staggering. Then he spun me round and took me by the shoulders with hands that dug into me so hard I thought they'd meet in the middle. I stared up at him. He was a big man, but the blackout had fallen and all I could see were the whites of his eyes and a whiter collar which circled his neck like a giant smile. Somehow we were already a distance from the pub. He leant his face close down to mine so I could taste his breath and feel it damp against my eyes. His own eyes bored into mine as if he was trying to read my thoughts. There was nothing in there but sheer terror, my heart hammering like a blacksmith. His face moved away but he kept hold of my shoulders which meant my hands could only flail like useless wands at my side. Then he squeezed and shook me so hard my feet left the ground and my head jerked all over the place and I couldn't stop it.

He set me back on my feet and let go. As I swung about waiting for the world to stop spinning, or at least the pavement to come up and hit me, I heard him laugh.

'The Lord loves you!' he declared as if I'd won a prize.

Now I saw the gentle glow of the far off pub door as it glinted off a row of teeth. 'He loves you so much he's sent me to this place of iniquity to rescue you from terrible deeds. Praise the Lord and rejoice in his name. Hallelujah!'

Glory, glory, I thought as the world spun. *This surely is peculiar.*

As the dizziness left, the minister's face took shape in the dark, well-fed and smooth beneath a cloth cap, all his clothes black, even the hat.

'I ask you, oh Lord,' he said, 'to cleanse this young person's soul and forgive her her sins and those she was about to commit and …'

'I didn't,' I said, finding my voice again.

'Lord protect her from evil and …'

'And I wasn't about to,' I said. Fury rose up in me as I backed away. 'Get away from me! I've lost my dad,' I said. 'I'm looking for my dad.' Then I shouted: 'Dad!' to make him think my dad was close.

I glanced round his shoulder. The street was completely dark. The wind whistled through. I heard voices but saw nothing and no-one.

'Help!' I shouted as three sailors floated past, weaving their way through the dark.

'Evening,' muttered one, and they vanished, laughing.

But the minister's arms were long and he seized me by my coat again and started pulling me along. I screamed as hard as I could but he had me so tightly by the collar I could barely make a sound. Helpless. Shop doorways flickered past. The street stank like a cludgie. The pub was far behind. We crossed another road to a door, huge and dark, barely visible in the blackout. It echoed beneath his fist and my head began to pound.

'Help!' I squeaked. 'Help!'

A slither of light crept under the door and lit our feet, so I kicked at his legs. But he was quick and I missed. Then the light died and I couldn't see a thing. Pitch.

The door creaked open to complete darkness.

'There you are, Mrs Brindle,' said the minister. 'Your light escaped beneath the door. The Lord will not be pleased, not to mention Mr Jackson, our very own ARP officer.'

I heard Mrs Brindle mumble an apology in the dark.

'I brought you a little lost lamb,' he said. 'Watch her. She has the devil in her.'

He thrust me forward into the darkness and the door closed behind me.

Chapter 24

My screams echoed round me like in the cave at Rothesay and it was pitch black dark. Mrs Brindle tried to grab me, but lashing out with my arms I kept her away.

'Come here, child, and stop that,' she said. 'We're only trying to save you!'

I felt for the back of the door and ran my hands over it for a handle, but there were only screws and nuts and sharp things sticking out.

'Get away from me!' I shouted and screamed until my throat was ragged and sore.

'Alright, my dear,' she said quietly when I'd stopped. 'That's enough. There's no need to make such a noise.'

A match shooshed to life and the yellow glow of a candle swam across the door throwing my shadow up against it. I yanked at the handle, a huge iron loop beside a giant keyhole.

'It's locked,' she said. She set the candle on a long dark cabinet. Its light grew still. Her face was scored with deep wrinkles and she was tall in a long white apron.

I kicked the bottom of the door. 'Help!' I shouted.

'Lord preserve me,' she muttered from behind. 'You might as well stop that. No-one will hear you and it's dinner time anyway. You'll no doubt be hungry.'

'Help!' I shouted.

'You can join us when you're ready,' she said. She lifted the candle and started down some stairs, leaving me in the darkness. 'God be with you.' Then I heard her mutter to herself: 'Dear Lord, I'll never complain about the good reverend again, if you just deliver me from this little devil.' Her shadow played on the walls then faded.

For a second I wondered if she was right and there was a devil inside me. I certainly wanted to kill her and the minister.

I held onto the bannister at the top of some stairs and chewed my fingers. A light glowed at the bottom.

'I'm not going down there,' I yelled. A long silence followed, then I heard the murmur of voices. I went back to the door and tugged again and shouted through but nobody came.

After a few minutes I smelled onions, and then heard what sounded like chairs being drawn over a floor. There was a silence, then Mrs Brindle talking, then a loud 'Amen' followed by the clatter of cutlery off dinner plates. It was dark there all by myself, and chilly with the draught under the big door all the time. I moved as far from it as I could and sat on the cold stone of the top step. Hunger pains shot through my stomach and it rumbled painfully. I felt for the photo in my pocket, but of course it wasn't there, and I cursed myself for coming, crying furious tears. How stupid I was.

I longed for Mr Tait and remembered Mr Tulloch saying how you couldn't do anything without a good breakfast. All I'd eaten was carrots. I shuffled down a step, and then another, and then another. I was shivering with cold and hunger, and if I couldn't get out perhaps I could at least get some food, if they'd give me some. I was halfway down when I smelled pork, which I loved and which Mr Tait loved too. At the bottom I stood up and wiped my nose and eyes with my sleeve, and waited for them to notice me.

There were trestle tables along which sat two lines of children, their faces turned towards me, all with identical expressions of interest but no surprise, as if seeing a twelve-year-old girl snivelling and covered in cuts and gentian violet was absolutely normal.

Mrs Brindle, who was at the head of the table, stood up. 'Now children, we shall say a special grace tonight and remember our little sister here.'

The children seemed tired, blank faces with mouths hanging open. We all eyed the plates on the table, each one with two fat little sausages.

'Ready?' said Mrs Brindle.

No-one answered.

'Dear Jesus,' they began, 'our friend and saviour, please look after our little sister in this her hour of need.'

'The Lord can't hear you, children,' said Mrs Brindle. 'Louder!'

'I'm hungry,' I said, trembling.

'Brother James, stop crying.' Mrs Brindle's lungs were strong. She banged her hand off the table and there was silence. 'You should be happy. Another lost soul is being saved!'

Brother James sat at the far end of a bench with a big square mouth. He was younger than Mavis and Rosie and his obvious terror took my breath away, what was left of it. Poor little mite. Beside him was a face I recognised, the boy with the stolen rolls. He winked at me without changing his expression, then lowered his head in prayer.

'For the wonders of God's bounty,' said Mrs Brindle waving her arm to indicate they should follow, 'may we all be truly grateful.'

While they prayed, Mrs Brindle laid her hand gently across the small of my back and I said a silent prayer of my own. 'Dear God. I don't know how I got into this mess. I only meant to find my dad, but now that I'm in it I need some help please, if you're not too busy. I don't believe these people are real Christians because real Christians are kind like Mr Tait and these people are …' I was so scared I didn't know what they were. 'Dear God,' I whispered, and then out loud, without really meaning to I said. 'Let me out of here, please.'

There was an immediate surge in the prayers and Mrs Brindle put her arm around me and squeezed my shoulders.

'Please God,' I whispered to myself, closing my eyes. 'I promise I'll never fight anyone ever again, not even Ella or George, please, and I promise to believe in you too.'

I waited but nothing happened. So I opened my eyes and waited for the praying to stop. They'd have to soon or their sausages would be cold.

I noticed the sausages were small with mashed potato and more carrots. My stomach rumbled. A row of cox's oranges, which are actually apples, were lined up down the middle of the table. I closed my eyes, lowered my head and put my hands together.

'For what they are about to receive,' I said to myself, 'may they be truly generous and give me some too.'

The prayers came to a sudden halt. I opened my eyes. Mrs Brindle had her hand up as if she was stopping the traffic.

'Children,' she said, and she began to unwind my scarf as if I was five. 'Our prayers are answered. You may eat and feel happy that the Lord has listened.' There was a hum of approval followed by enthusiastic clanks of cutlery. 'Sweet child,' she said to me, 'welcome to our family of rescued children.'

I nearly said, 'I don't need rescued. I need my dad,' but that would have been useless. She wasn't a lady to listen, I could tell. So I gritted my teeth and smiled. It was difficult not to just stare at the sausages.

'Thank you,' I whispered.

She indicated I should take off my coat and then shoved me towards a chair close to hers at the table.

'Sit,' she said. 'Brother Andrew, more soup please.'

Brother Andrew, who was the roll thief, threw me a disgruntled look, scooped three forkfuls of mashed tattie into his mouth and pushed back his chair.

When it arrived, the soup was as delicious as I'd hoped, though there wasn't much of it. Unfortunately the second course was one little sausage, only one for me, an even smaller carrot (yet more carrots), the teensiest daud of mashed tattie and not a speck of butter, obviously, being war-time. My apple was so sharp it made my eyes water. All in, I could have eaten three times as much.

No-one uttered a single solitary lonely tiny little word. Mrs Brindle sat down beside me at the end of the table and ate almost as swiftly as Brother Andrew, but with less slurping. I ought to have been home helping my mum, and not chasing my stupid dad or getting into bother with Jeannie and wee Bobby and bad men in Greenock. This was my punishment. It's not like I wasn't warned.

Then suddenly I heard Mr Tait in my head. 'I'm sure you were doing your best, Lenny,' he said, 'and the benefit of hindsight is a wonderful thing.' I imagined him frowning at Mrs Brindle.

'Was I?' I said out loud.

Andrew tittered. I drank my cup of water and blushed. First sign of madness, talking to yourself, so my gran always said.

But Mr Tait wasn't there to rescue me. It was down to me, so I asked him silently what to do, but there was no answer.

Mrs Brindle stood up and something heavy in her long apron clunked against my knee. The tables were cleared into another room and pulled against a wall. Mattresses appeared from nowhere. Mrs Brindle sat me and my chair by a barrel stove in the corner and directed proceedings in shrill decisive bursts. I held my hands to the heat and positively squirmed with pleasure. Then she brought a bowl of warm water and sat down with a vague smile opposite me to clean my face.

The door upstairs sounded just as she began. Mrs Brindle leant into the bottom of her apron, pulled out a gigantic key and headed up the stairs, stopping midway to turn back and pierce me with her eyes. I moved swiftly and smoothly out of the chair, grabbed my coat and, glancing back once at Brother Andrew, tiptoed up the stairs. The cool air from outside swept over me. The front door was open and I heard Mrs Brindle and a lady.

'She's looking for her dad,' said the lady.

'What does any of this have to do with you?' said Mrs Brindle sharply.

'I was helping her, but I got a bit of business,' said the lady.

'I'm sure you got a bit of business. You should repent, Rita, before you're killed in a bombing raid and go straight to hell.'

There was a pause before Rita went on. 'We're all trying to survive, Mrs Brindle. I got a customer and when I came out she was gone. I wasn't away long. I'm guessing your friend the minister got her.'

'Rescued her, and just in time, by the sound of it.'

'What if she wasn't lost? What if she is just looking for her dad?'

From the top step I could see the gap in the door and guessed who was beyond it.

'Probably a different child anyway. Goodbye, Rita,' said Mrs Brindle.

The door boomed shut. I launched myself towards it. 'I'm here!' I yelled. 'Get me out!'

But the scrape of the key told me all was lost so I ran back downstairs and threw myself onto the chair as quick as a flash.

'Wash then bed,' said Mrs Brindle with a glare.

The long white apron swung with the means of my salvation. Brother Andrew stared at me from a mattress, pointed first to me, then to himself and then up the stairs, then abruptly closed his eyes.

'What are you waiting for?' said Mrs Brindle in a voice like a machine gun. 'Ungrateful besom.'

I put my coat back over the chair and dabbed at my face with a cloth that was floating in the water.

Mrs Brindle stood over me then handed me a tiny towel. I followed her to a bench beside a large wooden rocking chair. She handed me a blanket and pointed at the bench, then set a single candle high up on a shelf and turned off the electric light. She pulled a thick woollen shawl around herself in the rocking chair. Unbelievably, I fell straight to sleep, deep impenetrable sleep, so exhausted I was.

It seemed no time had passed when I was startled by Brother Andrew. 'Wake up!' he whispered urgently in my ear. Mrs Brindle responded with a loud snore. Andrew put a finger to his lips and showed me a giant key. The bench creaked under me in complaint. We stole up the stairs taking the candle with us and had just made it to the door when a great boom-boom-boom sounded on it.

'Mrs Brindle!' came the unmistakable voice of the minister. 'Your light is showing. How many times must I tell you?' The snoring stopped.

I held the candle for Andrew until we'd found the keyhole. He put the key in the lock then looked at me and held up three fingers, one after the other. Downstairs, James began to bawl. Mrs Brindle's footsteps beat the stairs.

'One, two three, go, okay?' said Andrew. I nodded.

'Come on woman, what's keeping you?' bellowed the minister through the door.

'What do you think you're playing at?' said Mrs Brindle arriving at the top of the stairs.

Andrew dropped the candle, which went out instantly, and said his, 'One-two-three-GO!' The key ground in the lock, the door creaked open. 'Run!' he yelled. 'Go on.'

The colossal minister filled the door. I crouched low and scooted past and, thinking I was safe, turned for Andrew, but instead found the minister. Mrs Brindle shouted, Andrew screamed and then a roar from the docks shook the ground underneath us.

The minister had me by the shoulder.

'The devil will not get you,' he growled at me.

There was the tiniest pause of peculiarly complete silence.

Then all the bombs inside me went off at once.

'NO!' I yelled.

I can only tell you I made contact with his jaw because the rest of it's a blur, but my fight with Ella pales in comparison. My fist cracked against his face and a pain shot up my arm, but that's all I remember. And his yelp of shock. And my own cries as soon as the darkness fell. The moment I was free of him I stumbled into the night streets waving my arms until they hit a wall, and the rest of me soon after, then slid quickly along it until it ran out and I turned a corner.

The devil was not going to have me.

'Lord save me!' wailed the minister somewhere far behind. I heard him moan in agony, then Mrs Brindle shouting for Andrew, then there was quiet except for my own extremely heavy breathing.

Chapter 25

As if I'd been infected by the minister's religious excitement, I started muttering 'oh God, oh God' over and over, and shivered as though I was freezing cold, which I definitely wasn't, thanks to my exertions. But then suddenly I was. And then, immediately afterwards, I wasn't again. My whole body didn't seem to know what it was doing.

The boom of the church door shutting rang out through the night. I listened for footsteps behind me and dragged my shoulder along the wall, walking my hands across the surface as fast as I was able until I heard a whistle. It was too cheerful to be the minister, but I flattened myself against the wall anyway and hoped I wouldn't be seen.

'Andrew?' I whispered.

'Evening!' said a cheery voice. I made out a soldier's uniform, the whistle started up again, the footsteps passed and fell in time with the whistle and then faded down the road.

A thunderous groan sounded from the shipyards and sent shudders up the wall and through my back. *Don't panic*, I told myself as I sank to a crouch and willed my heart to stop thumping so I could think something sensible and get my bearings.

The air was suddenly full of roaring engines and

the bang of riveters, and their noise seemed to rise and rise. These were the reassuring sounds of my life in Clydebank: shipyards and docks, factories and motors, men shouting instructions, not threatening but business-like, containers landing on the quayside with supplies for hungry Britain, goods trains whistling their approach, thundering their departure. All strangely comforting, and they worked through the night because of the war.

So I stayed on my hunkers for ages until my heart slowed. A motor car crept past, honking a warning. A street sign flashed: Rue End Street, exactly where I shouldn't be. The last train was gone and I'd never find Mrs Strachan in the dark. What on earth to do?

My neck and mouth were tender, my arm hurt and my hands were ragged from the walls. In fact most of me hurt in one way or another, and when I tried to stand, I found my legs had gone so entirely to sleep that pains began to shoot up my legs as the blood rushed back in.

People approached, shadows in the blackout.

'Can't see a damn thing here,' said a man.

'Excuse you, mate. Watch where you're putting your feet, bloody great clod-hoppers you've got, if you don't mind my saying so.'

'Ouch, that's a wall! I'm sure that never used to be there.'

It was such a relief to hear someone giggling I almost joined in. They passed without seeing me.

Their laughter rang against the walls, a metal shaft squealed through a stirrup and light flared from a doorway allowing their silhouettes to slip through. The door clanged shut, leaving me in darkness but with a better idea of where I was.

There were no more train whistles up the hill, only the trundle of goods trains beyond the shipyard door and a tram which came humming round a corner and cut straight across the road a little further on, dinging its bell. I waited until it had passed then sneaked over the road and into a shop doorway. I needed a place to spend the night, somewhere I could be safe. I was utterly dog-tired, but scared to sleep in case anything happened. The doorway was smelly, like old cabbage and cludgies, but deep enough to hide in and be safe from the weather and any prying eyes. I crouched down, pulled my hat over my ears and held my nose until I couldn't any more.

But then I heard a voice I knew.

'You'll have to take me to the doctor, Mrs Brindle. The little devil's broken my jaw.'

'Are you sure it was the girl who hit you? Not Brother Andrew?' said Mrs Brindle.

'As God's my witness,' replied the minister. 'There's nothing so shocking as a child full of the devil.'

'Yes, Reverend, but I do believe there's very little can be done for a sore jaw, and the poor doctor's so busy with the men.'

'Are you a doctor now yourself, Mrs Brindle, that you know so much? May God forgive your immodesty.'

I crouched as still as still, hoping they wouldn't look my way, but Mrs Brindle had a small torch with her.

'Take the paper off that torch Mrs Brindle,' said the reverend, 'so we can see what we're doing here. I've already been caused enough harm tonight.'

'Well, Reverend, I don't think that would be wise. Mr Jackson the ARP is very strict and …'

'Mrs Brindle, have you forgotten you are doing God's work?' he said. 'Give me God's torch immediately.'

There was that Miss Weatherbeaten word again: immediately. I wondered if the minister and Miss Weatherbeaten were related.

The paper was for the blackout, to dim the torch. Everyone had to do it. I heard it scrunch and held my breath, but the beam went the other way. They were on a corner, a few feet away, but not facing me. I was dizzy trying not to breathe before they'd gone far enough not to hear me.

The rain was hanging in the air. I saw it in the shaded lights of a tram which tinkled towards me out of the darkness then faded into the night. I pushed back into the doorway and drew my coat around me. An old newspaper had been blown into the corner, not too damp. I could just make out **GIRLS SET TOWN A PROBLEM**. It should have been the other way round: **TOWN SETS GIRL MANY PROBLEMS**. I pulled the paper over my head and leant into the corner of the doorway. Stupid, that's what I was, for not listening to Mr Tulloch. Really it was all my own fault.

But sleep was impossible. It was noisy and I was too cold, too wet and too sore and my head was buzzing like a motor car, wondering how I'd got into such a mess. The docks went clatter-bang and the newspaper fell into the puddle beside me. Men were shouting, then their voices faded. A motor started, thrumming the air. Footsteps sounded on the road. The glow of a cigarette moved through the wet night then vanished. Someone muttered curses. Then, in a sudden burst, hurried footsteps drummed out and a man rushed past, then another, until suddenly one long scream rent the air and someone else yelled 'There they go! Over here!' and hundreds of pairs of feet thundered by. A lady suddenly appeared in my doorway, sheltering but not from the rain, gasping as if she'd been running. She didn't see me. A motor car shooshed on the road slower than you'd walk, its dimmed beam picking out the lady's legs, and a doorway opposite where two people huddled. Then darkness fell again and the lady left.

I ached for home, for my family, and was woozy with exhaustion. In my drowsiness I heard someone call my name. I tried to stand, but my legs were dead with sleep again and I my head light and dizzy. I gave my legs a shake and peered out and heard it again, my name, but from a different direction, which scared me awake: I was losing my senses. The next time it was high, quite shrill, and I realised it wasn't inside my head at all. I considered the ridiculous possibility that Mavis and Rosie had tracked me down all the way to Greenock.

'Mavis?' I said, willing my eyes to see, my ears to hear. 'Hello? Rosie? Are you there?'

The street was not empty, but I could only make out shadows of movement. No-one came to me or called again and I couldn't shout for fear of the minister. Perhaps I had imagined it, after all, just a cruel trick of my brain. Oh, how I needed Mr Tait. I stumbled back into the doorway and blinked and I thought I'd die of misery instead of cold. I was just about to risk it and shout when the minister and Mrs Brindle came by with their torch.

'What kind of doctor is he?' said the minister in tones of amazement. 'A man has his jaw broken and he's sent home by the doctor's wife? Without even talking to the doctor? There will be words. I shall write to the … . ' But I didn't catch who he'd write to because they were passing right in front of me and Mrs Brindle had me in her beady eye. I saw both her beady eyes in fact, which were glinting under her hat, but only for a split second, during which my heart practically leapt up through my throat and out my mouth. Luckily the minister was oblivious.

'Silly child,' she said and continued up the street. 'That's one little lost lamb we can forget about.'

I did an inward somersault for joy and whispered a secret thanks, but kept very quiet and extremely still.

'The devil will look after his own,' replied the minister before vanishing into the night.

So I had to wait and not call out for Mavis and Rosie and started walking the other way. After feeling my way along a wall, I found the great gap of a close mouth between two shops and decided to go in and hide. It was time to shout as loud as I could.

'Mavis! Rosie!' I called. 'Mum!' I hung in the shadows. 'I'm here! It's me!' I shouted for ages but no-one came and after about five minutes a door suddenly opened upstairs in the close and someone yelled down at me.

'They're not bloody here! Go and shout in your own close!' Then they mimicked me: 'Mavis, Rosie, Mum! … . Go home. Bloody young 'uns!'

'Sorry,' I said, wishing I could go home. 'It's just …' But there was no point. The door slammed.

I felt my way along the street and continued calling, but no-one answered and suddenly I couldn't bear my own voice any more, or the silence that followed, and

I came to the conclusion that I must have imagined them after all, which seemed so cruel, for my own brain to play tricks on me. I was suddenly utterly bereft and lost and plumped down on a doorstep and sobbed and shook, and then, just when I didn't think things could get any worse, I remembered little Bobby and the blob of spit, and then the things I'd seen during the bombing and which I shouldn't have looked at because I'd been told not to. These things used to haunt me like ghosts for weeks and months afterwards and make me jump, as if they'd come out of the dark and gone 'boo!' So all I could do on that doorstep was curl myself tight in a coalbunker door and cry and long for Mr Tait.

I forgot about my dad completely: what did he matter? I felt like a bruise throbbing, hurting inside and out, and that nothing could ever make the hurt go away. Mr Tait couldn't save me in that strange dark town bristling with things that weren't there and scary people who were. This fact was like those walls I kept bumping into: solid, hard, cold and utterly immovable.

I was so busy crying I didn't hear the footsteps until they were already at the close. I scuttled backwards out of sight.

'Lenny?' she said. 'Is that you?'

I kept back, not understanding. I knew that voice but in my confusion couldn't remember who it was.

A torch clicked on then swooped in at me. The light made my eyes hurt and I held my arm as a shield.

'Oh my God, look at you, you poor darling! It is you. You're a bag of rags.' She came towards me as I backed away along the floor. 'It's me, Rita, remember?'

she said. 'Don't be scared. Look.' She threw the beam in her own face. 'Outside the Lomond Bar? What happened? What did he do to you? Don't worry, I won't touch you.'

I could barely see her through my tears. Suddenly she got up and shouted out the close door.

'George! I found her! Over here. I'm in here. George? Where are you? Number ... there's no number on this.'

I wiped my nose on my sleeve, both sleeves in fact, and got up on my knees and shook myself to stop trembling. Rita vanished as suddenly as she'd arrived, but reappeared almost immediately to tell me to stay where I was before disappearing into the night again, taking her torch with her.

Had I imagined her too?

I wasn't used to crying like a baby. I didn't want to. I had to stop. We all had to be strong. There was a war on after all, as everyone was forever saying. We couldn't allow ourselves to go to pieces, my mum said so. Miss Read said so. The government said so. They couldn't all be wrong. I tried.

But Mr Tait never said that. He was always kind after the bombing, and he let me cry and listened when I was worried, and was quick with his big white handkerchiefs. I wobbled upright, straight and tall, wiped my nose and my eyes with the other side of my sleeves, and when Rita came back I tried hard to smile. She was a grown-up. She wouldn't understand. But I couldn't smile, no matter what, I couldn't.

'George'll be here in a minute,' she said. 'What happened? How did you get out of the crypt? That was clever. You gave the old rev quite an eye too.'

She unwound the scarf from her neck, handed it to

me and indicated my face.

'I thought it was his jaw,' I said. I mopped my face, noticing the perfume on the scarf.

'Maybe you got both,' she said. 'Well done. He's a nasty piece of work.' She glanced away and blew raspberries. 'You can blow your nose on that thing too if you want.'

This seemed rude and ungrateful but she insisted, so I blew and wiped and cleaned myself up, and finally she took a dry corner of the scarf and rubbed my hair with it and I stood straight and let her.

'Here's George coming,' she said.

I had thought George was her husband, but of course I was wrong, again. It took me a moment to realise it was my George, Bad George of Carbeth, originally from Clydebank, who I had inadvertently knocked into the canal the night of the bombing. He perched on the doorstep and dripped from the top of Mr Tait's hat, from the sleeves of his own jacket and from the cuffs of his working trousers, as if he'd fallen in again.

'There you are,' he said, and he put his two hands on his head as if his hat had been about to fly off and let out a huge sigh. 'At last! Thank God for that.'

'Why are you here?' I said. 'I don't understand.' The tears started. 'I want to go home. Where are Mavis and Rosie? I don't understand.'

Rita put her arms out and I let myself be wrapped in them.

'I've been looking all over the shop for you,' said George.

'I don't understand,' I wailed. 'Where's Mavis? How did you find me?'

'Jeez, Lenny, you're a mess. Why did you have to go traipsing about the countryside? And no, I didn't bring Mavis. Why would I bring Mavis? That would have been crazy.'

I didn't know whether to be relieved or disappointed. She was safe at home, so was Rosie. 'But I heard her,' I said. 'I don't know. I thought I heard them. I was looking for my dad. I want to go home now. I want to go to Carbeth. I don't want to find my dad now, not any more.'

'Why didn't you just ask your mum about him like I did?'

Perhaps it was the red scarf catching the light from Rita's torch, which seemed to be swinging about, up and down the close sides and sliding across the floor, but suddenly I saw red everywhere, as if it was raining red in the close. I broke from Rita.

'What exactly did my mum tell you?' I said, shaking the rats' tails out of my face.

'Nothing,' he said, shifting his weight against the doorway, 'except he might be in Helensburgh. Don't be angry. I came all the way here to find you. Mr Tait told me to keep an eye on you, didn't he? You know he did.'

That's when I fell to pieces, or at least fell down. I had this strange hot cold feeling up my back and neck and into the top of my brain. George and Rita disappeared into the darkness and the ground came up and struck me on the head. When I came to, George had gone and I was sitting on the bottom step of the close stairs leaning on Rita. Some light was escaping from the window over the road. The rain was vertical, the kind you know will last forever.

'There you are,' she said. 'Poor baby. George has gone to get you tea from the mission.' She stroked at her red scarf which was wrapped around my shoulders. Her lips were red again too. 'Shouldn't be long.'

'What happened?' I shivered. I was cold, so cold, and heavy.

'You passed out completely. Went down like a ton of bricks. When did you last eat?'

'I had soup and a sausage with Mrs Brindle,' I said. I wiped my tears with my fingers and felt new hot ones form.

'He'll be here soon.'

George came with tea and fish paste sandwiches.

'Thank you,' I said, with a sniff. 'Thank you, George.' Words I never thought I'd say to him. I started on the sandwiches, but it was hard because my nose kept running and a lump had formed in my throat.

'Right,' said Rita, propping me against the wall so she could stand. 'That's me away. You stay out of trouble, young lady, and go home safely with your brother, George. You can come back another day for your dad.'

'He's not my brother,' I said between sniffs.

'No?' she said. 'Who is he then?' She unwound her scarf from my shoulders.

'He's George,' I said stupidly, nibbling a sandwich.

'We're old friends,' said George, laughing. He looked down at me and smiled.

'Enemies actually,' I said with a sob.

'Well, he seems like a good sort of enemy to me,' said Rita. 'He's probably lost his job because of you.'

'Oh no! Has he?' I said. I put the sandwich down on my knee and wiped both eyes at the same time.

'Maybe,' said George. 'But it doesn't matter.' He crouched in front of me. 'Mr Tait told me to look after you and that comes first.' He squeezed my shoulder.

'Oh no!' I wailed. 'I don't need looking after,' I said weakly, and made a show of trying to shrug him off.

'Um, actually you do. George, make sure you do it,' said Rita. 'And get her home.'

She moved to leave but I held on to her coat.

'No,' I said. 'Don't go, please.'

'Listen love, I've got to go,' she said, catching my sandwich as it fell. 'I've missed half a night's work already.'

Then she wiped my cheek and kissed my head, gave me a hug that didn't smell good, got up and left.

I watched her disappear into the darkness and suddenly felt colder than ever.

But she came back.

'You'd better have this,' she said. 'Sorry, but nobody knew him.' She handed me the little photograph of my dad.

'Oh my goodness!' I said. 'Thank you!' It had a corner missing and the stripes of a boot on the back of it. I pressed him against my lips for a second, then wailed, 'I don't know what to do!'

George shifted over onto the step beside me where Rita had been. He put an arm round me and waited for me to stop shaking. When I looked again, Rita was gone.

Chapter 26

While I ate the fish paste sandwiches, George told me how he'd got there.

Mavis told Rosie where I'd gone, silly billy, so Rosie said to Mrs MacIntosh in the kitchen that I'd gone to find my dad. When my mum came home, Mrs MacIntosh told my mum and she went to find George at the workers' hostel he was in. George was having his dinner but he promised my mum he'd find me no matter what. And then she went home happy. So he says. I doubt it. She must have been worried sick. Anyway then he went to work.

'I thought your job was at John Brown's,' I said.

'It is,' he said. 'But some nights I'm a river patrol cadet too. Mr Tait got me started. The captain's a friend of his.'

'River patrol? What's that?' I said. He had given me his wet cap to wear, which was really Mr Tait's, because mine was sodden and we were walking back towards the dock with the teacup he'd brought my tea in.

'We go up and down the river checking for Germans and strange goings on. We only go as far as Bowling usually but I got them to pass me on to the crew for the next bit of the river and they dropped me at the pier at Craigendoran.'

At Craigendoran he heard there had been a stowaway and what she'd looked like and how the whole afternoon's schedule had been messed up because of her.

'And I thought, that's my Lenny!' he said.

And I said, 'I'm not your Lenny. I'm not anybody's Lenny.' Except Mavis, Mum and Rosie's. And Mr Tait's, of course, even if he did get George an exciting job on the river.

'That's not what I meant,' said George, with a sigh. 'Anyway, the patrol boat took me to Greenock, to here. Exactly here,' he said, pointing at a gap between ships at the pier side where we'd just arrived.

So George asked questions and generally followed his nose and, like me, wound up on Rue End Street in Rita's bar, the Lomond Bar. He asked there if anyone had seen a girl of twelve with dark hair and purple gentian violet all over her face and they said yes.

George then tried to order a drink at the bar to celebrate but the barman said it wasn't a nursery.

'Cheeky bastard!' said George. 'There's a war on, doesn't he know? Things are different now. I'm a man, working and everything.'

I bit my lip. He had, after all, rescued me, so for the time being it seemed only fair to give him peace.

Then Rita had appeared and told him about the photograph and the whole pub was in an uproar trying to find the photo of my dad. Somebody's pint got knocked over and another man's went missing and there was nearly a fight. George told me Rita felt guilty that she hadn't brought it straight back so she offered to help look for me. Then they bumped into the minister in the blackout, literally.

I began to shake just thinking about the minister.

'Any luck tonight?' Rita had said.

'There is no such thing as luck,' replied the reverend, 'only God's will.'

'And?' said Rita.

God had indeed brought the minister a lost soul.

'How lost?' said Rita.

The minister told them and offered to save Rita's soul too.

'My soul is safe, thank you, Reverend,' said Rita, and they watched him disappear into the dark heart of the Rue End.

So George had also been there when Rita called in at the church.

George and I stumbled along the shadowy quayside where a line of ships lay in darkness and there were plenty of things to trip over. He had me by the arm and was steering me along. Ordinarily I'd have told him to get off but for once he seemed to know what he was doing and I was too tired to argue.

'Where d'you think you're going?' said a voice. A face flashed in the beam of a torch, then vanished, a soldier. The light stole swiftly across our own two faces and died again.

'I found a fugitive,' said George. 'She stowed away on the *Lucy Ashton* this afternoon.'

'George!' I complained, but he squeezed my arm so it hurt.

'Aye, right! That's only a girl,' said the man.

'You mean you didn't hear the story? I'm taking her back to the ship,' said George.

'Yeah I did, but the *Lucy Ashton* went ages ago,' said the man, 'and no thanks to her.'

'The police, I mean, at the station on Princes Pier,' said George, and he pinched me.

'Ow! No you're not!' I said, right on cue and yanked at his grip on my arm.

'Hmm,' said the man. 'Alright, on your way, then, get a move on.'

So on our way we went and after a couple of steps George loosened his grip.

'You didn't have to hang on so tight,' I said, shrugging him off. 'It's not like I don't have enough bruises already.'

'You're not supposed to be here at all,' he hissed back and let go of me. Then he went on ahead and I fell head over heels on a pile of rope.

George came to a halt and laughed like he'd never stop. I was so tired I stayed there on the ropes and rubbed all my sore bits and wanted to die or at least sleep. But when I didn't get up or shout or laugh, he fell silent.

'You alright?' he said. 'Lenny? Where are you?'

I sank down into the ropes but they creaked and gave me away.

'I'm going over there to the mission to give this cup back,' he said somewhere in the dark. 'Just watch out for the rats.'

'Wait! I'm coming with you!' I said and hurried after him.

Then we were at a door. He pushed it open without waiting and suddenly we were in a warm bright place with steam billowing out of a huge shiny boiler on a counter. A lady was behind it and the rest of the big low-ceilinged room was full of tables with people sitting at them having tea and sandwiches and soup and smoking. There was a steady murmur of voices.

'Here's your cup back,' said George, landing it on the counter.

'So this is her?' said the WVS lady, raising an eyebrow. She leant across the counter at me and I noticed a crumb on her top lip. 'Bit of a mess, aren't you darling? What happened to you?'

'She got pulled in by a minister up on the Rue End,' said George, and he started explaining everything all over again.

I looked about the room and wondered if my dad had ever been there, or if he was there right then. It was mostly men in working clothes and a few in uniforms.

'Excuse me,' I said, interrupting George and his long showy-off explanation. 'Have you ever seen this man?' I held up the photo for the lady to see but kept a firm grip on the corner so she couldn't take it away.

'What on earth did you do to your hand?' she exclaimed. 'Let me see.' She looked it over, completely ignoring the photo. 'And the other one.'

'I had a fight with a few walls,' I said, with a sniff, as if to say, 'Haven't we all?' Everyone bumped into things all the time in the blackout. Some people even got killed bumping into cars, or rather cars bumping into them.

'Dearie me!' said the lady, rubbing her nose and knocking the crumb off her lip in the process. 'And what about your face?'

'She had a fight with a girl instead of a wall,' said George.

'Oh,' said the lady. 'Well, that's not so good. Fighting's not very ladylike you know.'

Yes, I did know that, I wanted to say, and also, *but you would not believe what's been happening*.

She put a giant lid on a pot on the stove beside her, leant across the counter and took my hand in hers. 'Ouch!' she said. 'Come round to the sink.' And without letting go of me she led me along the counter and in behind to a big china sink.

'So have you seen my dad?' I said.

'Yes, probably,' she said. 'I've seen everyone else's dad.'

She looked down at me and we both burst out laughing. I stopped when she turned on the tap and stuck my hand underneath it. She scrubbed off the blood and dirt that the rain hadn't removed as if she was cleaning carrots. It hurt like nobody's business. Then she took a dish towel and wrapped it round them so they were tied together and told me to go and sit with my big brother ('He's not my brother!') and she'd bring me soup and I could think about how I was going to get home.

George said the patrol boat would be back about half one in the morning. A big old clock the size of the moon said it was half past midnight, so there was no rush.

I told him I wasn't going.

'Not going?' he said, and the soldiers at the next table turned to look.

'I've nearly found my dad,' I said.

'No, you haven't!'

'Yes, I have,' I said.

The room went quiet.

'No, Lenny, you haven't. You haven't a clue where he is.' He tapped the salt cellar three times on the table.

'Yes, I do. I know where to look, anyway,' I said. 'And I know where not to go.'

The lady brought the soup. 'No squabbling, children,' she said. This cheered me up, George being called a child.

George scowled, sat up in his chair and threw an arm over the back. Then, without looking, he lifted the mug of tea she had brought him and took a drink. I could tell by the colour of his face and the way he sucked air, he had burnt his tongue. Then he turned slowly towards me and his eyes had gone small in the way that always scared me.

'I didn't have to come here,' he said, under his breath so nobody could hear. 'I didn't have to chase around all over bloody Greenock in the bloody rain for an ungrateful little runt like you. I could have stayed at home in bed.'

'I thought you were working on the patrol thing, on the river,' I hissed back. 'You're skiving from work.'

'I'm not. This isn't my night. I just hitched a lift. I'm working in John Brown's at eight in the morning.'

'You still didn't need to come.' I didn't feel good saying this and it wasn't how I felt either. I was so pleased he was there I could almost have hugged him, if he hadn't been George. But he was George and I had to remind myself how insanely nasty he was capable of being.

'You'd still be in that close if it wasn't for me,' he said. 'You can't look after yourself even for a day. Pah! I should never have said yes to Mr Tait. I should have said, there's no stopping that one, no looking after a nutcase like that.' He drew in a great sniff, crossed his legs and turned away from me.

I took a spoonful of soup and felt the flavour spread round my mouth. It was such a delicious feeling, so much better than Mrs Brindle's, that I had to close my eyes and follow the sensation as it moved down my throat and into my stomach. I went back for another mouthful.

'You're coming with me whether you like it or not,' he said. His eyes were so narrow I could hardly see the glint in them.

I went back to my soup and thought about my friend Mr Tulloch who always said I should have a plan. The trouble is my plans so often go astray.

Exhausted though I was, scared and sore though I was, I knew it just didn't make sense to go home. Home was a long way away, all the way back to Clydebank and over the hill to Carbeth, and anyway, I knew it wasn't home any more, even though it felt like it. Mum and Mavis and Rosie were my home, but George could take a message to them and I could stay and find my dad. Surely they'd understand that? George must understand, didn't he? I'd only have to come back again anyway and I could stay and help the mission ladies and maybe they'd let me have a little sleep in the corner for my trouble. Nobody would mind.

I yawned. The soup seemed to be that kind of soup, the kind that made you sleepy.

'Come on, let's go,' he said as soon as I'd put down my spoon.

'George,' I said. 'Thank you for coming here for me.'

His eyebrows slid down.

'No, really,' I said. 'Really honestly. If you and Rita

hadn't rescued me I'd still be in that close, frozen to death or maybe the minister would have found me again.'

He looked at me sideways.

'And, um, I made a friend on my way there.'

He nodded in that here-it-comes way.

'You're coming home,' he said, and stood up.

'I'm not,' I said, and I stood up too.

We glared at each other. The soldiers at the next table stopped talking again to look.

'Why don't you ever do what you're supposed to do?' he growled.

'Did you know my dad was in Helensburgh?' I said.

'Not until today,' he said.

'Did you know about Bobby?' I said, lowering my voice.

'Bobby?'

'My wee brother,' I said, even quieter. This was the strangest thing I'd said in a while and it shut me up for all of ten seconds while I fiddled with my fingers.

'Yup,' he said, at last. He lowered his voice. 'Mr Tait told me not to tell.'

I gulped. I wasn't sleepy any more, not even slightly. My ears tingled, the way they do when other people are talking about you. I plumped back down in my seat. Some men came in the door, letting a blast of cold air through the room. George sat back down too and leant over the table at me.

'Lenny … ,' he said.

I stared at him hard and made my eyes as small as his had been.

'Does my mum know?' I said.

Suddenly his hand flew up to his mouth. I flinched,

thinking he was going to hit me, but instead he started biting his fingernails as if he hadn't eaten in a fortnight. Then he leant on his fist and stared at the table. We sat like that for a long time with all the people shifting chairs round about us and the ladies serving up tea with such cheerfulness it made me want to go behind the counter and stay there forever and pretend.

'George,' I said, leaning over towards him. 'Do you know where my dad is?'

'No,' he said looking at me at last. 'If he's not in Helensburgh I've no idea.'

I thought about this for a minute. It was good news and bad news.

'Will you take me to my friend's house, Mrs Strachan, back up the main road and up the hill by the church? She's a very old lady and she said I could go there if I needed help. I can't go home. I need more time. You have to help me, George. You do.'

He sat back down in his seat and jerked his head towards the door. 'Home,' he said.

'I don't have a proper home any more,' I said. 'I don't have Carbeth or Mr Tait. I want my dad. Don't you understand?' We sat in silence for ages with the door banging shut every two minutes and some people at the back of the room laughing all the time.

'I hate my dad,' he said at last.

'That's not the point,' I said. 'I'm sorry you hate your dad. Please?'

He bent over, his head in his hands. I managed to keep my mouth shut. I know it wasn't like me.

'Okay,' he said after ages and ages more. 'But we've got to be quick getting you up there and you have to come home tomorrow. You have to promise.'

'Thank you, thank you!' I said. I rushed over to the counter with my soup bowl. 'Thank you to you too! Come on, George.'

First George had to go and tell someone he might be late for the boat, then we set off through the dark smoky streets back into town and the town hall with the big church next door to it where I had met Mrs Strachan. George held me by the wrist all the way because there was so little light. On the way I told him about the tram that nearly ran me down, deaf Mr Gregory in Helensburgh, the Germans on the truck, and Rocco. I made him promise not to tell Mavis or Rosie about Bobby or anything else so that I could tell them together myself.

There was no answer at Mrs Strachan's door so, remembering how she'd warned me about the Rue End in the first place, I nearly turned back down the hill, but George turned the handle and it opened. We found a fire dying in the grate and a candle which George lit with his matches. Mrs Strachan was in an armchair with a crochet blanket over her in every colour of the rainbow. She was snoring quietly so we didn't disturb her. The bed in the alcove was empty. I climbed in and wriggled down under the covers.

'This is strange. Do you think it's alright?' I whispered.

'Well, it's a bit late now, isn't it?' he replied. 'I'll come back tomorrow if I can. Don't forget your promise.'

'Tell my mum I'm alright.' I don't even remember hearing the door close behind him.

Chapter 27

Hours later I woke up feeling heavy and warm and blissfully happy. I had slept the rest of the night undisturbed, not even by dreams. I lay on my back and thought about how I'd like to stay where I was, in Carbeth, forever.

Then I thought I was in Greenock in Mrs Brindle's crypt after an ordeal with the minister so I opened my eyes double-quick to see if I had made it all up. Mrs Strachan was filling a kettle at the sink.

Her breathing was heavy, as if she'd just walked up the hill, but she was wearing a pink dressing gown and red slippers with bobbles on the toes. I watched her limp to the fire and set the kettle over it. Then she leaned to one side, turned on one foot and made her way back to the sink.

It was a single end like ours in Clydebank before the bombing. The window over the sink was steamed up and streaky but beyond it there was a bright sunny day. A loud clock ticked out the time and there was the crochet blanket over the armchair. Mrs Strachan set a teapot down at the sink.

'Good morning, dear,' she said, without turning round. 'What kind of trouble sent you here?'

'Good morning. Well … I …' I sighed and gazed at the ceiling.

'The Rue End?' she said, hobbling back to the stove for the kettle.

So I sat up and rediscovered how sore and bruised I was all over and told her about the minister and Mrs Brindle and Rita and George.

She nodded quietly. 'I did tell you not to go down the Rue End, didn't I?'

'Yes, I know, sorry, and I didn't mean to. It's just that I have to find my dad,' I said.

'You have to find some sense,' she replied, arranging breakfast things on a tray. 'Porridge?'

Mrs Strachan made the best porridge I've ever tasted. It was thick and gluey and made my stomach stick out I ate so much of it, plus I got to sit up in bed like we did at home if we were sick. I made a silent wish that by some strange fate Mrs Strachan would turn out to be my granny instead of the mean one I had.

'Greenock never used to be like that,' she said. 'It was always a bit wild but not like now. There are so many people now, all from different places and you don't know who anyone is any more.' She shook her head in exasperation. 'And of course a lot of our own have gone, evacuated or fighting or ...' She drew a breath and stopped.

I finished the porridge and she took the bowl.

'Better?' she said.

'Yes,' I said. 'Thank you.'

'You have nice manners,' she said. 'That's something.' She leant on the bed. 'Were you there when Clydebank was bombed?'

'Yes,' I whispered.

She stroked my arm. 'Were your family alright?'

'Yes,' I said, 'once I'd found them.' I didn't want to think about it. I didn't want to be asked. 'Were you here when Greenock was bombed?'

'Yes,' she said. She hobbled back to the sink with my porridge bowl. 'I was in that chair. I'd hurt my knee and couldn't move. My neighbours wanted to carry me to the shelter but I said, no, you go. You'll be quicker without me. What does it matter an old bat like me?' She laughed.

'Were they alright?' I said.

'Just a couple of broken arms and some burns.' She shrugged. 'We all hobbled around together after that!'

We sat in silence a minute. Then I showed her the photo.

'He's a handsome young man!' she declared. She was flushed from standing by the stove but sat down in the green armchair for a proper look. She stared at my dad in his little photo. 'I'd remember a face like that.'

I held my breath and leant over her shoulder.

'What's his name again? You're very alike.'

So I gave her both names.

'Oh yes,' she said, and laughed. 'A citizen of the world, I remember.'

She stared at the photo a while longer, so long I thought she might have fallen asleep, but instead she sighed and handed it back to me.

'No?' I said.

'Don't think so. Sorry. I'll have a little think. Maybe I'll remember something.'

She said both the Italian cafés in Greenock had been taken over for war purposes at the beginning of the war and later the owners were arrested with all the

312

other Italians. She also said there were lots of Italian prisoners in Greenock already and had been for ages. They were working alongside our own men and going back to camps at the end of the day. Of course, I didn't want to say but this particular Italian *was* one of our own men. Unfortunately, she didn't know where the camps were.

'I suppose the ones they arrested will be allowed back now Italy's not with Hitler any more,' she said. 'Your dad could be anywhere. I'm so sorry. Poor you. Good luck!'

I thanked her and left and set off down the hill, my heart doing somersaults. The day was brighter and Mrs Strachan had given me ideas about where to look. From her front door I could see Helensburgh beyond a glittery sea full of ships. The sky was a perfect blue with puffs of white racing across it. I went straight down the hill to the road where I'd met her the day before.

Outside the police station I waited for the courage to go in, but finding none went to the town hall first. It was much bigger than the town hall in Clydebank and even posher with pillars and towers and fancy windows.

But then George appeared in front of me and not only that he had Ella with him, of all people. They were both grinning their heads off as if they had just won a million pounds.

'Shouldn't you be at work?' I said. If I'm absolutely honest, which I always try to be unless there's a good reason not to, I was pleased to see George. I can't believe I'm saying this about bad George, but there it is. It was mainly because he was familiar, like an old blanket that needs a wash and is full of holes. But also, after meeting the minister I was nervous wandering alone, even in daylight.

'Hi, Lenny,' said Ella. 'We came down on the train.' You'd have thought no-one had ever gone on a train before, she looked so pleased with herself.

'Bully for you,' I said. I was not happy to see Ella.

'Did you find your dad yet?' she said.

'Mind your own business,' I said. 'What's she doing here?'

George seemed distracted by his fingernails.

'No need to be like that,' said Ella. 'I was just wondering. You're lucky you've got a dad. Mine's missing in action.'

George gazed off down the street, then took a pack of cigarettes out of his pocket and offered one to Ella.

'Thanks George,' she said, laughing at the horror on my face.

'You're not old enough to smoke,' I said. 'Neither are you, George.'

'Don't be so boring!' she said. 'You've got to get your fun while you can these days. We might all be blown to smithereens tomorrow.'

They went into a huddle, backs against the wind, and lit their cigarettes. Ella started coughing immediately, then laughed at herself, held the cigarette out to one side and batted the smoke away. George on the other hand blew out great clouds of smoke like he was used to doing this every day. His cloud drifted down the road like a ghost.

'Well, it's nice to see you again, George,' I said, 'but I've got to go.' I'd changed my mind about him being a bodyguard, not if he had Ella in tow. 'Bye!' I said and set off round the corner for the entrance to the temporary town hall.

'Wait!' they shouted and came after me.

'You don't need to come,' I said, hurrying away. 'It's fine, but thanks.'

As I came to the door of the town hall, a bride and groom and a whole wedding party were leaving. They sailed past me and went giggling into the shelter of the arches outside. The bride was so pretty and happy I couldn't help staring after her.

But I had important things to do and anyway George and Ella had clattered in behind me. However, they soon got bored standing in the queue with me, which was a long one, and sat on a bench whispering instead. Then a doorman, who looked so old and withered I was surprised he could open the big front door at all, told them to go outside if they wanted to talk and be silly.

It didn't take me long to find out I was in the wrong place, there being no mention of my dad in any of the ledgers. But the lady behind the counter told me where the right place was, the Harbour Master's Office, and about various other places which Mrs Strachan had also mentioned. It was cold in the town hall, even with my coat buttoned all the way up.

'C ... cold in here, isn't it?' I shivered.

'Hmm?' she said, busy writing something on a scrap of paper. It was a little map with two crosses on it, one for the Harbour Master's Office and the other for the police.

'I'd start with the Harbour Master,' she said. 'And don't worry about the police. You're too young to be arrested.'

I thanked her and went back outside. The wedding party were posing for a camera. George and Ella were by the next pillar posing for an invisible camera too. I pretended I didn't know them and hid in the doorway while the father of the bride came and chased them round the corner. Then I went after them as if I just happened to be going that way anyway. I decided to tell them a lie.

'I've to wait half an hour for the man to come back,' I said, 'the man who knows about these things.'

'You can be our witness then,' said Ella and she twirled her skirt, which was dark red with polka-dots.

'You shouldn't joke about that kind of thing,' I said. 'You know once you're over twelve even to pretend makes it legal and you'll be married to George for the rest of or life, or didn't you know that? I don't think your gran'd be too happy about that. I don't think anyone's gran would be pleased if their granddaughter married George. Just saying. In case you didn't know.'

'That's rubbish,' she said. She picked a gentian scar on her cheek and eyed me over her hand.

George's little lips twisted in a smile she couldn't see.

'Let's go and look at the ships then,' he said, and he put an arm round her waist as if she was his girlfriend, right out there in public, and I realised she must be older than me to let him do that. Was she his girlfriend?

'Yuck!' I said.

'Maybe I could get a job,' she said. 'I could pass for fourteen, couldn't I?'

'Easy-peasy,' said George.

'Lemon squeezy,' said Ella. 'Wow, look at all the sailors.'

'See you in half an hour, Lenny,' he said. 'No more

trouble please.' He waggled a parental finger at me, which I ignored.

When George and Ella came back to the town hall, I wouldn't be there. If they asked the lady where I'd gone, she'd tell them the Harbour Master's Office, but I'd have left there by that time too.

Chapter 28

After the noise of the street, it was amazingly quiet in the Harbour Master's Office. Everyone was incredibly busy. There were six people working so hard at their desks I only saw the tops of their heads. In the five minutes I stood waiting they only spoke in hushed tones as if there was a baby somewhere they mustn't wake. Through a closed door came the buzz of typewriters banging away like lots of bacon frying.

Then it was my turn.

I put the photo on the desk and pointed.

The boy at the desk wasn't much older than me. 'This your dad then?' he said in a loud voice.

'Yes,' I said just as loud, glancing round.

'Ssh!' he said. 'Let's see.' He put some thick glasses on his nose and looked at my dad for a long time. Then he said, 'He's not a seaman.'

'I know,' I said.

'But I know that face.'

Goose pimples crept up my back. I told him the names, both, Galluzzo and Gillespie, and he went and looked them up in a list.

'Nothing,' he said. 'Might have been a casual down at the quayside. If he's Italian the army might know or the police. I've seen that face though. He's a joker, isn't he?'

'The best.'

He gave me directions to the army office and the police (again) so I asked him to mark the army office on the town hall lady's map.

On my way to the army office I got lost and wound up down by the docks again, this time by an inner harbour busy with small boats and beyond that the big ships anchored out to sea. A million seagulls turned and squealed against the blue sky. Three ladies in khaki crossed the road and, while I glanced away to avoid being run down, they went off the edge of the quayside. No-one seemed even slightly worried but I had to go and look just to stop my heart beating so fast. But there were steps down and they clambered into a boat as if it was perfectly normal, then raced out of the dock holding their hats. As I watched them disappear beyond the harbour wall, I wondered how old you had to be to do that.

Then I spotted George and Ella over the road with a policeman who was at least a head bigger than George and two heads bigger than Ella. The policeman pointed back down the road toward the Rue End and I watched them follow his direction, then went after them at a safe distance. But a wind started up and a line of green army vehicles roared past, then a horse and cart piled with girders and soon I'd lost George and Ella in all the uniforms and the drum of engines in the docks. So I asked a boy about George's age in a polo-neck where the Army Office was and he told me where to go no bother.

The lady at the Army Office wasn't scary at all. She had dark hair pinned up behind her ears and buck teeth and was ages with Jeannie on the farm. She had the same green uniform all the other ladies had and WRNS on her shoulder. Ah, I thought. Wrens. I'd heard of them.

'Dunno, love,' she said, in an odd voice not from thereabouts and smoothed down the front of her uniform. 'Why don't you try the town hall?' She smiled and looked away.

I told her I'd already been there and showed her the photo. 'He's Italian,' I said.

She squinted at the photo as if getting too close to it she might smell him. Another lady came into the room, put some papers down and went out again.

'I know him!' said the buck teeth lady, coming to life. She snatched the photo before I could stop her and peered in close.

'Do you?' I said. My heart went boom into my throat.

'Yeah, but he's not Italian. Looks it.' She licked her lips and stared at the photo. 'But he spoke English, Geordie English, Newcastle or Middlesbrough or some such. I'm from Leeds me, see. That's how I know,' she said with some pride.

'Oh my goodness!' I breathed.

'Oh my goodness indeed,' she wheezed back. 'He was probably staying at Helensburgh, maybe … but I think they sent him somewhere else in the end. Might have been down at the docks for a while until they decided what to do with him. There was some problem with him being in the army or maybe he'd escaped from somewhere, maybe he was in prison. I don't know. Might have been someone else. I shouldn't be telling you all this stuff anyway. It's just as well you're only a child. I couldn't tell you if you were a grown-up.'

'I see,' I said, not seeing. 'Where, if not Helensburgh?'

'Goodness, let me think. One of the farms at the back of the town? One of the barracks? Don't know. Could be anywhere. We're short on healthy men, like.' She scratched her head with the end of her pencil and then chewed it, while I considered how Greenock seemed stowed out with healthy men.

'He is Italian,' I said. 'Well, his dad must have been anyway.'

'No, he wasn't, love. He was English. Had a gorgeous voice. Wouldn't have been in the army if he'd been Italian. But maybe that was the problem.'

'He's Italian, honest,' I said.

'Must be a different person then.'

'No, it's him. This is my dad.' I had to insist.

'What was his name now? I can't remember …'

'Lenny,' I said. 'Lenny Gillespie, or Galluzzo.'

'Oh, well done, yes,' she said. 'That was it: Lenny.' She didn't seem to notice the surnames.

'Well, I should know. He is my dad,' I pointed out, hoping it didn't sound cheeky.

'Silly me!' she said, her eyes pinned to the photo.

'It's my name too,' I said.

She said she couldn't quite remember. But then she brightened up.

'I think he was on the roads or clearing the bomb sites, and then one day he tried to join the Merchant Navy.' She said he shouldn't have been allowed down near the docks in the first place, and he nearly managed to join but then someone recognised him from being brought into town by the army. After that they stopped him working for a while. But the trouble was they needed men to do the work, so after a few days she saw him there again.

'I used to bring him soup, you see, because I don't think they were feeding him right at the camp.'

I remembered George complaining about enemy aliens getting better grub than the rest of us.

'But then my superior officer took me aside and said he was bad, with the ladies you know, and he drank, and that was that.'

Oh dear. The ladies. Plural. Not just Jeannie. And he drank. My stupid dad. Maybe I should just go home. I didn't want more surprises like Bobby.

But I nodded. Maybe she had more.

She smiled back.

'Sss … so how can I find him?' I said.

'Oh, yes, you want to find him. How did you manage to lose him? I mean, doesn't your mum know?'

I shook my head. 'We thought he was "missing presumed dead".'

'You have to be in the services for that, dear, I think, and he can't be in the services or he wouldn't have been working on the bomb sites or tried to join the Merchant Navy, would he?' She gazed up at the ceiling and said, as if she was trying to remember, 'There was a problem with being in the army though, wasn't there, or was it the navy?'

Feeling slightly cross-eyed, I made the mistake of trying to explain about him being in the army first and then arrested for being Italian, but then I saw she had glazed over and wasn't paying attention.

'You said they were deciding what to do with him,' I said. 'Who would that be? Who can I ask?'

'Um,' she said. 'Me, I suppose. I don't decide, but ask me.' She sighed and smiled at me. 'I'll go and ask my super.'

After a bit she came back to tell me I should go to the town hall and they'd check the missing persons book. She said she couldn't give me any information anyway, because of security, and bit her lip.

'I've told you too much already,' she said, although she hadn't really told me anything. 'But don't worry. He's sure to turn up somewhere.'

'How do I get to the work camp?' I said.

'The camp? Why do you want to go there?'

I sighed and considered what to say. 'I'm visiting relatives near there,' I said.

'Good idea. Maybe they'll know where he is.'

I felt my eyes cross again and went back out into the sunshine not knowing whether to be pleased or disappointed.

George and Ella were sheltering in a doorway further along the street, but didn't notice me. Grey clouds were moving across the sky like a blanket over the blue. A soldier hurried past, then a flock of Wrens.

'Excuse me,' I called to the Wrens, 'where's the police station?'

'Back that way,' said one. 'Up the hill. You can't miss it. Beside the town hall.'

'Thank you!'

Of course. I was so close I hadn't seen the tower. Mustering all my courage, I went in.

The policewoman at the desk brought out several ledgers and told me all the ways my dad had made his presence known. There were three breaches of the peace, two assaults, two thefts and one conviction for impersonating a service personnel. He hadn't been guilty of any of them.

'No, no,' she said. 'He wasn't *found* guilty, but that doesn't mean he didn't do it.'

This didn't seem right to me, I mean isn't that what courts are meant to do, find out if someone's guilty or not? But I had to take her word for it. Old ideas about my dad had already been proved wrong.

'Being Italian, some people didn't like him so some of these could have been made up, or maybe they couldn't be proved, and sometimes the court has to consider mitigating circumstances.'

I shrugged my shoulders.

'He might have had good reasons, like self-defence for instance. Maybe the sheriff didn't think a charge was worth bothering with or just liked him and wanted to help. I know he had the whole court laughing once. I wasn't there but he had the greatest excuses for impersonating a merchant seaman, like wanting to be one for instance. Amnesia was another one. That's when you forget who you are.' She laughed, although it seemed too true to be funny. 'I remember him, though. He'd have charmed the hind legs off a donkey.'

This was true. We were definitely talking about my dad.

'Thank you,' I said, but she wasn't finished.

'His given address was always the camp at Helensburgh. They bring them over in the boat in the morning and take them back at night, but I heard he got sent somewhere to work where he'd be less trouble, somewhere without women. Rothesay I think. They might know at the employment exchange. If you come back tomorrow I'll send a message up this afternoon.'

'I can go to the employment exchange. Where is it?' I couldn't wait 'til tomorrow. And what if they forgot or got his name wrong or misunderstood?

'They're very busy up there,' she said. 'They don't have time for children. Neither do I.' Suddenly she was sharp and unfriendly.

I lowered my head, sniffed loudly and waited. Someone else came in the door and passed through to a room beyond.

'Terrace Road, by the station, but you shouldn't really. No-one has any time to waste.'

'Thank you!' I said and beamed at her.

'Your dad was quite well known in Greenock for a while.'

'Thanks,' I said, as if she'd told me he'd started the latest dance craze.

As I left, I saw George and Ella sitting close together on a bench. They followed me up the street.

'Stop following me,' I said.

'Stop following me,' mimicked polka-dotty Ella.

'I can't. I have to look after you,' said George.

'In that case you can go to the barracks for me and ask for my dad,' I said. I regretted it as soon as I'd said it. What if my dad really was at the barracks and George found him before me?

'Alright,' he said with annoying cheerfulness. 'Fine. I'll go.'

'I'll come with you,' said Ella.

'I'll meet you back here,' I said, and chewed on my lip. The blue sky had vanished completely and rain clouds were gathering over Helensburgh.

'No, you won't. You'll have to come too,' said George.

'I can't,' I said. 'Children aren't allowed and I'd never pass for sixteen. You two would though.'

'Where's the photo then?' said George. 'Give us it and we'll go.'

Remember this is George who has held my head under taps, rubbed nettles into my face and thrown me off the upper branches of trees, but these are other stories. Trust me, George was not to be trusted, even if he had come all the way to Greenock for me.

'I lost it,' I said with as noisy a sniff as I could manage, and pretended to search my pockets and panic when I couldn't find it. George chewed his cheek while Ella twiddled her hair.

'Oh no!' she said, unconvincingly, as if I'd ever think she cared.

'I'm going back the way I came,' I said. 'See if I can find it.'

'You're lying,' said George. 'Why can't you just let us help you? Why do you always have to be so difficult?'

'Why are you here? Have you lost your job?' I said.

'No, stupid, I've left it. I've come to sign up for the Merchant Navy,' he said.

'What?' I said. 'What about the river patrol thing? And John Brown's? And … .'

'And what?' He stood there with his eyes all pinched and took another cigarette out of his pocket. Then he brought out the matches and lit it, pulling his cheeks in so hard he looked like a skeleton.

'You can't just walk out of a job. Mr Tait says you'll never work again if you do that. He says John Brown's is the best job in the world to have and you're an apprentice and …'

He wasn't even looking at me.

'What about me?' I went on. 'You're supposed to be looking after me.'

His head fell back on his shoulders for a second. He blew a long cloud of smoke up into the air above us then looked at me without answering.

'You're too young,' I added.

'Not for the Merchant Navy,' he said.

'Yes, you are,' I said. 'They won't take you. You're …' I couldn't think why they wouldn't take him.

'Too stupid? Too bad? Too annoying? Any of those fit?'

'Well, yes, actually, if you want to know,' I said. 'And you're not big enough.'

He laughed. He was tall, but he was skinny too. We were all skinny.

'I mean you have to be muscly,' I said. 'And you can't swim.'

'I won't need to swim,' he said. 'Swimming's no use to a merchant seaman.'

'But what if …' It was my turn to bite my lip. What if his ship sank like so many others? Surely he'd need to swim.

'He's going to be a hero,' put in Ella. 'You shouldn't try to stop him. That's just selfish.'

'Mind your own business!' said George, just as I was going to say the same.

'Well, that's not very nice,' she said.

'Shut up, Ella!' said George.

I splurted out a laugh but George glared at me. Ella sulked off and leant against the police station wall. The first spot of rain landed at my feet. I pulled my collar in tight and straightened my scarf.

'Mr Tait wouldn't let me join the Merchant Navy

because he said I was too young,' said George. (I always agreed with Mr Tait.) 'I'd have had to lie about my age and you know what Mr Tait was like about lying.'

'He wasn't your dad,' I pointed out. 'What about your dad?'

'What about him?' said George looking genuinely surprised. 'Anyway, even though there's a war on and the country needs every man, I think he just didn't want me joining, in case I got killed. If your ship goes down in the middle of the Atlantic you don't stand a chance, not unless you're very lucky and a rescue boat comes along.'

I thought about all the bedraggled souls down at the pier I had seen the day before and realised that must have been what happened to them. They'd been the lucky ones.

'Why are you doing it then? You don't need to. You're at John Brown's. It's protected. You can stay there all through the war. No-one would think anything of it. Mr Tait told me we're winning now. You could just hang on and wait and it'll be over soon.'

'Exactly,' he said.

'Come on,' said Ella suddenly. 'I thought we were going to the barracks.'

I looked at George. There was just no understanding boys. He glared back at me.

Ellie slumped against the wall again.

'That's the stupidest thing ever,' I said. 'I still don't understand why.'

George did that Mr Tait thing of taking forever to answer. 'You wouldn't understand,' he said and he blew a puff of smoke out the side of his mouth.

'Of course I'd understand,' I said. 'Why don't you try telling me? Why am I even bothered?' I threw my arms in the air and gazed down the street.

'Alright,' he said. 'It's *because* it's going to be over soon. Because we're winning. Because of everything you said. Because it's my only chance. It'll be over and everyone else, even Sandy for God's sake, even he got to join the war. And everyone will have stories to tell, everyone gets to be a hero, everyone except me.'

'What happened to Sandy?' I said. (Sandy was my old friend from Carbeth). 'Sandy never came back. I haven't seen him since last year. He could be dead for all we know. You don't want to be dead do you? That's idiotic.'

'Of course Sandy never came back,' said George. 'Why would he come back to Carbeth? Carbeth is for babies. He'll be spending his leave in town. Anyway, I don't have time for this. Not if I've to go to the barracks too.'

So I had to explain that sending him to the barracks had been a trick and that really I was going to the employment exchange, same as him, but for a different reason.

'My God but you're an annoying little cow,' he said.

And then Ella joined in and called me a dimwit and a selfish wee dough ball, so I had to cross my arms, stick my nose in the air and turn my back on both of them. But mainly I put my back to them because I didn't know what to think of George joining up and going away, because I knew I didn't want him to go to sea or join the Merchant Navy. This was something new. Ordinarily I wanted George to go as far away from me as possible. A week earlier and I'd have been cheering. Normally I wouldn't have felt my tummy tighten and my chest squeezing all the air out. So this was different, and I didn't know what to think.

But it turned out they didn't know where the employment exchange was, only that it was near the station which I had already passed. I knew it meant going back past the broken tenements which had been bombed and I didn't want to do that, but I was the only person who knew the way and it was the only way to go.

'Wow! It's just like Clydebank, isn't it?' said Ella, as if this made walking through bombed-out Greenock some kind of treat.

I held my nose against the old familiar smell and went on ahead of them trying not to look.

Then we turned up towards the station which was on Terrace Road and climbed the hill until we went over the railway line and beyond. The employment exchange loomed large and important and was guarded by groups of ladies chattering.

Chapter 29

The real guard at the door of the labour exchange was one very nice old lady in green tweed who sat at a little table smiling out a welcome. She asked us why we were there so she could send us to the right place. George was easy. There was a special desk on one side of the room with two men in sailor's blue and a short queue of two other boys and a man. Beyond this a line of ladies sat at a counter facing another row of ladies with pencils and notepads. The hum of their voices was steady like bees at a window.

Ella followed George to the sailors' desk but he sent her away again, so she bumped in beside me with a face like fizz while I was explaining what I was doing there, again.

'Are you her big sister?' said the old lady.

'Yes!' said Ella just as I said 'No!'

'You're very alike,' said the lady. 'Must be the gentian.'

I glared at Ella. 'This is Ella. We're not related,' I said. 'Go away, Ella. It's private.' I looked her right in the eye so she'd know I meant business. 'You're not family.' She wrinkled up her nose and slunk away out to the street.

'So he was in the army but isn't any more,' said the lady in a lowered voice. I nodded. 'Then he was Italian so he was arrested and sent to Helensburgh.

Then he did something to get arrested again, you're not sure what, and got sent to Greenock, and then he did something terrible again so he got sent away somewhere else. Is that right?'

'Sort of,' I said, and blushed. My dad didn't sound very nice. I glanced over at George who was leaning against the wall trying to look manly.

'But you've no idea where,' she said.

'No,' I said.

'Or why?'

I glanced at George again. This time he was watching me.

'Well, he's a bit of a one, isn't he, your dad?' She laughed and straightened out her green cable sweater. 'And you don't know any of these terrible things he's supposed to have done?' I shook my head. 'Or you're not telling.' Her mouth stretched to a grin and she patted my hand. 'Quite right, dear. Loose lips sink ships.' She nodded towards a poster on a nearby wall that said the same.

'They wouldn't let him join the Merchant Navy because of his being Italian,' I said as quietly as I could, ignoring the poster, 'but he still tried and now the Italians are on our side so I suppose he might have been allowed in the end, if he'd tried again.'

'He'd have come here if he was volunteering. What's his name, dear?'

So I told her.

'I've never heard of him, myself,' she said. 'And I couldn't tell you anyway, especially if he was Italian.'

I slid the photo across her table.

She picked up a pair of glasses, flicked them open and placed them on her ears as if the arms were made of glass, then drew in a sniff and held her breath. I held mine too and glanced at George who was at the front of his queue and had no idea something important was happening. The lady held my dad's photo between two fingers and thumbs. Her mouth pushed forwards as if she wanted to kiss him and this made lots of little lines appear on her top lip. Then she sucked both lips right in and at the same time her forehead came down over her eyes.

'That's why I didn't recognise the name,' she said, leaning forwards. She went on a whisper. 'He said he was Lawrence Oliver, Lenny for short, and that he worked in John Brown's and wanted to go to sea. I told him he should go back to John Brown's and he sang me a sea shanty and had everyone joining in.'

'Did he?' I said.

'Yes, he did,' she whispered and laid her specs on the table and the photo with them. 'It went "There was a laddie come from England, it was hey ho and away we go" or something like that, 'cause he's got that lovely northern accent, Northern English that is. Not everybody was happy about singing in here, but that man over there at the Merchant Navy table, the one with the moustache, he joined in.'

'Did he?' I said. I could hardly breathe for excitement.

'The other man didn't,' she said. 'But the lady in blue did and that one in the fawn Aran knit, and the three up the back in ladies recruitment added some harmony. Then he put it to the vote, once he had the whole room going, and everyone agreed he should be allowed to be a merchant seaman.'

'Oh no!' I whispered, and put my fingers to my mouth.

'The other Navy man was against it,' she said, 'the one in the hat, which he never takes off because he's an officer. Funny, that'd be rude if there wasn't a war. But there was nothing he could do. You can't not allow someone into the Merchant Navy just because he's charming all the lassies.'

Now my hands were over my whole face. I pulled the fingers down so I could see.

'But before he came back with his papers we found out the truth,' she whispered. She glanced around the room. I followed where she looked. George was leaning over a table with a pen in his hand. Concentration made him chew his lip as he wrote something on a piece of paper.

The lady poked my hand. 'It so happened that the lady in the Aran knit over there is the daughter of a bigwig police chief or something and your dad was already known for his choir-leading on the boat across from … but I can't tell you that.'

'H … Helensburgh,' I breathed, my powers of speech failing in the excitement. 'W … with the I … Italians. I already told you.'

She sucked in her lips again. 'I hope you're not a spy,' she whispered. 'We had one in here the other day.'

I shook my head. 'Really? A real sssspy?'

'Wait here,' she whispered. She picked up her glasses and the photo, which she held low at her side so no-one would see, and went across to the lady in the Aran knit. The Aran knit lady listened to her and shot a look in my direction, then whispered something back. George, on the other side of the room, was still bent over his sheet of paper but pulled back to scratch his head. I willed him to turn but instead he leant his elbow on the counter again and went on writing, or trying to. I've seen his writing: it's not very good.

Suddenly the door lady was back at her own table. She looked at me and shook her head. 'I'm so sorry but I've no idea where your dad might be,' she said. She glanced at the Aran lady and they smiled at each other. Then she lowered her voice and said, 'Go up Drumfrochar Road and keep going. Follow it up to the left until you come to the merino wool mills then after that follow it to the right and keep going up the hill. Southwards. Keep going south. Paper mills. Go to the paper mill.' Then loudly: 'Try the town hall or the travel office at Princes Pier.' Quiet: 'Follow the road, really, you can't miss it. Keep going south, always south.' Loud: 'Good luck!' Tiny whisper: 'Glentee Farm, almost at the reservoir.'

'Thank you,' I said, trying to look as upset as I didn't feel. Then I whispered, 'How far?'

'Far,' she said, 'and all uphill,' and she smiled as if she'd told me he was just round the corner.

'Thank you,' I said without containing my grin.

'Go now,' she said. 'You've a walk.'

'You can stop nodding now,' said Ella who suddenly appeared at my shoulder. 'Aren't you finished yet? What's George up to?'

The lady at the table squeezed my hand. 'Hope you find him.'

George was having an argument with the Merchant Navy man with the hat. As he stood up, the better to shout, his chair fell over backwards and two people at the next table rushed away. George's wee eyes went wee-er than ever. He pulled himself to full height and opened his mouth to speak. I couldn't look. I couldn't bear it. But he surprised me.

'Sorry,' he said.

'Pardon me?' said the man in the hat. 'I can't hear you.'

There was another long pause. George drew in his lips.

'Sorry, sir,' he said. 'Sorry. Sir.'

He sat back down.

The man in the hat leant back in his chair. I couldn't hear them any more but I guessed he was telling George he couldn't join up. George's mouth hung open and his eyes narrowed while the hat man shook his head and drummed the table with his fingers.

'Uh-oh,' said Ella in my ear. 'Trouble.'

'Poor George,' I said.

Then he reached into his pocket and laid a packet of cigarettes on the table alongside a cigarette that was already there. The man in the moustache pushed it back towards him and then the two navy men seemed to argue. Was he bribing them?

'You can't smoke on ships,' whispered Ella.

'How would you know?' I said.

'Lad down at the docks told me,' she said.

Then George stood up to leave, the cigarettes still on the table. His face was stony as he came towards us. But they called him back and soon George and the hat man were laughing and the other man seemed to be writing something on a piece of paper. He pointed to a clock on the wall above a poster which said **THE LIFE LINE IS FIRM THANKS TO THE MERCHANT NAVY** and had two merchant seamen gazing out to sea. The clock said five to one.

George stood up and shook their hands. He was grinning all over his face. I never saw him so happy. Come to think of it I couldn't remember seeing him happy at all, ever. So he had joined. So I was pleased for him. And I had found my dad, nearly. So why were the tears threatening to burst out of my eyes?

Chapter 30

George was understandably surprised by my tears, but no more so than me. He said it was because I was a girl, but I already knew girls were braver than boys, so I didn't listen to him. He paced up and down outside the employment place rubbing his hands while I stared out between the buildings where I could see the sea. The ships were all facing west in readiness, like Mr Tulloch's cows sometimes did in the field, all turned one way, waiting.

The clamour of the shipyards and the docks rose up, crashes and booms as if whole ships were falling over. A coal cart came clattering up the hill, the horse straining, its neck thrusting up and down with the effort. The rain had stopped again but the wind was freezing.

'You'll have to tell your mum for me,' said George.

'You ought to go straight home to your mummy anyway if you're going to cry like a baby,' said Ella. 'Shouldn't she, George?'

'Why don't you just tell her yourself?' I said, ignoring Ella. I batted the tears off in a way I hoped looked as if I didn't care about anything. 'And what about your own mum and dad, anyway? What about them? You'll have to tell them.'

'I've to go straight down for a medical at the

shipping office,' said George, ignoring me. He was smiling like he'd won first prize.

'That's nice,' I said. 'I've to go over the hill to the back of beyond.' I jerked my thumb up the road.

But Ella and I seemed to have become invisible.

'Then I've to get a letter from my dad or mum,' he said.

'Why?' said Ella.

'He's still a child, stupid,' I said. 'They need to give their permission. And how are you going to do that anyway? You know they won't let you, don't you?'

'I don't need it,' he said, waving an envelope at me. Then he read the letter that was inside. ' "To the Merchant Navy. I hereby give permission for my son George Connor to join you and go to sea. Yours sincerely Mr and Mrs Connor." I did that myself. No help from anyone.' His grin would split him in two if he wasn't careful. 'You could at least be pleased for me.'

'Yeah, you could at least be pleased for him,' said Ella. 'He did save your life after all.'

'I need some kit too,' said George in a faraway voice. 'Boots and waterproofs. A warm coat. What else?'

'He didn't save my life, did you, George?' I said. 'George?' He was checking a handful of coins in his palm and didn't hear. 'I wish you'd go home, Ella. This is none of your business, any of this. You should be at school or something or helping your granny peel tatties.'

Ella looked at the sky then laughed right into my face. I closed my eyes and stood as still as I could bear to, shutting out the sound of her fake laughter until she thumped me on the shoulder and I had to look.

She crossed her eyes, except only one of them actually crossed, and waggled her head at me.

'I don't have enough,' said George. 'What am I going to do? Oh no! There's only enough for a jumper. Not even that.'

But Ella and I were too busy staring each other out, me deadpan, her acting the goat. It wasn't hard and I would have won if I hadn't felt this great rush of happiness come up from my feet.

'George,' I said, grabbing his arm.

'I won!' squealed Ella.

'I found my dad!' I said.

'You're kidding!' he said. 'How did you do that?'

'He's over that hill,' I said. 'On a farm, I think, or a paper mill. What time is it? We'll have to go quick so we can get still get home to Clydebank. At least the rain's stopped.'

'You and Ella go. I've got things to do. The *Valpecula* leaves tomorrow early. I wonder which one it is?' He gazed out at the sea where the ships were glinting in a sudden burst of sunshine. 'They're going to take the last recruits out there tonight so I've got to get going. I don't want to get left behind.'

'The what? The *Peculiar*?' said Ella, delighted.

'Well, that fits,' I said.

'The *Vulpecula*,' he said. 'The man says it's after a star.'

'A star?' said Ella with a twist of her nose. 'Why did they call it after a star?'

'Peculiar, isn't it?' I said.

'Sssh!' said George. 'Loose lips sink ships,' he hissed. 'I shouldn't have told you anything. Oh god. I've done it now.' He checked up and down the street for spies.

'We'd better move.' He crossed the road and stood in a doorway. We followed him over and stood either side. '*Vulpecula*, *Vulpecula*, *Vulpecula*,' he said, leaning on one vowel and then the next.

'Tonight?' I said. 'That's a bit quick, isn't it?'

'*Vulpecula*, I think,' said George. 'Has to be.'

George had no money for clothes, not even for second-hand stuff from the Sally Ann. The money in my pocket seemed to chink louder than before as if there was a whole king's ransom in there instead of a few coppers. I was loath to give any of it up without finding my dad first. What if I had to stay longer? And I still had to eat. I totted up all the things I might need the money for and then I totted them all up again and realised I had no idea at all.

'What are you both counting for?' said Ella. She did a little dance, hopping on and off the step. 'Let's go back to the docks.'

'I need some of your money, Lenny,' said George. 'I'll pay you back from my first wages, honest. I'll send it to you at Ella's gran's. Go on. Please? I'll send you interest and everything, to pay for your trouble.'

'Yeah, come on, Lenny. Hand over the readies,' said Ella, on and off the step.

'Shut up!' said George and I together.

'Alright,' said Ella, backing off. 'No need to be like that. I was only trying to help. Just joining in.'

'Shut up!' said George.

Ella stomped off down the hill a little way and watched us from another close mouth.

If George had threatened me the way he usually did by towering over me and twisting my arm or promising various forms of torture, I wouldn't have given him anything, but he didn't. He set about persuading me with promises of trophies from foreign countries, tea from China, gum from America, fur from Finland.

'Russian dolls,' he said. 'I'll bring a Russian doll all the way from Russia. I just need the money now, otherwise I can't go.'

A sudden wind seemed to race through the close where we were standing, lifting my coat so it cracked against my knee. I thought of Mr Tait and how he wouldn't want George to go, how he'd hate the fact that George had lied and hadn't told his parents. How I'd have to be the one to do the telling. But aside from all that, Mr Tait had made George promise to look after me and now he was going. Didn't that mean he was breaking a promise?

'You're supposed to be looking after us,' I pointed out, one last time. 'What about Mavis and Rosie and my mum?'

'Only 'til you've found your dad,' he said.

I'd thought it was forever. 'But I haven't actually found him,' I said, 'not completely.'

'Lenny, don't be silly. I can't go to sea if you don't give me the money.'

'But I don't have much and I don't know what I'll need.'

I pulled the coins out of my pocket. I didn't want to. This was George. What was I thinking? He'd never bring me anything from foreign shores. He'd never send me the money. He'd forget I even existed.

He tried to see into my hand but I clutched it back from him. 'It's all I've got,' I said. 'I worked for it. I need it to get home. If I don't find my dad today ... .'

So he told me how much I'd need for a train fare

to get home and added on the price of tea and a roll and sausage at the station, and I turned the coins over in my hand. The hill I had to climb seemed long and steep and full of people I didn't know and places I wouldn't know how to find. What if I found another minister? Or the same one? What if he lived up the hill? I scanned all the people but they were just ordinary folk holding their coats tight against the wind, sailors and workmen and housewives, all hurrying about their business. An army truck passed up the hill with soldiers on the back. They didn't notice George and me because they were waving at Ella who was blowing kisses their way. Then a blue truck rattled down towards the docks with cages full of hens, feathers floating in its wake and a breath-stopping stink.

'Please, Lenny,' he said. 'Mr Tait would want you to.'

If I had been a religious person, I couldn't have been more shocked if you had said God was in league with the devil. I turned to stare at him.

'He would not,' I said. And I began to list all the reasons why Mr Tait would not want him to lie about his age and go to sea. Then I moved along the tenement wall for safety.

'Ella!' George shouted down the street. 'Ella!' then he turned to me. 'Ella's a stupid little idiot. So are you. Mr Tait told me to look out for you because he knew you'd go looking for your dad, and that it was only right that you should wonder. He told me to keep an eye on you until you found him because of how stupid you can be and the trouble you always get into. You've found him. Job done. I know we hate each other but do me this one favour and I'll send you a postal order from my first wage packet. I'll even send you interest. Ten percent. That's not bad, is it?' Then he shouted for Ella again but she only glared up at him and looked away with a flick of her hair. 'You were his favourite,' he said, standing over me. 'You don't need to worry about that. He always said butter wouldn't melt in your mouth.'

I didn't know what to say to that, but while I was thinking, there was the most almighty crash and roar from the dockside followed by a lot of shouting. We peered down the hill but there was nothing to be seen. All the hairs seem to stand up on my neck. The wind funnelled up the hill between the tenements and I stuck my hands in my armpits to keep warm. A lady in a pinny threw a bucket of dirty water into the gutter and I watched it hurry down towards the sea. The clang of the riveters rose upwards and George stood on the hill with his eyes shut and his hands clasped together against his mouth. It occurred to me he might be praying. Maybe Mr Tait had made him pray. Maybe George believed.

'Please, Lenny,' he said, as if he was praying to me.

I took a deep breath. 'Okay,' I said.

'Thank you!'

'But there's one thing.'

'Anything. Anything at all.' He was bouncing on his toes the way Rosie does.

I suddenly realised why George and I hated each other. We were too alike. Neither of us wanted, ever, to have to ask for help. It was ten times worse because next I had to ask *him* for *his* help. But I reckoned if he could do it, so could I.

'Can you follow me? I mean can you follow me over the hill to the farm or the mill, the paper mill, or was it a woollen mill? You see I don't even know. Once you've got your gear, I mean. It's just that I don't want the minister to find me,' I said. This was true but actually, if I'm honest, I was just scared of what I might or might not find.

He looked at me sideways. 'But I don't know when I'll be done,' he said. 'I don't even know where to go. This is Greenock.'

'Try,' I said. 'You could try. Mr Tait said … .'

'I know what Mr Tait said,' he said. 'But I'd never find you.'

I shrugged. Ella had sat down on the step of another close and was picking at the scabs on her face and staring off into nothing. She didn't look much older than me any more, just another girl whose dad had gone.

'Okay, here's what I'll do,' said George. 'I'll come as soon as I'm finished but you have to take Ella with you.'

'No way. I'm not going anywhere with her. She's waving at all the soldiers. Look at her.'

Ella was in fact waving at soldiers but none of them seemed to know she even existed.

'She's just stupid,' he went on. 'You could keep her out of trouble and make sure she gets back to Clydebank.'

'Nope.' I pulled my lips in tight so he'd know there was nothing else to say.

'Oh my God, Lenny,' he growled. 'She's the only person I know who's more of a pest than you. But it's a close contest.'

I crossed my arms and scowled in Ella's direction.

'What about your parents?' I said. 'I'll have to tell them you're going. That's not going to be easy. You owe it to me to follow. Mr Tait …'

'Stop yattering on about Mr Tait. I told you I'm coming, but you've got to look after Ella for me. I can't take her with me for my gear. Come on, Lenny. You don't want the old minister to get her, do you?'

I wouldn't wish the minister on anyone, not even Ella.

So it was decided. I counted half the money and gave it to George with Ella as our witness. Then we broke the plan to Ella. She turned red with fury first, then white when we both said we'd leave her and hurried off in opposite directions, then green when George wouldn't come back for her and finally red again when she came puffing up the hill behind me. I won't tell you what she said because it would make your ears burn although luckily she was so out of breath she only managed a few choice words.

Chapter 31

At the top of the road there was a junction. The road was called Hope Street of all things, which I might have pointed out if Ella had been someone else. It seemed like a good street to be in. We turned onto it and tramped along in silence staring in opposite directions, then went left at the next crossroad.

The possibility of turning a corner and suddenly staring my dad in the face was suddenly, well, staring me in the face. If I really was going to find my dad that day, I'd better be ready, and I wasn't. What would I say? What should I do? What could I hope for? I had no answers to any of these questions.

Somewhere close a machine hammered out, sharp, persistent, hard, and the drone of a colossal engine thundered and rattled. The sweet smell of sugar made us look around for the source but high walls everywhere kept nosey people out. The sugar was soon replaced by stinky whisky, a pong that hung and stuck in my nose and reminded me of Rita's pub. I rubbed the photo in my pocket and whispered to Mr Tait: 'I've nearly found him, Mr Tait, nearly.'

The pavement trembled and I yanked Ella back from the wheels of a lorry. Then a train chugged somewhere, and a metal screech rent the air. As we passed over a railway line we were engulfed in thick black smoke and coughed and wiped our watery eyes. The train let out a cheerful whistle and the wind took the smoke as quickly as it had come.

Very helpfully the sun pushed through just at that moment and cast long shadows of the factory gates and chimneys. We just had to follow the sun to find the south, didn't we?

We came to another junction. It was a big main road with factories left and right, left for the docks and right for up the hill. But straight ahead a smaller road beckoned and passed under another railway bridge. The sun shone through the gap, south. Perhaps there were mills beyond it too. I stopped for Ella who was trailing behind, her face glowing like her polka-dotty skirt.

'Come on!' I called and crossed the road to wait for her.

Ella was no longer her cheery annoying self, which was no bad thing. As we reached the railway underpass, three old men were leaning against the dank stone beneath it smoking and sheltering from the sun which was bright but not warm. The men smelled of burnt mince and vinegar so I had to hold my nose. But as we passed, they burst out laughing, snorting and sneezing, so I grabbed Ella and dragged her out the other side.

'Josephine and her skin of many colours,' said one.

'Somewhere over the rainbow,' sang another, and they all started coughing as if their insides were going to come out.

We kept going and we skirted a pond with the longest building you ever saw on the other side of it. There were piles of rope and the strangest glueyest smell ever. No paper or wool, but otherwise there were just a couple of houses, neither of which looked like a farm.

'This isn't right,' I said.

'What are we looking for?' said Ella.

'A mill,' I said. 'Don't you ever listen?'

'How will we know it?'

'It's a wool mill,' I said, 'but it's not here.' I turned and started back the way we'd come. 'We'll go back to that big road and turn up the hill. Hurry up. Why are you so slow? You're like an old granny.'

'Keep your hair on,' she said. 'What's the rush? Wait for me!'

I'd promised George to keep Ella out of trouble so I slowed down for her and we ran back through the underpass together.

'You lost?' said a man as we passed.

'No, thank you very much,' I said.

'Yes we are,' said Ella. 'What do you mean no we're not. We're lost. Let's go and ask them.'

So we stood and argued about whether they'd know the way and we wasted time trying not to waste time by going back and asking, until finally Ella went and asked.

'This way,' she said rather smugly and pointed up the long slow hill into the distance past all the factories and houses, exactly as I said.

Higher and higher we went until, instead of works walls and trains and lorries, there were piles of rubble, huge and jagged and blackened from fire, with slices of red brick wall lying on top of one another like giant carrot cake on a plate. A horse and cart sat in a space nearby which had been cleared and two men were throwing bricks and stones onto the back of it. Neither of them was my dad. Metal girders and pipes stuck out like lots of fingers pointing at the sky where the sun, now faint, shimmered behind the mist above the hill.

'What does a paper mill look like when it's at home then?' she said, echoing my thoughts exactly.

'Well,' I said, trying to sound as if I knew, 'there'll be a chimney or two, that's for sure, like those ones over there.' Two chimneys beyond a high wall were belching out black smoke. 'Not those though,' I said, hazarding a guess. 'Those are in the wrong place.'

'What else?' she said.

'Um … no windows and a big brick building. A gate, probably, with PAPER MILL or the company name on it.'

'What would that be?'

I didn't know. We passed more tenements, some with boards over the windows, like in Clydebank after the bombing.

'And corrugated iron sheds,' I said with some effort, keeping my thoughts away from our old house, 'and bales of paper.'

'What's a bale?' she said.

'Probably like a hay bale,' I said, not sure.

'What's that like then?' she said.

'Haven't you ever seen a hay bale?'

She shook her head.

'Well,' I said, 'a hay bale is a bunch of hay so a paper bale will be the same but paper.'

She laughed. 'You don't have the faintest idea.'

Hands on hips I glared at her. 'And what does that have to do with anything?' I said.

But she had nailed it because the truth was I couldn't remember what the lady in the labour exchange had said, not exactly. I thought I'd listened so carefully I'd never forget a single syllable, but actually I wasn't certain of anything except there was a farm and two mills, one wool, the other paper. But which one my dad was at was lost forever. There were names too. Duntocher Road? Drumtocher? No idea. And a farm. Glenlee? Glenree? I tried to remember, starting at the beginning of the alphabet: Glenbee, Glencee, Glendee, but soon realised it was pointless. South. I remembered that.

A lady came towards us in men's overalls. The pipe she carried on her shoulder bounced at both ends with every step.

'Excuse me,' I said. 'Is this D … Duntocher Road?' Duntocher is a place a few miles from Clydebank.

'Drumfrochar,' she said with a smile, and shifted the pipe higher onto her shoulder. 'Drum. Frochar.'

'Drumfrochar,' I said.

'That's the one,' she said. 'Got it first time.'

I thanked her and she carried on. Then I remembered all the other things I'd forgotten and ran after her. This time the pipe shoogled and swayed when she stopped.

'What about the wool mill?' I said. 'And the paper mill?'

'Just follow the road round to the left,' she said.

'And the farm,' I said. 'Glen … I've forgotten … Glen … tee. It was Glentee, I've remembered!'

'I don't know about that,' she said. 'Shouldn't you be at school or something? Why do you want to know all this?' Suddenly she wasn't smiling any more. 'This is heavy. I'm going to drop it if I don't get going.

I shouldn't have told you anything.'

'S … sorry,' I said. 'Thanks.' But she'd already gone.

'You should have said,' said Ella. 'Why didn't you tell her? About your dad, I mean. Why didn't you say? How are we ever going to find him if you don't ask?'

I watched the pipe woman turn in at a wide-open door and disappear. I could have asked her more but suddenly my tongue was doing that jelly thing again. How was I ever going to find my dad with a tongue like that? The thought of it all made me shake in frustration.

'Why, Lenny, why didn't you tell her about your dad?' said Ella.

A tractor came down with a load of hay on a trailer, in bales to be exact. It might have come from Glentee Farm. I waved at the farmer, but he was too busy watching the road ahead with his cap down over his eyes and his mouth thrust forward in concentration.

'Excuse me!' I shouted, and though I crossed the road and ran after him, he didn't hear me above the chunter of the factories. He was going too fast for me anyway. When I came back up the hill, Ella was nowhere to be seen.

I felt the hairs on the back of my neck rise and then goose pimples slid down my arms in waves, followed swiftly by a heat in my tummy like a volcano. *Oh Mr Tait*, I thought. *What am I going to do?* I ran to the nearest wall, leant on my arm and sobbed like I was being sick.

I'd only been there a minute or so when a lady came and asked me if I was alright.

'Yes,' I said, still hiding my face.

'You don't seem alright to me,' she said. 'She doesn't

seem alright, does she? What do you think?'

'Something must have happened,' said another lady. 'Poor pet.'

'I'm f … fine,' I said.

'What?' they said.

'I'm f … fine,' I said, and I lifted my head and glanced sideways at them.

'Let's see you then …' She stuffed a big spanner in her pocket and rubbed my back with her hand.

So I had to turn round, even though I didn't want to. I took a big breath. 'I can't find my dad,' I said. I told them I was looking for my dad who was missing presumed dead and I'd come from Clydebank and Helensburgh and now I'd lost Ella and forgotten everything the labour exchange lady said.

The lady gave me a rag from her boiler suit pocket to blow my nose and wiped her eyes with another. 'Oh dear,' she said.

'That's quite a journey on your own,' said the other one. 'Good for you, though, all that searching. Does your mum know you're here?'

'Very impressive,' said the first one. 'Why're you up here?'

So I reeled off Drumfrochar Road, the wool mill and the paper mill, and finally Glentee Farm, and asked if they knew it. Och, they said, it wasn't far, bit of the back of beyond but a lovely spot in the summer for picnics.

'He's not a conchie, is he?'

I had cheered up a lot by this point, feeling I had been brave after all. So I was brave again and told them.

'He's Italian, or I think his dad was. I just found out.

That's why he was sent to a camp. What? What's wrong?'

They had drawn back from me.

'I see,' said the first one. 'Italian, eh?' A glance passed between them.

Oh dear.

'He's not really Italian,' I said. 'It must have been his dad. He was in the army from the beginning. We went on holiday and he got arrested while we were away. He's English really.'

'I don't think we want anything to do with Italians,' said the first one.

'They're on our side now,' I said.

'She's only a wean,' said the other. 'It's not her fault.'

'Come on,' said the first.

'But Italy's our friend now. Wait! And everybody loves my dad.'

But they turned away and left me.

Chapter 32

'This way,' said Ella, striding past.

'Where have you been?' I shouted.

But I let her stride. Even though I wanted to scream and yell and knock lumps out of her.

She glanced back and nodded over the road, but didn't slow down for me. 'That man with the smelly cart. He says it's up here.'

How did I miss the huge dung cart on the other side of the road, with the smallest horse you ever saw? I don't know. But Ella forged on ahead so I had to hurry after her. The road veered to the left and went up at such an angle I thought I would fall over backwards. She crossed another railway bridge and I followed and we passed the biggest gate I ever saw, so big it had a building in the middle of it with a clock at the top telling me how late we were and we better hurry. Over the clock soared a factory the size of a kingdom with row upon row of huge windows. Some buildings had bars on their windows just asking to be run along with a stick, but Ella seemed to have a tiger chasing her the way she passed all of this without even stopping for breath.

Then it was fields and a farm with cows and mud and filth everywhere just like at Mr Tulloch's and I stood for a moment to breathe in the smells I loved. Perhaps this was Glentee. But some ladies in brown uniforms were carrying buckets and I realised they wouldn't let my dad stay there because of them, the ladies that is, not the buckets. Reluctantly I kept going.

Reluctantly because a wave of dread now washed over me, and even though I'd wanted to find my dad for ages and had travelled for two whole days to find him, it now seemed like the daftest thing in the world. Everything I had learnt about him made him a complete stranger and not the dad I remembered. I didn't want to meet a man who drank in pubs, got into fights, lied so convincingly and was often in trouble with the police. What would Mr Tait have thought? And what about Jeannie and little Bobby? ... I stopped and gazed out over the ships to Helensburgh and the green fields behind it which were lit up through a gap in the cloud. My stomach tightened. Who would do such a thing? Why was I even looking for him?

But he was my dad. I had come so far. Could I really just turn and go home and never know?

When I first saw my mum after the bombing, I was too scared to even look at her. It sounds silly now, but I was younger then and scared of her missing foot. We had all been through so much. But Mr Tait helped me. He told me this was the hardest part, seeing her for the first time, and that once this part was over, it would get easier. I'd had no choice but to believe him and actually it turned out he was right. There's nothing scary about my mum, not even her stump once you've seen it a few times. Mr Tait taught me how to be strong when I felt least able. He taught me to take my time when I wanted to rush or run away. He taught me to save my upset for when bad things really happened and not when I just thought they might, and he taught me how to gather all my strength when I needed it. Like there on the side of that hill on my way to my dad.

So I faced out over Greenock and the sea to Helensburgh and to Dunoon and to where the three lochs stretched off between them. I looked back down the Clyde River towards Clydebank and Glasgow and the Kilpatrick hills, and the other way out to sea. The mountains were turning brown with autumn, the trees red and yellow beside them. I pictured Mr Tait in his brown suit standing there with me admiring the view and what he'd say. 'Your dad's your dad,' he'd say, 'whatever kind of man he is.' I breathed in the strong fresh wind that was buffeting me from the hills and I took off my hat and let the breeze lift my hair. Then I faced into it, put my hat back on and straightened my coat and scarf. I thought that maybe, then, I was ready, or as ready as I'd ever be.

'Ella!' I shouted. 'Wait!'

She was like a demon. I finally caught up with her at the paper mill. It stank to high heaven, which was obviously why it was so far from the town centre. A muckier place it was hard to imagine. The stench was sweet, not in the mouth-watering way like the sugar factory, but cloying and foul.

Across the road a goods train waited by a warehouse with no windows. A chimney grew out of the back of it and blew dark smoke up the hill. Piles of paper as wide as desks and as high as chair backs sat on the train like something I'd seen in all those offices, but much bigger and all tied together with string. A crane was lifting these bundles up and a man stood on top loading everything into position. His shirt was rolled to his elbows and torn at the back and he wore a dark apron and moved in jerks, as if he was going faster than he was able. He glanced our way and shouted something, but I couldn't hear him.

'Come on,' said Ella. 'It's past here and up that hill. Hurry up or the man'll get us.'

The sun burst through the clouds, like an urgent reminder to head south, and glinted off a big sign that said NO SMOKING. Ella charged on in front. The path narrowed between bales of old paper piled high on one side and tin barrels all higgledy-piggledy on the other, then boxes in stacks like rickety old walls leaning to one side, and further down, two buildings of corrugated iron. It was all oddly as I had imagined it. The road squelched under my feet, softened by the rain, and everywhere there were mounds of old paper, curving and ready to fall. A sudden gust gripped these and the nearby autumn rowans and the air was suddenly filled with white and yellow 'snowflakes' dancing in the sun.

'I thought you were in a hurry,' she shouted back as the road curved out of sight.

'Coming,' I said, the urgency having seeped right out of me. The man on the train was watching me. He had stripy arms, not his shirt but the arms themselves, white and red like scars, but blue and green too. He had stopped to watch me and I couldn't help doing the same. Could it be him?

'Oi!' he shouted, though the wind took his voice. 'No minors allowed. Come out of there!'

So I made a show of moving then hid behind a stack of tree trunks and peered out, but he'd disappeared. I needed to think about Mr Tait again anyway, you see, because even though I'd gathered up all my strength on the hillside, I seemed to have lost it all again already.

'Oh, Mr Tait, I can't,' I whispered.

I missed him so much. Nothing made sense, and it hurt that, really, there was only me. Me imagining what Mr Tait would say. I felt my mouth quiver and pulled it down tight and tucked my hands into my arm pits. My heart beat hard in my chest and I closed my eyes the better to think.

This is what he'd say: 'Save your sadness for later. Where's your grit, Lenny? That's what you need right now, grit and bravery, and you have plenty of that. You have to gather up all your strength from the bottom of your boots and go and do what needs done. You'd better get on with it too before Ella finds him first.'

He was wrong about the boots. I've never had boots, only shoes. He always said boots. But he was right about everything else.

'Thank you, Mr Tait,' I whispered, and I opened my eyes.

There was a man standing in front of me. I squealed and staggered back against the logs.

'No children,' he said. It was the man from the paper train. 'It's dangerous, chemicals and stuff. Where's your friend?'

And then we stared at each other and all the courage and bravery and cleverness and sense drained right back down into my shoes again and I completely forgot to breathe. His arms were stained with dyes and burnt with chemicals and heat so that they were blistered and sore-looking. His hands were the same but leathery, even rougher than before. He held them out to me and when I shifted away from him he put them to his lips as if he was praying, like George before I gave him the money. My eyes suddenly burned and two huge tears escaped down my cheeks. My throat tightened and my head felt suddenly roasting hot. As if to help, the wind tugged at my tammy and I had to grab it to stop it blowing away. Then he put one of his hands on his head and the other on his heart and I saw the skin on his neck was like the chicken I plucked with Willie, which is not how it was before he went away. It made my legs tremble to see it that way and I thought for a minute I might fall over and not be able to stop myself. There was dye on his face too and the hair seemed to have gone from his forehead so that the hand on his head was actually on the skin and not the hair. It was like someone had thrown a bag of flour over him, the way what hair there was had turned grey and straggly, the same colour as his shirt.

I put out my hand and he took it and I added my other and the hat and he added his other too and we held on tight as if we were drowning in the sea and stared at each other. We were both trembling and squeezing our hands and the tears flowed down my face like rivers. He had no bunnet. He always had a bunnet. Everyone had a bunnet. Why didn't someone give my dad a bunnet? He drooped, the skin around his eyes hanging loose like an old dog's and red as if he'd been crying. And then I saw them glisten and felt my face crumple.

'Lenny?' he said, and at that exact same moment someone else shouted too.

'Lenny!' yelled a man. 'Where are you, man? I'm ready with another load here.'

'Coming!' my dad called back, letting go with one hand. 'Lenny, what are you doing here?' Our fingers were twisted together, locked so it felt like I'd never move them. 'How did you find me? Is your mother with you?' He looked up and down the lane between the mountains of paper. 'Where's Mavis? I can't believe this!'

His beautiful voice, like water when you're thirsty. He smiled but his mouth trembled and I knew mine was quivering too.

'No,' I managed. 'No-one's with me.' He glanced where Ella had disappeared. 'That's a friend. Mum's only got one leg now.'

'Yeah, of course, yeah.'

He put his hand out to touch my face but I flinched and he stopped and caught his breath.

'Because of the bombing,' I said, 'so she couldn't come. And she's working.' I wiped my face quickly with my hat.

He seemed surprised. 'Working? I heard she had a new man, that Mr Tait who used to bother her at Singer's, and you're all happy.'

'Who told you that?' I said.

'She did,' he said.

'She did? How?' I shook my head. That didn't make sense. How could she have? 'But it's not true. Mr Tait looked after us. He's our friend, my friend. Was.'

'Was?'

There was so much to explain but I didn't want to tell him anything, not about Mr Tait. I wanted to keep it all to myself, the precious truth. I loosened my grip and took my hand back. Then I turned my hat round a few times ready to go on my head. The wind kept flicking my hair in my eyes.

'Mr Tait died,' I told him, not wanting to, batting my hair away. 'Last month.' I bit my lip to stop myself crying again before I went on, and tried to gulp that sadness back for later, and watched the ground. 'He was very good to us. We were happy. It was him who told me you weren't missing presumed dead.'

'Good old Mr Tait,' he said, but not in a way he meant it, as if he didn't think Mr Tait was to be trusted. But seeing my frown, he added, 'for taking such good care of you.'

'Well ... he did and ... . ' What I wanted to say was *and you didn't* but I was too scared. It seemed all wrong. Not fair. But still true.

'I could do with a bit of looking after myself,' he said. 'I'm not very good at this job.' He let out a single laugh, like a donkey, and turned his arms over so I could see the wounds on the inside. 'I've only been here a couple of months. I was better at the last job.'

'Oh no!' I whispered. It looked so sore. I also nearly said, *Well, you should have behaved then and you'd still be there,* but I couldn't.

'Come here, Lenny,' said Lenny my dad. 'Let me see you. You've grown.'

'Well, what did you expect me to do?' I said, staying firmly where I was as if I was rooted there, stiff like a tree. 'I couldn't sit around waiting for you to come back so I could grow.' This was the kind of tone I always took with my dad, 'a bit of banter' as we called it in Clydebank. But it wasn't right. It was too close to the truth.

'No,' he said, 'I suppose not.'

We looked at each other for a second, then both glanced away.

'Did you put on the gentian so we'd have matching faces?' he said, turning back.

'Yeah, and so you'd be the only person who'd recognise me.'

He let out two donkey honks at that and I laughed a bit too, but I didn't want to laugh. This wasn't funny. It was upside down.

'Well, you are a bit long and gangly compared to last time I saw you,' he said.

'Gangly?' I said. 'I'm not gangly.' He stared at me. I was skinny and tired. 'I haven't eaten properly for a fortnight, longer.' This wasn't how it was supposed to happen.

'I'm sorry,' he said, rubbing his forehead. 'You're not gangly. You're like your mum, just younger. You're going to be a beaut.'

I felt my eyes narrow like George's, and like Rosie's when she was furious. I was thinking about Jeannie. We fell silent a minute. Then I remembered the row there had been last time I saw him and how my gran had insisted we go to Rothesay without him because it was all bought and paid for. He'd been arrested by the time we came back.

We looked at each other.

'I'm not the best dad in the world,' he said, in a quiet voice.

'You're still my dad,' I said, softening. 'I had to find you. Mum won't even talk about you. I thought you were dead. Mum let me think you were dead.'

'Lenny!' shouted the other man. 'What the hell

are you doing, man? That's a mighty long leak you're taking.'

'Coming, I told you!' he shouted. 'I was better at the milking,' he said, turning back. 'I'm all burnt to buggery now, me.'

'Why didn't you come to Rothesay with us?' I said. Questions I hadn't thought of until then began flooding my mind. Time was running out. 'You wouldn't have been arrested if you'd come to Rothesay with us.' My heart was in my throat. This other man might take my dad away and I wouldn't get to ask him anything ever again. This might be the only time I ever had with him.

'Yes, I would,' he said. 'They'd have got me sooner or later.'

'Why didn't you come? What was the row about?' I stuck my hat back on my head and pulled it right down around my ears.

'What row?'

'Before we went. You sent me and Mavis next door so you and Mum could talk. I heard it through the wall but I can't remember what it was about.'

'It was probably money, I don't know. We were always arguing about something. It doesn't matter.'

That was when my strength came back to me, flooding up from my pretend boots. I drew in as big a lungful of fresh air as I could manage and then blew it all out again.

'Dad,' I said, in a voice that meant business. 'It does matter. That was the last time I saw you. It was the last argument you had with Mum. I don't believe you can't remember. And I've had enough of grown-ups lying or not telling me the truth. I'm twelve years old.

I can milk cows, for heavens sake.'

'Really?' he said. 'That was my last job. Did you like it?'

'What? Yes, I liked it. Don't you think that makes me pretty able? And I can scrub and clean and cook, and look after Mavis and Rosie when Mum's working, which looks like being all the time from now on. I'm nearly a grown-up myself.'

'Who's Rosie? Did your mum and Mr Tait have a baby?'

I gasped. 'Eh? No!' I said, glaring at him. He really had no idea. 'No, not at all. We adopted her, even though we don't have two brass farthings to rub together. And see this?' I stuck my hand in my pocket, pulled out the rest of my money and showed it to him. 'I earned this. I had to. So I could come and find you.'

He reached out for my hand, a flurry of paper leaves floated between us and I whipped my hand away.

'When you're bigger you'll understand all this, Lenny,' he said. 'Your mum'll explain and you'll see we were just doing our best.'

'Dad, I saw people dying in Clydebank,' I said. 'I saw Mum's leg when it was cut off.' I paused for a minute. My chest was heaving while all those horrible things came back to me. 'Mavis saw stuff too in the bombing. We lost her for two weeks and she's never been the same since. Don't tell me I'm not old enough. Don't tell me I can't understand, like I'm an idiot or something. Tell me what really happened. Give me the truth.'

He rubbed his forehead and eyed me from beneath his hand, then pulled the top of his ear. 'You'd just be better hearing it from your mum, you know,' he said, shaking his head. 'She'll tell you what you need to know. She knows better what to say.'

I shook my head, exasperated. 'Dad! Why can't you just tell me what happened before Rothesay?'

He put his hand to his mouth and blinked at me, and blinked again.

'Alright then,' I said. 'If you won't tell me, I have things to tell you. I went to Helensburgh.'

He sucked his lips in at that and held his head in his hand.

'I met Rocco.' I suddenly realised I was trembling again, this time with rage.

He looked up and smiled. 'Rocco? Good man!'

'Yeah, Rocco was worried about me going looking for you on my own. He wanted to come with me but the farmer wouldn't let him. Not even Rocco had the guts to tell me. No. Not even Rocco, even though I think he wanted to. And then I found Jeannie.' I looked over at my dad who had dipped his head again so I saw dust and filth and scars on the top of his head. I even had time to notice a tiny spider up there. 'And Bobby.'

His head fell lower again and then bounced. He patted his chest with his palm then waved both hands in little circles as if to conjure up a reason for it all, and I saw that beneath the grime and the dye and the scars, his hands were the same beautiful sensitive hands that had held my own hands, the same ones he'd stroked my face with when I was wee but which had grown ugly and sore with work.

'He's so … so like Mavis,' I said, trying not to cry again but not managing. 'How could you leave us and make a whole new … ? Why did you do that?

How could you do that? *How*?' My throat closed up completely and I couldn't say another word.

I heard Ella tramping towards us on the muddy path but couldn't contain my sobs.

'Who's that?' said Ella. 'Is that him?'

I quickly wiped my eyes with my fingers. She had a man in a boiler suit with her. He was almost as ragged as my dad. I put a hand up to her but couldn't speak.

'There you are,' said the man to my dad. 'We need to get this load done, Lenny. It'll be dark soon.'

My dad didn't answer him. I glanced up at my dad and got a hold of myself so I could go on.

'We didn't even hear from you after the bombing,' I said, trying to ignore Ella and the man. 'We could have died for all you cared.' The tears ran freely down my face and I swatted them away like flies.

'I didn't know where you were,' said my dad with a sideways glance at the others. 'This is my daughter, Mr Archer,' he said. 'Her name's Lenny, like me, very like me.'

'And what are you, Leonard or Leonardo?' I said. 'Are you Italian or British, and does that make me Italian too? And does it really matter? It didn't matter enough to tell me.'

The truth is I hadn't really decided what I wanted to say to my dad because every time I'd tried to think something up, my mind had gone completely blank. Now it was all just tumbling out, one horrible complaint after another, and Ella and this man were standing there hearing it all too, and me weeping like the world would end. My head began to hurt. I rubbed it with my hands.

'Oh my goodness!' breathed Ella.

367

'You've got five minutes, Lenny,' said Mr Archer. 'Make it quick. Come on, lassie, let's leave them in peace. I said come on.'

'You want me to stay, Lenny?' said Ella.

'No,' I growled. 'No thanks, sorry. No, it's okay.'

She wandered off, glancing back every two steps, not wanting to miss anything.

My dad shifted from foot to foot. 'He's a good old boy, Mr Archer,' he said, 'but he's a bloody pest.'

'Why don't you have a bunnet?' I said. 'You always wear a bunnet. Everyone wears a bunnet. If you'd had a bunnet you wouldn't have burnt the top of your head and there wouldn't be any blue dye up there.'

'Where?' he said, feeling with a finger.

'Bend down,' I said. 'There and there and there.' He winced. 'And there's lots of green on your ear.' He obviously still had the habit of turning the top of his ear when he was thinking.

I was standing close then and could smell him. He smelled like the pub the day before, whisky and men not washing. He smelled like the mill too, sharp and dangerous.

'I dropped my bunnet in the boiler,' he said, taking my hands, gently this time, in his own. 'Boil that, I said. No, I didn't really. It fell in all by itself. The one before that went in the water on the way from Helensburgh. I was in Helensburgh for a while.'

'I know,' I said.

'Yeah.' He seemed to find a lot to look at in our hands. I was looking too and you never saw so many ragged bits of dark leathery skin with splodges of bleached white on his, and cuts and scrapes on mine. Hard-working hands, his, tougher than they'd ever been when he worked in John Brown's. I ran my fingers over his palms. He let me hold them, trembling a little, strange. They were always busy, always showing you what he was saying, but he'd turned quiet. After a bit, still staring at our hands, he went on.

'Lenny,' he said, 'I'd come back, but your mum wouldn't have me now. Not after, you know …'

I tried to speak but he stopped me.

'I'd have stayed if they hadn't arrested me. After that I just had to survive, you know? And now if I put a toe beyond that gate over there they're going to send me to that prison across the way.'

'What prison across what way?' I said.

He turned me round and showed me a dark building further round the hillside. It looked like just another factory to me.

'That one,' he said. 'They walk me back to the bothy on a farm up the hill and lock me in at night. There are three of us. I think about you all the time.'

'I know where there's a job,' I said. 'The farmer in Carbeth. His wife's having a baby and they have too many cows. You could …'

'Lenny, Lenny,' he said gently, and he tipped my chin up so we could look at each other. We stayed like that for ages. 'I'm sorry,' he said at last and looked away. Then he told me again how he could only work in the paper mill and sleep in the bothy and wait for the war to end. I stared at him, trying to decide if he was lying.

'The Italians are our friends.' I said, wiping my eyes. 'Mr Tait said so. They're on our side now. You're on my side.' This didn't sound right. 'You know what I mean.'

'I was always on your side,' he said. 'I have to go back to work now though.'

Mr Archer was shouting for him again. Ella would arrive any minute. She was probably watching us from behind a bale, without even knowing she was behind a bale.

'I wish you'd told me,' I said. 'About being Italian, I mean. It's important, especially if it makes me Italian too.'

'I'm not Italian and neither are you. I'm British. I was born here, in England at least. I don't even speak Italian, only bits your grandad used to say. I always had an inkling it was best kept quiet. Of course ordinarily there's nothing wrong with being Italian. Rocco's proof of that.'

Helensburgh lay like an accusation across the water, glinting in the sun, a thousand ships still at anchor in the water between, George's ship amongst them.

'A sea captain came up here one day with his binocliars,' said my dad.

'Binoculars,' I corrected.

'As I was saying, his binocliars, and after I'd played him a tune or two, he let me have a shot of them. That was before I threw my moothie into the boiler after my hat. Anyway I saw them over the water using this sea captain's binocliars, on the farm up there on the hillside, probably about the same height as this hill.' He gazed over the river.

'You saw them? What, Jeannie and Bobby?'

'Well, not exactly them but I saw the house, a wee speck amongst the trees. When did you say you were there? '

'Yesterday,' I said.

'Maybe it was you I saw then.'

'Dad!'

'What?'

'Anyway it was raining all yesterday.'

'Not all day.'

'Yes, all day.'

'You people with attention to detail. It's an affliction, you know. You ought to go to a doctor.'

'Doctor schmoctor,' I said.

But it wasn't funny. I turned back round and looked at the heaps of logs and old paper, the blizzard of scraps tumbling in the wind, Ella and Mr Archer waiting along the path. Time was running out and I hadn't said a fraction of what I could have said or asked enough questions or had any real answers.

'At least I know you're not dead,' I said. 'I don't know why she let me think you were.'

'She hates me,' he said. 'She has reason.'

'There's Bobby, I know, but wasn't that later?'

'Yes, Lenny,' he said quietly, 'that's enough now. Don't ask me any more. Ask your mum when you get home. And work hard at school.'

I stared at him. 'Why can't you just tell me? Agh!' I shook both my fists.

'Give your mum my love, and Mavis too,' he said, ignoring my outburst.

He sniffed and wiped his nose with the back of his hand then screwed up his eyes as if something hurt. I could tell I wasn't going to get any more. He turned the green part of his ear which meant end of story, no more information. I felt my blood boil. I'd had more sense and honesty out of Rocco and Jeannie than my own stupid parents.

'You're every colour of the rainbow. Does it hurt?' I said, hoping it did.

'No!' he said in quiet scorn. 'Well, yes, actually, it hurts like hell, but a man's got to do, and all that.' He smiled a little. 'Peas in a pod, you and me, eh?' he said. 'Tea for two and two for tea.'

'Not really. I've only got purple,' I said flatly

'You're not trying hard enough, girl!' he said, ignoring my tone.

Suddenly I felt very tired.

'There's work needing done, Lenny,' said Mr Archer. He didn't seem unkind or angry. 'The last car has to be loaded so it can go in time. You know we can't take any chances.' The two men met eyes and nodded. 'We're already behind, as you know.'

'Right, alright, just coming.'

'Come on, Lenny,' said Ella. 'Let's go and find George. We can say goodbye to him before he goes. You've found your dad now.'

'How is Mavis? And your mum, how's your mum?' said my dad.

'Mavis is fine,' I said. 'She's, well, she's …' I thought of Mavis rocking by the puddle like she was only three and I felt one of those pangs I'd had all day every day when I thought I'd lost her forever after the bombing. My dad had his hands at his mouth again as if he was praying, so I gave him the truth. 'She's nervous and sad and scared all the time. Ever since the bombing, she's never been herself again, even with … even with Mr Tait looking after her, even though she's got Rosie who's the same age to play with.'

He nodded and looked at the ground. Mr Archer made to move so we did too, back to the edge of the paper mill, slowly, as slowly as we dared.

'Mum's not really fine either,' I went on. 'She doesn't sing any more, not since Mr Tait got ill. She stopped when you went away too.'

He glanced at Mr Archer.

'I'd better get back,' my dad said, stopping.

'Why did you do it? Je … Jeannie and Bobby, I mean. What about us? Why didn't you …? Why … ?' A gust blew fiercely about us, so I lost my footing and bumped against him.

'I'm sorry, Lenny, I've got to go. Mr Archer's waiting.'

'Mum doesn't know where I am,' I said. I felt the blood drain from my face as I realised I had been stupid enough to get myself stuck in Greenock for another night. All this for a dad who wouldn't even give me the truth. 'I don't know how to get home.'

Ella was bouncing on and off a log, flicking her polka-dotty skirt.

'You won't get on a train without a pass from the travel office at the pier,' he said. 'I don't know what you're going to do.' He flicked a secret look at Mr Archer.

'But it's miles back to the pier,' I said. 'Even if we tried. I don't know what to do.' My voice was high with panic. I had no proper plan. How stupid. Even without Ella I couldn't stay with Mrs Strachan again. She'd already fed me and I didn't even know her.

Suddenly my dad grabbed me by the hand and bent down close. 'I've got an idea,' he whispered into my ear. 'I know how to get you home.'

Chapter 33

For a split second I hoped my dad's plan was him sneaking away with me there and then and coming home. Without meaning to, I had a whole new life mapped out for us in which he came to work at Mr Tulloch's farm, he and my mum were reunited, and we all went back to live in Carbeth. Simple really. Not difficult to understand at all. And clearly, seeing as both my parents loved me and had at some time loved each other, it was only a matter of time before they could leave all their troubles behind them and we could be united as a family again. I made that plan before I went to Helensburgh. It seemed so childish now.

Here, however, was my dad's plan: he was going to smuggle us out of there on a train, me and Ella that is. Not me, her and him.

He whispered instructions to me as he hugged me goodbye. I could barely take them in. After all, here I was saying goodbye already when I'd only just found him. It made me dizzy to think about leaving him so soon and with so little. Then he called Ella over and said something to her which I couldn't hear because, I suppose, I just didn't want to. And I was too busy trying to contain my panic and thinking, *No! It's too soon. Don't let the daylight go. I haven't finished yet. Stop the train. I don't want to get on.* My heart hammered away in my chest.

'But Dad,' I said, interrupting them. 'Can't you come too? I mean Italy isn't at war with us any more. It's all over the papers. Haven't you seen? They could move you to Carbeth, couldn't they? Please? Couldn't I at least just stay and chat while you work? I mean I'll just sit there near you. I won't be in the way. Please, Dad. Please Mr Archer? Please don't make me go. Please?'

Neither my dad nor Mr Archer spoke. Ella was suddenly there in front of me instead of my dad and I held my head and felt my face crumple, and over the top of my fingers I watched the two men walk away from me up the path until they disappeared behind a flurry of waste paper, merging into the piles of rubbish like ghosts until I couldn't see for crying.

'No!' I wailed, all hope being snatched away. 'Dad! Don't go! Come back!'

'He said we've to get away and hide,' said Ella. 'Come on.' She grabbed my arm. 'We haven't got long and I don't want to get stuck in smelly old Greenock for the night. This place stinks. Come on. Lenny!'

She dragged me down the path, and I followed her, blinded by tears and tripping over every bump in the path, the cold wind rushing up my legs. She yanked me in behind a pile of pallets.

'Okay, that's us away,' she said. 'What do we do next? What did he say?'

I had no idea. 'I don't know. I can't remember!' I gasped.

What did he say? What were we to do? I put my head in my hands. Mr Tait was in there. What would he say? I had to put my tears away for now and try to think. I held my breath and listened.

'Right.' I gave myself a shake. 'Don't say a word and don't jump,' I said before she could do either. I rummaged in my brain for what else my dad had said. What were we to do? Stowaway, we were going to stow away on that train. I told her this and she looked at me as if I was mad, which to be honest seemed quite likely.

'That train? There are no carriages,' she hissed at the tarpaulin-topped flatbeds that reached off into the distance.

I didn't know how he was going to do it, but we were to hide behind an old wooden railway hut with no roof and he'd tell us when to move. A green wooden structure stood near the line. It had no roof and no glass in the window. I didn't really care what happened any more, if we were caught by Mr Archer or got stuck in Greenock, but I did at least realise this was a silly way to think and not helpful. I crouched against the pallets and tapped my head to get my thoughts moving. Then I wiped my face with my scarf, pulled my hat into place and puffed my cheeks.

Ella peered out.

'Get down,' I said, giving her no choice.

'Ow!' she complained.

'Ssh! We have to keep low. Not a sound. Follow me.'

We tiptoed over cogs and wheels, bolts and tin boxes, round a ploughshare (in a paper mill?) and behind the remains of the railway hut.

'Lenny,' she whispered. 'I don't think this is a good idea. I think we should go and find George. He'll know what to do.'

'Don't be ridiculous,' I said. 'He's probably on his way out to his ship. Out there.' I pointed between some trees and a lorry load of waste paper.

'He's not really going, is he?' she said, searching my face.

'What?' I said, 'Of course he's going. What d'you think he was doing in that employment office? Saying hello to old friends?'

'Okay, keep your knickers on,' she said.

'It wasn't me who was thinking of taking them off.' This was something I'd heard about at Carbeth, ladies wanting to take off their knickers, and I thought I knew why. That shut her up for all of three seconds. But before she could scream and shout I put one hand over her mouth and the other at the back of her head to keep it there.

Somebody walked along behind the lorry we'd passed. The man whistled, then underneath the lorry we saw two legs in overalls and a pair of boots come to a stop. We held our breath and waited. A puff of smoke flew at speed round the back of it. Ella gasped and tore my hand from her mouth.

'Smoking? If this lot goes up!' she whispered. 'We have to stop him.' It was possibly the most sensible thing she'd ever said. But also the most stupid.

'Ssh,' I said. 'He won't be long. He's probably smoked here plenty of times.'

'Is it your dad?'

'No, those are boiler suit legs.' Couldn't she tell? 'My dad's in trousers.' Torn ones. Didn't she notice anything?

A shudder ran through the lorry, then the boiler suit legs crossed so we could see the underside of his boot.

'Oh dear,' I said. 'He's smoking the whole thing.'

'Ssh. Come on then, let's go.'

'No, I think we should stay here. Wait for my dad.'

Ella huffed, rearranged herself on her heels and leant back against the hut. In turn, the hut groaned and the boiler suit legs uncrossed and straightened, so we hurried on all fours further round the hut in case he might see us. The lorry door creaked open, slammed shut and its engine growled into life, billows of thick smoke rushing round the hut to join us.

I held on to Ella and we waited until the lorry had gone a short distance and creaked on its brakes. There was a noisy burp as the engine shut off again.

'Right then, where do you want them?' we heard in the distance.

'Now!' I whispered. I had done this many times of course, in school playgrounds and the woods at Carbeth, but never so it actually mattered. Keeping low, we sneaked round bits of engine and piles of rubbish and up along the goods wagons beyond them. Each wagon was piled high, with a black tarpaulin over the top. Along the track I could see my dad there on the ground tying the tarpaulin over the last carriage.

He glanced up at us and made a 'come on' sign down at his leg, and just as we got to him he lifted a bit of the tarpaulin and pulled out a bale of cardboard which was sitting on its own without another two on top.

'Up you go,' he said as quiet as he could.

He made a step with his hands, the way I've done lots of times trying to see in high windows. Ella, after some frantic persuasion, put her foot in his hands and jumped up into the space.

'Hold the tarp up,' he whispered. 'Come on, Leonora, you next. That's my girl.'

'Thanks, Dad,' I said as I stepped into his hands. 'Thanks, Dad,' I said as I took my place beside Ella, two little words I never thought I'd get to say and was scared I might never say again. 'Thanks, Dad,' I said a third time and slipped under the tarpaulin.

Someone shouted from the road, 'Lenny!' and Dad and I turned to see who it was: George, with a brown parcel under his arm. He waved to me, gave a thumbs up and pointed at the parcel. I put my finger to my lips and darted under the tarpaulin.

'It's George,' I whispered to Ella.

'Let me see!' she squeaked.

'Don't be a bloody idiot,' I hissed, taking a grip of her. She was worse than Rosie. 'You'll get us caught.'

'Nearly done, Mr Archer!' I heard my dad shout.

'That's George, Dad.' I said. 'He's my friend.'

My dad gave us some last instructions about getting off, then tied the tarpaulin tight, passing a rope underneath it and up to us. 'Pull that when you want to get off and not before. Understand?'

'Okay, got it,' I said. Had I? For once?

He patted the tarpaulin in reply and shouted to Mr Archer that he was finished.

'Come with us, Dad!' I said. 'Dad? Come too. There's room in here for you.'

There was a pause. All I heard was my heart beating in my ears.

He patted the tarp again and his voice was close to my head. 'Give my love to your mum,' he said, 'and Mavis.'

The train jerked forward and his feet scrunched on

the gravel so I knew he was walking beside us and then with one final pat he was gone.

'Dad!' I yelled. Ella screamed too and we tried to grab onto the bales. 'Dad!'

'I want to get off!' she screamed. We clung to each other as the train shook itself down and lurched forwards and we tried to jam ourselves against the walls of paper. There was nothing to properly hold on to and no protection from the clamour of wagons shuddering into life and the din and screech of wheels against rails. Neither was there any way of keeping the paper dust from our eyes and mouths or seeing anything at all in the total darkness under the tarpaulin.

Because it was my dad's idea, I'd assumed he knew what he was doing and it would be safe and easy to stow away like this. That's what dads do, isn't it, keep their daughters safe? But as we careered around the first bend at what already felt like high speed, Ella slid heavily against me and I in turn was squidged up against the canvas of the tarpaulin. We both squealed and fought against the force that seemed to shift us closer and closer to certain death with every jolt of the train. We knew the drop beyond the canvas and I for one couldn't help imagining the speed and violence with which I would hit the ground. Soon the bales at our backs, those nearer the front, because we were facing the end of the train, slowly moved backwards so that our little secret square was soon an oblong, and not a big one. Luckily the bales got stuck somehow, and with even more luck another bale came tumbling down on top of us and jammed at an angle in the gap before it reached our heads, boxing us in and preventing any others from coming closer. Our little prison had closed on all sides but one.

It was dark in there like you've never known, which was fine, really, to begin with. We had to keep our eyes tight shut against the dust anyway. But very quickly we had no idea which way up we were or how close to the edge or whether the oblong was shrinking and if we were about to be crushed. This meant we had to hold each other tight and keep feeling what was around us. We were not cold, quite the opposite. The bales protected us from most of the chill rushing past, except on the tarpaulin side which was icy. I knew immediately if I'd touched it.

Eventually we managed to stop yelling. The train slowed and blundered to a halt and I thought my bones would fall apart altogether with all the banging and shaking.

'Where are we?' whispered Ella.

'How should I know?' I said, shoogling the stiffness from my legs.

'Have a look then.'

'Sssh. Someone's coming.'

Suddenly a bang sounded and we were bounced two inches off our backsides, landing with an excruciating thud. I thought the lower end of my back was broken, and someone must surely have heard us squeal, but all we could hear was the scraping of metal against metal, the crack of a hammer and chains running over iron, then another bang and the same hammer and chains.

'Let's get out,' said Ella.

'We can't. We only get one shot,' I said. 'If we pull this rope and we can't get off here we'll fall off at the next bend.'

'I don't care. Let me out.'

'This is the wrong place. My dad said,' I said. 'He said we'd stop twice and the first time we'd hear more wagons being attached. That's what the banging is.'

'I don't care,' she said. 'Let me out. Now. Out-my-way!'

She grasped my face, her knee scudded into my stomach, then an elbow slammed into my ribs. If I'd eaten anything since Mrs Strachan's I'd have sicked it right up. She scrabbled for the rope but I had tucked it out of harm's way along the canvas behind me.

'Let me out! I can't breathe!' she growled.

'Stop it, Ella! We can't get out here.'

Full panic set in. She scratched at the canvas as if she could dig her way out. 'Give me it!' she grunted and threw herself against the canvas. A hand thwacked across my face, then a deluge of blows rained down as if there were three furious Ellas towering over me.

Another bang and we were moving again and mercifully Ella was thrown off me and landed full force against the paper, dropping immediately onto my bent knees. I whacked her until my knuckles hit the paper several times. She had me by my coat, her breath hot on my face. Another jolt of the train and her forehead crashed into mine, then she whimpered back onto her side, while I fell back to mine.

We both breathed heavily.

'Don't be so bloody stupid,' I spat. 'There's one more stop and if you so much as move I'll …' I kicked her so she'd know I meant it.

The train lurched to one side then back again and we grabbed each other for safety. I pushed against a bale to keep my place and neither of us spoke.

It was miles to the next stop. We braced ourselves

and listened to horses' hooves hitting the gravel, approaching then stopping short, then the wagon shook a little and shook again. No footsteps, horse or man, came near us.

'It's the next one,' I whispered. 'Right now we're safe. You should save being scared for later when we have to get off. We've been round enough bends to know the tarpaulin's not going to come undone. Just hang on and get your grit ready.'

'My what?' she hissed.

'Your grit,' I said. 'Bravery, courage. You just have to get your nerve up ready to jump when we get there. It's the next one. I'll get the rope ready so we can jump 'cause we won't have long.'

'I don't have any of that,' she said, 'that grit stuff.'

'Yes, you do,' I said. 'It's in your boots. You just need to pull it up.'

'I'm not wearing boots,' she said. 'Neither are you.'

I sighed. 'No, but you know what I mean. Being scared will only make you … scareder.'

I reached behind me for the rope and carefully brought it forward.

'What are you doing?' she said.

'Getting the rope ready,' I said. 'I told you.'

She leapt up and somehow found the stupid rope in my hand and pulled. The tarpaulin shook free just as the train pitched forward again and we were off. She crashed against the bales and bounced onto my knees again.

'You stupid idiot!' I shouted.

The tarpaulin flapped, gently at first but then, as we built up speed, it cracked like a whip. Outside, darkness had fallen. We felt the rush of cold air into our little compartment, which soon bit like a dog. I could see beneath us the silver line of some neighbouring tracks flickering and every so often a blue flash shone out from under us as metal hit metal.

The bale above us had loosened and shoogled from side to side. Ella squealed with every bump, then we turned a long but tight bend and the force shunted me closer to the edge.

At last the train slowed again.

'Get ready!' I said. 'This is where you've got to be brave.' I waited until we came crunching to a stop. 'Now!' I shouted, not caring who heard us.

I slid one leg over the side and shifted the rest of me towards it until suddenly I was on the ground with chunks of stone in my shoulder, completely winded.

'Lenny!' she screamed. 'Don't leave me. I'm stuck! I can't get out! Come back!'

I couldn't breathe or see her. I picked myself up and leant on the wagon. She wasn't stuck, only scared. She grasped my hand and started to edge out. But then the train bumped forwards an inch and I panicked, leant back and heaved with all my might. She came flying through and landed on top of me with her knees crashing hard on the gravel.

She got to her feet, squawking and squealing that she'd never walk again, so I grabbed her hand and tugged her away from the train across several other tracks. You never saw so many railway lines, a million of them like snakes side by side glinting in the moonlight. We heard and saw no-one and no-one came running, even with Ella screeching like a banshee.

We arrived at some rough ground where a row of giant pipes stood sentry. Beyond that was a road.

Moonlight slid off puddles while behind us our goods train roared and chuntered off again.

Chapter 34

Eventually Ella shut up about her knees. I mean, what were a few more scrapes in the circumstances?

The last thing my dad said was: 'Get a passenger train at Abercorn for the ferry.' I knew what the ferry was because I'd seen it from the other side. It was the Renfrew Ferry, but I'd never heard of Abercorn. You'd think finding a railway station would be easy, especially next to railway tracks, but all the station names had been taken down and it was dark. Thick clouds kept sliding across the moon.

'Where are we?' Ella whined. 'I don't like the dark. Maybe we should just hand ourselves in. There could be anybody out here. There could be, couldn't there?'

'Quiet, Ella,' I said. 'Stop being such a scaredy-cat. My dad said it's okay, so it's okay.' I took a firm grip of her elbow and wished that were true. I couldn't see the ground, but I was on my way home so I didn't care. 'This way,' I said, as if it was obvious. 'Head for the light. We can ask the way from there.'

A slither of light flickered round a window. Thank goodness for lax citizens and absent ARP wardens. Ella dug her fingers into my arm and we edged our way towards it until suddenly it disappeared. I pulled my coat tight and stuffed my scarf tight inside it. The wind was cutting. My stomach groaned and I realised

I was starving hungry.

A shadow came towards us, boots clicking on the tarmac.

'Oh no!' breathed Ella, and we clung to each other. Waited and listened. The footsteps were uneven and slow and as they approached we heard breathing. Then the clouds pulled back from the moon and the long white face of an old man appeared. Ella squealed and I poked her ribs to shut her up.

I was just about to ask him where the station was when I saw the station behind him, its roof lit up like glass.

'Station's that way,' he said throwing his thumb over his shoulder.

'Thank you,' I said.

'Last train's in five minutes.'

We hurried before the moonlight went, Ella whooping into the night sky in excitement. I bought us both tickets and we waited on the dark platform and argued about who was the biggest fearty, though to be honest I didn't care. The moon stayed out until the train came in and we climbed aboard, sank gratefully into the cosy velvet seats and Ella laughed her head off as if she'd won a watch. But the journey was short and too soon we were out again by the river.

All we had to do was cross it and walk home. The ferry terminal was a squat building by the slipway. As I stepped up to the pay desk, a surge of happiness lifted through me and a smile crept over my face.

'Pass,' said the lady.

'Pass?' I said, faltering.

'You need passes, both of you, or you can't get across.'

'We don't have passes,' I said.

She checked her fingernails, which were long and dirty, before going on. 'Well, you need them. You should be in bed anyway. Children out at this time, and look at the state of you. Next!'

I now plummeted to the depths of misery and stood uncomprehending at the desk with my mouth hanging open. The ferry engines rumbled into life and a whoosh of cold air grabbed me by the ankles.

Ella brushed me out the way.

'We had passes,' she said, 'but we lost them, and I've got my granny's medicine and she'll die without it. We've also been in a terrible accident and need to get home before our mothers think we've been killed.'

'Top of the class for inventiveness,' said the pay lady. 'Now get lost.'

'We'll pay you extra,' said Ella, so business-like all of a sudden. 'Please.'

'No, dear,' said the lady, softening. She leant forward so we could see the wrinkles round her eyes and gave us a brisk smile. 'I'd love to but I can't. Off you go. Who's next?'

We had to move away so a tall lady in a long flowing overcoat could get her ticket and then some other lucky people. They passed back again, down the slipway and up the ramp into the boat. One after the other they went, dark shadows moving in the dark, the moon no longer lighting us.

'It's not fair,' said Ella. 'What are we going to do now? Swim? I mean there has to be a way.'

Swim. For a moment this seemed possible. It wasn't that far and my dad taught me years ago. But good sense returned with one glance at the inky black

Clyde and I stood there feeling ragged and felt myself tremble.

'We'll die of cold if we have to stay here all night,' I muttered. 'Anything could happen. Oh God! I just want to go home.' My whole body seemed to ache with longing for my mum, Mavis and Rosie. 'I just want home.'

A bell rang on the ferry just as the tall lady in the overcoat passed us. She was fiddling with a large handbag, trying to find something in it. Ella went over.

'Excuse me,' she said, all polite. 'I wonder if you could help us? We're stuck on the wrong side of the river without any passes and our …'

'Your granny's going to die without the medicine,' the lady interrupted with a laugh. 'And you've been in a terrible accident.' She laughed again and the bell on the ferry tinkled.

'Um, yes,' said Ella. 'That's about it.'

'Not very good at lying are you?' said the lady.

'We just want to go home,' I said. 'We live in Clydebank and our mums will be worried sick. Please.'

The bell tinkled again and a man there called over. 'Mrs Buchannan, if you could?'

He meant if she could just hurry up and get on board, but I was thinking something similar. If she could just help us … .

'Good evening, Mr Bennett,' she called to him. 'I've brought my nieces. They've been in a motor vehicle accident and I'm taking them to my son, the doctor. I see his car is waiting on the other side as usual. Always a man for promptness.' Two headlights flashed across the water, right on cue. 'I just need to get their tickets.'

'Right you are, Mrs Buchanan,' said the ferryman, 'but never mind the tickets. We're already late.'

'Thank you, Mr Bennett. Come along girls,' said Mrs Buchanan. She went up the gangplank and we followed. What a surprise. I thanked God inwardly, thinking how he must exist after all but was playing rather cruel games on us.

'Thank you,' we muttered to Mr Bennett as we passed, avoiding his eye.

Mrs Buchannan perched herself on a bench and invited us to follow, so we did. 'Now, what happened to you?'

So Ella, like a complete fool, told her.

I didn't want to hear our story. I was there after all and was glad of a few minutes without Ella, and anyway I'd noticed a soldier standing by himself near the front. He was staring out at the opposite bank, but from behind he looked just like my dad, my old dad when he first came home on leave, before everything went wrong. As the ferry crossed that little stretch of water from one bank to the other I had a terrible horrible thought. At first it was too awful to bear and I pretended I hadn't thought it, but it seemed so true I knew I couldn't avoid it. This is what it was:

I had remembered my dad's instructions almost word for word. He told me what to do and where to go with absolute simplicity and straightforwardness and in such a way that even I, who had forgotten all the other important instructions in the previous couple of days, even I could remember them. But I knew my dad wasn't particularly clever at giving instructions. That wasn't it. He knew what to tell me because he'd made exactly the same journey himself.

He'd probably done it more than once, maybe even several times, and if he was able to sneak off like that without being seen or caught, why hadn't he come and found me and Mavis and my mum?

The ferry bumped up on the other side and I watched the soldier hurry off the boat, up the slipway and into the darkness as if he really did have his granny's medicine and she really was going to die without it if he didn't get there soon. Or as if there was someone he really loved who he just couldn't wait to be with.

All the other passengers flooded past me. Their feet rang out on the ramp and clattered up the slipway. Mrs Buchanan and Ella were last off, gossiping away as if they were old bosom buddies.

'Come on, Lenny,' Ella barked cheerfully, striding on ahead and clanking down onto the concrete.

Shards of light were escaping from holes in a nearby factory wall. I saw Ella and Mrs Buchanan beside a motor car talking to the driver. Behind me the ferry engines rumbled and cut out and an odd silence fell, heavy like the darkness, like my heart. The ferrymen were busy with the boat, calling to each other about the cold or the day's work. Whatever it was I didn't notice or care.

'Come on, Lenny, we're going in a real motor car, get a shift on, quick!' Ella's shins were dark with blood from her fall. Her polka-dotty skirt was torn on one side and her face was sprinkled with indistinct dark patches, like a brindled cat, but she smiled and showed her knees to the doctor and Mrs Buchanan, and the doctor insisted on the importance of cleaning wounds.

Mrs Buchanan got into the front seat beside her son.

Ella and I got in the back. This should have been fantastically exciting. I'd never been in a real motor car, only a bus. Ella ran her hands over the leather of the seats, drew faces in the mist on the window and then jammed herself between the front seats and watched out the front window. The moon slipped out of the clouds and dark figures flitted past in the dimmed headlights of the car: the soldier like my dad, a gang of boys, lingerers in a pub door, an old man in a torn shirt staggering down the pavement, a woman with a basket of washing who weaved her way past him while a young couple applauded. Dark walls with darker close mouths passed rhythmically with the speed of the car, then baffle walls flashed too close for comfort and I leant back in the seat, closed my eyes and fought back the tears.

They left us on the main road. I thanked them for their help and made some effort to smile, glad of the night to hide in.

'Wait 'til I tell … ,' said Ella, and she listed all the people she was going to annoy with endless stories of our journey, most of whom I'd never heard of. If I could have shut my ears I would have. 'What's the matter?' she went on. 'Aren't you glad we're nearly home? Aren't you pleased you found your dad?'

'Yeah,' I said, not wanting to talk.

'Mine's missing presumed dead,' she said.

'Yeah, you said.'

'That means he's dead but they couldn't find his body to prove it because he was blown to smithereens,' she said.

This was something I hadn't known, and I supposed it must be true, what 'missing presumed dead' actually meant, but how could she just say it like that? Didn't she care? I tried not to think of what happened to her dad. I knew about those things. I didn't want to know.

'That's … that's terrible,' I said, keeping my voice steady.

She didn't say another word.

In the end, my dad hadn't been missing presumed dead. Only missing, but not missing me.

We walked in silence while the old familiar sounds of the shipyards rumbled and banged in the distance. Swiftly we went, because of the cold and we hadn't eaten since the morning and because I had a million questions for my mum. I couldn't wait to see Mavis and Rosie again. I just wanted home, and the more I thought how much I wanted my family the quicker my steps became and the harder it was to swallow back my tears. We reached the end of the street and suddenly Ella grabbed my arm.

'I live up there,' she said, pointing up the hill. 'My mum's going to kill me. Friends?' She held out her hand to shake, which seemed oddly formal and something only men did, but when I reached out to take it she withdrew hers and whacked mine so hard it stung.

'Got yah!' she called and she ran up the street. 'See yah!'

'I hope you find a baffle wall,' I yelled, and by the sound of it she found one soon after.

The moon stayed with me all the way to number forty-three. I banged on the door and let myself in without waiting.

Chapter 35

Beyond the darkened hallway, behind a door, I could hear my mum singing, 'When I Grow Too Old To Dream'. She only sang when she was happy. Even for sad songs like this one she had to be happy, which she hadn't been for ages because of Mr Tait being ill and dying. But I couldn't hang about.

As soon as I opened the door the singing stopped and it seemed like everyone screamed all at once. Everyone except me that is because I was choked with sobs of relief. They were all in bed, Mavis and Rosie on either side of my mum who was sat up between them with a cup of tea cradled in her hands. Mavis and Rosie leapt up spilling the tea the length of the bed and swaddled me in hugs. I surrendered. I think otherwise I'd have collapsed in a shivering heap on the floor. Mum manoeuvred herself over the edge of the bed and held all three of us in one tight little bundle.

'I found him,' I said, as soon as I could get the words out. 'He's alive. You know that. But he's not coming back.' And then I cried because even though I didn't understand everything that had happened between my mum and dad, or to my dad since he was taken away, I knew he wasn't coming back, but I'd never actually said it, not even to myself.

My mum took my face in her hands and put her

own face close to mine and kissed my cheek then leant her own cheek against mine. She switched on the electric light and blew out the candle on the mantelpiece. Rosie ran circles round the room and Mavis clung tight around me, and I held on to her. A little fire glowed in the grate, fading after the day, and a basin of water sat ready on the floor beside it for the morning.

'Come here,' said my mum, leaning on the bed. She held me in her arms for a long time until I'd stopped sobbing and I closed my eyes and felt her warmth against me and the breath making her body move in and out, her hand stroking my hair. I think after a bit I was almost asleep, I felt so peaceful and safe in a way I hadn't felt for ages and ages. Rosie was doing a little jig and Mavis clung onto my hand, squeezing and squeezing it. In the end they both came and leant on us too until I woke out of my dwam and it somehow seemed funny so we all started to laugh.

'Right, Private Rosie,' I said. 'Back to bed. Private Mavis?'

'No,' said Mum. 'Let's get the fire going again and see if we can't clean you up. Mrs MacIntosh is already asleep. Listen.' We listened and sure enough through the wall were the round resonances of a snore.

'That's not Mrs MacIntosh,' said Rosie. 'That's Mr Weaver.'

'It's Mrs Weaver's mum,' said Mavis.

'It's coming from the kitchen, silly billies,' said my mum. 'It's Mrs MacIntosh, which means I can't heat up the soup for you, Lenny. She doesn't like us cooking on the fire because of the mess it makes of the pot.'

'I'll clean it up,' I said, wiping my nose with my hand. 'Or I could just have cold soup. I'm starving. I'll eat anything.'

She looked at me long and hard. 'You'll do nothing of the sort,' she said, changing her mind. 'You're going to get hot soup and while it's heating up we're going to sort all those cuts and bruises and … what on earth happened to you? Did your dad do this?'

'No,' I said. 'Of course not.'

So I sat on a packing case with 'Singer' on the side, and ate hot soup. Mavis and Rosie leant against me and my mum redd up the fire and sat in her wheelchair. I told them where I'd been, everything I've just told you really. But when I got to the bit about Helensburgh I saw my mum look off into the shadows and had to wait for a nod before going on. Mavis and Rosie took the news about Bobby and Jeannie in the best possible way, that is, they didn't even as blink, not even Mavis. I suppose they can't have understood, and it probably didn't matter anyway. It wasn't like we'd ever have to see them. It didn't need to be real for Mavis and Rosie.

By the time my story had arrived at the paper mill, Rosie was asleep and Mavis was trying not to be, so Mum and I slipped them easily into bed, turned off the electric light, relit the candle, and went back and huddled by the fire.

I had several important questions I needed to ask, but none more important than the one which came to me on the ferry. She listened in silence as I described meeting my dad at the paper mill, her fingers over her mouth. When I told her about the goods wagon she gasped.

'Oh my goodness,' she said. 'The idiot. What a

stupid thing to do.' The fire flashed in her eyes.

When I told her about Ella pulling the rope she put her hand on her chest and her lips fell open, dumbstruck.

'Oh no,' she breathed.

We both sat back in relief when I told her about the train from Abercorn to the Renfrew ferry in the moonlight. And when I told her about Mrs Buchanan joining in our lies, she laughed.

'Oh, Lenny, that's terrible,' she said, but went on in a whisper. 'You are so your father's daughter!'

Previously this would have seemed like a good thing, and of course on this occasion it wasn't even me, it was Ella. In the past I'd have been pleased to be like my funny old dad, but this time I needed answers.

'Mum,' I said in my serious voice.

'What?' she said in her small voice.

'When did you last see Dad? I mean, did he ever visit you? Did he ever come looking for us, that you know of, after the bombing or any time?'

I had decided to keep my eyes on her to make sure she wouldn't try to fob me off with something that wasn't true, one of her famous white lies. She'd probably think she was doing it for my own good. I had many arguments to the contrary, like everything I'd said to my dad at the paper mill. I was ready for the truth.

But her gaze didn't leave mine. Her head began to bob and her eyes crinkled at the edges, and then she gave one emphatic nod, closed her eyes and pursed her lips. I put my hand on her arm. She opened her eyes and a tear slipped out of the corner of both. She wiped them firmly away and sniffed loudly.

'He came to Carbeth,' she said.

'Carbeth?' I said, and hid my mouth in my hands.

'Someone round here told him we'd gone to Carbeth so he arrived one Monday when you were at school. He brought a big skein of blue wool as a peace offering, though what lorry that fell off I've no idea. That's what I made all those hats out of.'

'Oh,' I said. 'So this wasn't that long ago? Only this summer? A few weeks ago?'

'Yes,' she said. 'I'm so sorry. I thought it was best you didn't know.'

I showed both palms to the ceiling as if asking God to explain to my foolish mother that this was a gross insult. I squared my shoulders and was just about to give her some home truths when my prayers seemed to be answered.

'I realise now how wrong that was,' she said.

'What?' I said.

'I don't think I really understood how capable you are, much more than I was at your age. I should have told you. I should have explained instead of just telling you he wasn't coming back. I'm so sorry.'

I was completely gobsmacked. 'You let me think he was dead. Why did you let me think that all this time?'

She shifted in the wheelchair. It creaked and sighed.

'Did you ever think he was dead?' I said.

She stared at the ceiling a moment and chewed her lip. 'Yes, sort of,' she said at last, returning my gaze. 'I think I just hoped he was. It would have been so much easier. I didn't know definitely.'

I gasped and covered my mouth.

'I'm sorry,' she said.

'He's my dad!' I said, trying not to wake Mavis

and Rosie. 'How could you wish him dead?'

'I'm sorry,' she said again. 'I'm doing my best, you know. It's not easy. You don't know the full story.'

'So tell me,' I snapped. I got up and went to the window. The shutters were over and they were cold on my hand. I laid my forehead against them too and closed my eyes for a second until I realised I was shaking.

'Lenny,' she whispered. 'Let me tell you about when he came. Please. Come and sit with me.'

So I did.

It turns out my dad showed up at our hut. It was the first day Mr Tait had to stay off work because of being ill. Not such a good day. My mum was at the sewing machine by the window and thought she was seeing things.

'He came up the steps and in the door as if he lived there,' she said. 'He put this brown paper parcel on the birch bench. That was the wool. "I thought you were dead," I said, and I stood up and hugged him. For all that had happened, I was still, in that moment, glad to see he was alive. He was skin and bone, there was nothing to him. But then Mr Tait had the most almighty coughing fit so I had to go and attend to him.'

'Wait a minute,' I said, shaking my head. 'What do you mean by "for all that had happened"?'

She put her head down and stayed still for a minute. The coal shifted in the fireplace and she reached out and added three new pieces to the embers and wiped her hands on a cloth. She glanced at me then stared at the flames and the dust sparks rising amongst them.

'Jeannie wasn't the first woman he ... ,' she said.

'Or at least I don't think so.' She put her head back, closed her eyes and blew out until she sank like an old balloon. 'But your gran and Auntie May were convinced. There was a story going around, you see, started by another soldier your dad served with.'

This was the row before Rothesay, in June 1940, more than three years earlier. This was when Mavis and I were sent next door to neighbours and when we left him behind and crossed on the boat to Rothesay without him. My mum and I sat in silence a moment while I, at least, travelled back through time and pictured our house in Clydebank where so much had happened, so much I hadn't even known about.

'I never got to the bottom of it,' she said. 'It might all have been lies. And then he was arrested and I didn't know if he was even alive or dead. We heard there was a ship which had sunk with hundreds killed, you see, but no-one knew who was on it. I tried to forget all about him and I thought it was better you did too. Then after the bombing we had Mr Tait to look after us.'

'What happened when Dad came?'

So she told me. Mr Tait had sat in his chair by the fire, apparently eagle-eyed between coughs.

'Can you give us a minute, mate?' said my dad.

'Certainly, if Peggy would like that,' said Mr Tait, and he leant forward to get out of his chair.

'No,' said my mum, 'don't go, Mr Tait. It's windy out there and you're not well. Please. Sit.' My dad tried to object but she was firm. 'Mr Tait has been looking after us since the bombing, all of us, haven't you, Mr Tait?'

My dad threw Mr Tait a look that made my mum's

heart beat faster, then he stared back at her.

'So what's going on here?' he said. 'Are you two, you know, together?'

My mum said 'No!' at exactly the same moment Mr Tait said, well, nothing. Mr Tait got to his feet and steadied himself with the chair arm. My dad, tall but haggard, pretty much as I saw him at the paper mill but with a borrowed shirt, a jacket and a bunnet, squared up to face him.

'I'd like a word with my wife,' said my dad, 'a private word.'

'Peggy, I'll go outside and sit on the steps,' said Mr Tait. 'I won't be far.'

I watched as my mum paused to put another unnecessary piece of coal in the fire. 'I was scared,' she said. 'Your dad had a wild look about him and there was a smell of drink. I tried to calm him by offering him a seat, a plate of food, but the more he insisted Mr Tait go, the more I had to insist he stay. If I'd known why he'd come I might have let Mr Tait leave us in peace.'

'And why had he come?' I said.

Finally, she said, my dad turned red and began to shake, which my mum took to be rage. He sat down on the birch bench then stood up again wringing his bunnet between his hands. 'I love you Peggy. I always loved you.' He coughed and cleared his throat. 'But I need to tell you something before you hear it from anyone else.'

So he told her about Bobby and Jeannie and he promised he'd never see them again, which of course was an easy thing to do because, as I knew, he was normally under arrest in the bothy on the farm and if he got caught leaving he'd wind up in that jail. He told her he'd left Jeannie and Bobby and it had all been a terrible mistake and he'd gone to Greenock to work and wasn't allowed to come home to us, but that after the war we'd all be together again.

My mum stood there with her mouth hanging open for a full minute, so she said, until, she said, she could take in everything he'd told her and find some sort of sense or reason to it all.

'My dear Peggy … ,' Mr Tait began.

'It's alright, Mr Tait,' she said, cutting him off. 'I'll handle this. No, Lenny, we won't be together when the war is over. That would be so easy for you, wouldn't it?' she said. 'But it's not going to happen. I have a new life now and I've worked hard for it. Mr Tait and I both have.'

I don't know everything she said to him, but I've seen my mum when she's upset and angry and it's not something you want to be on the end of. And while she was telling him to go away and leave us all in peace, he was roaring that whatever happened he wanted to see his daughters, wee Mavis and me.

I put my head in my hands and pressed hard. It was like I could hear them, knew all the things they had said as if I'd been right there in the hut when it happened. My hands felt sticky on my forehead and my stomach ached. I wanted Mr Tait. I wanted it all not to be true and for them to stop shouting in my head. She fell back into silence and waited for me to come out of my hands.

'I suppose I was wrong about that too, about you not seeing him. You got yourself there anyway.'

I stared at the fire, which melted in the wash of

my tears. She came off her wheelchair and put her arms around me, holding me safe while I sobbed and shook and snottered into a handkerchief until I was all cried out. But I still needed to know.

'What happened next?' I said.

'Mr Duncan came and made him go. He went to the school to find you but no-one was there because it was the afternoon and you'd all gone up to the ropeswing on the way home. You'll see him again, darling, I promise. We just won't be together as a family again. I'm sorry.'

'I know,' I said. 'I know.' Though I couldn't really make sense of it.

'I don't know how he got to Carbeth,' she said. 'He shouldn't have been allowed anywhere.'

'I know how he got there,' I said miserably. 'The same way I got back today, stowed away on a goods train.'

'But tomorrow we're going to Carbeth,' she said, 'so we need to go to bed.'

'Carbeth? Why are we going to Carbeth?'

'Do we need a reason? But now that you've eaten you need to get some sleep.'

'Don't you have to go to work?'

'Yes, but … let's just go to Carbeth, alright? Sleep first.'

'What about Mavis and Rosie? Are they coming too? They should be at school.' It completely slipped my mind that so should I.

'Sleep, Lenny, first.'

I was toasty from the fire and so incredibly tired, my mind awash with everything she'd told me. She tucked me into bed with Mavis and Rosie then squeezed in beside us herself. I must have fallen straight to asleep, bathed in the glow from the fire and the warm bodies of my lovely family. Complete silence and total dreamless darkness.

It seemed almost no time had passed before Mrs MacIntosh banged on the door.

'Seven o'clock, Mrs Gillespie!' she called. 'Mrs Gillespie? Are you up?'

The floorboards creaked beyond the door.

'Mrs Gillespie?'

'Yes,' groaned my mum. 'Thank you.'

It was still dark, deliciously so. Mavis wriggled up close to me, and Rosie scrambled over the top of us both so she could be on my other side. My mum rolled over and cradled us with an arm. I wondered whether it was possible to make that moment last forever so I tried to capture it with all my senses, the warmth, the smell of their hair, their little snores, Rosie whispering skipping rhymes, Mavis fiddling with her fingers, my mum's soft long breaths making my fringe tickle my nose. When I opened my eyes, ages later but still too soon, there was brilliant light pushing its way past the shutters at the window.

'Mrs Gillespie!' insisted Mrs MacIntosh, from the hall. 'You're late!' Bang she went on the door again.

'Right you are,' my mum called back. 'I'm not going to work. I've got important business to attend to.'

Mrs MacIntosh went away grumbling, the floorboards complaining all the way back to the kitchen. My mum slid from the bed and opened one side of the shutters. Yellow light filled one half of the room. I rolled towards it and saw blue sky spread above the chimney pots of the tenements opposite.

'Carbeth,' I whispered, and a blizzard of leaves shot past the window. I sat bolt upright. 'Carbeth!' I shouted. 'Come on!'

We ate hastily boiled porridge and drank extremely weak tea with no milk. Mrs MacIntosh grudgingly let me have a proper wash in her sink and we all dressed as quickly as we could. It was cold, but we were so excited about the day that nothing really mattered. My mum had cut down her old dress that was torn under the sleeves from the crutches and it fitted me perfectly. It was just as well because I'd completely ruined the beautiful yellow and green dress on my travels. The new dress was longer than the last, hanging just below my knee, which meant many of my wounds were hidden. It was blue with embroidered flowers to cover places where the material had thinned.

We hurried down to Dumbarton Road, as best a one-legged woman can, and got on the tram to Glasgow and from there, the bus to Carbeth. At Craigton we pressed our noses to the window and waved at our friends on their morning break then got off just beyond the Halfway House pub and turned up the road to our hut. The wind sang through the trees and all the colours of autumn flew through the air or danced along the road with us. We passed George's hut and through the half-stripped trees the old man with his newspaper was outside his hut. I thought I saw Mr Tait standing nearby, but it was an old bush turned autumn brown. He seemed to be ahead of us too, hobbling home with his walking stick, but it was a sapling grown too far into the road. How my mind played these tricks I'll never know, but they were strangely comforting, as if he really was still with us, leading us home.

We were almost at our hut when my mum stopped in the middle of the road.

'Hold on,' she said. 'We have to make a detour, just to be on the safe side. We have to go to Home Farm.'

'Why?' we chorused.

'It's where the estate office is.'

'The estate office?' we said, and laughed at our ridiculous chiming together.

But suddenly all the happiness flew out of me. We couldn't afford the rent. That's what she said. She said we couldn't afford two rents, Clydebank and Carbeth. I hadn't thought about rent. I mean, why would we pay rent on a hut that Mr Tait and I had built? It seemed illogical. We'd even had to clear the ground. It was ours. Mr Tait's at least. And didn't it become ours now that he was gone? But rent was rent and we didn't have any.

The others crossed the road and headed down the driveway. I didn't want to go. I didn't know why we were going there. The last time I was at Home Farm was after Mr Tait died, when the red-faced minister climbed the hill to give a Sunday service and ask everyone to pray for us, and Mavis and Rosie cried so badly I had to take them outside.

But good old Mavis and Rosie seemed to have forgotten all that and were zigzagging across the driveway and tapping tree trunks at either side.

'Come on Lenny!' my mum called back. 'We haven't got all day.' Then she laughed and scratched her head. 'Actually, come to think of it we have.' She leant against an old fence post at the side of the road and waited for me to catch up. The wind held her hair off her face and her cheeks were apple red, like Mavis's used to always be before the bombing. Despite my mum's missing foot she leant erect on the old post, her head high on her shoulders, the cloth bag with our lunch hanging easily over her arm. 'I love you, Peggy,' I heard my dad say. 'I've always loved you.' Then Mr Tait coughed and coughed again. 'Peggy, my dear,' he said. I stopped on the path and closed my eyes. Mr Tait was in there smiling. I opened them again and there was my mum who everyone loved, smiling, her old self again, singing the song from the night before but without the words. Singing. Something was wrong here, or rather something had to be very right.

'Come on, Lenny,' she called. 'The factor's waiting.'

I ran over and took her arm.

'Why are we going to see the factor?' I said.

'Questions questions!' she said. 'Goodness me. You'll find out soon enough.'

And no matter how I badgered her she wasn't going to tell me.

We crossed the farmyard past the barn which on Sundays was the church. Inside two men were forking hay. The biggest horse you ever saw stood waiting by a stable door. The factor's office was beyond all this.

He seemed like a nice enough man but he suggested we girls wait outside. I set my chin, ready to insist. He patted the front of his woolly jumper, green with no holes, and waited for us to leave.

'Off you go then, you two,' said my mum. 'Lenny, you come with me.'

Rosie glared first at the factor, then at my mum, and lastly at me.

'It's not my fault,' I told her. 'I don't know what's going on.'

'Let's go,' said Mavis, throwing me a look that could kill.

But Rosie wouldn't move. She crossed her arms and the bottom lip came forward, the forehead down.

'Oh, let them stay,' I said. 'It's not worth it. You don't know the trouble it'd be to get rid of them.'

So we all huddled into the factor's tiny office and I waited with bated breath for what might happen.

The factor opened the drawer of his desk and brought out a sheaf of papers, sifted through them and chose one. On the other side of the table, our side, my mum went into her cloth lunch bag and brought out two pieces of paper which she unfolded, turned round and set in front of him. He picked them up and read them quietly. I read what I could upside down. LAST WILL AND TEST-AM-ENT. My heart began to beat faster.

The factor put down the papers. He shuffled his own papers together and put them back into the drawer.

'I thought you were going to ask for the advance rent back,' he said. 'Which of course I couldn't have given you, not without going through lawyers. I'm assuming you couldn't afford one of those. This changes everything. You have ten months' rent bought and paid for.' He smiled. 'There is just one problem.'

The smiles fell off our faces.

'I need his ownership papers,' he said. 'A will bequeathing the hut to you isn't enough. I can't transfer a land rent contract to you without ownership papers for the hut itself. I'm assuming you have them?'

My mum blanched. 'They weren't amongst his papers.' She said. 'Oh no. I don't know what to do.

They weren't in the hut when we left. I know that for certain because we cleared the whole thing. I thought we were leaving forever. I don't know what to do.'

The factor's face became serious. 'I can't give you the money, you know, if that's what you're after.'

'We're not after the money,' I said, before she could. 'Mr Tait and I built that hut, with help from George Connor and Mr Duncan.'

'And me and Mavis,' said Rosie.

'And these two,' I said.

'Then you need to find the papers.'

I was beginning to wonder if there was something that happened to people when they had a desk put between them and other ordinary human beings. There was a pause during which I thought I could actually feel all the sadness and anguish flood back into my mum.

'But, I don't know where to look. Isn't this enough?' She tapped the Will and Testament with her finger. 'Can't we draw up new papers with my name on them? Why is there a problem?'

'Sorry,' said the factor, with another pat to his sweater. He stood up and gestured towards the door. 'I'll be here all afternoon.'

I stood up too, full height, and shook my hair out of my eyes. 'We'll find them,' I said. 'Don't you worry, Mr Factor. We'll find them, won't we, Mum?'

'Well, Lenny, I don't know. I don't know what to think.' She stood unsteadily and I helped her to the door.

'We'll find them,' I said, conscious of my bottom lip doing a Rosie-like push forwards.

Outside a clear blue sky stretched above the trees

and the wind hummed and ahhed. We returned along the path in silence, a thoughtful little bunch.

'Why would Mr Tait lose something so important?' said Rosie. 'I don't think he ever lost anything important before. He kept everything safe in its proper place all the time.'

'Even us,' Mavis put in.

'He was always telling us to do that,' Rosie went on, ignoring Mavis. 'And if it wasn't in his Bible, he must have put it somewhere else.' Blah, blah, blah. Sometimes, often, I wished Rosie would be quiet and let us all think. She prattled on until we got as far as Mr Duncan's hut and his geese, at which point the geese gave us such a welcome, of sorts, that she fell silent at last. There we were, outside our very own front door. I listened for Mr Tait, the tap-ke-tap of his walk, his quiet voice, but he wasn't there. Suddenly it came to me.

'I know where it is,' I said. 'Oh my goodness, I know where it is! It's under his bed. He told me, or I think he did. '

I ran up the steps, in the door and through to Mr Tait's room. I was looking for a loose floorboard but all the slats ran sideways right under the walls, held there by the walls themselves all of which fitted perfectly, not a wobble amongst them. I was wrong again.

In the stove room everyone else was looking in the stove, around it, under it. We examined the birch bench from every angle, ran our hands along the ceiling supports.

I couldn't bear it and went outside to sit on the step. Oh Mr Tait, why didn't you just tell me exactly what you meant? 'Your dad,' he'd said, 'not far' and 'find' and 'under bed'. The sun came bursting between the swaying trees, flashing in my eyes and flashing again. 'Under the bed.' I turned round and peered through the steps beneath the hut, beneath Mr Tait's room, under his bed, and there it was: a short little tower of bricks, an extra one, like the supports round the edges. He must have added it later because it didn't quite touch the underside and wasn't supporting anything. I crawled in to examine it more closely. It really was just a tower, two bricks this way, two that, and lots of dead leaves. I shoved the leaves aside and dug at the bottom with my hands, the way a dog digs, until my nails scraped a piece of wood. 'Singer' it said, a word which appeared everywhere on all sorts of things all around our house, not least the sewing machine.

'I found it!' I yelled.

The earth around it was soft and loose and came away easily in my hands until I had a small box, maybe for spools, with a little brass catch on the front. I opened it. Inside it said 'LAST WILL AND TESTAMENT of John Tait'. Attached to it with a pin was a letter stating that the house on our plot belonged to Mr Tait, the very thing we needed.

I let out a yell and banged my head on the underneath of the hut in my hurry out. 'I found it! Look everyone. Where are you? Look!'

Beneath the Last Will were two postcards identical to the one of Helensburgh, one addressed to Mavis with the message. 'Daddy will always love you,' in big square writing. The other was for me: 'Dear Sweet Lenny, I miss you more every day. Daddy will always love you.' The postmark was clear on both: March 1942, a year and a half earlier. Mavis and Rosie clattered down the steps. I gave Mavis her card. She read it and handed it back. Rosie grabbed it from me and read it aloud. My mum came to the top of the steps.

'What have you found?' she said, but all the sounds of the trees and the geese and Rosie's nonsense got mixed up in my head. I crouched on the ground by the box and with shaky hands drew out a folded sheet of paper marked 'Lenny'.

'Lenny, my dear,' it said and I heard Mr Tait's soft gentle voice. 'I will probably be gone by the time you read this. Take good care of your precious mother, Mavis and Rosie and don't pay any attention to that fool George Connor. Here are postcards your father sent which your mother thought best to keep from you. I disagreed. You always loved the truth. Your very own Mr Tait.' Then near the bottom it said: 'Your father is in Greenock, but perhaps, knowing you, that will not be news.'

The letter fell shut. I pressed it to my heart. The geese let out a particularly loud blast of honking.

'Thank you, Mr Tait.' I whispered. 'Thank you!'

The End

Historical accuracy and the Barns-Graham family

Until very recently, the Barns-Graham family owned the land on which the Carbeth hut community sits. After the First World War, Allan Barns-Graham allowed a returning soldier to build a hut there and gradually a few more went up over the twenties and thirties. Then, in 1941, the Clydebank Blitz happened and hundreds of refugees from that devastating attack flooded over the hills to Carbeth seeking shelter. Responding to this need, the Barns-Grahams gave another piece of land for them to build on, like Lenny and her family.

During this period, the Barns-Graham family did not live in or even own Carbeth Guthrie House, which Lenny calls 'The Big House', but were actually in Carbeth House, a more modest building on the other side of Carbeth Loch in a wonderful spot with great views of the Campsie Fells. They were neither wealthy nor ostentatious. I have exercised artistic licence, and permission given by the family and the Wilhelmina Barns-Graham Trust, to place them in Carbeth Guthrie House, an elegant and rather grand place sitting aloof on a hill with its back to the loch.

The reason for this inaccuracy was simply practical.

Carbeth House was too far for Lenny to walk as often as I needed her to in the midst of all her other adventures. Carbeth Guthrie also offered a greater contrast in living conditions to those of the refugees and evacuees in the Carbeth huts.

Wilhelmina Barns-Graham was the daughter of Allan Barns-Graham and at that time an artist of the St Ives modernist art movement, having moved to St Ives in Cornwall in 1940. She is known to have visited the family at Carbeth on holiday during the war. It is not known exactly when.

Never having met 'Willie' myself I hope the portrait I have painted of her is somewhere near the truth, based as it is on what I have read of her life. I am grateful to the Barns-Graham Charitable Trust and to the current Allan Barns-Graham, her nephew, for their permission to include her in Lenny's story.

The paper mill at Overton to the south of Greenock actually closed in 1929 and the buildings were partially destroyed in 1939. I was working from an older map and did not discover this fact until that part of the book was written. It was so spectacular a spot for such an important moment, as visitors to Loch Thom will know, that it just had to stay in.

My apologies also to any church or church-goers in the Rue End area, or indeed elsewhere. The minister and Mrs Brindle are entirely fictitious. I needed something bad to happen and the minister obligingly presented himself. I'm sure the real churches in that area would have had their work cut out for them and they would have risen admirably to the challenge.

There may be other inaccuracies which have

slipped in, for which I take full responsibility and offer apologies.

For more information about Wilhelmina Barns-Graham please see http://www.barns-grahamtrust.org.uk.

Information about the Carbeth huts can be found here: http://www.carbethhuts.com/about.html

Information about Greenock during the Second World War as told by those who lived there: http://www.rememberingscotlandatwar.org.uk/Accessible/Exhibition/204/Port-Number-One

A note on Italians in Britain during the Second World War

Italy did not join the Second World War until the 10th of June 1940. On that day Italian Prime Minister Benito Mussolini announced that Italy would join Hitler's Germany and declared war on France and Britain. Until that point Germans living in Britain were considered 'enemy aliens' and each person was categorised according to the level of risk to Britain they were considered to be. Some were interned; others had certain freedoms withdrawn, for instance no radios were allowed and they could only travel with special permission. The system was inefficient and unfair, especially considering many of these people were Jews who had perfectly understandably fled the Nazi regime in their native country.

On the 10th of June 1940, when Italy became Britain's enemy, all Italians in Britain automatically became enemy aliens too. The panic in Britain was such that on that same day Italian businesses were trashed and Italians attacked in the street. Prime Minister Winston Churchill ordered all enemy aliens to be rounded up. 'Collar the lot!' is what he famously and rather shockingly said.

Previous to this only those Germans who were

considered a high risk had been interned. On the 11th June all categories of German aliens were arrested and interned along with all categories of Italians. One of the strange things about the Italian internment was that only men were taken. The women were left to struggle on alone without the main breadwinner and often having had their business premises seized along with their means of making a living. The interned Italian men were aged between sixteen and eighty, though there were also reports of internees as young as fourteen.

In Scotland many were herded onto trains and sent south to Liverpool. From there some were sent to internment camps on the Isle of Man while others were put on ships in terrible conditions of overcrowding and deported to camps in Australia or Canada, some to places of relative safety and peace, but others to dire circumstances and inhumane treatment. One such ship, the *Arandora Star*, was hit by a German U-boat on the 2nd July with the tragic loss of over 800 lives, including British seamen and soldiers, and German and Italian internees. Such was the chaos of the interments that no accurate records were kept of who was on the ship, so the exact number of dead and their identification is not entirely certain.

By September 1943 the tides of war had turned. Britain no longer believed invasion was imminent. Mussolini had been toppled and imprisoned. On the 8th of the month it was announced that Italy had signed an armistice with the Allies and had therefore swapped sides. This meant the internees were no longer enemy aliens. Most of those who had not already been freed were released shortly after this date, leaving interned only those known to be high risk, although some low risk internees were retained for essential war work. This may seem odd, but many sections of the ordinary population were also retained in various forms of employment, often without the option of moving to other work or negotiating better rates of pay or conditions. On their release, many Italian internees were allocated various forms of employment including farm work closer to home but not necessarily within reach of friends or family. Given the level of chaos during the Second World War, it's not surprising that many people fell through the various nets while others were inextricably caught in them.

For more information please read *The Scots Italians* by Joe Pieri, published by Mercat Press in 2005.

The importance of Greenock during the Second World War

Winston Churchill claimed 'the only thing that ever really frightened me during the war was the U-boat peril'. As a group of islands, Britain was essentially in a siege-like situation and nearly brought to its knees by the lack of incoming supplies. This was certainly Hitler's plan and one which very nearly succeeded.

To ensure essentials were brought in, merchant ships travelled in convoys and were accompanied by naval vessels for protection. German submarines, or U-boats as they were known, followed their movements in highly efficient 'packs' to torpedo and sink them wherever possible. Churchill named this the 'Battle of the Atlantic'.

The supplies they carried would have included food but also raw materials and equipment essential not just to daily life but to the war effort and the armed services as well. They also carried servicemen from all over the world including the colonies. For instance, two million American soldiers arrived in Greenock and were shipped south directly from Princes Pier railway station. Without access to the sea Britain could also not have transported troops to the Mediterranean and beyond to fight on the various fronts.

The Battle of the Atlantic was fierce and brutal. Somewhere between 75,000 and 85,000 people lost their lives, of which over 30,000 were merchant seamen, a higher proportion of loss than for any of the armed services in the rest of the war. In May 1943 the Germans partially withdrew so the threat, while not entirely absent, was at least diminished.

During the Second World War Greenock was known as 'Port Number One'. The Clyde, its estuary and the sea-lochs which stretch out of it formed a vast natural harbour in which ships could be built, repaired and tested and where the convoys could gather in relative safety before heading out to sea. Greenock therefore became a hub in which a great many of the houses were requisitioned for war work and which saw an invasion of a different kind – of servicemen of all Allied nationalities, of incoming workers to the factories and docks, and of Wrens, the Women's Royal Naval Service, who backed up the whole effort. Additionally those rescued or captured at sea were often brought through Greenock.

The effect on the local population must have been considerable, not least because the incoming population, despite the Wrens, was overwhelmingly male. There was some atrocious behaviour from off-duty, often traumatised servicemen, much drinking and frequent fights, not helped by the glamour of many of the overseas servicemen and their consequent attractiveness to local women.

But like Clydebank, Greenock was also bombed several times during 1941, most heavily in early May; and while Greenock's bombing was not as intense as Clydebank's, many parts of the town were also devastated, including a section of the town hall itself. The good people of Greenock did not have far to search for their woes.

Security was necessarily of the highest importance and information hard to come by. There were even women stationed to listen in at phone boxes for information being passed on. 'Loose lips sink ships' was a motto that was nowhere more true.

Some reviews for Mavis's Shoe

'Sue Reid Sexton doesn't flinch from giving her readers a gritty and sometimes heart-rending account of the trials confronting her young heroine ... This is ultimately a story of courage and survival as well as a highly readable and vivid account of one of Scotland's worst wartime disasters.

Esther Read, *The Scots Magazine*

'This haunting, beautifully written blend of fact and fiction captures the strength of humanity, the courage in adversity and the heartbreaking loss caused by one of the most tragic episodes in our nation's history.'

Daily Record

'Sue Reid Sexton's work with war veterans gives an insight into Scotland's most devastating wartime event.'

STV's 'The Hour'

'A moving new novel about a child living in Clydebank during World War 2 ... Sue Reid Sexton's work with war veterans gave her plenty of resources to draw upon when it came to capturing the feelings of survivors of war.'

The Sunday Post

'*Mavis's Shoe* reveals the shared trauma of war from Clydebank to Baghdad.'

Sunday Mail

'A remarkable story of a young girl's survival of the aftermath of the 1941 Clydebank Blitz.'

BooksfromScotland.com

'This is the first book to be simultaneously published in Braille in Scotland. And it's a great book. It's also good that it isn't in dialect – Glaswegian – it is Lenny Gillespie talking, so folk all over can understand it.'

Allan Balfour, Head Editor and Braillist at the Scottish Braille Press, who transcribed *Mavis's Shoe* into Braille

'Not just a good read – it is a book to talk about.'

John Sprott, Amazon review

'Compelling and contemporary fiction for our time.'

Jane Wilson, Amazon review

'A thoroughly engrossing read and a convincing evocation not just of the Clydebank Blitz … The author captures beautifully this young voice, which is simultaneously childlike yet disarmingly wise.'

A Hunt, Amazon review

'A fantastic read well worth the purchase.'

rugrat, Amazon review

'Sue Reid Sexton very convincingly brings that time, and its atmosphere, back again.'

Mr Arthur M Blue, Amazon review

'This is a lovely, compelling book.'

Simon Skinner, Amazon review

'Incredibly moving, at times made me smile and at times made me cry. Once I started it, I could not put it down.'

Pamela Hall, Amazon review

'I've heard many stories of the war years in Clydebank but nothing brings it to life as does this book.'

Scotland Jenny, Amazon review

'From the moment I picked it up I was there with Lenny a character that was so well written I could almost touch her, almost smell her … This is a fantastic book, a must read … Thank you so much Sue, please hurry up and write the sequel!'

Amazon review